NINE SOULS

A NATE TEMPLE SUPERNATURAL THRILLER BOOK 9

SHAYNE SILVERS

ARGENTO PUBLISHING, LLC

Shayne Silvers

Nine Souls

A Nate Temple Supernatural Thriller Book 9

ISBN: 978-1-947709-10-2

© 2018, Shayne Silvers / Argento Publishing, LLC

info@shaynesilvers.com

For updates on new releases, promotions, and updates, please sign up for my mailing list by clicking the '*Get My Free Book!*' Button at *www.shaynesilvers.com*.

CONTENTS

CHAPTER 1

I fidgeted with the cuffs of my dress shirt, staring at the most beautiful woman in the room. She stared back, a faint smile on her pale cheeks. Her white hair was shorter than when I had first met her, now brushing her jaws in a jagged, messy line that she somehow made look sexy and dangerous. She wore a silver dress that hugged her frame like a frosted candy coating.

I tried not to imagine myself licking it off her to see what lay underneath. But her growing smile told me she had read my mind. Was her smile amusement or... inviting?

"Just *do* something with her already," Alucard complained in a low growl. "Cradle robber."

Which was enough to snap my mind out of the gutter. I shot him a dark look, but I didn't need to defend myself out loud. Callie Penrose *was* younger than me, but only by a handful of years. We had spent a lot of time around each other recently, not as much as I wanted, but neither of us had taken that last step – possibly fearing what would happen the next morning. Two wizards with ties to Heaven playing pre-marital confession under the sheets could have all sorts of consequences.

I turned to the hard-looking man sitting near her. His eyes assessed the room out of habit. At least his eyes weren't glowing red at the moment. Roland Haviar, ex-Shepherd, now vampire.

As was usual now, Roland was flanked between two stunning brunettes with Callie sitting next to the unlikely trio. They wore playful smiles as they noticed my gaze drifting back to Callie.

"Are they taken?" Alucard murmured softly, discreetly gesturing to the two brunettes.

Roland had been a Shepherd – a warrior wizard priest who hunted monsters for the Vatican. But all that had changed months ago when he had been turned into a vampire. He and Callie had gone to the Vatican to save the two brunettes – fledgling werewolves – from a false murder charge. That act had broken the Vatican Shepherds, revealing both a traitor and Roland's new... affliction. The wolves had instantly become Roland's loyal companions – like every bad vampire cliché ever. His two familiars or something. I hadn't decided if the relationship was romantic or not. It was really hard to tell sometimes. They were very... clingy with Roland.

Long story short, none of them considered themselves employed by the Vatican any longer.

"You don't want to play with Paradise and Lost," I warned him, finally breaking eye contact with Callie to study the two brunettes. They had dressed to impress, proudly displaying their cleavage in tasteful but revealing crimson dresses. They knew they attracted attention. Paradise was taller, and Lost was shorter, but both could have been sisters.

The Reds – two teenaged weredragons – sat near them, studying the two wolves as if taking notes. Yahn, a tow-headed dragon shifter sat between them, much like Roland, and there was definitely some sinning going on somewhere in that triangle of teen angst, but I'd be damned if I knew exactly what it was. Yahn was either dating one or both of the red dragon sisters.

I let the thought go, not wanting to know. Especially since Alucard – the Daywalker vampire standing next to me – was their adopted father. Alucard and I stood elevated above the seated guests, who were mostly chatting back and forth with each other, and thankfully not staring at our every move.

Yet.

"Just ask Gunnar's pack. A few of them tried to play red rocket with Paradise and Lost." I shot Alucard a meaningful look. "It didn't end well." The two stunners turned to me as if they had heard me say their names – the names they had given themselves after all the chaos they had been through. They licked their lips at Alucard, their smoldering eyes practically inviting him to try his hand.

He coughed pointedly – whether at my crude reference or their hungry eyes, I didn't care.

My eyes flicked from place to place about the room, wary for threats. "Everything is fine," I murmured, letting out a breath. "Nothing is going to happen."

Alucard grunted beside me. His eyes caught a ray of the setting sun from the glass window behind us, flashing for a moment. He looked relaxed, at peace. Of course, the sun hitting him was like a constant battery, charging this new breed of vampire that didn't need blood to fang out. "Except a man is about to lose his life," he reminded me.

I nodded soberly. "It was bound to happen sooner or later. I'm surprised it took this long."

"Do you think we could have prevented this if we had been better friends?" he asked softly.

I felt Tory glaring at us from a few paces away on the modern-day execution block. The Huntress stood beside her, looking beautiful, but uncomfortable in her dress. I averted my eyes from her as I replied.

"No. Death comes for us all."

"He does," a new voice said. My sphincter tightened enough for my entire body to flinch at the arrival of the stranger. I let out a breath and shot the newcomer an anxious look. He was cleverly disguised in a well-fitting black suit, but no clothing could have hidden the depths in those eyes. His three *Brothers* watched over various points around the room, alert for dangers.

Of *any* kind.

"Little early. The body isn't even cold," I whispered to Death – Horseman of the Apocalypse.

He rolled his eyes. "So dramatic. It happens to everyone. Well, many, at least."

"What are you doing here?" I asked.

Gunnar, the Alpha werewolf of St. Louis, sensed the sudden arrival from a few feet away. He shot a panicked look at us and then swept his lone eye over the small gathering, checking exits for threats. Seeing nothing, he still didn't look relieved, almost as if he was about to approach and demand answers to why the Horseman of Death had arrived so suddenly. I waved a hand at him discreetly, mouthing *I'll handle it*.

He gave me a stiff nod before turning away to speak to the last person on the execution block.

"I have something to tell you, of course," Death murmured dryly.

"Well, wait twenty fucking minutes. We're about to start."

"It cannot wait. Your request has been answered. Three may enter, but three shall not leave. You have two days. Meet me at the Arch at Noon." I almost popped a button on my suit as I spun, but Death only stared back with an immortal grin – not of pleasure, but of... something. "Oh, and you might want to remove that before..." he indicated a few spaces away with his chin before waving a hand at the gathered crowd and the door at the far end of the room.

I glanced down where Death had indicated. Gunnar was busy talking in low tones with a woman in front of him. A dead mouse had been placed behind his foot. I frowned at it and then turned back to Death, but the Horseman of the Apocalypse was gone. I saw him stalking the perimeter of the seated guests, hands clasped behind his back, hyper vigilant. The woman speaking with Gunnar briefly glanced at me and then tracked Death's gait thoughtfully. Othello was no doubt wondering what her *kind-of-sometimes-boyfriend* had been doing on the stage where a man was about to be executed for the oldest crime of all time.

Alucard grunted beside me, his eyes noting the dead mouse. "I guess Talon wasn't as pleased with his role in this as we thought."

Organs abruptly belted out in a rehearsed melody, preparing the gathered crowd for the dark ritual only moments away. Everyone seated before the stage turned in their seats to see the doors at the far end of the room open. I used the distraction to swoop in and scoop up the dead rodent by the tail. I flung it behind me, aiming for a few potted plants near the wall.

Othello stared at me with wide eyes, but she was in no position to ask questions as she stood beside Gunnar on the elevated stage. I gave her a crooked grin, turning back to stare down the aisle between the seated witnesses – where the Executioner would soon appear. Gunnar's stone eyepatch glinted in the sunlight from the windows as he faced his death with a brave smile.

A young girl appeared at the open door. She flashed the crowd a smile, a mockery of the horror about to unfold.

And then she began to walk down the aisle, tossing flower petals to the left and right.

A beautiful Maine Coon wearing an ornate blue bow with shells of some kind woven into the silk ribbon followed the girl. He stalked with feline grace – that strut that wildcats had used to prowl the darkest corners of the world throughout history – as if considering how best to slaughter the young girl with the petals. His fur had been combed and his long, furry ears pointed high in the air, swiveling now and then to catch sounds none of us would have noticed, alert for dangers. He was easily fifty pounds and walked on all fours taller than many dogs. His tail twitched back and forth with agitation.

I tried not to smile as I dipped my head at him in gratitude.

"Jesus. He looks like he wants to kill us all…" Alucard breathed.

I let out a breath, taking in Talon's mercurial eyes. They did indeed shine with murder, but no one else seemed to notice. Gunnar deferentially lowered his beard at the feline, a silent *thank you*. Talon's eyes swept the ground at his feet, searching for the mouse I had just removed. Then he shot me a look and…

Winked. Which is weird as shit. Cats weren't designed to wink. Especially intelligently.

Gunnar frowned, glancing down, sensing nothing. But he did sniff the air, as if only just sensing the small death that had been there. He shot me a look and I shrugged guiltily.

"Maybe the dead mouse was a sign of what this is going to cost us…" Alucard whispered.

"Nah. Cats leave dead things behind for their owners all the time. It's like a…" I searched for the word, and then smiled. "An offering. A present."

When I heard no response, I glanced over to see Alucard frowning at me. "I don't think it was a present, Nate. Look at him. He wants to kill us. All of us. You, too."

"He won't kill me. Maybe you, Sparkles, but I'm safe. He's my Shadow. My guard."

"If you two can't shut the hell up for two minutes, I'm going to kick you out, no matter what Han Solo says," Othello warned in a growl loud enough for us to hear, but soft enough to be hidden by the *oohs* and *aahs* of the crowd as they fixated on the procession heading our way. Gunnar shot an anxious glare at us, hiding it from the crowd.

5

Othello was running this dark ritual, and she took her job very seriously.

I nodded, murmuring one last thing to Alucard as I watched Talon stalk closer to us, the cloth bundle at the base of his throat swinging back and forth. "He asked what he could do to strengthen the relationship between my other childhood friend. Ring bearer to Gunnar's freaking wedding sounded like a great idea."

But watching Talon now, and considering the dead rodent... I began to have doubts. Because Talon wasn't really a cat – that was just one of his shapes. He was naturally a bipedal feline Fae warrior – like a Thundercat. He had chosen his less threatening form for this event. And three things in this life made Talon the Devourer truly happy.

Murdering anything with a heartbeat.

Getting high on Fae catnip.

And chasing reflections of light on the ground.

Talon stalked up the steps toward the Alpha werewolf of St. Louis, and I held my breath.

He finally stepped to the side and sat down between Tory and Gunnar, turning out to face the crowd, and I let out a breath of relief.

"Are... those mouse skulls woven into the ribbon?" Alucard whispered from beside me.

I subtly glanced at Talon to see him licking his paw. He *did* have skulls woven into the ribbon, almost too small to notice. They gleamed wetly as if freshly acquired. He sensed my attention and turned to face me, paw still in the air. His lips curled back in a predatory grin.

The music changed to a different funeral dirge, and I turned, plastering a smile on my face. If Talon wanted to add some skulls to his ribbon as a small show of defiance, oh well. It was better than killing the flower girl.

"We're almost done. Nothing has happened yet. It's all going to work out fine," I told myself under my breath.

Then the executioner appeared at the end of the aisle, as radiant as an Angel of Death.

A collective breath went up as the audience stared at her with awed joy.

Ashley truly did look radiant in her wedding gown.

So why did I have a very bad feeling in the pit of my stomach?

We had enough guards here at Chateau Falco to prevent a war. Horsemen, werewolves, Odin's Ravens, the shifter students from Shift, even a few Kansas City Freaks.

We were safe...
But that feeling didn't go away.

CHAPTER 2

*E*veryone stared transfixed as Dean led Ashley down the aisle – my butler standing in as her father since this was a monster's only wedding. Gunnar's face cracked into a dogged grin, practically salivating as the setting sun glinted off her skin. Her red hair fanned down her back in wavy ringlets that, although it appeared natural, I was sure had taken the equivalent of a decade to prepare. Her face shone with joy, and as I studied the petite redhead, a ray of sunlight struck her eyes.

And I saw a monster within.

Because Ashley had gone to the Land of the Fae with me, and she had brought back a roommate. Not a different being or anything, but a new… awareness – Wulfra. She was the Wolf Queen to Gunnar's Wolf King – Wulfric.

This slip of a girl had also killed Hercules in hand to hand combat.

But she looked so *cute* in that wedding gown that I wanted to just gobble her up!

Sensing Gunnar beside me, I wisely kept this thought to myself. Talon had ceased cleaning himself and sat staring – like the Cheshire Cat – as she approached. The wedding party consisted of Alucard and me with Gunnar, Tory and the Huntress with Ashley, and Othello officiating.

Othello had computer hacked her way into getting a license to legally bind this wedding, rather than waiting the required short period of time for the paperwork to arrive. Knowing Othello, her illegal documentation was probably more ironclad than any legal license. Because she was one of the best hackers in the world. If she had heard me qualify that with *one of* she would have stolen my identity, robbed me of every penny that had ever even considered depositing itself into an account with my name, and likely would have buried me with billions of dollars' worth of debts that would take trillions of dollars in legal fees to disprove.

Because hackers could get vengeful when their skills were doubted. Rule of thumb, never piss off a passive aggressive person. Ever.

I could tell that Othello was loving every minute of this perfect union. One, because she was a romantic at heart. Two, because she was prominently displayed as the power behind the holy matrimony when she usually had to work from the shadows.

Ashley's gown trailed behind her as she climbed the steps to stand beside Gunnar. Dean gave her an awkward hug before passing her hand to Gunnar, who took it with a dip of his head in respect to Dean. The butler had been a constant figure in our lives since childhood, and was a de facto father to all my friends, but especially to Gunnar and me.

A whisper of a smile crossed his reserved face – but he hid it from others as he turned away and took a seat in the front row.

Othello cleared her throat delicately. "We are gathered here today..." I lost myself in her words, discreetly glancing about for dangers, because that prickling sensation hadn't faded. Either I was paranoid or something was wrong. But I saw nothing alarming, and knew the Horsemen 'Ushers' would make short shrift of anyone daring to interfere with my best friend's wedding.

I found myself staring at Callie again.

Remembering our recent travels all over the world. A few weeks of bliss. No real dangers, no threats, just a couple of kids having fun together. Not even romance, really. More just... feeling each other out.

I wouldn't have turned down a little feeling each other *up*, but even I can't get everything I want all the time. I saw her face bloom into an amused smile as she noticed my attention, and my grin turned roguish – full of smug pride. Spikes of fire abruptly pierced my shins and then tugged down like a fistful of scalpels.

I almost shrieked in alarm – a heartbeat away from calling up my magic whips to incinerate anything near me that could have even remotely been described as *bad guy*. I glanced down to see my murderous kitty, Talon, casually retracting his claws from my flesh, blinking up at me with fake innocence. To top it off, he extended his neck to rub his chin across my shins, purring happily.

I let out a breath, trying to mask my sudden glare. At a sound, I looked up to see Tory, Ashley's Maid of Honor, screaming at me with only her eyes. I suddenly felt every single eye pointed in my direction. I saw the flash of white gold in Tory's open palm and my eyes widened. The ring! It was inside the satchel at Talon's throat. Pretty much my only job as Best Man. I knelt down and detached the satchel, withdrawing the lone ring inside.

I heard a few chortles, but decided not to acknowledge them as I palmed the ring. At least they hadn't actually been waiting on me. I used my foot to gently nudge Talon the hell away.

Okay, not so gently. I tried to hurl him from the stage with minimal motion.

And the cat – not so gently – decided to use some freaky Fae strength to not move a millimeter, which meant my shove only caused me to wobble. Face heating in embarrassment, I glared down at the cat. As if nothing had happened, he arched his tail, wove between my legs a few times, rubbing along both of my shins and covering my pants in cat hair. Only then did he sit beside me, regally studying the crowd before us. He meowed, and the crowd swooned.

I looked up to see the Huntress glaring – as if it was my fault that the crowd's attention was split between me and Gunnar, or that Talon was stealing the show. Alucard coughed into a fist, trying to hide his amusement as I turned back to the bride and groom.

"The rings," Othello said.

Before Gunnar could even turn all the way, I had stepped closer, placing a hand on his shoulder and pressing the ring into his palm as he extended it my way. I was smiling until I noticed the look of tension in his single icy blue eye.

"Something is wrong," he whispered. "Be alert…" Then he was smiling and turning back to Ashley as if nothing had happened. His bride-to-be wasn't fooled, because her smile flickered for a moment before she replaced it with more forced enthusiasm than was normal for her.

A cold sweat ran down my back and I felt Talon tense at my feet, having heard the warning. With a flick of his tail, he sauntered off the steps as if bored. The crowd chuckled absently at that before refocusing on the two werewolves.

I saw Talon's eyes flash from a dark hallway a moment later. Then they were gone.

Alucard noticed and immediately tensed.

I didn't even hear Othello as my eyes scanned the room, searching for threats. I could sense Alucard using his vampire senses to pick up on any dangers, but with so many monsters in the room why hadn't anyone else noticed anything? What had Gunnar seen? Was he simply being paranoid? Surely, we were safe. The Horsemen wouldn't let any threats come in, and with so many allies around us it wasn't like we were in danger of being overrun.

Unless it was an army.

But we'd dealt with armies before, too.

A lone assassin had virtually no chance of success either.

I wasn't arrogant enough to believe we were untouchable. A suicide bomber could still do major damage. Maybe a killer had slipped in, fully aware he wouldn't survive his attack.

I knew one thing. Given the chance, I would make an attacker's head my wedding present.

CHAPTER 3

*G*unnar cleared his throat, but when he spoke his voice still sounded gruff.

"You irrevocably shattered my heart with a hammer." The room grew silent as if everyone had just sucked in a breath at the same time. Not the best opening, but Gunnar had always been better at *showing* rather than *telling*. "Because you saw the man I *could* be, rather than the man I *was*. Like a Master Blacksmith, you saw the potential in a lump of iron." I cringed. So far, he had told her that she broke his heart and that she was a blacksmith. "You beat the flaws out of me." Now, he'd added husband-beater. Alucard fidgeted uncomfortably beside me. Gunnar needed to wrap this up. "You gathered what remained, assessed it, and then added in those metals that had been missing. The fires of your love re-forged my heart and soul into something new, something stronger, something better. This new heart is too big for the shell of a man encasing it, but I will spend the rest of my life striving to be the man worthy of such a gift. To be the man worthy of standing beside you, the maker of my heart." He smiled at her. "If you'll let me."

Ashley nodded in a snotty-laugh-cry-hiccup motion as he placed the ring on her finger.

She stared down at her finger for a moment in wonder, as if forgetting she still had a part to play. But when she lifted her eyes, they smoldered with passion. It looked like Wulfra had a few things to say about this vow business.

My eyes quickly flickered over the crowd and locked onto Callie. I tried to pass on my concern without my face changing, because I was in the spotlight and couldn't very well alarm everyone in the room.

Her returning smile faltered. She feigned a casual look at the hallway where Talon had disappeared as if suddenly realizing what it might have signified. When she turned back to me, the violet flecks in her eyes seemed to flare. But she didn't move, not wanting to interrupt the ceremony.

But I was confident she was alert. As if having a sixth sense, Roland suddenly stilled, discreetly glancing over at her. Like a ripple, the two wolves at his side grew suddenly relaxed, prepared to shift in a moment if an attack came. But to everyone else – even though they were all mostly monsters – the wedding was going off without a hitch.

I now had four more sets of eyes scanning the room in a discreet fashion.

"I have not shattered your heart, Gunnar Randulf. Like a thief, I reached inside to steal it, but my hand was caught in a vise like a bear trap snapping shut. I was forced to hold onto a lightning bolt when I had only hoped for a man's heart." The crowd was silent, almost leaning forward. "I fought it, struggling against that trap, even considering losing the hand rather than risk that bolt of raw power incinerating me from the inside out." She stared back at Gunnar, and his eye crackled with desire, her words sparking the monster within. "You burned away my illusions, my-self doubts, my fears. You are my rock in a raging sea. I had only ever fought with my brain, using my education like a blade against my enemies. When I found myself..." her eyes briefly flickered to me and then the crowd, "in a world where my clever papercuts didn't hurt my enemies," the crowd chuckled at that, "you nursed me back to health. No! You showed me how to make new blades. You didn't *protect* me... you *empowered* me. And I will never forget that. The lightning of your heart, and the thunder of your voice, brought me face-to-face with my fears, helped me best them, and left a new woman standing in my skin. I would do anything for you." She paused, then turned to meet the eyes of the crowd, almost as if sharing it with each individual for a fraction of a second – but long enough for the subtle promise to carry weight. Then she turned back to Gunnar. "Anything."

She placed the ring on his finger and I actually heard him growl as he squeezed her hand.

A slow clap echoed in the immediate silence. I jerked my head to see a figure slowly standing from the seats near the back. He wore an arrogant smirk as he clapped his hands, and it was blatantly apparent that it wasn't congratulatory.

Not at all.

That clap was mocking. And as I studied him, I was entirely sure he was a werewolf.

Othello, clear as a bell, spoke over his clapping, her tone like a shard of glass. "I now pronounce you man and wife. You may now... *kill your prey!*" she hissed.

Something about her change of script just made it more romantic to me. But my soul is a dark, haunted, broken thing.

Gunnar and Ashley growled. Then they exploded into their Fae wolf forms, shreds of tuxedo and wedding gown raining down like confetti.

Wulfric and Wulfra – the werewolf royalty of St. Louis.

Suddenly unable to handle the size of Ashley's new werewolf-thighs, her garter snapped out into the crowd like a rubber band, and...

Struck Yahn right in his open mouth before falling into his lap. Everyone – even the asshole crashing the wedding – turned to look. Yahn slowly lifted the symbolic garter in his hands, blinking at it. Then the Reds stared at it for a moment.

Oh, boy.

As one, the three lifted their eyes to Alucard. He had taken an instinctive step forward, glaring at the three teens. They wilted in their chairs.

Any other time I would have burst out laughing, but the asshole in the room obviously took precedence. I turned to the bride and groom, arching a brow. They were now massive bipedal werewolves. Gunnar was all white, easily seven feet tall, and was flexing his diamond claws. His diamond eyepatch glittered beside his arctic blue eye. Ashley was shorter, but not by much. Her black fur was actually braided down her jaws and the ruff of her neck. It took me a second to put my finger on what was nagging at me, but once I did I couldn't un-see it. It looked like they had switched bridal clothes – Gunnar wearing white and Ashley in black.

Whips of power erupted from my palms as I called upon my magic. They coiled on the floor at my feet, popping and hissing with white light as my eyes scanned the rest of the room for additional threats – in case this was just a diversion. The rest of the guests had erupted into their own monster forms – if they had one – or had scooted back from the prick, like one would avoid the idiot holding a metal antenna outside during a thunderstorm.

He resumed his slow clap, smirking at Gunnar and Ashley.

"I think I'm going to like my new city. Very much..." he said with a grin.

Ashley and Gunnar snarled in response.

"Do we interfere?" Alucard murmured beside me – not sounding scared, but as if maybe we shouldn't get in the way of Gunnar on his wedding day. Or Ashley, for that matter.

"Do I look like I'm the authority on weddings?" I asked deadpan. "For all I know, this is totally normal."

CHAPTER 4

*G*unnar's chest heaved as he glared at the offending werewolf. I spotted the Four Horsemen at the door, staring darkly at the were-wolf's back. What the hell was this clown thinking? The more I thought about it – as everyone stood poised for murder – the crazier it sounded. He had no chance of surviving. He was surrounded by monsters and gods. Not even counting the fact that he stood inside Chateau Falco, my family mansion, the seat of my power.

Gunnar just waited, and I began to feel uneasy. Why wasn't he doing anything?

The man nodded one time, still smirking. "Not as dumb as you look. Smart to consider why I would reveal myself in such a vulnerable position. To wonder why I would reveal myself at all. In such a public manner. With so many blades, claws, and," he glanced at the whips of white energy crack-ling at my feet, "magic strings ready to cut me in half."

Ashley snarled as she took a step closer, but Gunnar let out a bark and she instantly halted as if he had yanked an invisible leash. She didn't look angry at Gunnar's command, but as if she was still visualizing the eviscera-tion of the man who had ruined her wedding day.

"Tell me why I shouldn't place your head on my wedding table as a trophy," Gunnar said in a tone low enough to resemble a minor earth tremor. "Because it's sounding more appealing by the second."

The man shrugged easily. "Because your entire pack will die if I don't walk out of here. I'm obviously willing to gamble on it." He held out his hands, grinning arrogantly. A challenge. He had revealed himself as a threat but hadn't shifted. "Want to throw the dice, pup?"

Gunnar growled, his claws elongating. Ashley stood motionless, a fraction of a second away from cutting loose. "You're mad." Gunnar finally said, relaxing. Then he began to laugh.

The man didn't seem to like that comment very much. He scowled at Gunnar for a heartbeat before composing himself. "Your pack's apartment complex is surrounded as we speak," he said in a low tone. "By twice their number. Your empire has fallen, Gunnar Randulf. You just don't know it yet."

"And what if I decide not to concern myself with your idle threat and instead slaughter your pack? Or, better yet, take them from you and leave you all alone?" Gunnar asked, actually glancing down at his paw as if inspecting a hangnail. "Because the more I listen to you whine and brag like an emo teen, the more I realize that the universe might have just given me a wedding present. I kind of want to kill you now, whatever your name is. Because I hate it when puppies yap at me while I'm trying to do grown up things."

The man didn't bat an eye. "My name is Zeus Fletcher, Alpha of Illinois, and I formally challenge your position as Alpha of St. Louis. I'll see you tomorrow morning. I wanted you to have at least one night of marital bliss, so didn't bother bringing my Second here with me. I'll have one of my people talk to your people to finalize the details. Neutral ground and all that." He cocked his head, frowning. "Oh. Any special requests? I'm feeling generous."

Gunnar yawned. "Do we really have to wait until tomorrow? I have a few minutes to spare before pictures." He glanced down at himself. Then the shredded tuxedo. "Well, that plan just went to hell. I guess tomorrow will have to do. Sleep tight." And he turned his back on Zeus.

I bit back a laugh as Zeus' face darkened. I released my whips, realizing they were unnecessary. I had thought werewolves were less... official. More snarling, less paperwork. Gunnar had killed the previous Alpha of St. Louis without all this red tape. But... Gunnar hadn't been an *Alpha*. He'd been a lone wolf. Maybe that changed things.

I realized Gunnar was speaking to Ashley – likely trying to convince her not to kill Zeus.

Zeus locked eyes on me and sneered. "Of course, you could always use your friends to do your dirty work... But that would make you look weak, proving that you're unfit to be Alpha. Then again, word on the street says you don't have a problem letting your friends do your dirty work. You've never had to face a true Alpha." Gunnar slowly turned to face him. Zeus frowned, as if remembering something. "Oh, that's right. You killed your predecessor, but he was just a pawn. The Brothers Grimm had already broken him when you came along. You've never had to stand up to an Alpha who paid for his throne with blood."

Then, before anyone could respond, he simply turned his back on Gunnar, the ultimate sign of disrespect. "I'll let you have tonight to fuck your bitch queen." Ashley actually lunged forward at that, but Gunnar held her back with a warning snarl – claiming this kill for his own. Ashley relented, but she practically shook with bloodlust as she watched Zeus walk away.

Zeus paused at the door, staring down the Four Ushers of the Apocalypse. At a look from Gunnar, they stepped aside. Zeus turned to give them one last look. He spent considerably more time appraising Ashley. He licked his lips, turning back to Gunnar. "If you put up a good enough fight, perhaps I'll even comfort your widow after you're gone."

Then he was walking away, chuckling to himself.

CHAPTER 5

*E*veryone turned from Gunnar, to Ashley, and then ultimately, to me.

I shared a long look with Gunnar before asking everyone to head out to the reception area. Alucard, Tory, the Huntress… look, everyone wanted to stick around for the private pow-wow, and they all began talking at once. I called back my whip and cracked it in the air, something I'd been working on for a few weeks. The sudden shower of white sparks silenced every protest.

I picked out the Reds from the crowd. "Sonia. Arya. Can you please escort everyone to the reception area? The Best Man wants to talk to the Groom." I shot a look at Gunnar and then Ashley. "The Bride can stay too, of course. I'm not feeling suicidal."

As angry as she was, that earned a flicker of a smile. She took a deep breath, shook her head, and then descended the steps. Callie was waiting for her as if by magic. She smiled at Ashley and then slowly reached up to brush one of the braids hanging near her massive jaws. "Very pretty," she said softly. Ashley let out a sniff, her head suddenly dropping as if about to cry. Gunnar moved as if to catch her, but Callie shot him a deadly look. He froze instinctively – subdued by only the power of her silent look. All women were born with this mysterious power, magical or not. Ashley straightened her shoulders and then wrapped Callie up in a tight hug, towering over the much smaller, white-haired wizard.

I shook my head in wonder, reminded that I would never understand these mythical creatures known as women. Gunnar had obviously experienced the same revelation because he cocked his head, watching curiously as the two began walking away, Callie speaking in soft tones to Ashley.

Alucard slipped off the stage with Tory, eyes locked onto the Reds and Yahn, no doubt to have a very serious talk about the whole garter situation. I grinned at their backs, not envying Yahn's fate. I locked eyes with the Horsemen Ushers, jerking my chin towards the reception area. *Keep your eyes open this time, Brothers.* Death nodded and the Four slipped away. I idly wondered how Zeus had even gotten into the wedding past all the security.

It had been by invite only. I shook my head, promising myself I would get to the bottom of it.

Roland and his two wolves had flanked Ashley and Callie without a word, taking it upon themselves to act as the wolf queen's guards. Ashley noticed immediately, dipping her head at Roland. But she bared her teeth territorially at Paradise and Lost. Callie calmly stepped back, but the wolves didn't appear to notice. Paradise and Lost dipped their heads and lowered their eyes – but I got the sense that it wasn't out of fear or weakness. They were acknowledging her authority here in St. Louis, but also firmly telling her they wouldn't rescind their offer of protection.

It wasn't two wolves submitting to an obviously stronger wolf. That wasn't even a question.

This was an act of respect.

Ashley watched them for a moment and then finally dipped her head like she had to Roland. Paradise, the taller of the two, cleared her throat. "We brought our luggage with us, so we have a few spare dresses that should fit you very well…" she offered carefully.

Callie waited, close enough to interfere if Bridezilla attacked. I hoped.

Ashley finally glanced down at herself, lip curling at her werewolf form, as if only just realizing she had ruined her wedding dress. "That… would be nice," she growled, her voice sounding hollow, as if the rage was fading, only to be replaced with regret at her tarnished wedding.

Paradise stepped up closer, holding out an elbow for Ashley to acknowledge, rather than grabbing the wolf queen unasked. Smart. Ashley stared at the offer for a moment before linking her arm and letting Paradise lead her away to a side room. "I hope you don't mind showing off a little skin…" she said, eyes mischievous.

"This might be the most fun I've ever had at a wedding," Lost chimed in sweetly, stepping up to Ashley's other side. "I've heard of trashing the dress afterwards, but that was hardcore. Mind if I copy your idea? Some day?"

Ashley turned a bewildered look from one to the other. Then she slowly bared her teeth. Lost grinned, so apparently Ashley's gesture wasn't a warning. It was hard to tell, being a human observer. The smallest thing could rile a wolf, and then what I would consider an obvious threat or challenge would elicit nothing more than a laugh. Or it was just their mysterious womanly ways. I shrugged. Greater minds than mine had cracked their teeth on that chestnut.

Roland followed behind the three wolves, speaking softly with Callie. They shot me one last look and I nodded at them, a silent command to guard Ashley with their lives.

Because maybe Zeus had lied about attending the wedding alone.

I turned to find Gunnar staring out the glass window behind the altar. The labyrinth stretched outside in the distance, the sun bathing it in an orange glow. Gunnar remained in his wolf form.

"Congratulations," I said, stepping up beside him.

His shoulders tensed at my voice. He was breathing heavily, eye distant.

"No one died," I noted.

He grunted. "Pity…"

I sighed, nodding my agreement. "How do you want to play it? Not that you need help, but if I can do anything…" I said this carefully. Because he was still in wolf form, and not as rational.

Understatement. He was a breath away from murder.

I didn't want him thinking I was telling him he needed my help. He didn't. I hoped. I was sure any help I offered would only make things worse. He would lose face with his wolves. Or some other political shit would happen. I didn't know much about werewolf politics, and Gunnar had never been a political schemer, so perhaps he didn't know either. Hence, the silence right now.

"No."

Expected, but the stubborn, stupid part of me wanted to press him. I didn't, but I wanted to. "Okay. What about my first question. How do you want to play this?"

The room was silent for a good minute. "We were supposed to go on our honeymoon tomorrow..." he said, voice shaking. Not with fear, but trying to hold back the river of fury now coursing through his veins. Zeus' challenge had tarnished his single moment of joy – the most important day of his life.

"Probably intentional," I offered in a soft tone.

He snarled at the window, claws flashing out. "I will rip the hide from his bones."

I waited for him to take a figurative step back from the ledge he was perched on. "Solid plan. What about his pack, though? What happens after?"

Gunnar was silent for a few moments. Then he turned to face me, and the pain I saw in his eye almost made me change my mind about killing Zeus myself. Gunnar was barely holding himself together.

This one day – his wedding day – had been taken from him.

And he wanted the world to hear his thoughts on the matter. To share his feelings about that.

His pack had been threatened.

He had been threatened.

The very first words Ashley had heard as his new wife had been a threat from another wolf.

His wedding ceremony had been stained.

And Gunnar seemed intent to repaint that memory with a healthy coat of fresh blood.

"You'll take care of it." I waited a few seconds. "Mind explaining these rules to me?" I pressed casually, showing no doubt in his capacity and capability to slaughter the other Alpha.

Gunnar nodded slowly. "I've learned bits and pieces from some of my pack – those who've lived under other Alphas in other cities. When a lone wolf wants to challenge an Alpha – like I did to win St. Louis – he can do so as long as there are other witnesses to the fact. To make sure it's fair. But when two Alphas have a pack – and mates – things must be handled differently. More... officially. That's why he waited until the ceremony was over."

My eyes widened briefly. Wow. That... was unbelievable. The prick had waited until Gunnar was married for a reason *other* than just being a dick? He really had been playing politics.

"What's different?"

"Spoils of war," Gunnar responded in a dry tone. "Terms. The pack merging together after. The fact that the packs need to hear the terms and then choose a side *before* the challenge."

I blinked. "You mean…"

Gunnar nodded. "Yes. My pack could choose to merge with his to prevent the fight, essentially neutering me. I could still fight, but what would be the point? My pack would have declared their preference – not me – so even if I won I would likely have to kill them. All."

I shook my head. "They would never do that." Gunnar didn't look as convinced. My mind raced. "This means you have the chance to win his wolves to *your* side…"

Gunnar shrugged. "Doubtful, or he wouldn't have waited. And I've got more important things to do tonight. I won't spend my wedding night politicking!" he snarled. He continued in a more reasonable tone. "Zeus has something up his sleeve. He waited for a reason. But what could he have that would convince my wolves to change sides?" I began to shake my head, but Gunnar interrupted. "Think about it, Nate. My pack loves Ashley and me. Wulfra and Wulfric. But… my ties with you have brought them directly into your fights. Every. Single. Time. My tenure as Alpha has been wrought with fighting everything *other* than werewolves. And all related to you." My shoulders slumped. I opened my mouth, but couldn't find the words. Gunnar reached out a clawed paw to grasp my shoulder reassuringly, but I stepped back in shame.

He sighed. "I wouldn't change a thing, Nate. And I doubt many of them would either. Look at what they got in exchange. Two Fae-touched werewolf leaders. No one else has that. No one."

I nodded sickly. "That doesn't directly benefit *them*, though."

Gunnar lowered his paw. "That's my fear. That Zeus will offer them something that directly benefits *them*. Empowering the pack, not the leaders. Bribing them."

I let out a breath, running a hand through my hair in frustration. "Okay, so what happens? You meet up tomorrow morning with both packs present, hold a vote of some kind, and then, what, duke it out?"

Gunnar shrugged. "As far as I know, yes."

"Okay, we need to—"

"Nate," Gunnar interrupted. My mouth snapped shut as I looked up at him. "Your work here is done. Right now, I'm going to go kiss my wife," he smiled distantly, as if only just realizing he hadn't yet had a chance to do that. Then he smiled wider. "Then I'm going to dance with her. Maybe shove some cake in her face if she'll let me. And then…" his eye grew dark and lustful. He didn't finish his sentence as he strode off the stage.

Rather than head to the reception, he approached the changing room where we had gotten ready. He had a change of clothes in there just in case – because he always carried a back-up. Even on his wedding day, apparently.

Before he reached the door, I called out in a sing song voice, mimicking the jingle from that *Hot Pocket* commercial.

"*Red rocket…*" I sang, smirking at him.

He whirled in disbelief. Then he burst out laughing. "I'll do my duty," he said, grinning. "But I probably won't call it that. I'd rather Ashley not die of laughter on our wedding night." Then, with a final shake of his head, still chuckling, he left me alone at the altar.

Realizing how *that* sounded, I let out a resigned sigh.

Time to crash this reception.

CHAPTER 6

I sat at the table Dean had set up for the wedding party, drinking my third glass of wine. Gunnar and Ashley danced across the floor to Ed Sheeran singing from the loudspeakers. They looked so happy together, like nothing had happened at the altar. Gunnar wore slacks and a white shirt and Ashley wore a red cocktail dress that complimented her hair. And prominently flaunted her cleavage. Gunnar might as well have been drooling when he first saw it. Paradise hadn't been lying. I smiled faintly, but inside my mind was racing. No matter what plans, schemes, and traps I had devised in my head, I knew they were all fruitless. Gunnar needed to handle this himself. This was a test as an Alpha. For him to prove both his power and his leadership skills.

It was an election in its most primal form.

A fight to the death.

I grumbled angrily, not familiar with feeling impotent when my friends were threatened.

I had reserved a private plane to take him to a remote, massive hunting lodge in the Rocky Mountains. The fridge was stocked with a week's worth of exquisite meals, and the grills were equipped to handle as much meat as they wanted to hunt and cook if they preferred that instead. The nearest house was five miles away, leaving them in the dangerous wilderness all alone.

So they could get their wolf on and hunt to their heart's content.

The place was packed with movies, music, blankets, and anything else they might need for their trip – even their luggage.

They literally had to hop on the plane – with nothing in hand – and they would arrive in their own personal paradise. The benefit to the lodge was that it was notorious for large hunting parties. Wild game abounded in the nearby mountains, and natural hot springs were only a few miles away if they wanted to check that out. Not some commercialized hot spring, but literal springs hidden within the mountains that you had to go and find for yourself.

I had placed wards on the property so that no magic could come within five miles. Hell, even I couldn't Shadow Walk there to pester them. They had a week of sheer bliss ahead of them.

Until Fuck-stick McWolf decided to make a play for power.

And I had been told to stay out of it. In fact, my close friendship with Gunnar might have even led to this confrontation. I needed to remain far away from it all. As did my friends.

Which made me want to go pick a fight with someone.

I scanned the room angrily, but none of the faces immediately pissed me off enough to kill. With a start, I realized that Raego had never shown up. He had told me he couldn't make the wedding due to travel, but that he would be back in time for the reception.

But… I scanned the room again. He wasn't here.

I unlocked my phone with a swipe of my thumb, typed in the code, and dialed the scaly bastard. I turned away from the crowd, swept up my drink, and walked away for privacy. He answered on the second ring.

"Yes, Nate?"

"Where are you?" I asked in a neutral tone.

"I won't be able to make it," he said, mirroring my tone exactly.

I frowned. "And why not? Gunnar is your friend. He got married earlier. Kind of a big deal."

Raego was silent for a moment. "Something came up."

I blinked. "Excuse me?" My voice was a low rasp.

"Something. Came. Up." He enunciated each word clearly as if I hadn't heard him clearly, rather than explaining his answer like he knew I had meant.

Now, Raego could be an upper-class prick. In fact, he usually was, but he often had a very good reason in hindsight. He'd gone to bat for me several times, but lately he had been very… distant. Almost reclusive. Something in our relationship had changed. Sure, he had been available if absolutely necessary, but it had been a struggle to get him to commit his aid. Ever since I had ridiculed his grandmother at the Dueling Grounds, I had seen very little of him on a day-to-day basis.

"What's going on, Raego? I feel like we need to have a chat. Catch up," I said through gritted teeth, trying to disguise my anger as concern.

"That won't be possible. Like I said, something came up."

I took a deep breath. "Maybe I wasn't clear. I'll see you later tonight. Better if you make an appearance at the reception like you promise—"

He hung up.

I yanked the phone from my ear in disbelief. As I stared, speechless, I realized that blue tattoos were pulsing brightly under my shirt. My Fae power responding to Raego's disrespect.

"Hey, hey. Easy, Little Brother," Alucard said from the shadows. I didn't even flinch in surprise, so focused on my phone. "Tell Papa Fang what's on your mind."

I let out a long breath. "The stinking reptile hung up on me." I finally looked up at him.

Alucard studied me thoughtfully, frowning. "Oh?"

"Said he can't make it tonight. Something came up."

Alucard nodded after a few moments. "Maybe we should go have a nightcap with him…"

A slow grin split my cheeks. "Like minds…" I said, clenching my fists.

Alucard's eyes flashed with anticipation, but he jerked his chin at my arms. "Might want to tone down the Smurf juice. This is a wedding, Little Brother," he reminded me in a neutral tone. After a deep breath, I gave him a stiff nod. He let his fangs show as he smiled. "We can always see how well blue and gold holds up against black. But not now. Later," he said, his eyes flashing gold for a heartbeat. I smiled back at him, appreciating his reference. His gold and my blue would meet Raego and his black dragon power tonight.

"That sounds fun. Maybe it would be wise to bring Tory. Just in case."

He took a sip of his drink to mask his frown. "I'll mention it to her." I saw his eyes dart over to where the Reds stood talking to Yahn. His frown grew harsher. "You should bring your purse. The one with the black dragon scales." Then he slipped away in the direction of the teens. He probably wasn't going to tell Tory. Someone had to keep an eye out on the Reds.

I chuckled at his back, responding to the air. "Yeah, that will definitely piss him off. And his piece of shit grandmother—"

"Generally, fighting grandmothers should be left to other grandmothers," a familiar voice said from behind me.

I grinned, turning to face Callie. Her silver dress clung to her waist like a second skin, and two silver chopsticks – doubling as weapons, no doubt – held her hair up in a crest behind her head. She wore silver bracelets that I was sure also doubled as some horrifying weapon, but she didn't need them. She was a weapon without blades. And I wasn't even talking about her magic.

She was a cute little killer. Not openly like the Huntress, but subtly, like a knife in the dark.

But her true weapon was her ability to read people. She was cunning, ruthless, and calculating – a chess player. I had reason to believe she didn't have as much confidence in this trait as she should – not that she denied it, but that she gave herself less credit than she deserved. She said it was just simple logic – like any savant would say when reciting *pi* to the thousandth digit.

"This grandmother is cruising for a bruising," I promised. "I already beat her up once, but the lesson didn't stick."

"I... see," she said in a dry tone, sipping from her martini glass. Like quicksilver, she slipped up beside me and wrapped her arm through mine, holding me close, possessively, and I had to fight not to lean in and nibble her neck. Even if she would kill me for it, I might have still considered it a fair trade. A dying wish.

But... I didn't. I had too much respect for her to treat her so casually. She was to be treasured.

"Walk with me," she said. She didn't wait for me to take the lead, but instead began walking me into the crowd, smiling politely at the various guests. After a time, she looked up at me. "The Angel didn't come," she finally said.

I nodded, not meeting her gaze. "I didn't invite him. Angels get kind of particular about premarital sex. Not to mention that the woman he protects is an Old Testament kind of gal. She probably wears Fire and Brimstone underpants," I added. "Not good party guests for us sinners."

She stumbled a step as if tripped. I steadied her with a frown, but she blushed, waving off my concern. "The two of you in the same room must have been a sight to see."

I sighed nostalgically. Maybe her shoes didn't fit properly. "Yeah. I actually do like the old bird. As infuriating as she can be…" I wondered what she had been up to lately. "But I didn't invite Eae. Didn't want to surprise you, and didn't want to risk ruining Gunnar's wedding with any drama." I let out a sigh. "Drama must have gotten an invite anyway."

"Gunnar is a big boy. He'll take care of Zeus." She didn't add that the drama likely stemmed from me. Zeus had made that pretty obvious – that he thought I was the power behind Gunnar. It meant a lot to me that Callie didn't say it. She knew I knew it, and didn't find it necessary to remind me. It was nice to know she respected me enough to not feed me comforting lies. All that mattered to Callie was that I was aware of it, and had accepted responsibility.

"What are you going to do about it?" she asked in a light tone, careful for none around us to overhear. Because the tension in the air was barely veiled. The guests here were as tight as any family. Tighter. A gang. To see Gunnar and Ashley openly challenged on their most sacred day didn't sit well with them. They wanted blood, even knowing that Gunnar didn't want their help.

And Callie was subtly asking how I could unleash a little pain without getting my hands dirty.

"You're pretty cool. For a broad," I said.

My foot was immediately swept out from beneath me and Callie was guiding me to the floor – appearing to all those nearby as if cushioning my fall. My drink crashed to the ground beside me.

But no one noticed the blade in her palm which was gently pressed against my throat as her eyes stared at me in false alarm for the guests' benefit.

The blade to my throat let me know what she thought of my snide comment.

I grinned, ignoring the people staring at us. "Looks like you saved me. How shall I ever repay you, My Lady?" I teased.

"How about you don't poke the dragon?" she murmured as the blade disappeared.

I discreetly assessed her body as she helped me back up, making sure she wasn't about to have a wardrobe malfunction – and that if she did, I would be ready to immediately assist her. She, of course, noticed my attention. She rolled her eyes, but she didn't move my hands from her hip bone – which I had grasped for… support.

She led me away from the concerned guests as if nothing significant had happened.

"Speaking of, do you want to see a dragon?" I asked her, thinking out loud.

"I'd rather dance," she said, not looking at me, but instead sweeping the room with her eyes, either checking for danger or searching for Roland.

"Well, you just noticed that I have two left feet."

"I'm willing to take that risk." She turned to look at me then, and her eyes were deep, the purple flecks calling to me like flecks of gold in a forgotten mine. "Sweep me off my feet."

It wasn't a question.

The music abruptly cut off and a glass chimed as Tory signaled her speech. Callie sighed in regret. I could have sworn she muttered a profanity under her breath, but it sounded more like a meditative mantra. Maybe I just didn't know the language she'd used.

But if it was profanity, I agreed with it. Tory had just taken this dance from me. And, worse, I suddenly remembered that, as Best Man, I also had to give my speech. But with Zeus ruining the ceremony, I felt like changing my planned speech a bit. Which meant I would be winging it.

Worst idea ever, right?

"You better go," Callie said with a sigh. "But I might be available for dragon stuff later."

I grinned. "Sweet."

There was an awkward pause, and then we both turned away from each other.

I felt like I was in grade school again. Neither of us daring to make a move, but enjoying the other's company. Oh well. It could wait. We would get our time. Some day. I hoped.

CHAPTER 7

I sat at the head table with the rest of the wedding party, listening as Tory spoke about Gunnar and Ashley. I didn't hear much of it, because I was too busy thinking of what I wanted to say. I had already prepared a speech, but it hadn't ever felt quite right to me. It wasn't fresh. I'd said it all before, and this was their wedding. It felt hollow to repeat the same platitudes here, now.

All too soon, Tory wrapped up and the guests gave light applause. Ashley's eyes were misty and Gunnar was smiling at Tory.

Tory had grown a lot since we first met – that night on the Eads Bridge where we had fought against a silver dragon during a high-speed car chase. Tory had never seen a dragon before, but that hadn't stopped her from doing her best to help Gunnar and I kick its ass. Afterwards, Tory had taken the biggest risk of her life and revealed her powers to the two strangers who had saved her. She'd bent a thick bar of metal as easily as a clothes hanger, and we had officially adopted her into our new club. Just the three of us back then. And look at how big our club was now.

My gaze swept the room, picking out several faces.

Alex – the kid we had saved from the Land of the Fae – a victim of the changeling operation the Queens still practiced. We had saved him, and then I had kind of adopted him. Except… he no longer looked like the kid I had saved. Somehow, he was now a tall, strapping twenty-year-old. His dark hair and dark eyes didn't scream *bad boy* – but he seemed like the guy who would steal the bad boy's lunch money. *Changed*, I thought to myself as I let my eyes roam.

The Huntress – an assassin who had worked for Rumpelstiltskin – once an enemy, but now friend, and babysitter for Alex – not that he needed that kind of help any longer. She was watching Alex out of the corner of her eye, and she looked deeply concerned. Troubled. *Change*.

Alucard – once an enemy vampire – now a Daywalker, and ally. *Change*.

I realized everyone was staring at me, and that they probably mistook my silence for aloof drunkenness. I sighed. Damn stereotypes. I stood, clearing my throat. I turned to Ashley and Gunnar, opened my mouth to speak and… the words died on my tongue. Because they were staring at me, and the compassion in their eyes told me that nothing needed to be said.

At least between us three.

But the crowd did need to hear something.

I turned to the crowd. "Gunnar is the best stray I've ever adopted." I heard him grumble unhappily and the crowd chuckled. I let the noise die down on its own as I studied the tablecloth. "They say that a dog is a man's best friend," I began gently, not looking up at the crowd. "That a dog can draw out the secret pain hidden in a young boy's soul. And fight off any future pain the young boy may face…" In my peripheral vision, I felt Callie staring at me, her glass held halfway to her glistening lips, forgotten.

I took a slow sip of my drink, setting it back down before anyone noticed that my hand was shaking slightly. I didn't want to go into details, because as far as most of the crowd knew, I had been born with a silver spoon in my mouth – a wealthy family, given everything I wanted. I'd abused that gift and had been a general nuisance for much of my life. A spoiled brat. I had admitted this to myself long ago. I had no more shame about it. That wasn't why my hand shook.

The crowd didn't know – I hadn't even known until just recently – that my upbringing had been much darker than they thought. Possibly dark enough to make them fear me.

That I was a human, a wizard, conceived and born in the Land of the Fae. Almost unheard of. At least I was pretty confident that I was the only one that had grown to adulthood.

I realized I hadn't spoken, and that everyone was waiting nervously.

"Gunnar healed me, true, but I think the saying has it wrong. In fact, it's bullshit. I think *he* adopted *me*. I had a pretty nice upbringing... but like all children, I had my demons. And my parents knew I would need a compass. A conscience. An ally. A... brother."

I looked up at Gunnar. He sat unnaturally still, watching me as he read between the lines. Like me, he had only recently learned that my parents had brought us together as children for a very specific reason – to help ease any subconscious memories of a childhood pet I'd had in Fae.

Talon the Devourer.

That even though my parents had been forced to wipe my memory of that dark, twisted place to keep my secret safe, they knew part of my heart would always feel broken – I would always feel like a part of me was missing as my subconscious mind struggled to remember my only friend from that other childhood in Fae. So, they had introduced me to Gunnar – a young boy who had also needed healing. A friend. A brother.

"Gunnar is my role model," I finally continued. "Always has been. Always will be." Then I let out a guilty grin. "He sets a pretty high standard, though, so don't expect miracles out of me. But I think failing to match his standards will still land me in pretty good company." I let out a tired sigh, letting the laughter and clapping die down as I finished my drink. I glanced at Ashley from under my brow, grimacing. "And now I have to share him with some chick."

The crowd erupted in laughter, and I saw Ashley smile faintly, a few tears falling down her cheeks. I smiled back, then lifted my empty glass to the crowd. "To the man who inspires me to be better. And the woman who inspires him to do the same. I couldn't ask for a better family."

Tory was grinning as she gave me an expectant look. I nodded back. In unison, we cheered out, "To Mr. and Mrs. Randulf!"

Voices shouted out, repeating our toast, and cheering on Gunnar as he kissed Ashley quite thoroughly. I stepped down from the table as I noticed Alucard discreetly trying to catch my attention from across the room. Roland stood beside him, signaling Callie over. The two of us reached the vampires at the same time.

Alucard cleared his throat. "I just got a call. It seems there is a meeting tonight I must attend."

"We," Roland corrected in a low tone.

Alucard nodded.

33

Callie and I waited for more, but nothing came. "You can elaborate any time now."

Alucard looked distracted. "The local vampires want to talk to me about something. And I heard the Mastership of St. Louis is up for grabs. Probably a coincidence," he muttered dryly.

"Locals?" I frowned. "I never doubted there were other vampires in town, but they must keep one hell of a low profile. I almost never hear about them."

Alucard continued in a very low tone so that no one could overhear. "The Sanguine Council – the global authority on vampires, not unlike your Wizard Academy – wants to correct that. I don't think they were satisfied with the previous Master's lack of ambition, so they gave him an early retirement." He gave me a stern look, letting me know this was confidential, and that the body would never be found. "For some reason, they're very interested in St. Louis. I can't imagine why," he added sarcastically, "nothing ever happens here..."

Thanks to Callie and Roland, I knew about the Sanguine Council.

Roland spoke up. "Perhaps this is a meeting about the upcoming meeting. To get a feel for you before tossing your name into the hat." Alucard didn't look pleased at that prospect.

"Ah, yes. The dreaded pre-meeting meeting." Callie watched the three of us, frowning. "Do you need any help? Someone to watch your back?" I asked. That might be fun. Better than antagonizing Raego.

Alucard shook his head. "No, this needs to be kept in-house. Showing up with an army – you – would send the wrong impression. Especially if they're intending to toss my name in the hat. And with Roland accompanying me – an ex-Shepherd – I think I'm both safe, and likely to inspire confidence. Or fear." He shrugged, as if one were as good as the other.

I glanced at Callie, who looked equally uneasy. Roland was new to the vampire thing.

"I'm pretty sure a Daywalker can win the vote," I said, hiding my disappointment that I wasn't welcome to join them.

Roland shook his head. "The Sanguine Council has been known to relocate vampires to certain cities they consider valuable. Kansas City is now run by a British Vampire named Haven. I'm sure you've heard that his two predecessors were murdered in the span of a year." He gave the three of us a very level look. I tried not to look guilty since I'd been somewhat involved in both of those murders – once with Alucard when we killed his sister, and once with Callie when we'd chosen the wrong night to rob Master Simon and were framed for his murder. I decided I'd rather not do anything further to attract the attention of the Sanguine Council, not wanting to answer questions about those two deaths.

"I'm sure the Sanguine Council already has their own prospects in mind for St. Louis," Roland continued. "And that he or she might have an agenda that does not align with your own. Whereas Alucard is local, powerful, and has prior experience as a Master Vampire. A Daywalker Master Vampire who has had dealings with the other powers in town," he added meaningfully, meaning Gunnar, Raego and myself. "He's both qualified and overqualified. But in the event that any of the locals has a different opinion on the matter, I'd like to attend the meeting as well." He smiled darkly. "And I need to get a better understanding of my new… family, since I will no doubt have to confront the Sanguine Council at some point in the near future."

"Long story short, we need to leave," Alucard added. "You still…" he hesitated. "Doing that thing you mentioned earlier?" He didn't know if it was a secret so was being careful.

I nodded. "I found someone else to join me. I'll be fine." I didn't tell him that my backup was standing right beside me, and he didn't tell me whether he had spoken to Tory or not. Trust. The glue to any solid friendship.

"Good. Can you extend our apologies to Gunnar and Ashley?"

I scratched my cheeks, thinking of my price. Callie punched me in the arm. "Yes, we will," she answered for me. I scowled at her, but finally nodded at Alucard.

The two of them left without a word, putting their heads together as they walked, minds wholly focused on the meeting ahead. I shared a long look with Callie.

Tory suddenly stormed over to us, closing her purse with a *click*. "Ashley just told me in no uncertain terms that she's about to leave the party to go take care of her husband. He's getting moody thinking about the fight tomorrow morning, and she wants to remind him of the finer aspects of marriage." She winked at Callie. "Alucard mentioned an errand you needed to run?" she asked me cautiously.

I rolled my eyes at her lame attempt at subterfuge. "Callie's coming."

She nodded as if stamping her approval on the subject. "Good." I was mildly surprised that Alucard had even brought it up with her. I was even more surprised that she seemed interested. Especially with Alucard leaving for his meeting. Ah. Maybe he hadn't told her about that. Well, that was his problem.

"Ashley said she's going to make Gunnar sing tonight. So, if you two are ready, I'd rather leave before that happens. Avoid the mass exodus of the guests."

I shrugged, glancing at their table. Ashley was laying it on thick, trying to keep Gunnar in good cheer. Knowing my friend so well, I recognized the tension in his shoulders and the faraway look in his eye.

"Let's go talk to his Royal Scaliness, the Obsidian Son. I'll get the car."

Tory grabbed my shoulder as I began to turn away. "I'd rather take the faster way if it's all the same." When I arched a brow in question, her lips thinned. "When the cat's away, the mice will play," she said, casually glancing back a few tables. The Reds turned away so quickly that it was obvious they had been watching. Yahn was staring into his cup as if trying to divine his future. "I'm sure Alucard can handle them for an hour, but I'd rather not push it." Callie muffled a cough. Luckily for me, Tory was still staring at the Reds and didn't notice my sudden panic.

I couldn't think of a way to tell her that Alucard had left without accidentally giving away something he maybe hadn't wanted her to know. But if she stayed and found out Alucard had left, that wouldn't be good either. So, I kept my nose out of it. "Overprotective much?" I teased.

She punched me in the chest. Hard. Tory could throw a car when she wanted to. Her punches were not dainty love taps. I rubbed my chest absently, knowing it would bruise. "Fine, fine. Let's find some privacy. No need to raise questions." I hoped the teens made the most of tonight, because I was going to pay dearly either way when Tory or Alucard found out.

I swung back to the hall we had used for the wedding and retrieved my satchel from an empty vase behind the altar. Callie and Tory gave me disapproving stares as I dusted it off and slung it over my shoulder, the strap crossing my chest. Since no one else was nearby, I held out my hands to the two beautiful women. As one, they put on their game faces and grabbed my forearms. I Shadow Walked, ripping our bodies to spiritual shreds and sending us to Raego's mansion in the blink of an eye. A pretty neat trick.

Shadow Walking was instantaneous. One second you were leaving, the next you were arriving. With nothing happening in the middle...

But not this time.

It seemed to be a night for new experiences.

CHAPTER 8

*C*allie gasped, and two silver blades whispered out from between the knuckles of both hands, leaving her with four forearm length silver claws.

Tory snarled, her eyes suddenly flashing green.

Like a badass, I blinked.

We stood in a world of shifting black fog about as high as our knees. Other than our own breathing, I heard no sounds, not even the wind that had to be billowing the fog. I also couldn't smell anything. The black fog stretched as far as the eye could see, almost like we were standing on a black cloud. Everything above the fog was dark gray. No hills, no dips, just flat nothingness. There was no apparent source of light – nothing above us and nothing on the horizon. But I could still see Tory and Callie, so there had to be light somewhere. I slowly turned in a circle in hopes of finding it. Or a door. Maybe a blinking sign.

And I suddenly realized we weren't alone.

Two tall figures in hooded black robes faced the other direction a dozen paces away. As one, their heads swiveled entirely backwards to stare at us. Their bodies didn't move at all as they did this, reminding me of an owl's ability to rotate their necks in almost a complete circle. Also, like owls, they cocked their heads in a sudden jerking motion like they had just spotted mice.

They also did this in complete silence. Not even a rustle of fabric from their robes.

They wore masks that resembled Calaveras – white skulls painted with elaborate designs of flowers, vines, or other geometric shapes, and often studded with gems, feathers, or anything else particularly colorful. They were also known as Candy Skulls.

Like those masks people wore during the Day of the Dead festival, although those were typically made of candy and given to children as gifts.

Or they were used as an offering to the dead – an afterlife snack.

Hence the name Candy Skulls.

I'd seen a few like them once before, and had hoped to never see them again. Nothing had happened – they had just watched me. But I hadn't wanted to repeat the encounter. Something was... wrong about them. Obviously.

These two confirmed my suspicions.

Their bodies slowly rotated to face us without a sound, revealing translucent blades from their sleeves. Either their arms were glass swords, or the robes were long enough to cover their hands.

The Calaveras lunged at us without a sound and I forcefully yanked the girls back since they both looked about to attack the approaching wraiths. I tripped over something unseen behind me, dragging the two women down with me into the black fog. I sucked in a breath instinctively, not wanting to breathe in the black vapor. But the blackness instantly disappeared and I realized I was lying on a manicured lawn surrounded by ebony statues. The night sky above us glittered with stars. I heard a bird chirp in the distance and released the breath I'd been holding.

We were in Raego's yard. Back from... wherever the hell we had just been.

Callie was panting. "What – the fuck – was *that?*"

Tory tugged me to my feet, warily eyeing a few of the statues as if they might hide a Candy Skull. I did the same before helping Callie to her feet.

"I have no idea. I've never seen a... place when Shadow Walking. I've always just appeared where I intended. I didn't even know there *was* a place between!"

Callie glared at me, studying my face. "What aren't you saying?"

I swallowed, and then let out a sigh. "I've seen those Candy Skulls before. Maybe not those exact two, but when I was fighting Castor Queen a few months ago, I saw them watching me. But that was near the Arch. Not in... whatever that place was."

"Do you know what they are?" Tory asked me, finally letting out a breath.

I explained the little I knew about the Calaveras and the Day of the Dead festival. "But I didn't find anything that said they were actually living... beings. Just the skulls." I shrugged. Living or not, they were obviously creatures of some sort. "Did you sense anything?" I asked Tory, having a sudden thought. She was a Beast Master, able to control shifters at will.

Anything with a beastly nature.

She shivered, shaking her head. "I tried..." she said softly. "There was nothing inside their heads. *Nothing*. Not even *anger* when they attacked."

Callie was shaking her head in disbelief. "Well, they sure weren't friendly. I think it's safe to say Shadow Walking is off the table until we figure out what they are."

I nodded. "Agreed."

"What about Gateways?" she asked, frowning thoughtfully. "Roland and I used one to get to the wedding from Kansas City. Think they're still safe?"

I thought about it for a second and finally nodded. "I used one yesterday and it was fine. At least you can see where you're going with a Gateway." I scratched my chin thoughtfully. "I don't think I've Shadow Walked since I saw those Candy Skulls in the first place. Months ago."

Callie seemed to be recalling her own experiences, but finally shrugged. "I think it's the same for me. I don't remember the last time I Shadow Walked." She met my eyes. "Maybe we should figure out exactly what Shadow Walking *is*."

My face reddened. I'd first learned to Shadow Walk from the Justices – the wizard police – and hadn't really considered any dangers. Masks... The Justices wore silver masks. Maybe wearing a mask kept you safe from the Calaveras. I realized they were both staring at me.

"Right." I let out a breath, noticing a silhouette in one of the windows in the mansion above us. The curtain shifted and the silhouette disappeared. "We should probably go knock. We'll figure out the other stuff later. Take a deep breath and put your game faces on. *Feel* the badass. *Be* the badass." Tory rolled her eyes at my pep talk. "We're not afraid of flower-masked creeps."

We picked our way through the lawn, skirting around the various statues – some human and some not. It felt like a cemetery with us walking between headstones. Actually, that was pretty accurate, because each one of these statues had been a person once. Before they pissed off the black dragon, King Raego. The Obsidian Son.

We made it to the base of the steps at the front of the mansion and began to climb.

Two dragons I didn't recognize opened the front door before we reached the top step. They were of Asian descent and wore crisp slacks and freshly-ironed dress shirts despite the late hour. Their suit jackets looked expensive and were perfectly tailored – not the typical folded collar I would find here in the States, but the Chinese style that looked almost like a very short, popped collar, or no collar at all. I'd heard a dozen different names for the style, but didn't know the particulars of each variation since I hadn't worn one before. Almost like a Kung Fu suit.

Their pupils were horizontal slits across their vibrantly blue irises – one slightly darker blue than the other – and they looked of similar genes, perhaps brothers. Blue dragons usually meant water or ice. Maybe lightning. They didn't smile and they didn't frown. They just held the doors.

I grunted as I walked past them, not bothering to be polite. Not if they weren't going to at least say hello. I felt the energy around them change and I slowed, turning to face the one on my right. "Did you have something on your mind, dear?" I asked him.

His blue eyes darkened and his pupil contracted slightly, but I didn't back down. Neither did he, but his pal at the other door audibly cleared his throat in warning. As if delaying to respond to his pal's warning somehow proved to me how dangerous he was, he finally broke eye contact with me. If the snort he let escape his nose had been even a smidge more obvious, I would have thrown him from the landing into the garden of statues.

Maybe my satchel had pissed him off, although I hadn't seen either of them look at it.

We entered the foyer of the sprawling mansion. The blue Asian dragons closed the doors behind us and waited, pointedly not looking at us. I spotted figures lurking just out of sight in the shadows of several halls, distant rooms, and upper balconies. The steady murmur and crackling of radios confirmed their presence. Raego wasn't taking any chances of an attacker breaking in and harming his people. It also made me reconsider yelling at the scaly bastard.

"Wait here," a bronze-skinned man with thick dark hair said in a clipped but courteous tone from the base of the stairs. He'd obviously been waiting for us. He wore slacks with a white dress shirt, and reminded me of an Egyptian man that used to work at my father's company. Not the same guy, but they shared similar features – a wide nose and stubble from cheek to neck that obviously grew back ten seconds after he shaved. He turned and calmly climbed the steps. I patiently turned to assess the dragons I could see, taking stock of the various eye colors.

Each unique color signified a different type of dragon – red eyes meant fire, blue could mean ice or water, and I had even seen silver eyes that represented chrome. Gunnar hadn't been too fond of that one. Silver and werewolves got along about as well as a tornado and a trailer park.

Their lineage also impacted how their dragon form would look. I idly wondered if the Asian dudes would look like Chinese dragons, complete with those long catfish-like whiskers. I almost asked, but then I spotted the handle of the dagger strapped to his chest, tucked under his coat.

Tory and Callie studied the house itself more than its occupants. Callie wasn't very familiar with dragons, but I didn't catch even the slightest indication of fear from her. She looked... bored. Well, bored with the people. But she did look interested in the artwork and décor.

Was that a psychological ploy to lower the guards' suspicion or did she genuinely like the décor? One never knew with Callie. It was fun to watch her at work, but even more fun to watch her victims when they realized they'd been mind-fucked.

I didn't like the fact that I hadn't recognized a single dragon yet. The number of armed guards in the shadows wasn't helping my mood either. Maybe I was just being paranoid. Perhaps these new dragons just had horrible teeth. And overcompensated by standing in the dark with guns.

The same Egyptian-looking dragon reappeared at the top of the stairs, dipping his head slightly. "The Obsidian Son will see you, now. If you will follow me." Had his gaze lingered on Tory? Raego knew she was a Beast Master – that she could shut down every dragon in the mansion with a single thought. He had to have warned all these new faces.

Was that why everyone was being so unfriendly? In fear of the tiny Beast Master beside me?

Maybe this guy just recognized Tory as the Reds' adopted mom.

Whatever the reason, they were justified in keeping an eye on Tory.

I just needed to find a way to use it to my advantage.

CHAPTER 9

*W*e followed our guide up the stairs. He led us down a hall, his tan eyes glinting in the warm lighting cast by the sconces on the walls. His eyes looked like molten sand, or... maybe I was just jumping at stereotypes. Egyptian – sand. As I studied them further, I decided they were actually more like aged ivory. That felt right. I wondered what kind of magic that signified.

We reached a large set of white doors, taller than necessary, and our guide opened them for us, announcing our names – even though we hadn't given them. Even Callie.

I entered the large office, not waiting for our guide to finish speaking. It wasn't that I had a problem with the guy, but I did have a problem with his boss.

Raego Slate sat in a thickly-padded leather chair behind a wide chrome desk. He had both elbows propped on the surface to support his chin resting on his interwoven fingers – like he was posing for a high school glamour shot. Even though he was flashing us an impish smirk, I sensed that he was tired. Exhausted, even. His eyes took in Callie with an appreciative study before moving on to Tory. His smile stretched just a bit wider at her, and he dipped his chin. What was that all about? His minions had been nervous around her, but Raego was... eager?

He finally turned to me, sighed regretfully, and then lowered his hands to wave at the open seats before him. "Team Temple, please, take a seat. To what do I owe this pleasure?"

I bit my tongue, sensing the ivory-eyed dragon still standing behind us and not wanting to give him a reason to call for backup. Raego was openly toying with my obvious anger. Someone should have told him that wasn't a healthy hobby. I set my satchel beside a chair and sat down.

"What the hell is going on lately, Raego?" I said with false cheer. Almost as if to an old friend. Almost.

He was nodding absently to himself as if making an inner decision unrelated to us. Then he seemed to remember I was there. He blinked those black eyes of his – iris and pupil practically indistinguishable. "Oh, you know. This. That. Things." His eyes flickered past me. "Thank you, Ivory. That will be all."

"I knew it!" I hissed under my breath. My triumph at correctly guessing the dragon's color overrode my annoyance at Raego's crap answer. I heard the door close behind us, signaling Ivory's departure and our privacy. Callie furrowed her brows at me for a moment as if debating whether or not she wanted to know what I had been talking about. Then she shook her head and resumed her study of Raego's office. I didn't sense anyone else in the room, but that didn't mean much. I glanced at Tory to see her letting out a relaxed breath. She didn't sense anyone either, or she wouldn't have relaxed.

Raego chuckled and then pressed a button on his watch. I heard a faint chime from several spots around the room. "Someone's always watching, but *now* we are private." He indicated a point near the ceiling with a slight gesture and I turned to see a security camera tucked into the crown molding. He had obviously just turned it off with his watch, because I could see a hinged metal cap covering the lens. The others I had spotted in the halls on the way up here hadn't had the cap.

Bookshelves took up an entire wall of the massive office, and three expensive leather divans formed an arc around a fireplace in the corner – which was crackling loudly. I smelled liquor in the air, but saw no glasses on the desk or tables. Interesting developments for a man who said he'd been out of town. Of course, that was over an hour ago, so he might not be lying.

I waited for more of an answer to my earlier question, but when it was obvious nothing else was coming, I leaned back into my chair and kicked my feet up onto his desk. I accidentally knocked down a glass figurine and it shattered upon striking the marble floor. I shifted my feet as I turned to look down at it and knocked a wooden box of pens over. "Whoops," I said, frowning.

Raego held out a hand as Callie instinctively made as if to scoop up the mess. I shot her a scowl as well, but she didn't notice. He then turned to me with a patient look, not upset, but not amused. "Is something on your mind or are you just here to annoy me?" he asked tiredly.

"Just clumsy. But now that you mention it, I do have a few things on my mind..."

He waved a hand for me to continue, but halfway through the gesture one of the fingers on that hand stretched into an inky black dragon claw. He focused his attention on using the tip of the claw to clean one of his human fingernails on the other hand. It wasn't a casual threat. It was literally just Raego's personality. Have a dirty fingernail – use my powerful dragon claw rather than wasting my time tracking down some nail clippers.

"The anticipation is killing me..." he said, not looking up.

"Gunnar got married. And you told me you would be there for it."

"I doubt Gunnar even noticed my absence. It was just a wedding. Statistically, he'll probably have another." Tory's fingers suddenly gripped the desk, denting it as she leaned forward. Raego blinked as if suddenly recalling his words. He waved his human hand, vaguely apologetic, but it felt more like he regretted that we had taken offense rather than him taking back the statement.

Raego had always been bad at recognizing even widely-accepted social behaviors.

"I can't be bothered with every social event that happens in this town," he muttered. I stared at him in disbelief, even glancing back at Tory, who was staring at him as if he were a stranger. He didn't sound angry, just utterly fed up. Exhausted. As if he gave no shits about no things.

He sensed the silence and finally looked up, his hand shifting back into its human form. "Politics are eating away my soul," he finally admitted with a yawn.

I blinked at him. "You're the Dragon King. Execute the politicians and stop being a dick."

He waggled a finger as if my point had been redundant. "Heavy is the crown."

I decided to change the topic, sensing Callie and Tory both watching me. "Strange things are going down in our city. Rogue shifters. A lot of... old

46

people are moving into St. Louis..." I said, emphasizing *old* in hopes he would understand I was referring to Gods and monsters.

He nodded, but his eyes suddenly latched onto a letter opener on the desk. He lifted it with a frown, as if realizing he could have used that for his nails rather than his claw. He grunted and tossed it back, turning to look up at me. "I'm sorry, did you ask me something?"

I let out a very patient breath. I hadn't spent a whole lot of time around Raego lately – only during life or death situations where all we needed to do was go kill things. But when I had first met him, I'd had my doubts about his mental stability. He shared tendencies with autistic savants. He could be brilliantly quick-witted if properly motivated, but without that motivation he was easily distracted and distant. Or maybe he could only function well when full of adrenaline. Conversations with no immediate benefit were the literal bane of his existence.

I briefly thought of those ancient kings who were almost legendary in their conquests but then lost it all during times of peace. I really hoped that wasn't the case with Raego.

I needed to motivate him, find the right trigger to engage him. Give him a purpose.

I leaned forward, almost pleading. "Can you help me keep an eye on our city? I think some bad things are coming our way, and we'll need to work together to get through it."

"I can't. I have my own shit to deal with."

I grunted. "Wow. I'm so glad I helped you earn your crown. It's the residual appreciation that I love the most. How you always repay the favor. This is your city, too, you know."

He sneered at that. "I can no longer help you. As you just pointed out, *too many* dragons remember that you helped me earn my crown." He met my eyes, the black depths of his irises seeming to ripple like hot oil, letting me know he was on the edge – dangerously close to shifting into his black dragon form – one of the rarest types possible. "I appreciate all that you've done to help me get here, Nate. We are friends, but it is time for us to go our separate ways. There *are* too many new faces in town, but I need to look after my own interests – my dragons."

"Well, three of those dragons are *mine*," I said through my teeth. Tory shifted beside me, silently reminding me that the Reds were technically *hers*.

"That wasn't a question, so I'm glad you didn't comment," I added towards Raego.

Raego rolled his eyes and turned to Tory, letting me know he was well aware who was in charge of the teenagers. "The Reds can go where they wish. But you will not keep them from me if they wish to return here. And I will not try to take them from you. Fair?" he asked her.

She thought about it for a moment. "Yahn as well." He nodded, looking amused. "Agreed," she finally said.

He continued to study Tory thoughtfully, and I could tell by the look in those black eyes that he was considering involving her in some scheme. Tory didn't need my help to stand up against Raego. She could have him eating out of the palm of her hand if she wanted to and he knew it. The only way to get to Tory was... through the Reds. Even though Raego had just assured her they were off limits, I suddenly began to have doubts, sensing loopholes in his promise. I opened my mouth to tell him to back off.

But Callie abruptly stood, cutting me off. I'd almost forgotten she was here. She scooped up my satchel and hefted it over a shoulder. "I left my lipstick inside," she said, patting the satchel. "Maybe Tory and I can go sit by the fire while you two catch up. It's rather chilly in here." Tory stood, rubbing her arms in agreement. I glanced down at the bag that was now in full view. I'd almost forgotten about it, but if Raego had seen it earlier he would have said something.

Clever, Callie... I thought to myself.

I turned back to see Raego's eyes pass over the satchel to instead watch the women walk away. Then he froze and did a double-take, his fingers suddenly gripping the table as they noticed the chain strap. I followed his gaze to see Callie sit down beside Tory as she reached inside the satchel with an empty hand, speaking softly to Tory. She withdrew her lipstick from the satchel and I managed to hide my surprise. I knew for a fact that her lipstick had never been in my satchel. She had deft fingers to pull off a sleight of hand that easily.

I cleared my throat, turning back to Raego. He slowly turned to me, eyes thoughtful. I smiled, batting my eyelashes innocently. He knew what that chain was made of. Dragon scales so tough that they supposedly couldn't be melted. Black dragon scales. Just like his own.

"Watch your back, Nate," he finally said, sounding as if he wanted nothing more than to go get some sleep. "A storm is coming. I'm not sure when, or who, but it's coming in like a high tide, and I fear we may all break under it."

"Then perhaps you shouldn't be cowering in your sandcastle," I urged, suddenly glad that Callie had left. Whatever she had done had changed something in Raego. "Team up with me. Whatever is coming will have a much harder time dealing with us if we stand together."

"Team up..." he mused, leaning back in his chair. "Under your rule, no doubt." I shrugged after a moment, not knowing how to answer his question. I definitely wasn't looking for any personal gain, but *someone* needed to coordinate things, and I had done pretty well coordinating numerous groups during the attacks that had plagued St. Louis in recent years. He sighed. "My people will not accept you. Even if I told them to. And I won't. Not without a direct benefit."

"Jesus, Raego," I growled, swiping the hair out of my eyes. "I put you in this throne. What more do you want from me? You know I'm not power-hungry. I'm not trying to dominate you."

A ghost of a smile crossed his lips. "That should be a thing. Domi-Nate. It's quite catchy."

After a moment of tense silence, I let out a faint smile. This was the Raego I liked. "No one else seems to think so..." I muttered.

He shrugged, silently stating there was no accounting for taste. "Let's not part with harsh words, Nate. I've helped you, you've helped me. Let's remember that. Perhaps we can one day stand beside each other again. If it benefits me and mine, of course." He winked.

I sighed. It wasn't what I had hoped for, but I understood. He wasn't speaking as my friend. He led the dragons. All of them. And even though he was in charge, it was likely that many dragons – possibly much older than himself – would only offer their support if they got something out of it. He worked for them as much as they worked for him. Give and take.

I also understood his position about teaming up under my banner. If the Academy had approached me asking me to quasi-submit to them for the betterment of all, I would have had a really tough time agreeing to it. He had a point. He needed to rule his own people. I needed to rule mine. Distant allies, not partners. Very distant, it seemed.

Like Gunnar had just made abundantly clear in regards to his wolves.

And Alucard, I guessed.

Why did it suddenly feel like I was being abandoned by all my friends? Or that a line was being drawn in the sand?

"Okay," I told him. "But if things get bad, don't be a stranger."

He watched me thoughtfully, not answering.

CHAPTER 10

Since that was as good as it was apparently going to get, I dropped the topic. Raego kept his eyes on the table, teasing a sliver of steel up with one of his claws that suddenly slid into existence again without any apparent effort. "I would like to speak with Tory about an internal affair, if it's not too much trouble."

I blinked. Then I laughed. "*Really*? You won't help me, but you want one of my people?"

"I am not one of your people, Nate," Tory snarled, suddenly standing beside my chair with Callie. I blinked at the two of them, then glared as I saw Callie trying to bite back her laughter.

Raego eyed Callie. "You might suffice as well. I've heard many interesting stories about Kansas City and the Holy Hitmen. Or Hit-woman," he corrected with a smile, eyes briefly flicking to the satchel on her shoulder. Well, the chain strap.

She didn't miss a beat, readjusting the strap casually. "Like you, I have enough shit going on back home. I don't need my first encounter with dragons to be political. And *Holy* hardly begins to describe me..." she added under her breath. Because she'd had some recent run-ins with the Vatican. Obviously, Raego hadn't heard about that. Or hadn't chosen to reveal his awareness.

Raego shrugged good-naturedly, shooting me a quick look as if to say *this is how you handle rejection.* I folded my arms stubbornly as he turned back to Tory.

Tory looked guarded, but intrigued. Because she wasn't stupid. Raego was the king of the dragons, and he was asking her for a favor. She knew that as dragons, the Reds might someday choose to be under his command. By birth, they kind of already were, in a way. But Tory was a Beast Master and their legal guardian. There was conflicting loyalty involved. Crossover.

But one day they might decide to step into the dragon family, and anything Tory did now could make that harder or easier for them, depending. Any decision here could impact them long term. For better or worse. That being said, what mom didn't want to stick her nose into a hornet's nest for her kids? Better than going in blind.

Tory helping Raego could be a huge benefit for them down the line.

Declining to help Raego could be a huge detriment for them down the line.

It was about risk versus reward.

"Regarding what?" she asked warily.

He was silent for a time, carefully choosing his words. "I need an impartial judge. The opposite of one of *your* people," he added, smiling at me. I grunted, leaning back in my chair. "With you being a Beast Master, I thought you might be an ideal candidate. Of course, my Council would have to judge your impartiality."

I shifted in my chair, not actually leaning closer, but almost willing to interrupt him. Council? Since when had the dragons had a council? They had Raego – their prophesied Obsidian Son – a dragon of immeasurable power who would one day lead them to greatness. No one had actually informed me what that greatness would entail, but his father, Alaric Slate, had been willing to murder his own son in order to get that power. Raego and I hadn't agreed, so had killed him, putting Raego on the throne instead.

Raego continued. "It would be best if the Council saw us at odds with each other, proof of your impartiality." He nodded to himself, a slow smile splitting his cheeks. By the look on Callie's face, she was sensing the same alarm bells as I was.

Tory frowned. "You want me to lie to your Council? Pretend I'm not working for you?"

He shook his head, still smiling. "No. I want you to do this for the dragons. Unbiased."

I opened my mouth to chime in, but then wisely closed it. Tory needed to make this decision for herself. Looking into her eyes, I knew she was well aware of the dangers – shifters and their games. Because Tory was the principal at Shift – a school for wayward shifters that she had saved from an illegal fight club operation run by another Beast Master. She had done so well running the school that she was now receiving applications for more new students than she could reasonably handle. Every shifter without a pack was trying to send their kids to her school, if for no other reason than to keep them safe.

It was in Tory's best interest to look after each and every student, regardless of breed. She'd made this point very clear a few times in recent months – that pack politics had zero influence over her students. If the student chose to leave, she wouldn't stop them, but no alpha was coming into her school to take fellow shifters away from her to pad out their pack. Unless they wanted everyone to see them put in their place by a tiny woman with the powers of a Beast Master.

And since most shifters valued power and their reputation, not many dared try.

What was so important to Raego that he would choose to use her as a judge? What was she to investigate? The only reason the dragons would need to hire a third party was if they didn't know which dragons they could trust. Some inner power struggle? If so, why wasn't Raego hiring her for himself? Something wasn't adding up.

"I want to be there for the meeting. As her guard. Nothing more. No influence. I'll even do my best to act meek when she yells at me if it will make your dragons feel better. But I want to know why. No games. What do you need her for?"

Raego studied me in silence, then arched a brow at Tory. After a moment, she nodded her agreement. "I want to know the full story up front. Everything."

Raego tapped his claw on the table. "You sure, Beast Master? Everything?" he whispered.

She nodded, but seeing that he wasn't looking up, she spoke. "Yes. Everything."

He let out a long sigh. "There has been a theft. An internal job."

I sucked in a breath through my teeth. Tory locked eyes with Raego. "Suspects?"

He stood from his chair and turned his back on us, staring at a display of stone eggs on a back desk that I hadn't noticed. They looked like dragon eggs. *Old* dragon eggs. I would have shrugged them off as figurines, but then I noticed the glass cases around them and the raised stands they were sitting on. They looked pressure sensitive.

Raego finally cleared his throat. "All are suspects... Including me."

The silence was deafening. Tory furrowed a brow, licking her lips slowly. "You mean to tell me that you're really hiring me to prove your innocence. That's a lawyer, not a judge."

He glanced over his shoulder, his dark hair whipping at the sudden motion. "No. I'm telling you that I trust your instincts to uncover the thief. I'm not hiring you to defend me, and I'm not hiring you to pin the blame on someone else. I'm hiring you to find the thief. If that turns out to be me, so be it." My eyes might have widened a bit at that. "And in point of fact, I'm not hiring you. I think you're the best person for the job, but the Council still gets to vote. You're working for the dragons. My people. Not just a single person."

"I hate to ask the stupid questions—"

"But you're so good at it, Nate," Callie piped up.

I ignored her, watching Raego's eyes. "Did you steal this... thing?" I asked.

Raego didn't answer immediately. "That's up to Tory to find out."

Okay. This was just weird. If Raego *hadn't* stolen it, why wouldn't he just say so? And if he *had* stolen it, why would he risk hiring someone as qualified as Tory? But... he wasn't hiring her, I remembered. Raego had said this mysterious new Council needed to vote on it. Why?

What game was being played? I shot Tory a warning look, mouthing *trap.*

She nodded and without missing a beat, mouthed *Reds.*

Which was the bait for the trap. She would risk anything for the Reds.

My mind raced with half a dozen scenarios – some good, some bad, but all needlessly complex. In my world, that usually meant she should have been running for the hills. But since this wasn't a storybook novel, and Tory was the kind of mom to risk her life for her girls...

"Let's go meet with your Council," she said in an overly calm tone. "Now."

I blinked at that. Then... I smiled. That was clever of her. Give them no time to maneuver. If they wanted her help, she would come in like a freight train.

Raego arched a brow at her, surprised and... excited? She held up a hand as he opened his mouth. "I'm not agreeing to it yet. I'm saying I will meet with the Council. I'll make my decision after. Or..." she trailed off with a shrug, "they could choose not to vote for me."

Was she planning on doing something to sabotage the vote? Piss off the Council? I frowned. That wouldn't help Raego, or the Reds, so I dismissed it. I shot Callie a look, but she shrugged, just as baffled as I was.

Unsurprisingly, the monsters were playing games. Or at least Raego was.

Raego glanced down at his watch and then grinned. "The Council is currently in a meeting. Let's go interrupt them."

I climbed to my feet. Bringing Tory with me tonight had been a bad idea. I grimaced at a new thought. And it would only get worse when she found out I hadn't told her about Alucard's meeting tonight, and that the girls she was doing all this cloak and dagger shit for were probably up to no good with Yahn right now.

"Sure, let's piss off this Council of yours. By the way, you're doing the whole King thing wrong. You're supposed to be a dictator, not let a group of bureaucrats dictate to *you*."

He glanced at me, amused. "King Arthur and his Round Table had it all wrong then?"

My blood ran cold at that, but I kept my face a mask, shrugging my shoulders in defeat. He couldn't know of my interest in King Arthur and his Round Table. It was just an idle comment.

Right. Just an idle comment. No reason to freak out and burn everything to ashes.

Callie watched me, slowly shaking her head. After spending a lot of private time with me recently, she had become remarkably aware of my inner workings. Seeming to be able to sense when I was worried about something, even though my face showed nothing.

Raego was already leading Tory from the room, leaving Callie and I to follow on our own.

The Kansas City wizard leaned in, whispering softly into my ears. Her shorter hair smelled like strawberries as a few strands tickled my nose. "I don't know dragons, but I know liars. I just can't decide if Tory is the victim, bait, or his personal wolfhound."

I nodded, wrapping my arm around her waist to guide her from the room, not wanting Raego to catch us whispering. I lowered my hand from her back after I got her moving and murmured under my breath. "Just watch. Tory's a big girl." *I hope.*

Callie breathed a sigh, nodding as she handed me back my satchel.

"Chop, chop, Temple. I would hate for you to get lost," Raego called over his shoulder. He glanced back, smirking. Even though his eyes were black, they somehow managed to sparkle in the lighting. "Or would I?" he added, laughing.

"Fucking St. Louis," Callie muttered.

"Fucking dragons," I corrected as we hurried to catch up.

CHAPTER 11

We strode up to a door with two male dragons standing guard outside, bodies too lazily relaxed to be anything but experienced killers. Like resting lions. One was a tall, thickly built thirty-something guy with scars on his face and a crooked nose. His hair was buzzed close to the scalp and he leaned against the wall with his arms folded.

The other was dark-haired, also buzzed close to the scalp, but his scars were across the top of his head. He had a thick dark beard and one long eyebrow wider than most mustaches, making him look perpetually angry. They must have gotten the scars before they became weredragons because dragon shifters had incredible healing abilities.

All in all, they positively screamed *friendly*. Especially with those big guns at their hips.

One look at Raego and they said, "Da," in unison before uni-brow rapped on the door in a specific beat. Russians? That was new.

They pulled it open without waiting for a response. Raego strolled inside first, tugging Tory after him as if escorting her to a ball.

Not wanting to be left outside with the guards, I strolled past them, ignoring their sniffs.

Callie sniffed them right back, and then let a grimace pass over her features before continuing through. I hid my smile as I stared at the five dragons seated at the table before us. And when I say *us*, I mean Tory, Callie, and myself. Because Raego was busy pouring himself a drink near a bar to our right, as if forgetting we were here or that anyone was here, for that matter.

Which meant we braved the stares of the five dragons all alone.

I only recognized one of them – Gertrude – Raego's grandmother. The last time we had met, I had flicked her in the eyeball with my finger nail and then blown her snout right off her face. But since you couldn't actually die at the Dueling Grounds, here she was.

"Well. This is awkward…" I said, shifting from foot to foot. "It's Dirty Gerty."

There was a collective intake of breath from everyone in the room at the blatant disrespect I had shown the seemingly harmless little old lady. But I knew better than to let my eyes deceive me. She wasn't harmless. She was over four hundred years old, and liked to be in charge. The last time I had seen her, Raego had been very careful around his Gram Gram, and described her as *controlling*. I'd never mixed well with that type. I waited for Raego to step in to defend her, but he didn't. That was a change for the better. Wasn't it?

Her cheeks flushed a deep purple and she pulled back her lips to show me her teeth. Her blue eyes were flecked with gold, which were made all the more vibrant by her inflamed cheeks. Pleased with the reaction, I decided I liked Dirty Gerty better than Gram Gram.

I dipped my head, seemingly apologetic. "Where's that swanky purse you had last time we met?" I had used it to blow a supernova into her ribcage at the Dueling Grounds, so she probably remembered. "I was hoping to have some girl talk. Maybe compare bags." I lifted the chain strap of my satchel with two fingers, hefting it up and down, giving them a chance to see it was made of black dragon scales – scales that everyone thought were impossible to melt down and re-forge.

Her sneer faded, and I felt her companions shift uncomfortably in their seats. She seemed to regain some of her composure, avoiding looking at my satchel and turning to the other dragons.

"This is Nate Temple. I'm sure you've heard of him. More's the pity."

Judging by the stiffening of shoulders, she was right. I released the strap and waved politely.

Their faces hardened, but they didn't speak. Gertrude pointed to each, introducing them.

Baron Skyfall was an older black man. He was bald as an egg and had dark freckles on the skin just below his bright orange eyes. In contrast to his shining dome, he sported a short white beard – looking to be made of bulletproof cotton since I couldn't see the flesh through the hair. His orange irises stood out starkly against his skin. He was a tall bastard, easily twice as wide as most men, and had a thick neck. From what I could see he was obviously buff and I knew that if he got to his feet he would tower over me. Much bigger than Gunnar, but differently proportioned.

He smiled at me with very white teeth. "Wotcher cock," he said in a distinct British accent.

"Watch his *what?*" Callie gasped in disbelief.

Baron Skyfall grinned back at her, but I spoke first. "A greeting," I told her, meeting his eyes. Those orange irises seemed to roil with flame. That phrase was also used to mean *watch your clock*, as in, your ass. A greeting and… a warning. Or was it a threat? Callie repeated the phrase under her breath as if committing it to memory. I only recognized it because I had spent quite a bit of time in London recently – in some of the seedier neighborhoods where cockney slang was more frequently used. Did he know about my travels? I turned to the next dragon.

Chu was next in line. He laughed in the face of stereotypes by sporting a long, thin goatee – his mustache hanging down below his chin in thin strips like ribbons of silk, and his wisp of a chin patch hung between it, a little thicker, but not by much. He wore his hair tied back in a gray ponytail, not a strand out of place. His suit matched the two blue dragons I had seen at the front door, and I wondered idly if they were his sons.

He stared at me like a big stinky asshole.

His gray hair let me know he was old, but there was no way for me to guess the number. Gertrude looked to be in her sixties but she was over four hundred. Chu looked to be in his mid-fifties, but he maintained the youth of a Shaolin Monk ready to Zen my ass into oblivion. I squinted at him, letting him take that how he pleased. His slate gray eyes narrowed further.

Enya had skin as pale as milk, and her long wavy hair was the color of spun gold – but with hints of red when the light caught it just so. She wore a layered silk robe, almost inappropriate enough to be a nightgown, and had a long thin neck. Her open robe informed me that she was very well developed and proud of it. She didn't appear to be past her early forties, but those emerald green eyes were darkly inviting. A cougar on the prowl. I fed her ego with a smile. Her reply was to slowly lick her teeth. Subtle, she was not. This Russian was trouble in a silk bow.

The last was Malik, a caramel-skinned man. He apparently found his book more interesting because he didn't bother acknowledging me. He was lithe and thin but looked as strong as wire. His dark hair hung to his shoulders and I caught a faint yellow glow to his eyes as he turned a page in his book. I was pretty sure that he was Egyptian like Ivory.

Which brought up an interesting point. Almost everyone I had seen so far tonight had been a stranger and seemed to closely resemble these Council members. Except for Baron, but there had been those guards lurking in the shadows with radios and guns. Maybe they were his.

Four old dragons from various parts of the world in a Council with Dirty Gerty... I'd overheard that Raego's grandmother had been causing nothing but headaches since she came to town. Nothing major, just the grumblings anyone would make over their grandmother living with them. But I hadn't heard anything about her running a Council until tonight. Had Raego given her this Council to get her out of his hair? A peace offering? Or was this a power struggle? It might even be a check against Raego's... absentmindedness.

Maybe this Council wasn't a bad idea. Like a Board of Directors to keep the trigger-happy CEO in line.

But everything I had learned so far from Raego, the added security, all the new faces... It just didn't feel like one big happy family. And whenever a group of older, wiser patriarchs and matriarchs coordinated together to assert their will on a younger relative, it rarely worked to his benefit. Then again, I had always been suspicious of groups. It was far too easy for individuals to get swept up in their hidden agendas.

Raego piped up, addressing the Council. "This is Callie Penrose, a wizard from Kansas City. She... well, kills assholes, I guess." He turned to her, beaming energetically. "Ever killed a dragon, Callie?" he asked before slurping loudly from his drink. "Nate has."

I got ready to throw down.

CHAPTER 12

*C*allie arched a brow at Raego, momentarily caught off guard. "Not yet."

Baron Skyfall's booming laughter doused the tension in the small room like a wet blanket. Malik snapped his book shut at the sudden sound. Callie smiled back at Baron, shrugging. Since Malik had been so rudely interrupted, he set the book down with an impatient sigh and deigned to grace us with his unbridled attention.

Raego pointed at Tory. "This is Tory Marlin. Thought you might want to interview her for the... investigation." They nodded politely, but didn't seem particularly interested at the mention of interviewing her. "Oh, and she's a Beast Master," he added, as if he'd almost forgotten.

That caught their attention. Malik even scooted back in his chair, eyes narrowing. Enya leaned forward, cocking her head thoughtfully. She was smiling, I think. I was too busy making sure she wasn't about to fall out of that robe. Chu blinked slowly, but I saw his fingers twitch.

Dirty Gerty spoke up in a casual tone. "She is also beholden to Nate Temple."

"I am beholden to *no one*," Tory snarled angrily. "If you don't want my help, stop wasting my time. I've got plenty of other things to do." She turned to leave the room.

"Finally, a good idea," I muttered, turning to follow her. I stumbled into her back and fell down onto my ass. I frowned as she slowly turned to look down at me, eyes very cold.

"I don't think anyone asked you for your opinion…"

I scowled angrily. "This is a shit idea, Tory, and you know it—"

Tory gave an annoyed shake of her head and walked past me. She whipped out a chair and sat down across from the Council. "It would be rude to not at least hear you out."

Callie glanced down at me, shrugged, and then joined Tory at the table. I climbed to my feet, grumbling unhappily. Rather than crawling up to the table like a kicked puppy, I sauntered over to Raego, holding out my hand for a drink. He pointed a finger at the bar and then jumped up to sit on the counter. My eyes narrowed. The bastard. Not even in his own house. He wasn't going to serve me a drink. Then again, the thought might have never crossed his mind.

I poured a healthy splash of something amber colored into a glass. I sniffed it, felt my eyes water a little, and grunted in approval. Then, with no one else to impress, I climbed up onto the bar beside Raego, ignoring the perfectly empty bar stools. In fact, I propped my shoes on them, watching as Dirty Gerty spoke to Tory.

Callie propped her chin in her hands, observing silently. Looking more curious than anything.

Dirty Gerty cleared her throat, interrupting Chu in the middle of his question. He didn't look pleased, but he didn't challenge her. Interesting. "With Raego bringing you into this, I can't help but wonder if your loyalties lie with him. If you can be trusted. We can't have a biased judge." She did a good job of appearing to be a responsible Council member, with only the best interests of the dragons at heart. Not accusing Raego, but bringing up a valid point.

"This is fucking ridiculous," I muttered to myself, rolling my eyes.

Raego shrugged, sweeping the Council with a disinterested look. "Then tell her *no*. I don't give a shit. I only brought her here because you wanted someone trustworthy. Independent. At least we won't have to be concerned about her being mentally manipulated as she investigates."

Silence filled the room as the other dragons considered that. "He has a fair point," Baron said.

Tory looked over her shoulder at me. "This might take a while, Nate. I'll see myself home."

I blinked at her. "You don't have a car…"

"Raego will arrange for one." And there wasn't an ounce of subservience in her tone. Quite the opposite, actually. It hadn't even been phrased as a request. Raego went entirely still.

I could sense heat rolling off him in waves. I knew he wanted Tory to look into this… theft or whatever, but that didn't mean he was okay with being disrespected.

He finally hopped off the bar. "It's your funeral, girl." And he left. Without me.

I caught what looked like a brief flash of triumph in Dirty Gerty's eyes, but she was turning to Tory with an apologetic look before I could confirm it. Tory was playing a dangerous game.

But she would risk anything for the Reds. Even playing Dirty Gerty against Raego, it seemed.

I wasn't concerned for her immediate safety, because I knew that with a thought, she could have the five Council members simultaneously braiding her hair, feeding her grapes, painting her nails, drawing a bath, and ironing her dress.

But… the dragons knew that, too. They wouldn't play her game. They would attempt to *manipulate* her. Use leverage to bend her to their will. Or plant a knife in her ribs when she wasn't looking.

I was confident Dirty Gerty had plans. Raego had plans. Each Council member had plans.

Tory smiled at the Council. "Now, where were we…"

Callie made her goodbyes as she excused herself from the table, but the Council hardly seemed to notice as they nodded along with Baron Skyfall as he spoke to Tory in a basso rumble. We walked out of the room in silence. I glanced back before the doors closed to see Gertrude studying Tory thoughtfully, as if wondering how best to cook her before eating her.

Seeing my attention, she gave me a sniff of disdain. No love lost there.

We ignored the two guards as we retraced our steps down the hallway in silence. Raego was nowhere in sight, and it looked like we weren't worthy of a guide any longer.

Putting Tory and the dragons to the back of my mind, I spoke softly to Callie. "The werewolf duel is tomorrow, and we probably need to let Roland know about the Candy Skulls. Make sure he doesn't decide to go Shadow Walking any time soon."

In reply, Callie's face grew suddenly slack, as if only just realizing Roland might be in danger. She stopped abruptly, breathing heavily as her eyes grew distant. Then she flung her hand in front of her with a snarl. A flaming Gateway crackled into existence in the middle of the hallway – in full view of the guards outside the door to the Council. She snatched hold of my wrist and tugged me after her as if we were fleeing an anticipated explosion. I half jogged, half stumbled through the Gateway just as the dragon guards roared behind us, and landed on soft grass outside Chateau Falco. Talon and Carl were bare-chested and sparring under the light of the moon not ten paces away.

The two spun with their blades facing us, jaws set as they stared down the dragons shouting from the other side of the Gateway. Callie let it wink shut as she locked eyes with me. "I'm going to go see if Roland's back yet." She patted Talon and Carl on the shoulders before walking back to my mansion at a brisk pace.

Talon and Carl stared at me, the question unspoken but obvious.

"Don't ask me. I just live here..." I eyed their weapons. "Why are you sparring? It's nighttime."

Talon shrugged. "I'm a cat. I'm nocturnal."

Carl waved his claws at his white scales. "Does it look like I get a lot of sun?"

I sighed. "Keep those blades sharp. We're leaving soon..." And I told them Death's message. That it was almost time to go to Hell. Everyone else thought we were taking a quick trip to Fae.

I only needed to keep that secret for a few more days. After that, it wouldn't matter.

It was late, but I couldn't sleep yet. I had a few things to do. Regrettable things, but I would pay any price to keep my friends safe. Whether they wanted me to or not. And since I was already planning to go to Hell, I decided there wasn't much harm in making a deal with a demon.

I just hoped I had time to complete the ritual before the sun rose or I would lose my chance.

"Time to get to work," I muttered under my breath as I opened another Gateway, ignoring Carl and Talon's urgent shouting behind me as I stepped into darkness.

～

I stood cloaked in the shadows of the stygian, abandoned warehouse. These wretched demons preferred the inky darkness. Their crimes could be better hidden. I stared them down with the fury of a pissed-off wizard that had nothing to lose. All I could see of them was a faint reflection in their predatory eyes. "You will listen in silence or I'll strip the flesh from your bones."

Their eyes narrowed, with outrage or hesitation, I couldn't be sure. All I knew was that I couldn't turn my back on them. And I couldn't give them an inch or I would be overrun.

I told them what I needed.

After some time, they came to some agreement. "What's in it for us, wizard?"

I told them.

Even though I couldn't see anything but their eyes, I could practically feel them salivating with raw hunger. I had offered their favorite form of currency, even though it may cost me my life.

Dealing with these creatures was a last resort, but they were the only ones I could trust.

"Do we have a deal?" I finally asked them.

Their spine-tingling cackle was the only response necessary.

CHAPTER 13

The wolves had somehow convinced King Midas to host the duel. Since he owned vast tracts of land all over town, he hadn't had any problems finding a nice, secluded spot for a little bloodshed. He also owned the Dueling Grounds – where Achilles and the Minotaur ran the supernatural Fight Club of St. Louis – so had experience hosting organized fights.

Which really wasn't much different from a duel.

But as I swept my gaze from left to right, I wondered if it was really distant enough. Because it looked like we were hosting a charity marathon.

Hundreds of people milled about the small valley tucked between wooded hills somewhere in the northern section of Midas' farm – an expansive tract of woodlands and pasture.

I'd been walking around, getting a feel for the place, and wishing I had grabbed a coffee thermos. I'd spotted a bleary-eyed Tory a while ago and waved at her, hoping to get some details on her night. She had calmly walked up, slapped me hard in the face, and warned me never to lie to her again before storming away. From that encounter, I somehow surmised that she had learned of Alucard's meeting last night and hadn't been happy with me for keeping it from her.

She hadn't even bothered to ask me about the Reds, but they were wandering around here somewhere. I had seen them when I first arrived, sitting in the grass with Yahn. I decided not to warn them about Tory's temper, but maybe they already knew because they had avoided me.

I was still wandering around, growing impatient, when I saw Callie approach Tory. I realized I had slowed, smiling in anticipation of the oncoming slap. But much to my dismay, the two spoke for a few seconds before wandering off together, hugging like old friends. I scowled, rubbing my cheek as I swept the valley, focusing on the werewolves.

Gunnar and Ashley's pack had broken down into what looked like highly disorganized pockets and huddles. But if you knew what to look for, it was actually kind of alarming. Each wolf – also called a *claw* – actually belonged to a predetermined group – or *paw* – of five wolves. Furthermore, each *paw* was partnered with three others, making a *ghost*.

Five claws made up a *paw*, and four *paws* made up a *ghost* – twenty wolves.

Ashley had taught it to them once it became apparent that the pack was getting too large to easily coordinate during times of war. Like with an army, discipline and order saved lives. These smaller, lightning-fast units were both incredibly nimble to maneuver, and easy to bunch together if necessary. It was much more efficient than a few hundred wolves running around chaotically.

There were at least twenty Ghosts – four hundred werewolves – loosely arranged around half of the make-shift ring where Gunnar and Zeus would fight. Some of these Ghosts were human while others were wolf, also seemingly at random.

I was pretty sure it was organized chaos. It was obvious that none had chosen to switch sides.

Light rain began to fall. I glared up at the clouds, realizing I had left my umbrella near my seat with Alucard and Roland. I was tired, feeling particularly useless, and obviously grumpy, thanks to Tory, so I used my magic to create a transparent dome that I let hover over my head. The water struck it and rolled off, leaving me perfectly dry. Whenever anyone nearby noticed, I shot them a very dark grin until they ran away with their tail tucked between their legs.

Literally or figuratively – since many of the attendees *were* in wolf form.

I glanced at Zeus' pack of a hundred wolves. It seemed he had exaggerated last night, or hadn't realized how big Gunnar's pack actually was. In contrast with the St. Louis wolves, they sat in neat, orderly rows like they were gearing up for a Colonial musket battle. They all faced forward towards the ring. The three rows closest to the ring were wolves, the next few rows were kneeling humans, and the rest of the pack stood behind them.

And for the most part, they didn't make a noise.

Like they had all been bred in some science lab or military school. Maybe they were just that scared of their boss. Othello had done some research on Zeus Fletcher, but she hadn't come up with anything that useful. He seemed to be one of those ex-military, private types – living on a hill in the middle of the woods with trip-wires surrounding his cabin full of guns.

The non-wolf attendees were careful not to wade too deep into either pack, respecting the imaginary lines that marked each territory.

But Talon, being a raging dick, walked over to Zeus' pack, picked a nearby spot in full view of them all, and pissed on a tree. Carl stood a few yards back, staring down the wolves the entire time. Talon shook twice before lowering his kilt, and then the crazy bastard pawed his boots in the dirt before walking away, like a cat cleaning his litterbox. Carl kept staring at the wolves as he held up his claw for Talon to high five him. Only then did they turn and walk away.

But that was the extent of our involvement in the matter. Because Gunnar had reminded me – personally upon my arrival – that this was strictly to be handled by him.

"This is wolf business," he had said in a firm tone.

Tired of walking, I approached my seat to find Alucard and Roland using my umbrella, smirking at Talon's act of defiance. They had been silent about their meeting last night, even though I had pestered them several times already. At least the cloud cover would protect Roland from the sun, although I knew he had a stash of some special sunscreen that could protect him for short periods.

It looked like we all had our dance cards and wouldn't be sharing partners.

Talon, Carl and I were secretly going to Hell.

Gunnar and Ashley were about to fight a duel so they could hopefully go on their honeymoon.

Roland and Alucard were attending secret vampire meetings.

Yahn and the Reds were stealing kisses, avoiding the adults like the plague.

And Tory was working as a private investigator for the dragons.

I let out an angry sigh, but I wasn't quite sure why. I didn't want to stick my head into anyone else's problems, but... I was used to it. Us working as a team. And now...

Talon and Carl strutted our way, sitting in the grass beside me, glaring at the wolves across the ring, who actually seemed to be snarling back. "I can't wait to go to Hell," Talon purred in a tone that even Roland and Alucard couldn't have overheard.

"I hear it's beautiful this time of year," Carl agreed just as quietly, his tongue flicking out to catch rain drops.

Tory and Callie approached from behind us and both Roland and I jumped to our feet. Roland instantly wrapped an arm around Callie, leading her away to talk in private. I approached Tory, not sure if I wanted to apologize or demand answers about the dragons. I'd taken the slap like a man, so I deserved something for my trouble. I opened my mouth, but she held up a hand.

"I will not speak of it, Nate. Don't meddle. Please." She very discreetly flicked her eyes beyond my shoulder, back towards the trees to her right. I sighed, turning my back on her and muttering under my breath as if angry that she had just shut me down. Then I let my eyes sweep the area, as if taking in all the Freaks present for the fight, and annoyed that Tory wouldn't talk to me. I was sure not to let my eyes linger on the area she had indicated, but even still, my heart skipped a beat.

Baron Skyfall leaned against a tree in a bowler hat, watching Tory for a moment before his eyes drifted to the wolves closest to him – those against Gunnar.

Tory murmured under her breath, as if talking to herself, but loud enough for me to hear. "Seems I have a tail... Ah, irony."

"Is *Baron* actually his first name or is it a title?" I muttered. "The others only had one name."

"First name."

I grunted, debating sauntering over to ask him a few pointed questions, but thought better of it. Not my problem. I let out a growl and sat back down. Alucard waited five seconds before standing up to talk with Tory. I waited to hear the slap he deserved, but instead saw her hugging him tightly. My eyes narrowed and I picked up a twig beside me, snapping it in half violently.

Why was I the bad guy in this situation? The world was unfair. I didn't see what the big deal was. Yahn liked the Reds – both of them – and believe it or not, they obviously felt the same. Why were they so adamant about keeping an eye on them? Sure, it wasn't a traditional relationship, but they were dragons, and I'd heard all sorts of crazy stories about them.

A steady hush settled over the valley as the hulking Minotaur entered the ring. "Finally," I breathed, sitting up straighter.

I needed to see someone *else* get slapped around.

CHAPTER 14

The Minotaur wore his fighting gear – spiked tridents on the tips of his aged ivory horns – and he stomped into the ring as if expecting trouble. He halted in the center and snorted into the air, sending a puff of fog to burst through the thick ring in his nostrils. The rain only emphasized his muscles, matting down his shaggy fur to reveal the thick slabs of muscle covering his body. He wore a set of prayer beads on his chest and a tattered skirt of some thick blue cloth with white embroidery on the hem. The white was stained here and there with flecks of blood.

His eyes narrowed as he spun in a circle, glaring at everyone in silent warning. Then he bellowed, but to me it just sounded like a murderous *MOO!*

The sound somehow shared both the anguished cry of a beast being slaughtered, and the victorious roar of the beast doing the slaughtering. Like a homicidal harmony.

You know how they combined a bunch of unique animalistic sounds to make that T-Rex roar in the dinosaur movie? This was kind of like that. A mixed drink of seemingly random animals, but spiked with an extra shot of nightmare juice.

It made the hair on the back of my arms stand up, and anyone who hadn't been paying full attention suddenly whipped around to see what was happening. An old man slipped into the ring, wearing a brilliant white suit and a pair of expensive leather loafers. Because this old man was kind of a big deal, he had someone holding an umbrella for him.

A full-grown chimera walking on his hind legs.

The monster was easily ten feet tall, larger than even the Minotaur, and it held that tiny black umbrella in a thickly furred paw as big as the old man's head. The chimera was a demonic hodge-podge of three different kinds of monster. Above the shoulders it was a fire-eyed, horned ram. On the chest was the head of a snarling lion. But to top it off, a hooded cobra as thick as a python made up its tail, wavering back and forth as it hissed in every direction.

And it was holding an umbrella for the little old man – King Midas.

But where had he gotten a pet chimera? This one was much bigger than the chimera I knew.

The white-haired old man cleared his throat audibly as the Minotaur and chimera flanked him on either side, the Minotaur facing Gunnar's pack and the chimera facing Zeus' pack.

"We gather here today for respect and power. Gunnar Randulf has been challenged for his position as Alpha of the St. Louis werewolves by..." he leaned closer, listening as the Minotaur leaned down to speak into his ear. Midas nodded, turning back to the crowd. "Zeus Fletcher, Alpha of a pack in Illinois." The Minotaur leaned closer, and Midas nodded after a moment. "*The* pack in Illinois," he corrected, dipping his head at Zeus apologetically. "I'm not too familiar with the shifter nations unless they're for sale. Old men must have their hobbies, after all," he chuckled. But the glitter in his eyes put the lie to his words.

I hadn't noticed Zeus Fletcher standing before his pack of wolves. He had both feet inside the ring and a thickly muscled woman stood beside – and slightly behind – him. She was easily over six-feet-tall, and thicker in the arms and legs than I was. Considerably.

Zeus didn't acknowledge Midas' comment – just glared ninety degrees to his right towards the edge of the ring. I followed his gaze to see Gunnar staring at him, his eyepatch glittering.

But he wasn't standing with his wolves behind him. There was literally no one behind him.

I frowned. Why wasn't he standing before his pack, directly across from Zeus? And where was Ashley? Wasn't she his second in this fight?

I scanned the perimeter of the ring, searching for her, and saw her standing directly across from Gunnar, glaring at Zeus and the woman. Was this some tactic? Divide and conquer? Midas didn't seem to mind, and neither did the challenging wolves. Although they did look curious.

Midas cleared his throat again. "Asterion," he said, and then stepped to the side.

The Minotaur cleared his throat, and then spoke in a low, deadly tone. "I have lived for thousands of years, and killed many." Zeus' pack studied him with renewed interest. "I am the Minotaur. I'd like to clear the air. I have heard whispers as I walked through the crowd that this arena may in some way be tainted by our history with Gunnar and Ashley Randulf…"

Murmurs of agreement and protest, both, began to drift through those gathered, and I found I wasn't the only one of my friends leaning closer. What was this all about?

As if on cue, Gunnar and Ashley both strolled forward, staring at Zeus and his partner as they walked towards Asterion. Neither looked at the Minotaur as they approached, leveling their flat, murderous glares at their challengers. It was… oddly chilling.

Gunnar stopped before the Minotaur and then tugged off his shirt, leaving him only in his khakis, his hair plastered back against his skull as the rain poured down. Many of the females behind Zeus grumbled their appreciation, and I saw Zeus' face tighten angrily as he noticed. Gunnar's open chest faced the Minotaur but he kept his face locked on Zeus, flashing a smile as he spoke. "Missouri wolves don't turn their backs on pain." Without warning, the Minotaur slashed his head down, scoring a diagonal gash across Gunnar's chest from pectoral to stomach, drawing blood. I gasped as the blood continued to flow. That had not been a shallow cut.

Gunnar didn't even flinch. Then… he laughed, a great echoing sound in the valley.

"In fact, we kind of like it," he told Zeus with a wink. Or a blink. Whatever.

And the Minotaur slashed again, this time from the opposite direction, making a bloody X across Gunnar's chest. Gunnar's torso was a sheet of blood as he smiled at Zeus. Then as slowly as I had ever seen him shift, he morphed into Wulfric, over the space of fifteen long, excruciating seconds. As he stretched taller and taller, his pants popped, snapped, and a button flew off, sparkling as it whipped off into the crowd. I barely noticed Talon's instinctive reaction as he jumped to his feet as if to chase it down. Then he grunted in embarrassment and sat back down.

Fur slowly sprouted all over Gunnar, instantly painted red as the slowly increasing downpour of rain spilled down his chest, spreading the blood over his snow-white fur. His arms elongated, bulging with thigh-thick muscles, and diamond encrusted claws erupted from his fingers as his snout finally erupted from his face, his teeth chomping at the empty air.

His crystal blue eye never blinked as he stared down Zeus.

Ashley interrupted the stunned silence with a sudden shout. "GERI!"

I spun to see the chimera slash across her chest just like the Minotaur had done to Gunnar.

"This might be the greatest day of my life..." Carl hissed, leaning forward hungrily.

I ignored him as I stared at Ashley. Why were they purposely injuring themselves before the fight? I would have thought this some kind of ritual, except every wolf looked just as startled as the rest of us. Well, Zeus' wolves looked startled. Gunnar's wolves looked... proud.

"FREKI!" Ashley snarled, and the chimera slashed her again, making a gory X across her chest that matched her husband's. Then she duplicated Gunnar's impressive feat of slowly shifting into Wulfra form – which had to be painful. Before now, I hadn't even known it was possible.

But I knew one thing. It was a very poignant display of their confidence, control, and willingness to bleed for their pack.

Ashley dragged a claw through the blood of the first wound. Then she dipped another claw into the blood of the second slash. "For Odin's wolves, this bride will make a wedding dress out of your hide..." she snarled, staring right at Zeus' second. Then she licked up the blood and waited, chest heaving.

The Minotaur stared at Zeus. "I hope this shows our... neutrality."

In answer, Zeus and his second exploded into their wolf forms. They were big – huge as hell, in fact – but not as intimidating as Wulfra and Wulfric – who had chosen their wild Fae wolf forms. But I'll say this, before I had taken Ashley and Gunnar to the Fae, I had never seen them look as deadly as the two challenging werewolves.

Midas called out in a clear voice, vacating the ring with the Minotaur and chimera.

"There will be blood. Submission or death. St. Louis or die."

74

And the crowd went wild.

CHAPTER 15

The two Illinois wolves didn't waste any time, going straight for Gunnar's bad side, although they did eye his diamond coated claws warily. The woman only managed one swipe of her claws before Ashley jumped onto her back, did a cool spinning thing with her legs wrapped around the woman's neck, and the next thing I knew the poor wolf was sailing across the ring.

But Ashley was running in an instant, chasing down the airborne wolf with inhuman speed. Ashley caught up to her right before the wolf was about to land again, and hammer-fisted the back of her neck so hard that the wolf yelped – once at the blow, and a second time as her face slammed into the mud. Dazed, the wolf tried scrambling to her feet, but Ashley kicked her elbow so hard it hyperextended with a loud *pop* that almost seemed to echo in the valley.

The wolf howled in agony, clutching her broken arm as she writhed through the mud. Zeus whirled at the sound, his instincts urging him to help his fallen packmate. Or avenge her.

Ashley had been waiting for that look, and with his full attention on her, she blew him a slow, mocking kiss. Then she reached down, grabbed her opponent by the neck fur, and proceeded to drag the wolf through the mud towards the center of the ring.

Zeus didn't notice Gunnar was now standing directly behind him until it

76

was too late. Gunnar grabbed both of the wolf's ears and swiftly ripped them off. Zeus roared, jumping away. Gunnar flung the ears into a puddle as if they were trash.

"Sweet Jesu—" Roland abruptly cut off when Callie blindly elbowed him in the ribs. He blushed, but didn't actually draw his eyes away. "This is unbelievable..." he amended.

I nodded distantly. This wasn't a fight, this was retribution. For ruining their wedding day.

Carl and Talon acted like a couple of kids with their first video game, bobbing and weaving as they watched the fight, breathing heavily as if trying to mimic the moves in the ring.

Paradise and Lost now sat beside Roland and Callie, watching the fight as if taking notes. Whether as ideas on how to counter Gunnar's strengths, or to learn new moves for when they got back home to Kansas City, I wasn't sure. They were pretty new at the werewolf thing, but they had spent a few months training with the Shepherds in the Vatican, and then a few more months training with Roland. Callie had told me they were scrappers in every sense of the word, but formidable. Cunning and quick to learn from their mistakes.

Ashley had her opponent on her back and was slapping her in the muzzle repeatedly. The woman found a sudden boost of strength and kicked up with her feet, tossing Ashley into the air.

Zeus snarled, his ears bloody holes, and slashed out with his claws. Gunnar didn't lean back far enough, and one of the claws raked his face, but his stone eyepatch took much of the hit. Gunnar didn't acknowledge the pain, but instead grabbed the offending arm and sliced it clean off at the shoulder. Zeus threw back his head and howled in agony, blood fountaining from the wound as he clutched the other paw over it to staunch the bleeding. He thudded to his knees, whimpering as the flesh tried to regrow – the werewolf gene actually doing more harm than good in this scenario, because if that wound closed, I wasn't sure if it was possible to reattach the arm. Then again, it seemed the only place Zeus would be visiting today was a morgue.

"Ashley! Need a hand?" Gunnar called out, circling Zeus thoughtfully.

"If you have one to spare," she growled, climbing back to her feet to glare at her opponent.

Zeus' arm thumped into a puddle, right beside Ashley. Her opponent went entirely still, and then slowly turned to look at Zeus, who had now fallen onto his face in a puddle of bloody mud.

So, she didn't see Ashley scoop up the arm and stab her through the kidneys, but her head did drop down to see her Alpha's claws suddenly poking out of her stomach. Ashley slashed her throat, panting as she let the woman fall.

"You never should have let him come to my wedding."

Then she stomped over to Zeus, glaring down at him, nothing rational about her movement. Zeus struggled to rise with his one remaining arm. Gunnar let out a rough bark at Ashley. She halted instinctively and took three hurried steps back, ducking her head low, but still panting from the adrenaline. Gunnar had claimed the kill for his own, and Ashley obeyed.

Gunnar squatted down beside Zeus. "Answer me truly..." he said in a very soft voice, but the silence of the crowd let it carry to all of us. Zeus bobbed his head woozily. "Did you challenge me because you really thought you were a better alpha, or were you just looking for a fight?"

Zeus' head began to loll and Gunnar gripped his snout, lifting it to look into the man's eyes.

He died of blood loss without giving Gunnar an answer.

Gunnar finally turned away and saw his wife. His lips curled and his ears tucked back at the wounds raking her chest – but his lone eye shone with pride. Both at the outcome of her fight and her ability to do so injured. He placed an arm around her shoulders and turned to face Zeus' pack.

He cleared his throat. "You are free to go back home. I have no interest in Illinois. But mark my words... If you come back to St. Louis with this type of shit again, you better fucking bring an army. Because once we're through with you, we *will* come to Illinois. To burn your homes to the ground. Then we'll come back home to celebrate." He let that sink in for a few seconds. "We don't play games here. None of the petty dominance shit. We don't do pissing contests. It's really very simple. I – just – run – this – city. *Period.* You want to see what a real pack is like, then you need to talk to them," he said, pointing. Two men I hadn't met before stepped up obediently. The two couldn't have looked more different. One was a tall black guy with a flat-top and bushy beard, and the other a scrawny looking white guy with unruly brown hair. "I can't promise any openings," Gunnar continued, "but I understand that many of you might just be here out of obedience to Zeus Fletcher. Your choice."

The wolves shared looks back and forth, but no one spoke.

Gunnar slowly lifted his arms, and his wolves began howling in a low rumble. As Gunnar's arms stretched higher, so did the pitch and volume, until Gunnar held his hands over his head, staring down the pack with his one icy eye. The howling made the very air vibrate.

"This is my family, and I take *care* of my family. You have one week to decide."

And he left the ring with Ashley, walking straight for me.

Alucard was shaking his head. "I'm glad we don't have to deal with this kind of shit."

Roland was staring off at nothing, but the comment jolted him from his thoughts. Vampires had to deal with all sorts of cloak and dagger shit. I'd rather have an open, honest fight any day, and it looked like Roland leaned more towards my way of thinking.

Gunnar and Ashley had been... merciless. I couldn't blame them, not after Zeus tarnished their wedding day. Watching them approach, I noticed their wounds had already begun to stitch closed. They were still open and raw, but not as horrifying to look at as they had been. The four lines across his face from Zeus' parting shot didn't look too serious, and probably wouldn't even leave a scar, but I winced inwardly seeing them up close.

Gunnar halted before me, still in wolf form. The two wolves he had pointed out at the end of his speech trotted over with robes and bottles of water. Very thick, expensive robes. Gunnar and Ashley shifted back to human form, accepted the robes and drinks with murmured thanks, and then sat down, motioning for the two to join them.

I jerked my chin at the other pack, who were now huddled together in a tight mass. "Shouldn't you make sure they leave town before you head out for your honeymoon?"

Gunnar shook his head, smiling faintly. "Firstly, nothing will hold me back from my honeymoon." Ashley purred her approval in an entirely inhuman sound. "Secondly, the duel is over. Zeus challenged me on my turf. I won. They have the choice to flee back home and establish a new Alpha among themselves, or stay here and submit to my pack."

"What about option three?" Paradise asked thoughtfully. Gunnar looked at her and she wilted slightly under his bloody stare. "Where... they wait for you to leave and then attack your pack?" she finished in a hesitant whisper.

Lost was leaning forward, eager to hear the answer.

"Well, that might throw a wrench in the honeymoon," I said out loud.

CHAPTER 16

*A*shley smirked. "I doubt four-to-one odds against them sounds very appealing."

Gunnar nodded absently, studying the distant pack. "Even with fair odds it wouldn't come to that. But it will make more sense if we circle back to that question in a moment." I found myself listening intently as he took on a lecturing tone. "There is one absolute – the Alpha is the law. Period. Every wolf agrees on this. It's simply in our genes. If a wolf decides to *not* be part of a pack, he's essentially choosing to be an Alpha... his *own* Alpha." He waited to make sure we were all on the same page before continuing. "If a wolf disagrees strongly enough with the Alpha's methods – if he's corrupt, not taking care of the pack, or not keeping them safe – they can challenge him. The winner becomes the new Alpha, and his word is now law."

Paradise and Lost nodded slowly. Their eyes were haunted with the memories of their own experience. They had been abducted and turned by werewolf rapists. All because the Kansas City pack had fled when a demon came to town, so there had been no one to stop the sons of bitches. Until Callie and Roland came along, killed them, and freed Paradise and Lost.

The two fledgling shifters had a lot to learn about how wolves interacted – and a lot of prejudices to overcome, thanks to their past. It was why they had been spending some time with Gunnar's pack lately, trying to learn from a good example. And how to defend themselves, of course, but they seemed to have a knack for that.

Paradise spoke up. "What if they had sufficient numbers and chose a new Alpha right now?"

Gunnar shrugged. "There is a two-week period where they may not attack."

The two girls frowned in unison. "Why the hell would anyone agree to that?"

Ashley leaned forward. "Without this law, an entire pack could challenge Gunnar's right to rule, one by one, with the real Alpha sitting back and tossing his lower-level wolves at Gunnar until he was too exhausted to continue. Only then would the Alpha step in to finish it. That is why there is a two-week rest between duels." Her eyes grew distant, but she didn't continue.

"That!" I pointed, leaning forward. "What was that look on your face?"

Gunnar waved a hand. "A third party only has to wait one week to submit a challenge."

I frowned. "That seems like a big loophole..."

Gunnar shook his head. "Not really. Two packs are unlikely to work together. Why would they?" He saw the look on my face and sighed. "Let's pretend Zeus had an Alpha friend and they wanted to team up to take me out. What's their purpose?"

"Kill you, obviously. And take your pack."

Gunnar nodded. "Let's say they succeed. Who gets my pack? You think after two dominant Alphas just invaded me they're suddenly going to decide to share? Split my pack down the middle? To *both* be Alphas? Can you imagine the chaos?" he asked, waving a hand at the five hundred wolves around us. "The confusion as this family goes to Zeus, that family goes to the other... No. They would turn on each other within *hours* just to stop the infighting. The winner would end up trying to take all three packs." He let that sink in. "So, why bother teaming up in the first place? Much easier to pick off the smaller pack, acclimate, and then challenge the next pack if you think you can handle it. But pretty soon, your pack will be too big to efficiently manage, and will likely split off. Full circle."

I found myself nodding, taking it all in. I laced my hands through my hair. "Where did you learn all this? You two don't have prior experience with packs..."

Ashley answered. "It kind of just came to me over in Fae. Like an instinct…"

Ashley had gained something in Fae, for sure. And not just strength. She had been like a general. I had always attributed it to her experience as interim CEO of my old company, Temple Industries – applying her corporate management skills to the pack. Because many corporate bosses studied *The Art of War* by Sun Tzu, which pretty much applied to the werewolf thing.

And a lot of other things in life, if you thought about it.

"But we didn't really put it all together until after my last trip to Fae. We were trying to figure out some internal matters and got to talking with these two clowns," Ashley said, smiling at the two wolves who had sat silent during the conversation. "Meet Drake and Cowan," she said.

Drake was the scrawny guy with the wild mop of hair. His eyes glinted with mischief as he smiled at us, dipping his chin. "Pleasure." His eyes might have lingered on Paradise when he said it, but it was hard to be sure. I found myself smiling as if I had found a new drinking buddy.

Cowan, on the other hand, had a face like a block of stone, as if he took everything seriously at all times. His skin was almost charcoal dark and his eyes were chocolate brown. He was the kind of guy you wanted with you in a dark alley. The way he looked at Gunnar and Ashley, was nothing short of devotion. "Greetings. I'm the balance to his chaos," he said, jerking a thumb at Drake. He said this without humor, just a statement of fact.

Drake chuckled and gave us an easy shrug. "Truth. Like peanut butter and jelly."

I wasn't sure if that made any sense, but I think I knew what he meant. They were pals.

Ashley rolled her eyes at Drake. "They've been with us for about a year, slowly working their way up the ranks, but we hadn't spent much time around them, personally. They said our plans were solid and we got to talking. They were drifters from a pack on the East Coast and decided they didn't like some of the decisions being made…"

"What was so disagreeable about the other pack you were in?" Roland asked.

I had almost forgotten he was present.

Drake answered. "They came up with some crazy ideas that only seemed to benefit the few at the top." Cowan grimaced as Drake continued. "They wanted to establish regional and local Alphas that all bowed to one king."

I nodded slowly. "Not unlike Corporate America with its District Managers, General Managers, and Store Managers..."

Drake nodded with an angry gleam in his eyes, even after all this time. "Sounds great, but it wasn't. Like Gunnar just explained. If you had a problem with what your local Alpha was doing, and he wouldn't listen to reason, what did you do? Challenge him?" Drake shook his head with a humorless smile. "No way. Because your local Alpha was good friends with your district Alpha, and you didn't want to piss *him* off. And if you went over your local Alpha's head, the entire chain would come crashing down on you to set an example. And that's just *one* aspect.

"Because we're talking about territorial killing machines who don't like submission. But to give him a handful of Alphas to submit to? Each level more important than the previous?" He whistled, shaking his head. "It got out of hand quicker than we ever imagined. No one knew who to turn to, who to trust, and the Alphas just kept getting angrier and angrier. We started seeing the corruption – some of our female wolves called to audiences with the King, and not ever coming back. When we learned that they were being used as leverage to keep our own local Alphas in line, we realized it was too late to stand up. The King was basically taking hostages from all over his kingdom, preventing any of his minions from rising up."

Cowan cleared his throat. "It was madness... We got out before it imploded, leaving the entire area in chaos, duels from sunrise to sunset, deaths by the hundreds as the local Alphas tried to claim their independence while the district Alphas fought to keep their territories."

Gunnar nodded grimly before turning to Paradise and Lost. "It's in our blood to be dominant. That's how wolves are in the wild. As human as we think we are, we share that wildness. Denying it only results in chaos. We live in balance, or we die."

Carl and Talon were actually napping, apparently bored to exhaustion with the lecture.

Gunnar spotted them and grunted. "We have a plane to catch," he said, smiling at his wife. Ashley grinned eagerly. Gunnar spoke again, this time addressing all of us. "Drake and Cowan will be in charge in our absence. We promoted them last night to our seconds in command. Since Ashley is technically my Mate, we decided it didn't make sense for her to be the liaison between me and the pack."

Drake noticed my frown and held up his hands in innocence. "I argued with him about it but he wouldn't take no for an answer. I know what you're thinking, though, and you don't need to worry. I have zero interests in being an Alpha. I didn't even want to be second in command." Cowan looked horrified at the idea, shaking his head adamantly.

"Which is one reason you two will do well," Ashley said. Then she turned to the rest of us. "Also, they couldn't challenge us even if they wanted to. They've sworn their lives to us. They literally cannot challenge us or do anything to put us in harm's way. For this oath, they may speak freely to us without fear of consequence. Which will benefit the pack as a whole."

Gunnar nodded, settling a stern glare on the two wolves. "Keep my pack safe."

Drake and Cowan nodded. "On our lives, Wulfric."

I glanced at Tory, who had been strangely silent. She gave me a faint nod. Well, if she approved of these two, and Gunnar and Ashley did, that was about as good as it could get. Not that I had any say in the matter. And they had sworn an oath.

I let out a deep breath, climbing to my feet. Gunnar had asked me to back off and leave the wolves to him. I needed to do so. Otherwise, my interference could cause him even more problems. Like the one he'd had to resolve today. This Alpha, Zeus, had come to town full of piss and vinegar because he assumed the real power behind Gunnar was me, and that he would have an easy victory. My meddling – although with the best intentions – had cost him something.

I couldn't make that mistake again.

"Let me call the pilot for you two lovebirds," I said, wrapping an arm around Ashley and Gunnar's shoulders.

Drake and Cowan began barking orders to the wolves. I didn't bother waking Talon and Carl, hoping they would wake up in the empty field and have to find their own way home.

A six-foot-tall lizard man and a Thundercat walking the streets of St. Louis, or better yet, calling an Uber. They would have a long walk.

I glanced back to see Callie nudging them with a boot and grunted.

"Spoil sport," I muttered under my breath.

Gunnar chuckled. "You've got it bad, man. So bad..."

Ashley giggled, squeezing my waist.

I sighed, refusing to acknowledge the truth to their statement.

CHAPTER 17

Gunnar and Ashley had left without further fanfare. Murdering two wolves was good enough.

I had tried cornering Tory before leaving the fight, but she had told me, loud enough for Baron Skyfall to overhear as he coincidentally walked by, that she had work to do. She didn't say it harshly, at least her eyes had let me know it wasn't personal and more for show, but it was also apparent that she fully meant to handle it all on her own.

I let her. But I did tell her to keep an eye on her students from Shift, just in case this was some ploy to take them away from her. Or use them against her.

Tory had been a cop so I had no doubt she would get to the bottom of the theft. But that was my concern. That her skills as a cop would lead her to an answer that would put her, the Reds, or the students at Shift in danger. Or any of my friends. That the dragons might be angling to gain control of the Beast Master to use her against my friends.

Everyone had parted ways to head home, leaving the other pack under discreet surveillance.

Talon licked his paws incessantly beside me until I shoved him in annoyance. Alex walked beside us through the twisted overgrown path at Chateau Falco, eyes alert out of habit. He had been kidnapped one too many times in his life, and now kept an eye on everything at all times.

But he would be a lot harder to kidnap now that he wasn't a kid. I studied him out of the corner of my eye, still uneasy about his recent developments. He now resembled a tall, strong, dark-haired guy ready to take on a college campus. In the past few months, he seemed to have aged five years. Pan had checked him over repeatedly but found absolutely nothing wrong. His only suggestion was that his time in Fae had messed with his aging, or that perhaps his body was trying to catch up to the age it would have been if he had never been kidnapped by the Fae.

On a very surface level, I was kind of glad for it. I wasn't really father material.

And it was nice not to feel the sharp paranoia whenever we went out in public together – that someone might recognize the kid beside me as the one who went missing years ago, and think that I had kidnapped him and held him prisoner this whole time. With him looking like a young college student, I was able to breathe a little easier.

He was no longer gangly and awkward – thanks to all the training my various friends had been giving him. Alex had no magic, so every one of my friends jumped at the chance to teach him how to defend himself and kill his attackers by any means necessary. He was a fast learner. To catch him up on his education, I had put him in school with a bunch of ex-murderer monsters.

I told you. I'm not good father material.

He had been in his early teens when I met him, so it wasn't like he had much else to learn by that point. He didn't intend to become a doctor or teacher or anything so disciplined. He wanted to be... well, like me. I decided to put him to work in my bookstore, Plato's Cave, most nights. He wasn't a manager yet, but he was infinitely better than Alucard had been.

As a result, Othello had been able to step into more of a CEO role of both the bookstore and Grimm Tech – my supernatural technology company. We were only just now announcing ourselves to the market to introduce some of our prototypes and gauge interest.

Of course, not all the products were available to the public. Because they were my weapons.

With Alex's determination and work ethic, I could eventually see him doing quite well for himself at Grimm Tech if he so chose. He had a knack for seeing the forest through the trees.

But as we walked through the trail, he just listened. Intently.

Talon kicked a rock with his velvet slippers. "And the Welsh Bible had nothing else to say?" We'd gone over this a dozen times already, but I could tell he was agitated so obliged him.

I shook my head, thinking back on the book Yahn and I had... borrowed from the Vatican recently. We had given it back after copying everything we needed, but all in all, it hadn't been as helpful as we had hoped. It had given us some answers, but like life usually worked, it only gave us additional questions.

"It filled in some blanks, but nothing majorly helpful."

"And he still sleeps?"

I nodded. "Weird, right? Van and Baba say they found him that way. Like a cryogenic sleep."

"What is a cryogenic sleep?" the words sounded strange coming from the squat, five-foot kitty-cat-man. He didn't carry his white spear at the moment, but his leather kilt made steady whooshing sounds as we moved, and I thought I heard metal hilts or cross guards clinking in hidden pockets. Not that he needed blades. He was dangerous enough with just his claws.

I thought about how to explain it. "Like how Sleeping Beauty was in a living sleep, but couldn't wake up until Prince Charming gave her a kiss." Alex frowned, silently repeating the words as if doing so would impart understanding.

But Talon hissed. I flinched, ready for danger, but heard only birds chirping. I rounded on him. "I will not kiss this Knight," he growled, his thick, beardlike fur quivering. He even had his long, furry ears tucked back low.

I let out a tired sigh. "No... that wasn't what... never mind. The knight is alive, but he can't wake up. At least, we don't know *how* to wake him up."

"How do we know he *is* a Knight?"

"Well, Van Helsing and Baba Yaga seemed pretty sure, but there's no way to know until we can actually talk to him. I'll point out that Matthias also thought he was the real deal, and he spent years looking into this stuff."

He nodded slowly, not looking happy, but acknowledging the opinions of three old and powerful supernatural persons. "I still don't understand how no one has found the knight these past centuries. And if the Mad Hatter is so interested in this topic, where is he?"

"Being a hermit somewhere, I guess. He took that fight with Castor

Queen... hard," I finally said, trying not to remember too many of the details. "Why are you asking about all this again?"

His claws extended and he resumed cleaning them with more force than necessary. "I'm bored." He met my eyes between licks of those lethal claws. "Very, very bored."

"We'll see action soon enough..." I muttered, thinking about our upcoming trip. To Hell.

Alex shuddered instinctively. He – and everyone else – thought we were taking another one of our frequent trips to Fae. And Alex had particularly bad memories of that place.

I actually was taking Talon and Carl to Fae, but just for a brief recharge before heading onto our final destination – Hell.

Heh. Final Destination. Hell.

If any of my friends heard about that they would have tied me down to a chair for a year.

We continued down the trail, heading back to the mansion. For fun, I had taken Alex and Talon out to see my old childhood hideout – Chateau Defiance. Alex had smiled distantly, but it had seemed to sour Talon's mood, reminding him that we had been unknowingly separated after childhood, and that I had found a new best friend – Gunnar – to replace him.

The two were still trying to come to grips with who actually held the Best Friend Title Belt, rather than accepting that it didn't have to be one or the other.

The walk back to the mansion had been brittle rather than pleasant, thanks to Talon's mood.

All in all, I was ready to get out of town. My friends didn't need or want my help anyway, and I had always hated sitting on my hands.

First, we would go to Fae.

Talon and I had spent a lot of time there recently. Well, that was relative. We had only gone a half-dozen times, fearing the time slippage in the real world. I had hoped to find a calculation that would let me know how much an hour in Fae cost me in the real world.

But that had been a big fat failure.

The first time we went, an hour had cost us a day. The second time, an hour had only cost us about four hours. Repeated attempts yielded even more varied results. Basically, there was no logical explanation for the time slippage, no way to calculate it ahead of time.

And no way to explain Alex's suddenly rapid aging.

Wylde – my inner Fae – had tried to tell me it was futile, but I had refused to listen.

Wylde...

The two of us were becoming less... distinct. Each trip to Fae brought us closer and closer until I had hard times distinguishing my thoughts from his.

The short of it was that I had been conceived and born in Fae by two human wizards. My parents had broken into Fae to steal a few things from the Queens – an Hourglass and a War Hammer – and as a result had found themselves trapped there. They hadn't been romantically involved at the time, but being locked up in a cave for long periods of time has consequences. Something about that specific chain of events had tainted me. I was a Manling Fae or something equally bizarre. A Catalyst. I didn't have pointed ears or anything, because I wasn't actually Fae. I was just born there.

My parents named me Wylde.

They kept me there for years, still hiding from the Queens. Until Pan – the Wild God – came along with a rescue kitten warrior he had found in a ransacked city. I had named him Talon the Devourer, and the two of us had fast become friends. Pan agreed to help keep my parents – and me – safe from the Queens. He kind of shacked up with us like a crazy distant uncle.

To everyone's surprise, I soon showed a knack for Fae magic. The only way I can think to describe the power was... primitive. Wizards in our world can use magic – fire, ice, wind, earth – and manipulate it to their will. But it must obey the laws of physics.

Fae magic kind of had its own unwritten set of rules, and physics was more of a quasi-flexible set of guidelines rather than concrete rules. For example, I could pull starlight from the air, use a moonbeam as a spear, command tree-people – things like that. Like I said, bizarre and not easily categorized. If I wanted something, I just kind of tried to do it. There were still rules, I think, but the drunken shaman who must have come up with them forgot to write them down.

It was more like an instinctive, primitive knowledge – *fire hurts. Knives cut. People die.*

When my parents were finally able to escape Fae, they blocked my memories and took me back to earth. Since they had used the hourglass stolen from the Queens, time hadn't passed in our world – luckily, because we had spent the better part of two decades over there – and when I stepped foot on earth for the first time, I was a child again.

And I had no memories of Wylde, Talon, or the Fae.

So, I got to grow up again, totally unaware of my past.

But Wylde had spent those years haunting the Land of the Fae as some kind of spirit memory.

Reunited, Wylde and I had a lot of growing pains to overcome. He needed to be recharged by occasional visits to Fae, and I wanted to wring out every scrap of Fae magic he knew. Each visit to Fae brought us closer together, merging our lives, memories, and powers. I wanted to know – and feared – the final result of that merging, of becoming one person again.

I was a Catalyst. *Cue dramatic thunder and lightning*, I thought to myself.

Whatever the hell a Catalyst was, my parents had been pretty confident I was one.

Pan hadn't known what it meant – because my parents had never told him. For Pan, the Wild God, to not know something, it had to be a doozy. Which meant I needed to go to the source.

To talk to my parents. Who currently resided in Hell. Or… at least the Underworld. Gods kind of used the terms interchangeably, informing me that there were many dimensions in the Underworld – some were paradises, and others were eons of torture and anguish.

My parents were now legal citizens of the Underworld, and Death could no longer take me on a short trip to see them because I had a lot of… *dangerous* questions. I had argued with him.

He had stared me dead in the eye and said, "The fact that you even *know* the questions is what is limiting me from taking you to them myself. The act of awareness has eliminated that path. The only way down now is to *pay to play*."

He wouldn't – or couldn't – tell me what that price would be. Like a big girl, I had to buy my own bus ticket for this trip. I had told him to set it up.

Remembering Death's comment from the wedding sent a chill down my spine. *Three may enter, but three shall not leave…* I had told Talon and Carl about it – the two I had chosen to join me because they were both other-worldly and scary as hell – but they hadn't known what to make from it, other than the obvious. That we might not all make it back.

This hadn't changed their minds. Both had piped up that they were willing to remain down below in order for the others to get back.

I had thoughts on that, but I had accepted their offer of support, not sharing my opinion about Death's cryptic warning. I blinked as we finally stepped out of the woods and Chateau Falco loomed ahead over the manicured lawns.

CHAPTER 18

$\mathcal{T}$alon purred approvingly as he stared at the house. I smiled distantly, remembering growing up here and getting into all sorts of trouble. Seventeen-thousand-square-feet of places to hide, explore, and desecrate. Gunnar and I had had a blast as kids.

But I was beginning to learn that it was much larger than the blueprints told. The house was actually alive. Literally. Because a powerful Beast named Falco was magically bonded to it. Secret passageways, hidden levels, and odd distortions in space likely doubled or tripled its size.

And now... Falco was pregnant. But that was on a need-to-know basis.

A large alicorn – a fancy name for a winged unicorn – with long black feathers sporting red orbs on the tips like a hellish mockery of a peacock, slashed great divots in the ground in the distance near the labyrinth beside the mansion where a large crystal I had bought for him hung from a high branch. The alicorn snorted and neighed, but it sounded more like a vicious snarl as he clawed his razor-blade hooves and barbed horn into the ground, attacking dozens of...

Rainbow reflections zipping back and forth across the ground.

Alex chuckled. "I don't think I will ever hate something as much as Grimm hates rainbows."

I smiled, shaking my head. Grimm fucking hated them. More than anything. His brother, Pegasus, had even told me that Grimm traveled across worlds – plural – to hunt down rogue rainbows and destroy them. Apparently, his horn could... kill them. Even though they were just reflections of light. I heard a shattering glass noise and then a triumphant scream from Grimm.

Pegasus, the fabled winged horse was napping in the grass, but lifted his head at the sound, nodding his amused approval at his brother's accomplishment.

"Wow. He really *can* break them. I've never heard him actually get one!" Alex whispered.

"Is that Carl?" Talon asked, ignoring Grimm and the flickering lights – which also annoyed him to no end, being a cat. He pointed to where a giant white tree had recently stood, but now only a wide circle of ash, coal and charred husks remained. I had thrown my War Hammer at it.

Allegedly.

I squinted and saw a tall, albino lizard in armor made of leather straps with his hands on his hips. Carl was an Elder – dangerous creatures who had been banished from earth long ago. By everybody. Like that one guy at the party no one wanted around, turning the music down and hiding when he knocked at the front door. I didn't quite know why Elders were so feared.

No one would talk about them.

Carl was staring at a cute little treehouse in the center of the chaos. It had been in the tree when it burned down, but for some reason hadn't burned away. It resembled a tiny, fort-sized cottage made of white wood. Kai – the Beast who had briefly resided in the tree had made it for Alex, saying every boy needed a treehouse. No other explanation had been given. It had just been there one day. Only a single shoot from the giant white tree had been found unharmed, and Alex had planted it with loving care beside the treehouse as if in memory of the Beast – Kai – who had briefly resided there. They'd been close friends, even if only briefly.

Kai had decided to knock up Chateau Falco before becoming a martyr.

His death had struck everyone hard, but no one harder than Alex and Falco. The lone sapling seemed to be healthy, sprouting a few new leaves since we had planted it.

"We better go stop him from... whatever he's doing," I said as I made my way towards him.

A few minutes later we stepped up behind him. Other than his ear holes constricting, he didn't immediately acknowledge us. A plaque had been hammered into the earth beside the cottage and tree. It said *Kai, a free Beast.* Alex – the one who had put it there – read the words with a sad look on his face before walking over to Pegasus and sitting down, pulling out his phone as he leaned into the winged horse's ribs.

Pegasus nuzzled him for a moment before resting his head back down. Alex stared at his phone in silence, occasionally swiping with his thumb. Probably reading another book related to King Arthur. He'd read most of them by now, but had seemed particularly interested in the story about Tristan and Isolde. He was determined to help as much as possible on the whole Round Table and *Sleeping Knight-y* issue, resorting to even fictional tales to try and find answers that might help us figure out what was so important about it. Or what we needed to do to wake the Knight up, and what to ask him when he did wake up. Anything was helpful at this point since Matthias Temple was hiding out in solitude and not helping.

"Is it getting bigger?" Carl finally asked, interrupting my thoughts as he turned to me.

I frowned at him, then peered at the tree house where he was pointing. "It's a treehouse, Carl. Wood doesn't just get bigger—"

But I cut off abruptly, staring at it harder. Was it bigger? I couldn't actually tell because I hadn't ever measured it, but... something was different.

I glanced back at Alex since the treehouse had initially been built for him by Kai. He was smirking to himself as he read. I spotted motion near the house and turned to see Alucard jogging our way, not in a rush, but as if glad he had spotted us.

Talon had his head cocked, staring at the treehouse. He saw Alucard – now within earshot – and pointed a feline paw at him. "I have heard Alucard talk of wood that can grow. He called it the *D.* Tory didn't look pleased when he spoke of it, so perhaps it's a secret... Ask him about this magical D."

I coughed into my fist, wanting to burst out laughing, but also wanting to stretch this out as long as possible. Alucard had skidded to a halt, rubbing his ears as if he hadn't heard correctly.

Deciding to be mature for once, I shot Alucard a warning look before answering Carl. "It's a treehouse, Carl. Wood can't grow on its own. This wood is dead."

"The wood is dead. Long live the wood," Alucard chimed in, ever helpful.

I glared at him.

Talon grasped his arm conspiratorially, as if making sure Tory wasn't nearby. "Nate says wood can't grow on its own, but I heard you say otherwise. Tell us about this secret D."

I subtly began shaking my head from behind Talon, warning Alucard to put a stop to this before it got out of hand. Carl was leaning close to Alucard, practically on the balls of his feet. A very serious look settled over the vampire's face and I let out a sigh of relief.

"I must understand this world better," Carl pleaded. "You are always teasing me about things I don't understand. Tell me about this growing wood. This D."

Alucard sucked in a breath, eyes twinkling as he tried not to laugh. Then, with a straight face, he gave Carl exactly what he asked for – the Legend of the D. "It's very rare, but I'm not supposed to talk about it. I've found most women are very good at finding the D. You just have to ask them. Politely. It's a secret they don't like to share."

I groaned, opening my mouth to stop the madness.

"Why do women love the D?" Carl asked, tongue flicking out through his inky black teeth.

Ohmygod. Alucard shrugged hesitantly, leaning down to whisper. "Ask the Huntress. Tell her you know of her love of the deep wood and want to know the secret to growing the D."

"Carl—" I began, but the Elder was nodding to himself and striding up to the house.

"I will get to the bottom of this," he called over his shoulder.

Talon was staring at the two of us, frowning as Alucard struggled not to burst out laughing with Carl in earshot. "You're a dick, Alucard," I sighed.

He grinned. "What harm is there? You said you three are leaving soon for Fae."

Talon, not wanting to prove his ignorance, chose not to ask anything else. He probably didn't trust us to tell him the truth. The thing about Carl was that he was the only Elder on earth. And since his kind hadn't been around humans for quite some time, he had no understanding of our ways. Especially not sarcasm or crude humor.

He provided endless joke material.

Talon, having grown up in Fae, was also ignorant of many things about humans, but having spent his life around semi-human Fae, he had at least a basic enough understanding not to make himself the brunt of too many jokes. He was also notoriously vicious and would likely torture anyone who pushed him too far, or pulled a prank on him.

But Carl? He fell for everything.

"I just hope he doesn't wear his red heels when he asks someone about the D," I muttered, glancing back at the treehouse. It did seem bigger. Maybe. Or maybe it was just because the question had been asked and the possibility had entered my mind. One of those tricks of the eye. Someone tells you to find something specific in an inkblot, and you can suddenly see it, when in reality, no such thing exists. Your mind simply shows you what you tell it to see, connecting random variables into the outcome that you told it to find.

Alucard's voice grew more serious, making me look up as he spoke. "Can we head inside? We need to talk."

I nodded, not liking the dread in his tone.

CHAPTER 19

*W*e sat in the Sanctorum, sipping rare fifty-year Macallan that Mallory had left out. He usually kept it hidden from us. Maybe he'd left it out as a gift since he knew we were heading to Hell. He was the only other person I had told about our travel plans. Or Falco's pregnancy.

Talon was lying on a couch a few paces away near the waterfall that occupied one wall of the massive cavern turned private library. The ceiling was easily fifty feet high and covered in gems to represent constellations, and railed walkways marked each floor – complete with rooms, bookshelves, and furniture. I'd barely managed to explore the entire place. Only in a cursory fashion to make sure nothing dangerous lurked behind one of the closed doors. Some trapped demon or something.

Other than dusty piles of books, manuscripts, and strange artifacts from all over the world, I hadn't found anything concerning. Some of the rooms seemed more like ancient antique stores than anything, with tan sheets covering the furniture, shelves, and lamps.

On the main floor sat an ornate desk that had belonged to my ancestors, those former Masters' Temple. Our family had always used the title for the head of the house, but it had only recently come to my attention that it used to have actual meaning. The original Master Temples used to be Makers – those extremely rare beings who shared headspace with a Beast, a creature of unknown origins and powers. One of those Beasts had actually been freed from her partnership and had instead been fused with the mansion we now stood in.

The mansion had even been named after her – Falco.

The ground shook with a faint hum for a moment as Falco acknowledged my thought. I could speak to her, in a way. We kind of had a mental intercom system.

Either Falco was acknowledging my thoughts or she was having another mood swing from her pregnancy. Before Kai had died, he had told me to take care of his coming son. I felt familiar gooseflesh roll up my arms as I thought about that. A baby Beast. What the hell was I going to do about that? Not only was I incapable of taking care of human children, now I had to do so with a celestial baby… thing?

I sighed, shaking my head.

Regardless, this area of the house had been locked away for hundreds of years. Falco only gave access to this part of her… body… to those true Master Temples – those who were or had once been Makers. Since Kai and I had briefly teamed up, making me a Maker, I was the first Temple to see this room since the 1800's when Matthias had been Master Temple.

I heard a rustling of feathers and glanced up to see two sets of beady black eyes watching me from the third tier. Hugin and Munin, Odin's ravens.

They were on my family Crest, but I had originally taken that as more of a figurative symbol, not literal. I'd been wrong. The two bird brains loved hanging out with me, not telling me things, not helping me, not making my life easier in any way shape or form – things like that.

Talon glared up at them with open hatred.

They often tried to use him as target practice when defecating. Seeing he was safe for the time being, he turned away, his tail twitching and his ears rotated in their direction. I turned to Alucard. "Well?" I said, sipping my drink.

He looked tired. "The meeting was… enlightening. They were very interested in meeting the both of us. Roland, because of his past, and me, because of the Daywalker thing."

I nodded. "Anything I need to be concerned about?"

Alucard hesitated, as if debating whether or not to answer. "In a way…"

He took a drink as if readying himself. "Have you ever heard of White Fang?"

I frowned. "The book?" He shook his head. "I guess not, then. What is it?"

"Not a *what*, but a *man*," he emphasized, watching me.

My pulse began to quicken, not understanding where he was going with this. "Just say it plainly. No need to drag it out."

He nodded. "I'm trying. It's not anything I've been able to verify. Basically, someone seems to be planting seeds of discord with each family of supernaturals. But no one knows who he really is because he hasn't actually taken credit for it. People have begun to call him White Fang." He grimaced, searching for the right words. "In a way, he's kind of like an anti... *you*, I guess. You've been gathering various flavors of monster together and giving them a home or support or whatever you want to call it. This man is doing the opposite. Encouraging the weregorillas to break away from you when the Greeks invaded. Telling the vampires that they need to encroach upon their neighbors. And..." he let out a deep breath before meeting my eyes. "Possibly encouraging Zeus to challenge Gunnar."

I blinked. "You're kidding, right?" He shook his head, face deadly serious. "Why?"

"I think it's retaliation against you. This person doesn't like what you've done. He's trying to break up everything, go back to the way things were before you began knocking people down."

I grimaced. "He prefers anarchy?" I spat. "Or does he just want everyone to solidify their boundaries? And how many groups are we talking about? I'm not even sure I know all the families in town. Wolves, dragons, gorillas, Greeks, vampires..." I shrugged. "Who else?"

He pursed his lips. "I'm still trying to confirm that. There are supposedly seven families – or nations – in town. But many of them have kept a low profile as a result of your *high* profile. None of them have wanted to catch your attention for fear that you will roll over them, too."

I blinked at him. "Roll over them, too?" I laughed. "What is *that* supposed to mean? I'm not in charge of any of those families."

Alucard blinked at me. Talon grunted. I turned from one to the other, frowning. "You might not be in charge of them – directly – but you helped put almost all of them in their position of power. Think about it. Gunnar," he said, holding up a finger, "is your childhood best friend, and he took over the local werewolves as a result of drama that fell on you." I grimaced, nodding. "Raego. You practically handed him his throne, and not just for St. Louis, but for the *world*. And you embarrassed his grandmother."

"That was not my fault. The Academy brought her into it. I didn't even know she existed."

"Ah, the *Academy*. You've shut them down repeatedly, even declared war on them."

I closed my mouth, realizing that anything I said wouldn't really change the facts.

"You shut down an Angel and his Nephilim, and now the Angel is a guardian for one of your old employees. A fucking Angel, Nate..." he said in a low tone, leaning forward. "The Greeks. You set up their Fight Club, now one of the premier sources of entertainment for all Freaks – those with the invite, anyway – giving them a lot of financial muscle."

"The gorillas don't like me," I said, latching onto one of the other factions.

Alucard shrugged. "Yeah, you fucked up there. You almost had them." His smile turned amused. "But you scooped up a Beast Master, one who can control *all* shifters. And she runs a school – that you founded – of independent shifters, beholden to no packs. Some consider them an army in training..." Then he pointed at himself. "And you have a Daywalker Vampire living at your house." He finished off his drink, letting me absorb everything. "None of this is even considering your other friends – Talon, an Elder, the Horsemen... Or your enemies – the Syndicate, Makers, Athena," he waved a hand, not bothering to list all the people against me, whether they were now alive or dead.

Talon was watching me, looking impressed. I wasn't sure I had ever laid it all out like that.

"And now you're friends with a Kansas City celebrity, Callie Penrose. Who has been making similar waves in her half of the state. And she just broke the *Vatican*. Do you see why people are concerned? They liked the way things were. Before *you*. And this White Fang is encouraging that while not taking any credit for it. Basically, lighting fuses all around town."

"Who is it?" I asked, my voice like a rusty nail scraping concrete.

Alucard shrugged. "No one knows, but everyone talks about a werewolf wandering around town. Big son of a bitch. Gray. I checked with Gunnar before he left. Definitely not a part of his pack. Everyone says he is responsible, but I've never seen him. He's a ghost."

"What did you mean about him leading Zeus Fletcher here?"

"It makes sense," Alucard shrugged. "White Fang is stirring up trouble, and suddenly Zeus arrives to challenge Gunnar." He leaned forward, eyes grave. "I overheard Drake and Cowan talking to Gunnar. They said Zeus had an official invitation to the wedding, Nate."

I growled at that. Someone had given him an invite? Definitely not Gunnar. "Zeus is dead, now. No more rebellion against Gunnar. Or the Temple throne," I added sarcastically.

Alucard was silent for a moment, as if not wanting to continue. He finally sighed. "White Fang met with the gorillas today. One of Gunnar's wolves was on patrol, keeping an eye on Zeus' pack. He saw White Fang leaving the gorillas headquarters. The wolf tried to catch him but failed. White Fang is rumored to be very fast. As soon as the gorillas heard about the wolf on their turf, they chased him down with tenacity, threatening war if Gunnar's pack crossed into their territory again."

I blinked at Alucard, shaking my head. "War? A handful of gorillas threatened war against a pack of *hundreds* of wolves?" I asked incredulously.

Alucard nodded soberly. "That's exactly what I'm talking about. White Fang is inspiring people to act. Encouraging them to stand up by feeding their paranoia. Everyone is gearing up for something big, and none of them are working together. Like I said, this White Fang isn't uniting them *behind* anyone, just *against* each other. And against you. And with all the new faces coming to town, everyone is trying to solidify their property lines, so to speak."

I reached over to the bottle and refilled my glass, thinking. "White Fang…" I took a big gulp of my drink, growing angry. "I don't want anyone behind me. They can do whatever they want. But it benefits no one to go to war."

"It's a little late for that. I'm pretty sure it's a foregone conclusion."

I squinted at Alucard suspiciously. "Is this why everyone is pushing me away? Why Gunnar didn't want me to interfere? Why Raego treats me like a stranger?"

"Pretty sure." He managed to look mildly embarrassed as he continued. "It's also why… I was called to the meeting last night with the vampires. They wanted to make sure I'm not one of your pets. Which means… I'm going to need you to give me some space as well. Roland and I are heading to the Sanguine Council tomorrow. To nominate me for Master of St. Louis. The only reason I was picked is because I'm obviously strong, and... I made it abundantly clear that you held no sway over me. At all."

I just stared at him. I was hurt. Even if Alucard was only doing it to get control over his vampires, it still hurt. Anyone with ties to me was fair game. Because of this White Fang.

"I... see," I murmured, fighting not to shatter the drink in my hand. Talon also looked torn between murdering Alucard and understanding the big picture. I faced Alucard. "Does this mean you actually want me to get out of your hair, or that you are just doing it for show? To become Master of St. Louis."

Alucard closed his eyes. "It needs to be authentic."

"Get out, Alucard," I said through gritted teeth, setting my drink down. "Just... get out."

He sucked in a breath – even though he didn't need to breathe – but I turned my back on him and walked away.

My fucking hands were shaking.

CHAPTER 20

I realized I was standing before the Round Table, studying its little streams of liquid silver and gold that circled the surface in a constant flow. I studied them, breathing deeply. *Be the stream.* I heard Alucard leave, but didn't acknowledge him. I felt Talon walking up to me.

"I need a fucking mantra," I said, not feeling at one with the molten metal stream.

"Want me to kill him?" he asked, not an ounce of hesitation or judgment in his voice.

I rounded on him. "No! Christ, Talon. I'm pissed, but not at him. Not really. I'm pissed that he has to do this. This fucking White Fang prick. He's twisted everything around."

Talon arched a brow. "Alucard doesn't have to do what he did. He could walk into their home and slaughter all opposing vampires. I think the Sanguine Council would approve. Bold."

I studied his eyes and realized he was being completely serious. That was actually the option he considered most beneficial. A murder spree.

My pet kitty was a psycho.

But... he might be right. Alucard was strong enough that he could have done as Talon suggested. But which was better? Murdering a bunch of scared vampires to make a point, or to do it the way he had, by having the balls to tell me to my face that he needed to cut ties to me.

"If White Fang doesn't stand to gain anything, why is he stirring up trouble? And if he was working with Zeus, why is he still here?"

Talon shrugged. "Perhaps you will let me kill *him*? It won't take me long."

I thought about it for a few moments before shaking my head. "No, not yet. If anyone sees you around town hunting White Fang, it will only put truth to his claims. Everyone will think I'm trying to silence him. That I really do fancy myself some kind of king." I swore under my breath, turning back to the table, trying to find my center. What was the best way out of this?

At least Gunnar's pack had taken care of their own problem. Killing Zeus.

But who else was facing similar issues in town? Who were the newcomers people kept talking about? Was there perhaps some kind of unified group and Alucard just wasn't aware of it? Was White Fang causing chaos in hopes that I would shut everyone down and remove his competitors for him? But to plan that, he would have to have some kind of plan for after – how he intended to handle Nate Temple after I cleared the field of all these families.

"We'll be busy with our own problems soon. Let them fight over St. Louis. It's not important. We've dealt with bigger wars than their petty power plays. We'll sit on the lawn and watch the city burn."

Talon purred. "Spoken like a true king."

"Where's that squirt bottle?" I muttered, patting my pockets. Talon hissed instinctively. I'd actually sprayed him with one a few times – a small squirt bottle I had carried around in my satchel for a few days.

The house rumbled again and then let out what sounded like a sigh. The ravens burst into flight with a squawk but roosted again once the house stilled. Talon purred at their discomfort, but he studied the walls for a few silent seconds before turning back to me.

"How long until that stops?" he asked. Talon knew the truth. He had been there when I found out. I'd also told Pan and Carl, just in case. But that was it.

I shrugged. "I don't know. She hasn't been very talkative lately. Maybe it will take a century or something. Or an hour. Without her talking to me, I'm not sure. And the way Kai made it sound – that Beasts weren't supposed to be free, or to procreate outside of their bonds with a Maker – I'm not sure she would know the answer either. I think this is new to everyone."

Talon sighed. "Any thoughts on *them?*" he asked, not pointing openly, but flicking his eyes towards the ravens who were watching us in silence.

"They haven't spoken to me in a while. Just watched. Ever since the fight with Castor Queen when they bravely flew away," I said loud enough for them to hear. The two ruffled their feathers in response, but didn't comment. I growled in frustration. I had spoken with Odin. Twice. He'd been kind of a dick, but not more so than I had expected. Cryptic as hell, but that was par for the course with gods.

But the second time I had seen him, he'd brought a hooded figure into this very room to… look at me, I guess. Odin had asked the wraith if he was satisfied, and then the two had disappeared. I had shrugged it off, assuming it had been Death being a creep. But it hadn't been my Horseman pal. No one knew who he had been, and neither Odin nor his ravens had deigned to inform me who they had brought into my home, into my most secret room in Chateau Falco.

Some god? Goddess? Friend? Enemy?

I had no idea, but knowing that Odin's ravens were on my family crest didn't make me feel any better about it. It just made me feel like I was a pawn on a board, and that Odin was moving me about as he saw fit.

The more I thought about it, the more I wanted to get to Hell so I could start killing things. But it wasn't time yet. "I'm going to the Fight Club tonight. I feel like letting off some steam."

Talon purred. "That sounds positively delightful. Can I come?"

I thought about it. "Only if Carl will stick around Chateau Falco. Just in case…" Talon sighed in understanding. In case Falco decided to deliver her Baby Beast. I needed someone strong here when that happened, in case the Baby Beast arrived in this world hungry and scared.

Only to find a dozen appetizing treats walking around.

My friends.

Since I had no idea what a Baby Beast ate, I didn't want to risk it.

"That is wise. I'll stay here with the albino." He sounded as if he was volunteering for torture. I rolled my eyes, motioning for him to follow as I left the Sanctorum and entered the long stone tunnel that led back to the house proper. Purple flamed torches flared to life ahead of us. I glanced back to see the Round Table silently lowering back into the floor and shook my head.

When all this was over, maybe I would just move back to Fae with Talon and my Baby Beast.

CHAPTER 21

$\mathcal{W}$e walked through the halls of Chateau Falco. Armored statues and priceless paintings lined the halls and the thick woven rugs stretching down the floor were decorated in swirls of muted colors that fit the colors in the paintings of each section of the home like a leather glove. The entire mansion had been tastefully decorated over hundreds of years so that the vast size didn't just feel like a vacant storage building. It felt like a home. Not just to me, but to those who visited as well. I could always see it in the eyes of my guests, that look of contentment and concealed wonder as they took in the polished chandeliers, the shining woodwork, and the overall feel to the space. But maybe it was just a result of being inside a living Beast.

After a few minutes of walking we came upon one of the living rooms. Dean, my butler, was polishing a wooden bookshelf, taking care of one of the million details necessary to keep the place up to his exacting standards.

Carl was speaking with the Huntress a dozen paces away from Dean, but I could tell the Butler was listening. The Huntress was an immortal assassin who had once worked for Rumpelstiltskin before I had taken him out. Van Helsing and Baba Yaga had also been working for him – having made a deal with him in their youth. They hadn't read the fine print of their contracts with Rumpelstiltskin – Silver Tongue – and had wound up bound to serve him for hundreds of years. He used those agreements to coerce people to work for the Syndicate – a group of rogue wizards who stood against the Academy.

But I had taken care of the Syndicate, too.

Alucard's accusations echoed in my ears, taunting. Maybe he had a point.

I hadn't seen the Huntress very much recently, and her relationship with Tory also seemed strained, letting me know it wasn't just me she had been avoiding. I was pretty sure it had to do with Alex's sudden changes – from a young teen to a young man. It didn't sit well with her. The Huntress hadn't ever been very fond of children, referring to them as *it* more often than not. But she had begrudgingly taken Alex under her care – opening up a heart she hadn't known existed within herself – to give him the love he so desperately needed.

The love of a mother. It had cost her something to do that.

Except now that brief purpose had been ripped away. Because he no longer had boyhood needs. Like any young man, he was trying to find his own way. It was ironic that now that he was more self-sufficient – which she had originally preferred – she was more uncomfortable than ever. And the fact that it messed with her... messed with her.

I realized Dean, who had many problems with Carl, namely his penchant for wearing high heels and leaving dead skin around the house, was now pretending the two beside him didn't exist, his face a deep red color as he focused on polishing the wood.

I heard a loud *slap* and spun to see Carl gripping his cheek and the Huntress storming away with fire in her eyes. Luckily, she hadn't noticed Talon and me or she might have wandered over to give us a similar display of affection. Carl turned to us, his lizard mouth seeming to frown. He blinked his clear eyelid several times and flicked his tongue out upon seeing us.

"She wouldn't tell me of the D. She just struck me."

I couldn't even come up with a response.

But Talon could. "If it is such a closely guarded secret, perhaps you just need to keep trying. Ask the others. Temple has many women on the grounds."

"That makes it sound like I have a dungeon of naked chicks stashed away here," I argued. I turned to Dean, who was staring at me. "I don't, do I?" I asked him, and was rewarded with an even darker blush to his cheeks. I sagged my shoulders in mock disappointment.

Talon ignored me. "The best answers are found through quiet contemplation and determination. Perhaps meditation will help you learn the secret on your own." Talon pointed at the stick in Carl's hands, the one that he had picked up outside before leaving us to find the Huntress. "Elders are powerful. Try using your natural gifts to make this D grow. Or to learn if this wood even is this magical D."

Carl nodded absently. He looked at me, and seemed to remember something. "Did you upset the sparkly one? He left without saying goodbye to me. I specifically remember you telling me to always say goodbye to friends when they left. And something else when they arrive..." he added, scratching his scaled lips thoughtfully.

"*Hello*. You say *hello* when friends arrive."

He pointed the stick at me. "*That's* the word! *Hello*," he mused, as if getting a feel for the strange word. "Sparkula said neither. He just left."

"Don't worry about it. He's got some stuff to work out. Hey, can you keep an eye on the house with Talon tonight?"

Carl shook his head. "I will be here, but I will be busy with my D. If anything..." he glanced at the walls thoughtfully, well aware of Falco's pregnancy, "strange happens, I'll be available, but I must not be disturbed unless absolutely necessary. I'm sure Talon understands." Talon muttered darkly under his breath, but Carl cleared his throat. "Goodbye." Then he spun around, crouched low, and sprinted away from us down the hall at a dead run. I was pretty sure I heard him talking to his D as he ran.

"No running in the house!" Dean shouted, but he sounded resigned, knowing it was futile.

I turned to Talon to find him smiling proudly. "I do not understand why this D is amusing to Alucard, but now I'm in on the joke, right? I did the funny." He sounded very pleased.

I sighed. "Sure, Talon."

Carl was simply too easy to tease. Even those who didn't understand a joke could tease him about them. I was pretty sure this was Talon's way of not becoming the brunt of the joke. To team up with us rather than admit his ignorance about... whatever this D was. But if Carl wanted to go find a quiet spot in the house and talk to his stupid stick, I was going to leave him to it. Better than him pestering more women. He was weird enough that no one would expect someone had put Carl up to it, simply thinking he was being his usual weird self, talking to a stick.

I wanted to go yell at Alucard and make him take it back and explain the joke, but...

Alucard had already left.

"If we hadn't let Alucard play this joke on Carl," I muttered out loud, "maybe he could have helped us tonight. That's called Karma." I turned to walk backwards down the hall as I attempted to explain it to Talon. I sensed Dean watching me with a disbelieving frown. "When you play a joke on someone, the universe has an uncanny ability to turn around and—"

I bumped into something solid and heard a grunt before ice water splashed all down my back.

I yelped, spinning to see Alex holding an empty glass of water. He stared at me, face turning from initial anger to fear as he realized who he had just dumped water on.

Dean cleared his throat, and Alex's face paled even further. The young man ripped off his shirt and crouched down to begin mopping up the mess, forgetting me entirely as Dean began storming closer. Alex's muscled chest was soaked as well, and I heard Talon grunt behind me – whether amused by the karma or impressed at Alex's drastic change in body type, I wasn't sure. Or maybe my bodyguard had fled the scene rather than risking Dean's wrath.

With a last hurried swipe, Alex scooped up the ice cubes and turned to run back the way he had come. "I'll be right there, Pegasus!" he shouted. And then he was gone, leaving me to face the legendarily temperamental Butler God.

Dean stared down at the still slightly wet floor and then at me. My shirt continued to drip onto the floor, making a bigger mess. Even worse, it was mixing with the dried dirt on my boots, leaving the floor muddy. I sighed, muttering under my breath as his eyes burned through me.

I realized Talon was no longer behind me. The coward.

"This was *not* my fault," I said. The Butler God arched a brow, pointedly glancing down at my dirty boots. I let out a breath and bent over to untie them. Dean sniffed, not mentioning the fact that I had obviously worn my dirty boots inside when I knew very well he had told me not to dozens, if not hundreds, of times. He folded his arms, silently watching me. I tucked the offending boots under my arm and stormed towards the front door to leave them outside – like I should have done in the first place. I was going to go take a long, hot shower.

"Fucking coward, running to your winged horse rather than face down my butler."

"*Language*, Master Temple…" Dean warned from over my shoulder.

I turned to bare my teeth at him – but only after I verified he was no longer looking at me – and stomped away.

I made sure not to run. Because, *rules*.

I fantasized about the Fight Club tonight, wondering who I would have the chance to murder.

CHAPTER 22

$\mathcal{I}$ had chosen to take a long bath instead, hoping the soak would help clear my head. Then I had spent a few hours reading a few of the gathered books on King Arthur we had collected. My frustration had quickly returned as I found nothing useful in the stories.

This Knight saved this damsel. That knight fought that monster. Lady of the Lake. Merlin. Guinevere. Blah blah blah.

Not that they weren't fun stories, but when I was looking for hard facts, they lost their value.

Now, I sat on bleachers packed with a hundred or so Freaks from St. Louis. Wolves, dragons, robed mystery guests, vampires, and a mess of Greeks from Achilles' bar. A fiery sunset hung on the distant horizon like a ball of molten fire. A ring of flickering torches around us held supreme darkness at bay. I'd never really learned what was beyond the ring of torches, but I knew monsters lived out there. When I had first met Grimm, he had been hanging out in there, murdering things, before introducing himself to me by attacking me.

Luckily, since I was the last Temple, his horn hadn't harmed me. Something about unicorns not being able to harm virgins or the last of a bloodline. I definitely wasn't saved by my v-card, because I had misplaced that thing a *long* time ago.

Grimm and I were now pals. Hell, he was my Ride. Capital R. Because I was the Fifth Horseman of the Apocalypse – the Horseman of Hope. At least, I had been offered the job. Because the Four Horsemen were dicks, they hadn't told me whether I was officially a Horseman or not, but I definitely had some new powers as a result. My magic could turn white with Heavenly Fire of some kind, basically, supercharging my wizard's power with Bible Juice.

And if I put the Mask on – which was currently disguised as a coin on a necklace hanging from my throat – my skin turned to some kind of diamond grit and I grew skeletal wings and claws. But that had only happened once.

Death had told me that I would know when the position became official, and since I was still questioning it, I considered myself still on the bench while the Varsity Team managed the field. I wasn't sure I wanted to be a destroyer of men during Armageddon.

But maybe that was what the whole Catalyst thing was about. My unique birth in Fae.

I really needed to get some damned answers from my parents. They had read an old text while on a trip in England, and it had led them to their brilliant plan of robbing the Fae Queens for that Hammer and Hourglass. I needed to find out what they learned. What they read. What events led to my birth.

Because all of those super powerful gods and legends – Pandora, Achilles, Shiva, Ganesh, and basically anyone I had ever met who had lived a few centuries or more – spoke of a War that was coming. The All War.

And if I was this Catalyst, and possibly a Fifth Horseman…

I had never been a fan of coincidences.

"Tomorrow," I reminded myself under my breath.

I felt those beside me shift uncertainly at my random comment. I looked up at them, ready to laugh it off, and found them averting their eyes. Some of them even grimaced, as if not wanting to be seen near me. Some even got up and walked away.

I opened my mouth to ask a question and then stopped. Alucard had mentioned White Fang turning people against me, but I didn't want anyone knowing he had done so. Or knowing that I cared if they were turning against me, because even that might play into White Fang's plans. So, I kept my trap shut and tried to ignore the veiled glances I was getting from the various Freaks sitting in the stands outside the Dueling Grounds.

I let my eyes scan the crowd outside the ring. Dirty Gerty was here with her Council, and Tory wasn't far away from her. Not a part of her circle, but hovering just outside it and looking agitated. I didn't spot anyone else I recognized – or, at least no one that I personally knew or was friends with, but I hadn't seen everyone. And with the tight crowd, I would have had to walk the perimeter of the ring to get a look at every face. Not caring to do so, I stayed in my seat, wishing I had a friend to chat with while I waited.

But I knew I would be poor company, so hadn't bothered to ask anyone. I had considered asking Callie, but with her friendship with Roland, and the fact that he had been in the meeting with Alucard, I had decided not to. I also hadn't wanted to bring her into the politics apparently bubbling up in St. Louis. Especially not if her name was already being mentioned by this White Fang as another concern. I definitely didn't need everyone seeing us together and perhaps making her an even bigger target.

All this pleasant drama condensed into a white-hot fire in my belly.

I was ready to fight.

Leonidas and Achilles were currently sparring in the ring, sparks flying as they fought spear to spear. They both sported gashes and cuts, but neither looked near exhaustion. They were actually laughing as they spun, twisted, lunged, and leaped into the air, spears whistling around in a lethal blur before whipping out in a flurry of stabs that rarely seemed to strike home.

An even match, or close enough to it. This fight could go on forever.

As if coming to the same conclusion, Achilles finally lowered his spear and stepped back, grinning at Leonidas. "Let's let someone else play for a while. They didn't come here to watch us fight for four hours."

Leonidas grunted. "I'll get you one of these days, Myrmidon," but a whisper of a smile split his bearded cheeks. Achilles rolled his eyes good naturedly before turning to Asterion and signaling for him to announce the next contenders.

The Minotaur glanced down at a paper in his hands, rubbing a sausage-sized finger down the list before stopping and grinning. He lifted his head to the crowd.

"Nate Temple!"

"About fucking time," I muttered, climbing to my feet.

I entered the ring like a starving lion. At this point, it wasn't even about winning or losing. I just wanted to hit something. And since no one could actually die at the Dueling Grounds, I could cut loose without consequences.

The crowd was eerily silent, as if not wanting to be heard cheering for me. This only proved Alucard's warning about White Fang. I looked at Asterion, wondering why he hadn't called my contender. He was frowning at me.

"You want two on one?" he asked in a low tone.

I nodded.

"That's... unfortunate."

I ignored him, walking to the center of the ring, wondering which two unlucky bastards were about to get bitch-smacked by one grumpy Master Temp—

"Raego Slate!" Asterion bellowed.

This time, the crowd went even quieter. But only for a moment. Then they burst out in a frenzied roar.

I spun to see Raego, the Dragon King, step into the ring, frowning at me. He didn't look pleased at the bad luck. I wasn't necessarily happy with the pairing either, because Raego was a badass and I really didn't want to lose against him. But... he was also involved in this shit show going on in town. Somehow. And his whole investigation thing with Tory smelled fishy.

Asterion let out a blood-curdling *Moo*, silencing the crowd as he held up a hand. The crowd hushed, murmuring to each other in small pockets, wondering what Asterion was waiting for.

"And... Alucard Morningstar!"

The roar of the crowd was deafening this time, and a red film of rage washed over my eyes as I saw the Daywalker enter the ring beside Raego. He also didn't look pleased, but he was masking it for the crowd, not daring to show anything in his eyes. Because if he did, it would only show his friendship with me, which he apparently no longer wanted.

"Authentic," I said loudly, but casually, reminding him of the word he had used. I studied the two of them lazily. "This will be fun. The location could be better," I added with a dark smile.

A subtle hint that it was unfortunate we were about to fight in a place where none of us could actually die. Raego and Alucard's faces grew harder.

"We three kings..." I sang in a soft tone. Then I flicked my hands, not even glancing down as white whips of fiery lightning erupted from my palms. They were made of pure magic, and since this fight was going to be much harder than I had bargained for, I wasn't about to play games. They wanted to show the city they could stand up to me? That they were big boys?

Okay.

The whips scorched the earth as I strutted closer in a fluid stroll.

"Heavy is the head that wears the crown," I said.

And then I struck out at both of them simultaneously to the sound of the roaring crowd.

CHAPTER 23

I muted the crowd with a mental effort as I lashed out at the two of my friends. Two friends who – whether for good or bad – thought they needed to step out of my imagined shadow, or at least make everyone in town think so.

They thought I was trying to take over St. Louis? Whether they truly believed it or not, enough people did, and now here we were.

My whip crackled through a sudden cloud of black smoke where Raego had stood. My other whip struck only a cloud of embers as Alucard darted out of the way in a flash of golden light. I saw him zip to the other side of the ring, so I focused on the black cloud before me. From the depths of that shadow, a hulking figure suddenly appeared, black wings flaring wide as the dragon roared and then launched himself at me.

I laughed as I spun, flinging out a handful of dust.

Raego's massive jaws snapped onto the dust and then his mouth flared wide as he gagged, trying to spit his black vapor – a thick, roiling fog that would turn me into an obsidian statue. I knew he could also spit fire, an almost liquid black flame, but I wasn't concerned anymore.

Because thanks to my dust, he wouldn't be doing much of either.

I flung my hands wide as he continued to gag and cough, still trying to spit flame while ignoring the searing pain in his mouth. A powder I had

119

devised at Grimm Tech that essentially – when combined with saliva – turned to a gooey, waterproof paste.

Basically, I had slapped a big wad of bubble gum over his fire holes, or whatever it was that let a dragon spit flame.

Two flames from the flickering torches outside the ring suddenly zipped through the crowd, interrupting the cheers as the fireballs whipped past their faces, maybe even hitting a few of them if I was lucky. The fireballs struck my palms and then doubled in size before turning an icy blue.

I slapped them into Raego's cheeks, gripping his massive head with both hands as the flame splashed over him, burning. Acrid smoke billowed up as Raego tried to scream. I dipped my head close and kissed him right on the snout before jumping back, laughing at his pain, embarrassment, and fury.

Which was when Alucard struck me like he was Helios running late to work.

I felt my ribs crack – a muted, popping sound – as I went cartwheeling through the air. I saw Alucard standing in front of Raego protectively. I managed to fling out my hands, summoning two clear whips – not elemental destructive power, but more like elastic cords – and threw them.

They cracked over Alucard's shoulders, and I saw him grin.

But I hadn't been aiming for Alucard. The clear whips hit Raego's outstretched wings.

They latched on like anchors, halting my flight, and suddenly whipping me right back at the two opponents like a pebble in a slingshot. I held my legs up and released my whips, smiling as my boots lined up with Alucard's stunned face.

I miscalculated and only managed to clip his jaw before my legs went wide and...

Well, I rode him to the ground with his face in my crotch. I think I've heard it called a tea bag, but I was moving too fast for it to be funny and the blow to the groin made my kidneys and back explode with inner fire. His back slammed into the earth, relieving the pressure somewhat as I sat on his chest, gripping his hair like a steering wheel.

Alucard gasped for breath – heh – as we slowed, struggling to get free. Raego suddenly towered over us, jaws wide to gobble up the tea-bagging wizard.

I threw myself clear, hobbling away on shaking legs as I tried to ignore my aching back and groin. Knowing that Alucard would be livid for making him look like an idiot and that I wouldn't be fast enough to escape Raego's teeth, I instinctively Shadow Walked to get out of the danger-zone and strike the black dragon from behind.

Whoopsies. Forgot about not Shadow Walking.

I was suddenly standing in that gray world of roiling black fog. And two of the Candy Skulls stood only ten feet away from me. This close, they towered head and shoulders over me. They cocked their heads in those fitful, jerking motions and three glass blades – like claws – erupted from the end of each sleeve where their hands should have been. Then in silent and awkward jolting movements, they drifted in to slice me into wizard tri-tips. Sweat popped out on my skin as I stared into those haunting skulls, the beauty of the painted masks distracting me like those beautiful predators in the wild. The flowers, whorls, and almost tribal designs in vivid blues, pinks, reds, and yellows seemed almost alive, writhing across the surface of the bone Calaveras. I was momentarily frozen in horror. It was like their gaze drew me in and bathed me in fear and self-loathing.

With great effort, I managed to lower my gaze, and felt my strength and willpower instantly return. I frantically scanned the shadow world for my opening and saw it.

Behind the Candy Skulls was an oval of shimmering, clear glass hovering in the air.

Hoping that glass could take me somewhere better than this place, I sprinted at them and ignited white blades before me – the only sound in this strange world seemed to echo like a cavern. I hadn't wanted to use whips and possibly attach myself to whatever the fuck these things were. I slashed down and out, intending to slice them from clavicle to hip, or knock them clear of my path to the suspended glass.

My swords tore through them like a fire in a library, slicing through their bodies but not seeming to do them any lasting harm. They shifted away from me with the blow as if trying to diminish the impact, to roll with the punch.

Which was all I cared about. It gave me enough room to slip past them and dive face-first for the hanging glass, which I realized up close looked like a fogged window showing the Dueling Grounds. I felt heat as the Calaveras claws scored across the heels of my boots as my nose touched the hazy window.

I flew through it to the sound of shattering glass.

I twisted to hit the ground on my back, panting wildly from my fear of the other place. I scooted backwards on my ass, eyes latching onto the opening I had just used. In falling shards of translucent glass, I saw the Calaveras staring at me with heads cocked, but as those shards continued to fall, they simply evaporated to reveal the other side of the Dueling Grounds.

I heard the crowd still cheering as if nothing had happened.

Then a fist grabbed me by the back of my shirt collar and threw me across the ring.

I didn't land on a soft mattress as I slowly rotated in the air.

My face landed on a black-scaled fist so hard I thought I heard a *pow!* sound effect before everything went white for a few moments. My vision slowly came back and I found myself on all fours, barely holding myself up.

"Stop," I whispered, trying not to throw up. "Stop…"

"What is he saying?" I heard Alucard ask from the other side of the ring, his boots striking the ground as he came closer.

Raego, naked and in human form, suddenly stood before me. "I don't know…"

"Candy…" I whispered desperately, trying to let him know that our fight didn't matter. Needing to know if anyone else had seen what just happened. That other place.

"I think he called me Candy. Smart-mouthed asshole."

"Is he concussed?" Alucard laughed. "That was a pretty solid blow he took to the jaw."

I tried to shake my head. "Did… you see the… Candy Skulls?" I finally rasped, head slowly clearing and nearly able to somewhat raise my head.

"STOP!" Asterion bellowed, cutting off conversation. "The fight is over. A draw."

I grunted, not giving two shits about the crowd or the fight as I stared at the Minotaur who was running my way, his boots seeming to make the ground shake. Achilles wore a frown as he watched from the sidelines, obviously just as surprised – and not pleased – with Asterion's decision.

"Temple was done for!" someone in the crowd shouted out. Several chimed in their agreement. It sounded like it came from the group of dragons. I thought I saw Baron as I glanced over at them, but was too woozy to be sure. I definitely noticed the whites of Dirty Gerty's teeth as she smiled at me. She was probably more upset than anyone, wanting to see her grandson make me look a fool in front of so many people.

Achilles, sensing that something was obviously amiss, turned a cold stare onto the crowd, silencing them in a heartbeat. "Myrmidons!" A dozen men in sleeveless black vests and black khakis suddenly melted out of the crowd, wielding spears as they formed a perimeter faster than they should have been able to do on such short notice. "The next person who challenges or comments on this fight will see what a spear through the throat feels like before they leave. Even though it's not permanent, you will feel every sensation. And the same sensation for your next six visits to Fight Night."

The crowd collectively snapped their mouths shut.

Achilles turned to Asterion and dipped his head, but his look was curious. The Minotaur helped me to my feet, watching me with concerned eyes. "You... saw them?" I asked.

His lips curled back. "I saw nothing. But whatever you think you saw must never be mentioned again," he said carefully.

I frowned. "You know what they are?" I whispered, aware of Raego and Alucard both studying me. They kept their faces neutral so that none of the crowd sensed any camaraderie between us – if there was any, I wasn't sure anymore – but their eyes danced with questions. Was this a stunt of mine or was something really wrong? Fights were very rarely called off, and I was pretty sure that the only draw I had ever seen was between Achilles and Leonidas earlier tonight.

"I know nothing. Neither do you. Neither do they." He jerked his chin at the crowd. "I cannot say anything else. Can. Not." He said, clipping the words with emphasis. "Whatever you think you saw is probably very dangerous." He grimaced, and then, as if coming to a decision he didn't like, he leaned closer as he guided me away, barely audible as he spoke. "The more who know, the more dangerous they will become. Awareness breeds more... of *them*."

I blinked. What the living fuck was he talking about? He couldn't tell me what he knew, and was warning me to not say a word to anyone? How the hell was I supposed to figure out what they were if I couldn't ask anyone questions about them? The more people who knew, the more there would be next time? I needed to warn Tory and Callie – make sure they hadn't told anyone.

"You took a nasty blow, Temple. Everything okay? You were doing very well for yourself, at first. Pity the fight had to be called off." I glanced up at the new voice to find Achilles before me. I nodded, shaking off Asterion's support as I struggled to show a strong face for the crowd that I sensed staring at me.

The crowd had seen me go from kicking ass to suddenly getting my ass kicked.

"How long was I gone?" I asked carefully.

Achilles cocked his head. "Gone? You did your teleporting thing. Maybe a fraction of a second?" he asked, glancing at Asterion. The Minotaur nodded, his face a blank mask.

"Right..." I said tiredly. It had been minutes, or at least one full minute. But... why was there suddenly a realm full of homicidal Candy Skulls when I tried to Shadow Walk? Was that why it was called Shadow Walking? Was there supposed to be some realm we had to pass through, and up until recently, we'd been somehow dodging it? Cheating the Candy Skulls of their free meals? "Must have tripped or used more magic than I thought at the beginning of the fight," I said as an excuse. I glanced up to study the crowd with a quick sweep of my eyes. "You guys mind calling out the next fight? I'm sick of these assholes staring at me."

Asterion nodded, whipping out his pad of paper and walking back to the center of the ring, calling out a name I didn't recognize. Achilles studied me with a thoughtful frown before finally shrugging. "Get some sleep, Temple. You're a hot mess." Then he was walking away.

I glanced back to see Raego and Alucard watching me from across the ring. Their faces were emotionless. Then they were slipping back into the crowd. With a tired sigh, I shuffled out of the crowd, intending to catch my breath and clear my head in a lone section of bleachers. I couldn't show weakness here, but I did want a freaking minute to relax.

I looked up to see two wolves staring at me.

Drake and Cowan. They weren't smiling. "Look angry. Very, very angry," Drake murmured, barely moving his lips – as if hoping to disguise the warning.

"That won't be hard," I muttered.

"We need to talk. Now, Temple. Gunnar demands it," Cowan said in an angry tone.

I managed to keep the scowl on my face, even though I was suddenly very concerned. Gunnar wasn't accessible right now. He was on his freaking honeymoon. And I couldn't tell if these two were actually angry or just pretending to be.

"Lead the way, mutts."

CHAPTER 24

I followed them over to the ring of torches, far away from listening ears. I folded my arms as I stared them down, aware of the eyes watching us. "Talk," I told them in a cold tone, forcing myself not to rub my throbbing jaw. I took a breath, testing my ribs. They ached, but not too badly. I knew that if I had died here, I would have woken up back home, healed. But what if I had only been injured?

"We brought the pack here to let off some steam after this morning," Drake told me. I nodded, wanting him to get to the point. "But we also wanted to catch you on neutral ground, almost as if by coincidence..." he continued, not smirking, but something playful and dangerous lurking not far below the surface. For anyone watching, looking like he was delivering a warning.

"I'm tired, Drake. Did Gunnar really have something to tell me?" I was sure to keep my voice low just in case we had listeners.

Cowan shook his head, folding his arms. "We wanted to open communication lines with you." He said nothing further, kind of making his statement seem ridiculous. Instead, he kept his eyes on the crowd, looking annoyed to be seen anywhere near me, performing a duty he wasn't particularly happy about. Was that for the witnesses or was it genuine?

Drake cleared his throat. "We were... approached today. By a big gray wolf. A stranger."

I cursed under my breath. "White Fang…"

They shared a long look with each other, startled, but not showing it. "That was the name he went by, although he sounded amused when he said it."

"Because it's more of a nickname. Did he warn you to turn against me, too?"

They shared an even longer look. "Not in so many words. But he did warn of a new threat to the pack. It seems Zeus had an Alpha King – the self-declared Alpha of the Midwest. This king is not too happy about the turn of events with Zeus. He's bringing his pack to St. Louis. Soon."

I tried to keep the shock from my face. "But Gunnar isn't here."

"I don't think he's coming to challenge our Alpha. I think he's coming for war. And White Fang made it sound like this king sees himself as above the… antiquated shifter laws. It's exactly like what we fled back East. But they seem more successful with it here. He's wants retribution for Zeus. Either to take Gunnar's pack or to kill Gunnar and then take the pack."

I frowned. If White Fang worked for Zeus – and ultimately this king – why had he warned Drake and Cowan? "Why have you come to me?" I asked warily, remembering that Gunnar hadn't wanted me to get involved in wolf politics.

They shared an uneasy look. "We know how this looks, that we have experience with this kind of… leadership structure. These *kings*," Drake said the word as if it tasted foul on his tongue. He shook his head, a flicker of anger swiping his wavy hair to the side. "I will die to keep the pack together, with or without Gunnar. I have sworn an oath, but would have done the same without it."

Cowan seemed to realize Drake was on the edge of anger. "Seeing as how Gunnar holds you in such high esteem, we had hoped that you might truly have a way to get word to him."

I frowned. I actually didn't. I could get us about five miles from their cabin – the ward I had given him was that strong, per his request, since he would be hunting often with Ashley and hadn't wanted to risk anyone catching them off guard while out in the wilderness. But getting within five miles of the cabin wouldn't help. Within the ward, we'd have to travel on foot. In the mountains. Likely in snow. It would take a very long time, and anything could happen here in St. Louis while we did. And once we were within the ward, we would also be out of range for any magical communication. Or even cell phones, for that matter. There were no towers.

I told them this and their faces let me know their frustration, but only because I was so close to them. Anyone else would have taken it as disgust for simply talking with me.

"Then we seek guidance," Cowan said. "What would Gunnar say if we took his pack to war? I can't see any other option, but if this pack is as big as White Fang says, we might need assistance. And... Gunnar made it clear that we were supposed to handle things ourselves rather than ally with *anyone*. The restriction for seeking aid wasn't just about *you*."

That made me feel marginally better, but I still wanted to scream. What was White Fang's angle in this? Was he part of this king's pack? Or was he doing an act of good will for his fellow wolves, rather than the chaos he was sowing elsewhere?

"My resources are at your disposal, but I fear the long-term consequences of that, thanks to White Fang. We might just win this war to find every other faction in town against your pack because you teamed up with me. Besides, I'm heading out of town tomorrow. Do you know when they are going to get here?"

"Several days. They are taking their time. Moving almost a thousand wolves is not a fast process. White Fang says they are coming like a people meaning to settle down and stay."

"And do you know where White Fang's loyalties lie?"

Drake spoke up, now composed. "He told us he was not part of this king's pack or ours. I don't know if that makes him ally or foe, but he did warn us. I couldn't get a good read on him."

"Why didn't you fucking capture him, then?" I snarled, taking a step forward before I realized it. My chest struck Cowan's solid outstretched arm.

"Might want to take a deep breath, Temple. We don't react well to aggression..." his eyes were very cold, and it was no longer for show. I took a breath and stepped back. He was right.

But my reaction pretty much guaranteed those still watching us saw that we definitely weren't on friendly terms, which I guess was good for the wolves. I didn't want the other families in town ganging up on Gunnar's pack because they thought we were allies.

"This is like a fucking gang war," I muttered. *"West Side Story* or something."

Drake merely nodded, breathing deeply himself. Probably trying to shake off his adrenaline before he did something stupid at my aggression.

"What I meant was that you should have questioned him further."

Cowan openly yawned. "Capture a lone wolf who had just warned us of an attack? That would have shamed us. And Wulfric."

I grunted. Well, that could be true. Another scheme of White Fang. Turn the families on the wolves for capturing White Fang when he had *only been trying to help.*

"Is there anyone in town you could team up with instead of me? Someone that would benefit you without drawing the attention you're trying to avoid? Raego?" Because the dragon king had a veritable army at his command.

"Not him. The dragons have closed ranks. They're not getting involved with anyone. And anyway, it seems their King is letting his Council run the day-to-day affairs."

I frowned. That was news to me. Raego was shirking his duties? Or maybe this Council was just getting in the way and making him impotent.

"I'm the last person you want to ask for help right now, but even if you wanted me, I'm leaving town tomorrow. Non-negotiable."

"Who tells a billionaire what's non-negotiable?" Drake asked, cocking his head doubtfully.

I shook my head. "You don't want to know." I thought about asking Tory to help them. She had her students, who were all trained killers, but that would also make Gunnar look weak.

And she was currently working with the dragons. Who weren't helping anyone.

Was this part of White Fang's ploy? Get everyone busy and closing circles so they wouldn't help each other out? So, this Midwest King could come in and scoop up a treasure? But White Fang had told Drake and Cowan that he didn't work for the king. Was his plan to ultimately take Gunnar's pack for himself? But then why warn Drake and Cowan?

Talk about a clusterfuck. And even if Gunnar did want me to help out, I didn't have time to do so. Because I had an appointment in Hell that I couldn't reschedule, according to Death.

"We will figure something out," Drake said. "But it's best if we stop talking. Oh, and if you see Paradise and Lost, tell them I said *hello*," he said with a straight face, but his eyes danced with mischief.

I grunted and turned away.

Without bothering to say goodbye to anyone, I stepped out of the Dueling Grounds into an empty field. I took a deep breath and gagged at the smell of fresh manure. Too fresh.

I looked down to see I was standing in a fresh pile, steam curling up around my boots.

I yelled at the top of my lungs, unable to maintain control of my temper this time. I stepped out of the manure, untied my boots and then opened a Gateway back to Chateau Falco. I tossed the boots upright into the cow shit and stepped through the hole in the air.

The last thing I saw of the field was my pair of four-hundred-dollar boots sitting in a pile of cow-shit and the introspective part of me determined it was the perfect representation of my life.

I strangled my introspective self and stomped up to my mansion in my socks.

It was officially this wizard's bedtime.

CHAPTER 25

*I*t had been a long morning, the various women of the house demanding that I make Carl stop his research into the D. Hiding my smirk had been hard, but the ridiculousness of it all had helped curb the last of my bad attitude.

Tory had swung by, demanding to know where Alucard was. In careful terms, I told her I didn't want to get slapped again and that was that. It wasn't that I didn't want to tell her the truth, but that I didn't want to bring back my dark mood. Also, I wasn't sure where she fit into White Fang's big plan. I didn't want to tell her anything that would make her stick her nose into something that could get her killed. Or anything that would make her demand answers from the dragons – which might put her and the Reds in danger.

On that note, she had followed up with, "Where are the Reds? Or Yahn? I keep missing them..." her motherly glare was in constant motion, as if searching the room behind me to discover them hiding. When I didn't immediately answer, she looked back up at me.

I smiled as I said, "Welcome to being a mother to teenaged girls."

She didn't find it as humorous as I did, judging by the slap to my cheek. I was only thankful she hadn't used her full strength. Luckily, my wounds from the previous night hadn't remained upon leaving or she might have accidentally killed me.

Before she could leave, I grabbed her arm. She spun, slapping my hand away. "I have to find them, Nate. I don't have time for you to pester me."

I almost lost my temper at that. "Are you *kidding* me?" I whispered.

That caught her attention. She seemed to deflate, taking a deep breath. "Sorry."

I nodded slowly, glad that I didn't have to point out her double standard. "I saw them hanging out on their sunning rock in the Solarium. In plain sight. They're just being teenagers. Taking advantage of your... work for Raego."

Her face clouded over. "I am *not* working for *Raego*."

I waved a hand. "Whatever. The Council, then." She huffed, folding her arms beneath her breasts. When it was obvious she wasn't going to offer anything up, I pressed her. "Find what you were looking for? This thief?"

She just folded her arms, looking tired and frustrated, but not willing to answer me.

I sighed. Worth a shot. "You'll figure it out. Just a reminder, but I'm leaving tonight and might be gone for a few days."

Her eyes took on a hungry shine. "Fae. That sounds so much easier than St. Louis."

I grunted, arching a brow. "Right." Fae would be easier than St. Louis. And Hell.

She smiled at my look. "I know. I'm being irrational."

I nodded carefully, placing an arm over her shoulders as I led her down the hallway, sensing that she needed to burn off some energy. "Let's go find the teens." Tory began to talk conversationally. Hearing nothing of value, I listened absently as I let my eyes trail over the halls, smiling in memory at some, cringing in horror at others. Memories of breaking something or getting into trouble about some prank Gunnar and I had thought we could get away with. Some of these spots in the hallways were where Dean or my parents had finally pinned us down to chastise us for our recklessness. And little things like that stuck in a kid's mind. Now, it was funny, but that instinctive clench was still there. Kind of like parents could still say your name in that tone and you might flinch, even though you were a grown adult now.

My smile withered away as I remembered that if all went well, I would be seeing my parents soon. Not in the best of locales, but that I would get to see their faces again. Or souls.

I sensed Tory staring at me. "Sorry. Thinking about Fae. What were you saying?"

She studied me critically for a few seconds before repeating herself. "The Council and Raego disappear often. When I ask them about it later, they shrug it off and tell me to stop worrying about their daily planners and find the thief. But if I can't ever question the suspects, how do they expect me to find the thief? Last night, for example? I couldn't find any of them. Then Alucard mentioned that he was going to the Fight Club, so I figured I would at least accompany him. But he was as closed off as I've ever seen. And who do I find? The fucking dragons. All hanging out like a family dinner, but no one had informed me about it!"

I nodded, not giving any advice.

We walked in silence. "I know what you're doing. I appreciate it, but it also pisses me off."

I smiled, not turning to face her. "Oh?"

She shoved me with her hip. "Thanks for not letting me lean on you. Even when it bugs you as much as it does me." She let out a sigh, shaking her head. Then she stopped in the hall. I turned to look at her and she had her hands on her hips. "I completely forgot with all the stupid dragon stuff. Why the hell did you fight Alucard and Raego last night? And that part at the end?"

I considered telling her the truth, but saw way too many problems with that. She was working with the dragons, and I wanted as few as possible knowing about the Candy Skulls. But she needed to know not to talk about it, too. "Remember those things we saw on our way to visit Raego after the wedding?"

She noted my vague description and nodded. Then she froze, her eyes shooting wide. "Oh, shit! You tried Shadow Walk—"

I held up a hand, cutting her off. "Yeah. Instinctive. I forgot about the dangers. They almost got to me. I felt like I was there for a minute or more, but Achilles said it was like any other time I Shadow Walked – a fraction of a second. I was dazed and my opponents pounced." I tried to let her know with my eyes that the fight wasn't important. "We mustn't talk about those things we saw. Not to anyone. I'm actually on my way to find Callie to tell her the same. There are some... dangers in sharing the information, apparently. So just keep your trap shut. You women and your gossip—"

She began tapping her feet, giving me the mom look and I grinned. "Just kidding. But I am serious about speaking of... them. Don't. I'll take care of it. I'm on it." I wasn't *on it*. Not at all. But she had plenty on her plate at the moment.

"Fine. I won't tell. To be honest, with the dragon stuff, and the Reds hiding from me, what... we saw completely slipped my mind."

I held up my hands in a *there you go* gesture. "Keep it that way." I held out my arm for her to rejoin me and she finally did. We made our way to the front of the house. A thought hit me and I stumbled. Tory frowned at me, a concerned look on her face.

What if... I didn't make it back from Hell? What if White Fang did something to put Tory and the Reds in danger. Her students...

I checked that we were alone before continuing on, speaking quietly. "Keep an eye on everything while I'm gone. There are... things going on in town, and I think the dragons are just the tip of it. I don't want to scare you, but someone is stirring up trouble. Chateau Falco will always be a safe place for you guys if things go badly while I'm gone."

To emphasize this, the house rumbled all around us – but much stronger than normal. It cut off abruptly as if interrupted. Tory glanced up at the ceiling warily. "What's up with her lately? She's more... vocal. But less vocal at times, too."

I nodded, but I wasn't about to tell her. *Oh, yeah. My house is just pregnant.* "Maybe she caught a bug or something."

Tory gave me a look, but I didn't let her break my resolve. "If you need anything from me, ask fast. I'll be leaving tonight."

She thought about that. "I better not. It's not just that I don't want to, but that I want to abide by the terms the dragons gave me. A verbal contract. Even though they read the fine print much more closely than I did."

I chuckled. "They *wrote* the fine print."

She grunted. "What's so important about going to Fae again? If it's just another recharge, you might not be gone that long. But if it was something big, you would have asked us for backup."

I was silent for a time. "Maybe you're wrong about both points..." I felt her watching me and felt bad for lying. But I did it anyway. "I never know how much time will pass while I'm over there. So a recharge could take days. I'd rather you be warned ahead of time than be wondering what happened to me if I was gone longer than anticipated."

She sighed. "Otherwise we'd be checking up on you every hour."

I gave her a very serious look. "No. You promised."

She swore under her breath. "I know. We won't ever go there without you. Just a figure of speech. But... what about the other thing? You said I might be wrong on both points."

I shrugged. "Maybe I don't want to always ask for your help." I felt her shoulders tensing, ready to berate me for being so stubbornly stupid, but she saw me smiling at her with a raised eyebrow. She blinked. Once. Twice. Then it hit her.

"Just like we've been doing to you..."

I snapped my fingers. "Bingo. My problems are not always your problems."

We walked on in silence, nearing the front door. She squeezed my side in a brief hug before detaching and turning to look up at me. She looked... scared. "I know things are crazy right now, Nate, but don't do anything stupid. Even if your friends are doing exactly what I'm warning you not to do right now." She smiled guiltily as she said that. "But... I think it's just growing pains. We've been through hell lately, and I think everyone is just trying to tighten up their boots, take a breath, and check their foundations. See who they are without *you*. So that they have a better sense of self-understanding the next time something goes down. To understand what they can handle on their own, and what might require... assistance."

I smiled, nodding. "I know. It sucks, but I get it."

"Right. Well, stop being so emotional about it. It's disgusting."

I rolled my eyes and turned as if to walk away. "Take care, Tory. You'll do well."

"Damn right."

When I glanced back, she was gone.

Likely to burn down my Solarium when she caught them cuddling with Yahn.

CHAPTER 26

$\mathcal{I}$ glanced at the small study off the main entrance, saw the crackling fire, and went to take a seat. I didn't pour a drink from the nearby bar. I didn't read any of the books beside me. I just stared at the flames, focusing on my breathing. We were going to Fae soon. To get a recharge before we went to Hell tomorrow. Since I hadn't told anyone about that part, they all thought we were leaving for Fae tonight and that we wouldn't be back for a few days.

With luck, we would get back from Fae and off to the St. Louis Arch to meet Death before anyone noticed we'd returned. I hadn't told any of them about our planned trip to Hell, because, come on. It was *Hell*. They would have spent a year calling me nine kinds of idiot and then demanding that they should come with me.

Not this time.

Just me. And the two wildest bastards I had ever met. Talon and Carl.

Talon was my first best friend. But he was also my Shadow – a self-appointed bodyguard. Fearless, ruthless, and savage.

And Carl was an Elder – one of those mysterious creatures who had been banished from our realm a long, long time ago for being very, very naughty. But he was my stiletto heel-wearing buddy. And if he was that feared, maybe he had a few tricks up his sleeves. I also knew nothing scary fazed him. Only the normal, human things rattled him. Going to Hell would likely be an adventure for him. And the women of the house would finally stop hearing about the D.

"Here he is," a deep voice called out from behind me. I glanced over my shoulder to see Roland standing in the entryway with an umbrella. His crimson eyes gleamed, reflecting the firelight. Callie stepped into view behind him, wearing a hoodie. The tips of her now short white hair poked out to kiss her jaw.

I patted the couch invitingly. "Here I am. But I'm leaving soon. What's up?" I felt two other shapes lurking behind them but not stepping into the light. I rolled my eyes. "They can come in, too. If they wipe their paws. Dean isn't fond of messes." I heard a responding pair of growls.

Roland grunted. "It's not that they don't want to come in. It's that they think they need to guard me from... well, everyone."

"Paradise and Lost are high-maintenance, and their relationship with Roland is... unusual," Callie added, smirking from beneath her hood.

"Whatever. You're just jealous we took him from you," one of them argued.

Callie slowly turned, but Roland gripped her arm warningly. Not threatening her, but as if begging her not to kill his puppies. Callie jerked her arm clear. "If you took him from me, I don't remember it. We can do a reenactment if you want. Like, now."

They mumbled something unintelligible, and Callie turned back to us with an amused smile, arching a brow at Roland as if to say *See?*

He let out a sigh and plopped down into one of the chairs. The one furthest away from the sunlight shining through a window. Callie sat beside me, crossing her legs as she propped up her fancy, calf-high leather boots on the table. Her Darling and Dear boots. As if to emphasize this, she glanced at them for a second and she was suddenly wearing leather moccasins – like house slippers. I rolled my eyes.

"Wish my satchel did cool things like that. You must have been shopping on the clearance rack when you picked it out."

She slapped a palm down on my thigh, laughing. "I think your purse has plenty of neat features. Stop bitching." She studied the room for a second before turning back to me. "Where's Alex? I haven't seen him lately, and that kid is usually stuck to your hip."

I sucked in a breath. "He was at the wedding." She frowned, trying to remember.

"The tall dark and handsome guy?" Paradise called out helpfully. I winced, but nodded.

Callie's eyes looked confused. Then they widened. "Wait... That guy was... *little Alex?*" she asked me slowly, enunciating the words as if making sure I understood.

"They grow up so fast, don't they?" I said uneasily. Roland was watching us with a frown.

She was staring at me. Hard. "We should talk. Later," she said very intently.

"Yeah, you should. I think we can all agree on that!" Paradise hooted from the hall. Roland's cheeks blushed at their not-so-subtle meaning.

Callie and I continued to stare at each other, her hand gripping my thigh. "Later," we both said at the exact same time. I wasn't sure which question she was answering, and from her thoughtful frown, I could tell she suddenly wondered which question I was answering.

The story of our lives.

Roland cleared his throat loudly. We turned to see him staring at her hand on my thigh, and she quickly yanked it away. I kept my face innocent. "What can I help you with?" I asked.

"You've spoken with Alucard?" he asked me guardedly. I nodded, my humor fading. He sighed, sensing my reaction. "I'm surprised he's still among the living," he said with faint cheer.

I grunted. "I didn't kill him. He's heading to the Sanguine Council. And we're not friends."

Roland hesitated uncertainly, and I felt Callie turning to look at both of us individually, obviously not having known about any of this. But she didn't interrupt.

"With things between you suddenly... complicated, I thought I might join him," he said casually. I felt a smile tugging at my cheeks so tried to mask it as I nodded. He wasn't just doing this for me. He had as much reason to meet with the Sanguines as Alucard did. Those ancient vampires. They were the Masters of the Master Vampires. Like the U.N. of fangers.

"For me? How altruistic..." I said, deadpan.

He glared at me, actually looking embarrassed, and I burst out laughing. "You need to work on your deviance. The Sanguines will eat you alive, otherwise. Take that soul of yours and lock it in a locket. Heh. That wasn't even intentional!" I said, nudging Callie with my elbow.

"Good, because then it was only *unintentionally* lame," she said, rolling her eyes. I bumped her with my hip in retaliation. It felt nice to just sit down and relax for a minute. With her.

Roland was nodding. "I'll try to hide my feelings better. No soul. Check. But you're right, of course. I think the Sanguines are very eager to speak with me regarding my past, if the vampires in St. Louis are any indicator. I thought joining Alucard would at least make me only half as notorious. Better than being the center of attention if I went by myself later."

He was fingering a chain around his neck, not even aware he was doing it. I leaned forward, wiping the humor from my face. "I appreciate it. Keep him whole for me, will you? I'm not... happy with him, but I understand his decision." He nodded stiffly.

Then a ghost of a smile crossed his face. "I've got experience with... handling vampires."

I snorted. "Yeah, maybe find a middle ground. I don't think they value a Shepherd's social skills as much as you think. But... now that you're one of them, I can see them trying to corner you into giving up secrets, intelligence, or maybe even wanting to lock you up in a coffin forever. I can give you something to help with an easy exit..." I said, reaching into my pocket.

I had a few of my... well, the nickname had stuck, whether I wanted it or not.

Temple's Tiny Balls.

In actuality, they were glass marbles that could open a Gateway back to Chateau Falco. Smash one on the ground and leap through. Land back here, with the backing of my friends and my house suddenly protecting you. Strong enough to keep almost anyone safe if they needed an immediate sanctuary.

Roland eyed my pocket warily. "I can still make Gateways, Temple. Callie warned me not to try the other thing." I nodded at that, almost having forgotten. "Keep your balls to yourself, thank you very much."

Callie burst out laughing.

I scowled at the two of them. "What if they take you down and Alucard needs to get *you* out."

Callie's laughter abruptly cut off. "Take it, Roland," she snarled.

He held out his palm obediently, seeing the truth to my words. I handed one of the balls to him, explaining what to do and where it would take him.

I also handed one to Callie, just because. She stared down at it in silence, lost in her own thoughts.

"Regarding the other means of transportation. Don't talk about it... about the things we saw. It apparently makes them stronger. More numerous, possibly." Callie's face paled. Roland frowned, wanting to pepper us with obvious questions. I shook my head firmly. "I can't talk about it. And neither can Callie," I added, shooting her a meaningful look.

Callie studied me in silence for a few seconds before giving me a resigned sigh. "Okay." She mimed zipping her lips shut.

Roland let out an annoyed sigh. "Do you mind if Paradise and Lost remain behind? I'd rather not take them with me. I don't want another reason for the Sanguines to have interest in me, and I don't know how they would react to so many vampires in one place." He said all of this loud enough for them to hear from the hallway.

"Sure. They can stay here if they want." At Roland's reaction, I let out a breath. "Or grab a place in town." Roland nodded in embarrassment. "I can give them some of these," I said, holding out more of the glass marbles.

Roland nodded thoughtfully. "I'll let them decide where they stay. But it's probably best if they remain neutral. Keep an eye on all parties, not just your friends."

"You two should probably get back home soon. Make sure this craziness isn't spreading."

Callie nodded, tucking her hands behind her head. "I'm heading back today. Looking into some... real estate for Roland."

Which made sense. With him not being a Shepherd anymore, it wasn't like he could live in a church. But I didn't like the idea of Callie heading back home alone. I also knew that if I even breathed that thought aloud, she would carve my ears off, so I kept silent.

She'd be fine.

Roland cleared his throat. "Alucard will be waiting for me," he said, climbing to his feet. Callie did the same with a resigned sigh. She suddenly wrapped me up in a hug, whispering into my ear. "Wherever you're really going, don't do anything stupid or I'll kill you."

My tongue actually tingled for some odd reason. As if the mere proximity of her lips so close to my jaw made my mouth salivate in anticipation. I grunted as she pulled away, calling upon my testosterone reserves. "I'll be fine. I always am."

She tucked her hair into her hood and shot me a very considering look. "Like I said. Careful."

I rolled my eyes. "Get out of here, Bible Thumpers."

Surprisingly, Roland laughed just as hard as Callie. His cut off sooner, as if startled by it, but at least he had laughed. Baby steps.

I extended my hand to trade grips with him. "You're a good man, Roland. You don't need anyone's permission to stay that way. It's in your DNA." I told him, referring to his past as a Shepherd. If anyone could be a man of God and a vampire, it was him.

He gripped my hand fiercely, his voice rough with gratitude as he mumbled, "Thanks."

Callie nodded out of his view, silently thanking me with her eyes. I shrugged.

I stood in the doorway, watching them leave, lost in the lingering smell of strawberries in the air. Callie's perfume or shampoo. Or maybe just her... Strawberries and sunshine—

"Have you two boinked yet?"

"Gah!" I shouted, jumping as my heart thundered out of my chest. I had forgotten all about the two werewolves behind me. "What the hell?" I shouted, rounding on Paradise and Lost.

"I can smell your dirty lust, wizard," Lost said with a cunning grin.

Paradise nodded. "You really should just get it over with. Everyone says so."

My face flushed. "Scram, you two. Go find this White Fang asshole for me if you're bored."

They shared a look in silence. "That's not a half-bad idea. Of course, no one told us to do this. We're just two nosy werewolves in a new city. Staying at a hotel that we paid for. Nothing to do with Nate Temple..."

A slow smile crept over my face. "How... industrious of you. I'd hate to keep you."

Without a word, they slipped past me. One of them had a phone to her ear as if calling a cab.

If they could find White Fang... maybe they could do some good while here.

I was whistling as I walked back into my house in search of Alex. I wanted to talk with him before I left. I wanted to make sure he could take care of himself in my absence. And if my absence became more... permanent. I wanted to introduce him to my librarian.

Pandora.

CHAPTER 27

*A*lex and I walked through the halls of the Armory, following the sounds of a harp near the balcony that always seemed to end up being the favored gathering spot. At least most times I had been here we always ended up in that area.

"It's very dangerous here, Alex, but I'll keep you safe. Just don't touch anything. Pandora doesn't like her things to be touched." Alex nodded soberly.

I stepped through an archway and saw Pandora sitting on a cushioned stool, eyes closed as her fingers brushed the strings of a golden harp the size of a man's torso. She had a distant smile on her face and leaned forward as if trying to hug the harp, or perhaps bring her ear closer to the sounds her fingers made dancing across the strings.

I smiled at her, enjoying the tune. It was light, jubilant, and... faint. As if even though I knew I was in the same room as the harp, I was actually hearing something far away in the middle of the woods, echoing through the foliage. Some nymph luring me to my death.

I shivered and turned away at the macabre thought. I'd heard songs like that before, and they were nothing like this. It was just... so entrancing. Almost the entire back of the room was actually a sandstone balcony over-looking a dry deserted wasteland. Not sand, but dry cracked rock, withered gnarled trees no taller than a man, and patches of dead weeds. No signs of life.

In fact, I wasn't entirely sure where it was. If it was somewhere real or something from Pandora's imagination. Because this was the Armory – a supernatural weapons cache that my parents had tucked away into this pocket dimension. Pandora was their librarian – or perhaps she was one of the weapons to be kept from mankind – and she answered only to me.

Well, she would also answer anyone I had let into this place, but ultimately, she had my best interests at heart. She had an encyclopedic memory of everything stored here, and almost seemed to share the soul of the place. Knowing with a thought whether anything was missing, where something was, or if anything was wrong with the place.

One time not too long ago, she had almost committed suicide in order to prove her loyalty to me, and as she had crept closer to that moment of no return, the Armory itself had begun to fade more and more – the walls becoming vague, shifting columns of smoke and fog, like dust caught in beams of sunshine.

I also knew that Pandora was kind of dangerous in her own right.

Which you couldn't tell by looking at her now. A young woman with olive skin, perhaps freshly eighteen – although her smoky eyes made me think of two-thousand years of hot, steamy nights – and a fragile, yet pleasantly curvy, body.

She and Achilles might have been friends with benefits – or something more serious.

I watched Alex spin in a slow circle, jaw hanging open and eyes peeled back as he murmured to himself when he recognized – or thought he did – some particular piece. Because ornate wooden tables – all different shapes, sizes, designs and dimensions – displayed ancient items. Scrolls, wooden books adorned with precious metal locks, an ivory tusk with a golden cap on the broken end, bowls of treasure, thick glass vials of strange liquids, a glass orb full of shifting yellow smoke, weapons of every nation, some gleaming silver with priceless gems set into the hilts and scabbards – and even...

I realized I had walked closer to a black spear, my hand outstretched to touch the black wooden haft – not looking too dissimilar from the wood of the Huntress' new bow. One end of the spear was tipped in six inches of silver that depicted four howling, agonized faces, as if to represent each cardinal direction. The other end featured a matte-black spear tip that seemed more of a cross between a sword and an axe – an arced, deadly concave shape maybe two feet long. A black-roped braid wrapped three times around the wood, as if holding the blade in place, and from the rope hung two black silk bags about as long as the blade itself.

The blade itself was black. Not painted, but as if forged from a black mineral of some sort. The blade's edge was polished into a dark gray – as if that was the best that could be done with the dark metal. The reason for the odd shape of the blade was obvious. A single red ruby the size of a goose egg was set into the thickest section of the blade, right in the center.

I frowned at it, something about the overall look tickling my memory.

I realized my fingers were about to wrap around the wooden haft when the music suddenly ceased. "Hello, my Host," Pandora called out. "And who is this tasty-looking specimen of a man?" she purred in a suggestive tone.

I grinned at Alex's yelp, turning to find him reaching towards a stand of ornate swords. I wasn't sure if his yelp was in guilt for almost touching the merchandise or Pandora's hint that she might like to touch *his* merchandise. Tall and strapping he may be, but experienced with the ladies, he was not. He stammered awkwardly, brushing a hand through his longish dark hair. "Al—" he attempted to state his name, and almost jumped to find Pandora suddenly six inches away from him, staring almost vertically up to look into his eyes.

He actually flinched as her fingertips touched his chest and trailed down his shirt. The caress stopped at his belly, but didn't break contact. His face was beet red as he struggled not to stare down her transparent, flowing toga. Until she had stood, I hadn't realized how translucent the toga was. It was entirely see-through! As good as, anyway.

"Al," I repeated, grinning, "the lady killer. Lock up your daughter—"

"Alexander Arete…" Pandora whispered under her breath.

I flinched. "What was that?" I asked, leaning closer. I must have missed part of it.

Pandora shivered as she took a step back, clasping her hands behind her back, which did nothing for Alex's shame, only flaunting her assets. She turned to look at me, took a breath, and then bathed me with a radiant smile. "I spoke his name."

Alex cleared his throat, attempting to avert his eyes without appearing rude. "I don't use that name. My biological father was never around."

"Can you so easily change your height? Weight? Eye color?"

His mouth opened and closed a few times, and she clucked her tongue, her lips glistening.

"I... no, what?" he finally asked in confusion.

"I'm referring to you dismissing a name because your father accidentally made you. A name is a name is a name. You are not adopting the man with the name, you are accepting a heritage. Just because your father was a bad apple doesn't mean the family tree should be cut down. The tree might yet one day produce a succulent, crisp, sweet—"

"Apple," I interrupted hurriedly. "Christ, Pandora. You're going to give him a heart attack," I muttered, watching as Alex desperately struggled to find something in the room without even a *hint* at femininity to its shape.

Pandora blinked, looked him up and down again, and then beamed delightedly. "Oh! Oh, my. You brought me a *virgin*? How viciously cruel of you..." she said, winking at me.

If possible, Alex's face turned even darker. He was about to die of shame. "What was that about his name?" I asked, trying to give him a minute to compose himself. "Did you say Arete?"

"You know I did, Nate," she responded tersely.

"Right. Well, I guess I'll just cut to the chase since you can read my mind anyway. There's no use drawing it out. Does his name have anything to do with this?" I asked, holding out my palm. The brand of my family Crest stood prominent, even though a burn, still remarkably clear even after the skin had healed. So clear, in fact, that the word *Arete* was still legible on the blade of the spear crossing the shield. The other weapon crossing the shield was a scythe – like Death carried – and that blade was etched with *memento mori*, which meant *remember, you are mortal.*

"What an interesting looking blade..." she said casually. I frowned at her, glanced at my palm, and then turned back to her. She sighed impatiently. "Yes. The same word. Coincidence, I'm sure," she added dryly, turning away from me.

I turned to Alex. He shrugged. "Right. Is it, though? A coincidence, I mean?" I persisted, following her.

"Of course not," she snapped.

Her tone made me pause for a moment. I found my eyes lingering on her cute little rear, and looked up hurriedly. I heard her chuckle and scowled. She could read minds, damnit. "Anyway," I said. "I brought him here to see if you could give him a weapon. Something to help him defend himse— Hey! Where are you going?" I shouted at her back as she began walking away from me. Then she was gone. I saw her appear at the opposite end of the room, entering a hallway.

Then she disappeared from view again. "Um. Was that a no?" Alex asked.

"Follow me," I growled as I jogged to catch up. Alex was hot on my heels as I followed her soft steps around one turn, down another hall, and then two more turns before I caught her sexy toga-nightie disappear through a dim doorway. How fast was she? I was almost running.

I skidded into a hot, humid, steamy room, eyes searching for her.

And saw some breathtaking side-boob.

CHAPTER 28

I gasped, spinning back around. Alex stood behind me, gaping openly like a deer caught in headlights. "Stop looking, Neanderthal!" I hissed, slapping him in the stomach with the back of my hand. He finally averted his eyes, and I risked a glance over my shoulder to see Pandora slip over a rock ledge and into a steaming pool. She let out a languorous sigh and a husky giggle. Her eyes sparkled at me through the steam. "He'll see a lot more than that before the night's through..." she whispered in a highly inappropriate tone.

I coughed, holding out a hand for Alex to stay back. "Hey, Pandora. Did you... drink decaf or something this morning? Accidentally get possessed? You seem... different."

"Because I'm undressing a man with my eyes? Or because I'm speaking plain truth?"

I blinked, unsure which of those I was supposed to answer, or if they were both rhetorical questions. "Right. Um. Alex is a kid. Let's start from there. Then we can progress to the part that Achilles probably won't be a fan of you doing... that first thing."

She laughed throatily, motioning for Alex to step closer. "Achilles and I walk different paths, now. Trust me. Our last... talk," she said this in an amused tone, "was a make-up celebration. A farewell banquet. But this..." she purred, splashing the water playfully.

I felt Alex looming behind me and pushed him back. "Down, boy. *Down!*"

Pandora laughed again, and the tone sent a shiver right down to my toes. "Be easy, Nate. I mean him no harm. I'm just glad I was chosen for this... onus."

I glanced at Alex, mouthing *onus* in a question. He shook his head and shrugged.

But he looked ready and willing to find out. To take one for the team.

I was giving serious thought to disbanding Team Temple. The founder got none of the perks.

I studied her silhouette. I could barely see her through the steam. Well, that wasn't true. As I tried to make her out, she suddenly became very clear because she had lapped over to the edge closest to us. Then she placed her arms flat on the rim of the pool and rose up to lean on them.

I blindly flung up a hand behind me to cover Alex's eyes, defending his virtue as I glared at Pandora. "Lower, if you will. I can see your suckle-knuckles."

She blinked, then glanced down at her prominently displayed chest. With a sigh, she slipped down into the pool to lean back against the far edge again, facing us. I squinted, then made the hand motion for her to get lower. She snarled, but obeyed. I finally dropped the hand behind me that had protected Alex's eyes. "You're safe, Alex. You can look now." I said, turning to him.

He was two feet to the right of me, having been in plain view of her show. "What?" he asked.

Pandora laughed as I shot Alex a disappointed look. "Dad says *no*," I finally said, folding my arms as I turned back to Pandora. "He's a kid."

Pandora took on a lecturing tone. "He actually is not, Nate. Often, when the Queens take a boy in their Changeling market, the child stays the same age as he was when first taken. They are able to slow their own time for... maximum benefit. Alex was their prisoner for years in human time... Why else do you think he has aged so abruptly now that he is back... home?"

I was shaking my head, but Alex had gone deathly silent. I looked at him and found him frowning at his own memories. As if... finding truth to her words.

I glared at him. "Are you telling me that you don't remember how long you were there?" I asked incredulously.

He didn't respond, looking troubled. But... if what Pandora said was true, other things began to make a lot more sense. I wasn't sure why he had aged the way he had. Pan hadn't known either. We were sure it had something to do with Fae, but time normally worked the other way around. Spend a night there in Fae, and a week could have gone by on earth. But… I had also found that there was exactly no reliable way to judge the flow of time between the two places.

Unless… one used the Hourglass my parents had left me. As a child, I had spent over a decade there, almost two decades, and returned to find zero time had passed. Because of the Hourglass. But… this was fucking crazy.

Another point against me was that Alex *had* been taken years ago in human time – at least according to the Syndicate member I had spoken to. So, he was either catching up to the age he would have been as a human or… Pandora was right. Or both.

"Let's say you're not wrong. Why have you turned on the Aphrodite charm all of a sudden?"

"He must be strong for what is to come. A mortal… kind of. No magic… kind of. There are many things my touch could unlock within this young *man.*" Her voice cranked up to eleven on the pornstar vibe. "If he cares to take a quick dip, of course."

"Stop! Both of you stop!" I said, sensing Alex taking a step towards the pool.

They did, turning to look at me. I ignored Alex, knowing there would be no reasoning with him. He wasn't in the right headspace. Heh.

I rounded on Pandora. "Swear three things to me. That you will drop dead – forever dead – right this second if you have lied about anything in this twisted conversation. Promise that Alex is truly an adult, that anything you two do next will not harm him, and that this has nothing to do with your lust. I'm serious, Pandora. I'm all he has, and if I'm going to do at least one thing right as a stand-in father, it's that I won't let a monster eat him up, even if that monster promises joy."

She stared at me, and slowly nodded.

Then she snapped her fingers, and the very air suddenly seemed to still all around us as she climbed out of the pool, the water dripping down her oh-so-scrumptious body. I glanced over at Alex to find him staring at the pool unblinking. I saw the throb of his pulse in his neck, but his eyes were locked onto the pool as if eating Pandora with his eyes. Except... Pandora wasn't standing in the pool.

Not a single muscle moved on his body. Not even a breath. Just the pulse.

I turned to Pandora, alarmed. "He is fine. I didn't think he needed to hear this next part. This is for you."

I frowned, opening my mouth to argue and my heart stopped as her body shimmered. She was suddenly taller, her body shifting, stretching, and rounding out in places. Her hair shifted from the thick brown to a white bob of straight hair, longer at the jaw than in the back. The curtains of the familiar white hair hung like blades, and those lips...

I looked up, staring into those pale blue eyes with violet flecks. "Callie..." I breathed. Even knowing it was an illusion, I could hardly breathe.

One side of her lips curled up in a smile and she gripped my hands in hers. Her skin was flushed from the heat of the pool, warm against my calloused fingertips. And... still wet. She slowly, deliciously, knelt before me. "If all I wanted was a wild ride for personal pleasure, I know the way to your heart," she said in Callie's voice.

My heart thundered against my chest as I slowly nodded, careful to avoid openly staring at her naked body to make sure Pandora had made an accurate depiction. My peripheral vision betrayed me, soaking in all that wet, tight skin, and I realized I was panting heavily.

Then another thought hit me. Pandora could read my mind. This illusion was probably drawn directly from my own mental catalogue of Callie – obviously not naked – but my assessment over the last few months had apparently been very... thorough.

I blinked and it was suddenly Pandora again, but still in the same position. Utterly naked, kneeling at my feet and holding my hands. Alex grunted in surprise to suddenly see Pandora kneeling before me rather than the ultimate vision of a naked chick climbing out of a hot tub.

"I swear that Alex is an adult. That this is not personal for me. That this will only arm him for what is to come, and that it will not bring him any lasting harm. In fact, his decision today will only lead to potential beneficial consequences down the road. For both of you." She waited for me to process her statement. "But I won't promise that I won't enjoy every single second of it." She glanced to Alex with a wink. "I'm sure he'll enjoy it, too."

I grunted. "Lasting... what do you mean lasting harm?"

She sighed. "You know that knowledge sometimes causes brief, *initial* pain. I'm not speaking permanent. Working out with weights *hurts*, but makes you *stronger*. To earn callouses requires blisters, first. Nothing *lasting*," she enunciated, holding her arms out to either side, giving us a healthy dose of more boobage.

I slowly nodded. She was right. Almost every time I had gotten stronger, learned something helpful, gained more power... I had tasted pain of some sort or another.

"But he has a choice," I repeated. She nodded soberly. "And better things happen to him if he says yes." Her eyes twinkled darkly and I glared. "Better things happen *long term*." I sighed. Her grin stretched even wider at the word *long*. "You know what I'm saying! He will be stronger, safer, better able to protect himself if he says yes."

She drew a cross over her... heart. "I swear it on my life. On anything you so choose, in fact."

I scratched my chin, not feeling at all comfortable with this. I finally turned to Alex. "Well, I may not be the best father figure, but I'd say I'm right up there," I muttered, rolling my eyes.

He surprisingly had lost the dazed look, as if taking everything she had said to heart. Which was better than I could have done at his age. Whatever age that really was.

"Then live long and prosper. Need a minute to consider your decisio—"

"If I say yes, I will be strong enough to help Nate when he needs it?" he asked in a serious voice, staring straight into Pandora's eyes.

She nodded. "It is the only way you may help rather than hinder Nate in the future. I swear."

He swallowed. "Yes. I'll... do..." he shifted uncomfortably. "Yes."

I rolled my eyes. "I'll wait in the main room. See you in thirty seconds—"

"Goodbye, Nate. I'll return him tomorrow. And don't forget to pay the piper. The world depends on us paying our own debts."

And I was suddenly standing outside the door to the Armory. I glared at the giant wooden door of carved wildlife. The fish darted back and forth in the pond. The reeds shifted and swayed in an unseen breeze. And the wolf... I squinted in disbelief.

He was dry-humping something in the bushes.

I scowled at him for good measure and stomped away down the hall back to my office. "The fucking luck!" I bellowed, my voice reverberating off the walls. "All the crazy shit I've had to go through for a power boost, all the hard choices I've had to make, the consequences… But he gets to bang my librarian!"

I pulled out my phone, glancing at the time, and let out a sigh. It was time for me to get ready to leave Chateau Falco. And I was actually eager to do so.

My house got more ass than I did these days.

The halls groaned, mocking my plight. "Can it, Falco. No one likes a braggart."

I stormed further down the hall towards my office as a new thought hit me. I spun, cupping my hands around my mouth. "I'm telling Achilles!"

Of course, there was no response.

CHAPTER 29

I left the office in search of Carl and Talon. They had cell phones now, but it was kind of a one-way communication device with them. When Talon could manage to touch the screen with his paw rather than his fur, it worked fairly well, but with the pads of his paw being so much larger than a human fingertip, his responses were often utterly useless, although always hilarious.

For example, he had just responded *Poop*, when I texted him to meet me in the Sanctorum. Staring at my keyboard and using a little brain power, I was pretty sure he meant to type *OK*. But he might have actually gotten that one right, so I typed back *Hurry!*

Carl, on the other hand, was cold-blooded, had scales rather than warm flesh, and sported wicked claws. He had been useless with the touch-screen device and had given up on even carrying it after a few days. To solve this problem, I had gotten him a flip-phone that he could answer by simply opening it. Then, seeing the Reds decorating their new phone cases with sequins and glitter, Carl had insisted we have an arts and crafts night to bedazzle the shit out of his new flip-phone.

He really was identical to a gullible pre-teen girl. From the mid-nineties.

But he hadn't answered when I called, so I was forced to scour the halls and scoop him up to make sure he was ready to leave.

After ten minutes of fruitless search, I finally spotted Othello standing motionless outside of one of the living rooms. She was staring at something, face stricken. I slowed, frowning as I approached. Then, realizing she still hadn't sensed me, I prepared to pinch her ass. But I heard murmured chanting coming from the room ahead of her and my curiosity overruled my need to annoy her. I stepped up behind her and whispered, "Hey," as I glanced into the darkened room.

There sat Carl on the couch not five feet away, his back to us as he stared down at his lap. "Grow, D, *grow*! I command thee!" he hissed urgently into his lap, again and again, like a mantra. It looked even worse as he began rubbing his hands together out of sight in front of him.

Othello shot me a concerned look. "Jesus... What..."

I sighed. "It was supposed to be a joke, but I didn't think he would take it this far."

"Oh. So he's not... doing what it looks like?"

I shook my head. "He's talking to a stick Alucard gave him. It's a long story."

"Someone needs to tell him to stop. He's creeping everyone out. Even more than normal."

I nodded. "Carl. CARL!" I repeated when it was obvious he hadn't heard me.

He stilled, then turned to look at us. "I think I almost had it. I almost felt something." He saw Othello and flung out a claw excitedly. "You!"

She took a step back reflexively, placing a hand over her chest in confusion. "Me?"

"Do you know the secrets of the D?"

Before she could respond, I placed a hand on her back, shoving her closer. "Othello is a master of the D." She whirled, slapping my hand away and glaring at me. "Fine, she *isn't* a master of the D," I amended, smirking at her smugly.

She opened her mouth to argue *that* before realizing that I had her trapped. Declaring she was a master of the D – a reference to her nighttime hobbies – would only cause Carl to kidnap her and demand answers. Admitting she wasn't... I almost wanted to laugh. She scowled angrily instead, muttering dark promises under her breath. Carl finally cocked his head, flicking his black tongue out to test the air. "Did you need something?"

I scrubbed my hand through my hair. "Yeah. It's time for us to go. You ready?"

He climbed to his feet, nodding as he tucked the stick into a pocket. "Of course."

Othello eyed the hallways warily, making sure we were alone as she walked with us. "Are you really doing this?" she whispered. I frowned at her, not liking her underlying tone.

"The Fae isn't so bad if you stick to the path—"

"Don't bullshit me, Nate. Death told me the truth." She looked... well, frightened.

I let out a long sigh, cursing the Horseman. Just because he was kind of dating her didn't mean he needed to blab my secrets over pillow time. "It's important."

She let out a frustrated breath. "It always is with you. Just... be careful, Nate. I don't like the feel of the city lately. Lots of weird customers at the bookstore." I arched an eyebrow at her and she threw her hands up. "I didn't think they were that big of a deal until Death told me about your trip, and then the fight with Zeus, and just like a storm was rolling in, the bookstore is suddenly empty of customers. Everyone is battening down the hatches, and that usually means you're about to do something incredibly stupid."

I scowled but she stared back defiantly. "Fine. I'll be careful. I'm bringing Talon and Carl. They'll make sure I'm safe." A new thought hit me. "If you're sticking around, can you make sure Alex is okay?"

She nodded. "What about the Huntress?"

"She's... having a hard time with Alex's changes."

She nodded knowingly. "Okay." Then she grabbed my hand and pulled me in for a very tight hug, burying her face in my neck. "Be safe," she demanded. I nodded, placing a hand on the back of her head and rubbing her hair with my thumb. Then she nipped my neck playfully. "I *am* a master of the D, and you *know* it!" she hissed. Then she pinched my ass, shoved me away, and was storming down the hall. "Goodbye!"

Carl watched her curiously, nodding thoughtfully. "No, Carl. That is not how you usually say goodbye to someone." He frowned, looking even more confused.

With a sigh, I continued on. I barely saw the house as I walked, patting my satchel absentmindedly as we made our way to the Sanctorum. Since we were actually going to the Fae first, it was the most convenient point of entry, and I had found a way to make sure I landed where I intended now, rather than plopping down somewhere in the middle of nowhere – or perhaps in front of the Queens' army or her prison.

It now took me straight to the cave where I had been raised with Talon. But we had one more stop before going to Fae. Since I didn't want anyone knowing about that either, I had decided to let everyone think we were going straight to Fae, now. They wouldn't ever find out anyway.

I had everything I could think of for my various destinations, and even a few things I wasn't sure if I would need. But since my satchel could hold as much as I wanted – like my own pocket dimension – I had packed it with all sorts of potentially useful stuff. Extra weapons Talon and Carl had set out, food, Grimm Tech prototypes, clothes, and medical supplies. To find what I needed, I only had to think of what I wanted, reach my hand inside, and it would be the first thing I touched.

Anyone else trying would be unable to do so, which was important. I had tested it out with Talon, hiding a Fae Catnip pod inside, as well as a bunch of trash. After the sixth piece of trash, he had finally upended the satchel and shook it out, shocked to find only more trash raining down from the satchel, even though he had seen me put the catnip inside. Apparently, I could allow certain things to fall out of the bag, but still hide back what I wanted. Or I could prevent anything from falling out. Darling and Dear made some pretty sweet stuff. I still needed to meet them in person, but it would have to wait. I'd visit Kansas City again soon. Hopefully.

Talon had handed the pack back to me, letting me know with his murderous eyes that I better hand over the catnip. Wanting to keep breathing, I had reached inside and handed it over. He had grabbed it greedily and then flinched at the rustle of wings, then sprinted from the room as Hugin and Munin dove after him, cawing and screeching at him.

I had everything I thought I would need and was ready to leave. Talon stood from the couch as we entered the Sanctorum, absently patting the armor he wore over his furred chest – which was new. Nothing extremely fancy, well, it didn't look too elaborate. But it was a design based on the dragon scales I had once taken from one of Alaric Stone's silver dragons. I had found a way to make a single scale duplicate into armor that covered the wearer. I had initially tried it with Ashley, and although it had worked, she had given it back as fast as possible, not appreciating having so much silver on her body. It was an easy tweak to modify it for Talon so that he now stood before me in a dull gray metallic armor that had the flexibility of a second set of skin – since it was made out of scales, a dragon's skin.

Carl had picked up his things from a side room and was now buckling his leather straps all over his body. White blades poked out from sheaths and holsters all over his chest, legs, arms, wrists, shoulder, back, and even a few around his ankles. Those blades were made from the bones of his fallen enemies, and although ancient looking, I knew they were razor sharp. He looked like a skeletal, scaled porcupine. He shook his neck and a horned fan sprang out around his neck like a lion's mane.

The two turned to me expectantly. They were both covered in scales, looking eerily uniform. I glanced down at my own leather jacket, plain tee and dark pants. No fancy armor for me, but I had plenty of weapons – both offensive and defensive – at my disposal. To be honest, I was more concerned about what kind of magic I would have access to once I got to Hell. Because whenever I went places, I seemed to adopt some of the powers of the place – and the consequences had been both a rush of power and horror at what I had been able to do.

And I never learned of the cost, until later.

Thinking of that, I frowned, recalling Pandora's warning about paying the piper. But which piper was she talking about? Something in Fae? Here? My Horseman Mask? Something else?

I shook my head and flung out my hand, ripping a hole in the air. Falco reverberated behind me, as if begging me not to leave, or maybe saying goodbye. "I'll be back, Falco. Don't worry."

Talon's fur stuck straight out, realizing I was talking to the house. He knew about it, of course, everyone did, but that didn't make it any easier to accept. Me having a conversation with either a house or an unseen celestial being hidden behind the walls. Either one was enough to make your sphincter slam shut like the vault at Fort Knox.

A rainy hut appeared before us, and the smell of wet mud and vegetation drifted through the hazy opening. At the edge of the opening, white sparks and fire crackled and hissed, as if I had actually burned a hole through the fabric of reality. I shivered at that, recalling the Candy Skulls. If they were now consequences of Shadow Walking, what were the consequences of Gateways?

I let out a breath. Whatever they were, they wouldn't stop me from going.

Story of my life.

I stepped through the Gateway and into the rain. Carl and Talon followed, eyes alert, listening as I gave them the information that would keep them alive for the next ten minutes.

CHAPTER 30

J took a deep breath, smelling the air, eyes darting about, ears focused to hear the smallest sound other than the steady patter of raindrops. I even tapped into my Fae magic, fumbling with it to try and get a better sense of everything. It was still somewhat awkward for me to use – working better in the heat of the moment than for casual, everyday things – but it at least gave me heightened senses enough to be certain we weren't about to be surprised. I studied the hut before us, facing it squarely, watching the dim candlelight in the dirty center window. It was a sagging, decrepit building made of ancient, waterlogged wood. The porch was slanted, and other than the candlelight, it looked uninhabitable.

I reached into my pocket and pulled out a small metal pen. I thumbed it on and blue laser lights shot from each end, a thin beam made more visible thanks to the overcast skies and heavy rain. I was sure to aim one end at the candle light, and shuffled a few steps laterally until I was confident the beam of light was ninety degrees at the wall of the building. I glanced over my shoulder, eyeing the other laser beam pointing into trees that looked like any of the others surrounding the clearing with the hut. I marked the spot, turned my back on the candlelit window and began walking away from the house.

Talon and Carl silently fell in step with me as we made our way to the woods. After a few minutes of walking through the mud we crossed into the tree line. I kept my eyes on the trunk I had marked with the laser, occasionally glancing behind me to make sure the house still sat behind us. So far, so good.

The path began to grow thicker, the mud deeper, even trapping our boots, making us struggle to continue. The smell of damp rot increased, and I heard Talon snort. Then he sneezed a few times. Carl's eyes squinted to bare slits, his tongue flicking out to taste the air as everything grew darker and gloomier with each step.

Low growls suddenly rumbled out of the nearby foliage. "No talk, no touch, no eye contact!" I snapped at Talon and Carl. "I warned you about this."

They stiffened obediently, their every predatory sense urging them to ignore my demand. But they listened, shoulders tightening as fingers rested on hilts of the weapons at their hips. *Thank you, Dog Whisperer*, I thought to myself.

I continued walking as if I hadn't heard the growls, eyes latched onto the tree I had marked. The growls grew harsher, angrier, and I even heard footsteps crunching over soaked twigs, the snapping of jaws, and saw fiery yellow eyes in my peripheral vision – stalking us.

Then a blast of hot air struck me in the face as I took the last step between me and the tree.

The gloomy woods were gone and I stood in a sunlit clearing. Talon and Carl each sucked in a breath, spinning warily to look behind us. A shimmering wall of gloomy darkness stood behind us, like a dirty window into those rainy woods.

Talon shared a long considering look with Carl before they both turned back to me. I grunted and walked ahead. Towards the freshly painted house – like a vision of what the water-logged hut had been when first built. Fresh paint and the smell of cut timber filled the air.

Mallory – in his human form, rather than his natural form as Pan, the Wild God – burst from the door, eyes glinting with the promise of death. He wore no shirt, and his white-furred chest did little to conceal the slabs of muscle over his body. A thin cord hung from his neck, adorned by a lone set of pipes that rested on the tufts of his chest hair, partly concealed by his thick, well-groomed beard. Charcoal brushes of color swept back from his temples, breaking up his long white hair which was tucked back in a baby ponytail – or possibly a man bun.

He wore jeans but no shoes, as if we had just woken him from a nap. I spotted the feather tattoo on the back of the hand he raised to shade his eyes as he looked out at us before sweeping the rest of the clearing for danger. I waved at him, not slowing. "How is he?" I asked him. "And where are Baba and Van?"

That was when I realized that the silence was brittle, and that Mallory's face hadn't changed.

He turned his back on me and walked into the house. I glanced at Talon and Carl. Without a word, they took up places on the porch, glaring out at the peaceful clearing as if expecting an ambush. I followed Mallory inside, ready for anything.

I saw an empty bed and flinched, spinning slowly to search for its occupant.

Mallory stood with his beefy arms folded over his chest beside a couch. I looked down to see Van Helsing sleeping, and frowned. Mallory stomped his foot hard enough for me to feel it through the wooden floor from a few feet away. Van didn't even shift, even though the sound was enough to wake him from all but death. Mallory pointed a finger to a rocking chair in the corner of the house and I froze. Baba Yaga sat in it with an unfinished blanket on her lap, and long needles still in her hands. She had been knitting – I leaned closer, inspecting the unfinished design – a skull amidst a field of flowers. I shivered at both her decision of a blanket and at a small birdhouse on the bookshelf beside her. It had... chicken legs.

I slowly turned to Mallory, eyes wide. "Where the living fuck is he?" I rasped, pointing back at the empty bed.

Mallory shook his head in answer. "Gone. And I can't get them to wake up. They are not harmed, not in danger of even being harmed, but they will not wake."

I swept the room, suddenly very afraid. Was something else in here? Some trap? Some spell for the unwary? Whatever had spelled them all to sleep, but had woken up the other occupant?

Mallory spoke as if sensing my thoughts. "The danger is gone. There is no spell left. *Someone* did this, not *something*."

I clenched my fists in fury. "Matthias," I snarled, my vision flashing red at the edges. "What the hell? Why? How?" We had added the camouflage, the traps... and no one but the people in this room right now had known about it. Talon and Carl had only heard the details less than ten minutes ago.

Pan grunted. "I don't know, but it was definitely him. I can sense Maker all over this place. But how did he find it?"

I took a deep breath. "You sure it was him? You haven't told anyone about the precautions? At all?" he shook his head harshly. "The how doesn't matter right now. He did this. But why?"

"He did say he was interested in the Knight..." Mallory added.

"But he also said he was going away for a while. Our last meeting was... hard on him."

Mallory grunted. "Not hard enough. Or..." he trailed off, scratching at his chest hair absently. "Maybe hard enough to make him do this?"

I swore. Then I began to pace, scraping together anything we had learned, which wasn't anything at all, really. No understanding of why the Knight of the Round Table was important, or even which Knight it was. One of King Arthur's fabled heroes, we were certain, but not which one. Or why anyone should give two shits about him.

My eyes settled on the sleeping forms of the guards who had failed to keep the Knight safe. "You're sure they're okay?"

He thought about it, finally giving me an uncertain nod. I grimaced. He sighed in annoyance. "I can't be sure without waking them up, and I dare not wake them up until I'm sure. I think it's temporary. He... put their magical natures to sleep. Somehow. Since they rely so heavily on that aspect of themselves, their mortal body followed suit. I still sense magic in them, so I don't think he... removed it or anything."

I gasped. "*Removed* it! He can do that?"

Mallory shrugged. "I'm only hypothesizing. I don't know what he can do. He's been alive for centuries, and spent the majority of that time in Fae. Who knows how that changed him? The Mad Hatter," he grunted sourly, kicking at the leg of the coffee table. I didn't see a plate of food or a drink in sight, otherwise I might have thought them poisoned. Pan met my eyes. "Who can know the mind of a Tiny God? And he did tell you that the Knights were once one of his pet projects..."

I finally glanced at the birdhouse. It had been Baba's Familiar – a sentient house that walked around on chicken legs. It could grow to any size, and usually walked around as a hulking, cloaked monster with a bone-beaked mask like one of those Renaissance-era doctors. Now, it looked like a toy figurine of that, the size of a birdhouse.

A wooden door on the birdhouse suddenly popped open and a wooden piece that looked like a tiny bird skull shot out as the hut erupted with sound.

CHAPTER 31

I had rolled to the side, curling up behind one of the couches with crackling white fire around each fist. "CUCKOO! CUCKOO! CUCKOO!" a chirpy voice rang out three times and then went silent for a few seconds.

I peered over the edge of the chair, searching for Mallory. He rose up from behind the couch holding the sleeping Van Helsing so that I could only see his eyes and the top of his head. Carl and Talon burst into the hut, blades out and hunched over, prepared to slaughter.

"CUCKOO! CUCKOO! CUCKOO!" the birdhouse rang out again.

Carl and Talon took one sweep of the room before turning to watch Mallory and I peering over separate couches, obviously terrified of the birdhouse.

Nothing happened.

I slowly climbed to my feet, squinting at the birdhouse. It looked like one of those cuckoo clocks – at least the wooden piece extending out from the tiny open door did. I jumped as the birdhouse rang out with its stupid chime again, before stomping closer to glare down at it.

A small slip of paper was pinned to the bird's skull extending from the open door. The bird wore... a tiny fucking hat, basically confirming who was responsible.

Matthias Temple.

165

The Mad Hatter.

But... not many would understand the significance of that tiny hat. Just those close to me. Mallory was suddenly standing beside me, frowning down at it. Before I could reach for it, a furred paw shot past my shoulder and snatched the piece of paper, shoving me down to the floor with his hip. I glared up to see Talon hunched over me protectively, as if expecting the cuckoo clock to explode behind him.

Nothing happened. We shared a long, concerned look, and he handed the piece of paper to me. I climbed to my feet, reading it out loud. It was written in elegant calligraphy, like a carefully penned letter from hundreds of years ago. A forgotten skill these days.

"The King is Dead. Long live the King. Much that was lost to history can be found down a rabbit hole."

I blinked at it, my voice echoing in the tiny hut.

"One of these days..." I muttered, handing the paper to Mallory. The moment it left my hand, it burst into flame for a fraction of a second, so hot and fast that it didn't even have time to burn Mallory before disappearing. It didn't even leave any ashes in the air. The bird skull and hat crumbled to ashes and the tiny door closed on the birdhouse.

I shivered as I wondered what damage that message had done to Baba's Familiar. Had Matthias... surgically implanted it in there? That hadn't been the Familiar's head, had it?

I studied the bodies around me, wondering if they would suddenly wake now that Matthias' message had been delivered to its rightful recipient. They didn't.

I turned to Mallory. *"Rabbit hole* is kind of obvious..." I said.

The skin at the corner of his eyes crinkled as he nodded. He didn't state the obvious. That it was likely some kind of trap. "Maybe too obvious," was all he said.

I nodded, thinking. "Well, we were headed there next anyway. Just for a recharge before..." I waved my hand, not wanting to say it out loud. Mallory's lips tightened and he flexed his fists. He was one of the few I had told about my plan to go to Hell. Because he knew everything about my past anyway, and even though he didn't like it, he knew that was the only place I could get answers. From my parents.

Because they hadn't even revealed all their secrets to him, and they had made him promise to kill me if I became a power-hungry dictator with no impulse control.

We needed that recharge from Fae – we needed any additional strength we could get. But the time-shift in Fae presented a problem. Because even spending an hour in Fae could take a lot of time in the real world. But an hour was all we needed, enough time for me to meditate and calm my thoughts. Wylde needed his energy drink – Fae Bull. We would just have to be fast, because we dared not risk missing Death's escort to Hell.

"If Matthias meant any harm, I'm sure he would have killed Van, Baba and her house. They obviously didn't pose a threat to him..." I hoped I was right. "I'll need you to look after these three. When they wake up they might have something else to tell us. Or... we'll need to try and wake them up ourselves," I added with a sigh.

"I'll keep them safe. Maybe take them somewhere else if I'm confident it won't harm them."

"I'll be in touch."

"This will be faster than heading back to Chateau Falco," Mallory muttered. "At least I can do something to help."

He waved a hand and a shimmering curtain of hazy green light appeared before us, seeming to sparkle. Beyond that glimmer was a cavern. A familiar cavern.

"Home sweet home," Talon murmured.

"Thanks," I told Mallory, extending my hand. He gripped it with his, and we both stared down at the feather he had tattooed on the back of his hand – identical to the one I had drawn there one day as a carefree child. He'd had it permanently tattooed there as a symbol of his love for me – even knowing that he could someday be tasked to kill me. Luckily for me, we had gotten past that stage, and I didn't have anything to fear from Mallory. I squeezed his calloused palm and let go, turning to step through the door to the Land of the Fae.

Talon and Carl followed me without a word and the door winked shut behind us.

I let out a breath. "Meditate. Calm down. Relax," I reminded myself.

A silver blur erupted out of my peripheral vision and slammed into my chest, riding me down to the ground and straddling my hips. A sweet, seductive purr tickled my ears. "I've missed you, my sweet," she cooed before licking my earlobes.

"Shiny!" Talon roared, and I heard a struggle as Carl fought to restrain him.

"Relax!" I shouted as the body jumped off me, hissing back at Talon. "She's a friend! Barbie, stop shining. He really hates it. Or at least stay still long enough for me to talk him down!"

The nymphomaniac sprite nodded, stepping behind me as I began to shout at my kitty cat.

CHAPTER 32

*C*arl went to sit on a rock at the mouth of the cave when it became apparent that the naked silver chick meant no harm, Talon was no longer trying to kill her, and that Talon was being yelled at for attempting to do so.

Talon still shot hateful glances at Barbie, even though he now recognized her from my first trip over here. Barbie was a silver Fae sprite that fed on sex. She was pretty cool once you got past the whole sex thing, which most couldn't.

I'd also kissed her once and told her I loved her, which she seemed to recall quite vividly, trying to rekindle something that had never been kindled – me. I had explained repeatedly that I did love her, but not as a physical love. No lust. A familial love. A friendship love.

"Friends can have sex. Even some royal families have sex. I don't understand the problem."

It had taken me a few minutes to get past *that*, and all the while Talon was losing that instinctive anger as he stared at her – sometimes agreeing with her, and sometimes baffled at her thick-headedness.

I sat across a glowing orange stone that gave off heat. It wasn't really a stone, but an orb of molten lava that maintained its spherical shape on its own, discharging heat. Much like a fire.

But since we were in Fae, nothing was as mundane as simply having a fire pit.

"Oberon is furious that you let Matthias return. And with a guest, no less," Barbie finally said, answering the question of why she was here, having reluctantly accepted my answer on *no means no*. She didn't bother putting on clothes, though, saying they chafed at her skin.

I shared a look with Talon. "Matthias came here? You can verify that?" I asked, careful to keep my foreknowledge to myself. I had been pretty sure Matthias' note implied he had taken the Knight to Fae, but having verification show up at my front door the moment I arrived, and neatly wrapped up with a silver sex sprite demanding satisfaction made me uneasy.

"Did I not just say so, Manling?" she pouted.

"Where are they now?" I asked.

She glanced at me, not speaking for a few moments. Then finally said, "We do not know. No one knows. That is why Oberon was so upset. He sent me here to find answers…" she said, waving a hand absently at the cave around us. "He warned me of wards, but I felt none. At least, nothing that tried to stop me."

I leaned forward curiously. Originally, my parents had placed wards around this hill so that anyone searching for them would not find their secret home in the cavern. But when I had last met Oberon, he had told me that the magic was fading from the place. Still strong, but not as strong. He'd made it sound like he couldn't wait for the ward to drop so that he could explore the cave himself in my absence.

I almost said my next thought out loud, but remembering who I was speaking to, I closed my mouth. I had kissed Barbie, told her I loved her. Perhaps that let her find the place without issue? Or maybe the ward was entirely down, now. I wasn't concerned too much about that, because we had scrubbed the walls of all evidence that I had ever been born here. Pan had made sure that my parents hadn't hidden any other secrets in the cave – a stash of weapons for example, since they had been so keen on robbing others and storing their stolen goods all over the worlds. *Worlds*, plural.

The place was clean. No fear of anyone finding out anything specific on my past. By now, I was sure everyone knew I was a Manling born in Fae because I had shut down both Queens' armies when they tried to attack us. But I still didn't want anyone ransacking my home, seeing the cave paintings I had drawn with my dad. Smashing cups or plates I had once shared with my mother. Basically, this place was *mine*, and I would rather wipe it out myself than learn that anyone else had come snooping around.

I pondered Barbie's answer. "If you know Matthias is here, and that he brought a guest, how do you not know where he is?"

Barbie studied me with a flat look. "I know the sun exists, but I do not know where it hides when the moons rise thrice."

I sighed. I thought about explaining space to her, but remembering I was in Fae, perhaps my answer wasn't right when it came to their sun and moons. And I didn't want to get caught in a long discussion that she would have problems following.

As curious as we were about Fae, they were just as – if not more – curious about us Manlings.

"Pah. Let's be done with this. The Hatter is back where he doesn't belong, but once lived. And you are here for something. The Queens want your head. Why bother gallivanting in Fae?"

I sighed, waving Talon out of the cavern. He furrowed a brow, the scars that seemed to bisect his eyes prominent in the orange glow of the cavern. Then he was gone, his steps utterly silent.

"I like his slippers," Barbie whispered, suddenly kneeling before me. Christ, what was with these crazy women all trying to give me a heart attack by kneeling naked before me?

She placed her hot palms on my thighs, staring up into my eyes. She squeezed. "Answer me or I will devour your pleasure."

I tried to pull back, but her fingers suddenly dug into my thighs like claws.

"Fine. Just… give me some space. Please?"

She released her finger spears – if reluctantly. I made as if to move and she instead leaned her cheek on my thigh, staring up at me as she held my calves. It was a very great effort not to stare down at her, because even looking at her eyes, I had a direct shot at her every asset in my peripheral vision.

"I came here to recharge. To clear my head. And this is not helping."

She laughed, a bubbling gurgle like a fresh stream tumbling over loose rock. "I knew I sparked your fire, Temple. Or is it Wylde?"

"Both, technically."

"In one neat meat package, I get the fiery souls of two powerful men.

You're making it harder for me to restrain myself from gobbling you up, Manling..." she complained.

"Well, how about this?" I asked. Then I began to tell her, in brief, what I had been dealing with since we had last spoken. I knew I could trust her, because she had been there for me repeatedly, even standing up against the Wild Hunt, and losing some of her sisters in the process. She had been following Wylde at that point, but she had also served me before she knew about that. So I told her. About all the chaos. The fighting. The infighting. Matthias. My parents.

I didn't tell her about Hell, or the Round Table, mainly because she interrupted me.

"If you won't let me sex you, at least let me learn you."

I frowned. "You mean teach? Teach me?"

She folded her arms below her breasts and I shifted in my seat awkwardly, crossing my legs. She grinned, licking her teeth as she glanced down at my concealed interest.

"The Fae..." she began, then tapped her lips thoughtfully, "do not negotiate."

I chuckled. "Funny, because all I've seen your kind do is negotiate and make deals."

She arched a brow at me. "You misunderstand, Manling. We make deals when it is more advantageous than killing our foe, or risking death by attacking superior forces."

I thought about that. "Okay. We do that, too."

"Of course, you do. Did I not just tell you that, Wylde? You are Fae."

I blinked. "No, I meant humans. Manlings. They do much the same. And... I'm not Fae. I was born here, but born a Manling."

She waved a hand dismissively. "Semantics. But humans are weak, petty creatures. We deal from strength and power. You... 'deal' by finding cowardly ways of stabbing your opponents in the back, all while pretending to be friends. We do it for prestige. A stunning victory. For fun."

I frowned, shaking my head. "You are describing the same thing two different ways. We are the same. We double-cross each other, make deals, and go to war just like the Fae."

"Ah, but do you? When we double-cross, all know it is coming. The only thing to discover is from which direction and how beautiful the victory will be. Or if you can turn it on your foe at the penultimate moment. You humans play with trust. Pfft. Trust is a Manling dream. Only power thrives."

I thought about that in silence for a few moments. She had plenty of it wrong... but not all of it. She actually had a good point. When humans tried to stab each other in the back, it was usually slimy and cowardly. Very rarely was it appreciated as a tactful move between equal parties. In fact, everyone considered it tasteless when it was between two powerful parties.

It was not... *respected*.

But in the Fae, they applauded camouflaged mischief. Beautiful assassinations. Gorgeous murder. Epic betrayals. And... it was different. They established the rules up front. Always. Creating the rules of the game, knowing that the only true way to have the most beautiful victory was to abide by every single constraint, and still outmaneuver your opponent.

I finally turned to her and gave her a slow nod. It wasn't a perfect explanation on her part, but then again, maybe that was intentional. The Fae liked to leave a lot of discovery to the student.

"Think about what I have not explained in your own time," she said softly. "And a stronger lesson will be learned." I nodded. "Now, when subterfuge is not worth the effort, there is war. Domination. Supreme annihilation. Such sweet, savory things, the screams of the fallen."

I felt a shiver inch down my spine as I watched her eyes almost glaze over with a silver shine. Her body shuddered as if she had just taken care of a personal need, and then she was looking at me again. "What is ours, is *ours*. We protect it at all costs. Nothing may take it. Ever. St. Louis is *yours*, is it not? Your parents' *home?*" I felt a surge of anger rush through me, but more than that. Pride. Defiance. Territorial rage. Before, I would have brushed it off as Wylde's influence, but that line was becoming blurred lately, and it felt entirely natural to experience his take on events. "You must fight for it."

"Yes. I guess it is mine. But don't my friends need to stand on their own?"

She cocked her head. "Why would they need to do that? Are they not your allies? Are you not a Manling? The city is *yours*."

She leaned forward, flashing her teeth as she gripped my chin. "*Claim* it. *Take* it. Make it *so!*"

CHAPTER 33

I shifted away from her feverish fingertips. I struggled to clear my throat, thinking on her declaration. She didn't understand how my world worked. But... was that such a bad thing? "What if the people of St. Louis don't want me to take the city?"

She scoffed. "Then they can *move*..." she said with a feral grin.

I nodded absently, considering the pros and cons of her advice. I don't know how long I sat there, but I suddenly remembered that I shouldn't just be hanging out in Fae. I hadn't even meditated yet. "Barbie, I need to—"

"You need power, Manling. To fill that vacuum inside of you, that raging, burning, starving hole in your soul..." Her skin glistened as if misted with sweat as she stared up at me.

I nodded stiffly. "I was going to say meditate, but... yes. That."

"I'll take care of it. Sitting alone may do wonders for the mind, but I think my Wylde Fae could do with something a little more... primitive..." she purred. Then she unhooked my legs, flinging them wide apart.

The tips of her breasts were like hot coals pressed against my knees. I tried to rise but she grabbed my wrists and yanked me back down to a sitting position. Her wings abruptly flared out behind her – silver butterfly wings as thin as a coating of frost on the grass at dawn.

They folded over me and the tips touched my back like icy fingers, the opposite of her fiery torso against my legs. And then she was slowly writhing up my crotch, licking her lips as her fingertips brushed my inner thighs. I realized I was no longer trying to get up, but trying not to explode from raw lust. Stone shattered under my palms as I squeezed the rock I was sitting on.

Her fiery breasts dripped sweat now and she breathed in ragged pants as she slowly – oh, so slowly – glided up my body until her chest was in my face.

Her sweat tasted like strawberry juice.

My skin sizzled – not in pain – but as if my senses had ignited, chock-full of a drug that made me taste smells and see sounds. All while that delicious Fae flesh pressed into my face. Her fingers danced across my shoulders and she was whimpering as she slowly sat down on my thighs, straddling me as she locked her heels behind my back, trapping me.

She gripped a fistful of my hair and pressed my face into her sweet-tasting, sweaty chest, hard. Electric current zapped into me from every single point of contact with her flesh against my clothes, as if nothing was between us. And I finally felt that hollow space inside of me – one I hadn't even known existed – roaring as floodgates of power gushed into me. Not any new, strange power, but more as if I was being replenished, fed, rested, and massaged at the same time. I felt close to bursting as she yanked my head back, my cheeks sliding across the sugary flesh of her breasts to look up into her silvery eyes.

She stared down at me... and I blinked. It was no longer lust in her eyes, but... affection. Concern. Empathy. And... love. Ever so slowly, she inched closer with her lips. I closed my eyes, and she kissed me on each eyelid – each touch like that moment in a particularly gripping movie when you knew the next words spoken by your favorite character were going to squeeze your heart until your eyes instantly watered up and your throat grew tight. Not a sad feeling, but a triumphant, glorious feeling of overcoming. Where your emotions were so vigorously raw from the tension, that all it took was that one statement to crack the floodgates of your soul to let the emotions pour out of you.

Then she kissed my forehead and I fell back, not knowing up from down.

She caught me in her wings, holding me protectively as I panted, struggling for breath. Tears poured from my eyes, falling down my temples as I let her hold me.

I felt as weak as a kitten.

More exhausted than I had ever felt after a fight.

More alive than I'd ever known.

And... complete for the first time in what felt like years.

No questions filled my mind. No doubts. Just... confidence and resolve.

"Are you... finished, Wylde?" I heard a vaguely familiar voice call out somewhere nearby. It took me a minute to recognize the creature as a Carl. No, not *a Carl*. My friend, Carl.

Unable to speak yet, I simply lifted one of my hands and gave him a thumbs-up.

"We'll just wait. Outside. I guess."

I slowly looked up at Barbie, who was still straddling me. Her back arched and chest out as her wings held me like a silken hammock. I hadn't ever really thought about her wings before. No bones or anything. Just... ribbons of dreams. I shook my head and licked my lips.

"I feel... exhausted," I rasped.

She chuckled, and then heaved back. I didn't have time to shout as I was suddenly flying. I landed on top of Barbie, my body pressed against hers, staring down into her eyes from only an inch away.

She blinked – her silver eyelashes much longer than I had ever noticed. "I gave you the fuel, but now you need a spark," she whispered. And she flashed forward to bite my lower lip.

I felt a drop of blood hit my tongue, as well as something else velvety and wet, and then I was surging to my feet, hands clenched into fists as I roared. I felt as if I was standing beneath a waterfall, struggling to stand, but knowing that if I could last one moment longer I would win.

The sensation stopped and silence washed over me. All I could hear was panting.

I glanced down to see that Barbie was gone, only a silver butterfly pressed into the cavern floor. I bent down, suddenly alarmed, but realized it was just a piece of metal, intricately carved and detailed. "Claim it..." Barbie's voice whispered, no louder than the breeze. "Have no fear. I know where your heart lies, Manling, for I have tasted it. My gift was an act of pure love, as you once gave to me. But even repayments can be... enjoyable..." and with that, her voice faded, the silver butterfly in my fingers throbbed warmer for a moment, and then I knew she was really gone.

I stared down at it for a moment, and then out at the cave's entrance.

I smiled, and then began to laugh as I tucked the butterfly into my satchel. I had a lot to think about. But right now, it was time to get to work.

Still, that was the best sex I'd never had.

CHAPTER 34

*W*e had returned from Fae to find that it was almost noon the following day, cutting it very close. Talon and Carl had been silent, merely watching me as I told them what to do. They didn't question, comment, or even speak unless I asked them to. Which was good enough for me.

Death was waiting for us in front of the Arch. Talon and Carl wore deep hoods to conceal their appearance from the dozen or so humans walking, eating on a blanket, or tossing Frisbees around the area. With it being broad daylight, all it would take was one close inspection under those hoods to start a panic. Luckily, no one paid us any attention.

Death opened his mouth to say something, but then hesitated, studying me. "You seem… well. Alive. Full."

I grinned. "Ah, irony. Bringing life to the Underworld. I had an energy drink."

He continued to watch me in silence, then finally glanced at my companions. "It is time to depart. Not that it matters at this point, but are you ready?"

I nodded smugly. "I've taken any precautions I could think of. Even printed out copies of the *Mappa dell'Inferno* by Botticelli. A map to Hell based on Dante's *Divine Comedy*." We had spent days studying the famous painting, staring at the inverted funnel shape until we had nightmares. Well,

I had nightmares. Carl had seemed eerily peaceful and well rested afterwards.

Death chuckled, but it slowly grew into a great booming laugh. "You think *that* will save you? As if we would let humans publish an *accurate* map!"

I squinted at him, my confidence wavering. "Well, it can't hurt," I argued stubbornly.

"Just don't use it. That map is so much toilet paper."

I kicked a boot into the grass angrily. "You couldn't have told me that earlier? I spent a lot of time reading this kind of stuff. Hours..." I muttered, suppressing a shudder at the nightmares.

"Well, unless you'd rather give up your soul, we best get moving. Hopefully you brought some good walking shoes." He turned and began walking to the center of the Arch.

I nodded as I followed him. I glanced at the dozen or so people around us, but it was almost as if they didn't see us at all. I waved at one, curious. He was only ten feet away. He smiled, but his eyes let me know he was looking past me. I glanced the other way to see he was staring at a friend who was getting ready to toss a Frisbee. I held out my hands, flipping both off simultaneously. They didn't react at all, and I shivered.

I hurried after Death, not wanting to know how he had managed to conceal us from the humans. "Now that we are here, can you finally tell me who's in charge down there? There are so many options, but I really doubt it's Lucifer. That's kind of discriminating against everyone else if he's in charge."

Death turned to face me. "One lesson you should already know..." he said in a tight, frustrated voice. "Is to not say certain names out loud. And that's a long list of names. It's not like earth, Nate. You say the wrong fucking name down there, and you have no idea what kind of shit storm will rain down upon you." He stepped backwards, and the world flashed black for a moment, revealing the Grim Reaper, the Horseman of the Apocalypse, holding his wickedly lethal scythe, taller than his own body. His mask – a human skull, but slightly elongated – flashed into place, and I again considered the impact craters visible on its surface, wondering what sort of a caliber bullet would have left a mark on his Mask.

Then he was Hemingway again, a man in a sharp suit.

Flicker.

179

Death.

Flicker. Hemingway.

Flicker. Flicker. Flicker. Back and forth, faster and faster...

Then we were suddenly standing in a dead landscape. Condensed clouds of drifting, shifting, black fog roiled and crashed over each other with such mass that as one crested and struck another, the weaker of the two dispersed like a wet water balloon hitting pavement, evaporating in an instant. The land was dead. Ash covered the earth in knobby, distorted pale pillars like precariously balanced stacks of totaled cars, and as I took a step, the pale earth beneath my boots puffed up into the air as if it weighed almost nothing. Such fine immolation that it could make the dust practically float like feathers. The sky crackled with black lightning in the distance, seeming to somehow throb with pulses of darkness rather than flashes of brightness – like a sudden shade thrown over the moon.

Speaking of... I looked up at the sky, staring at those shifting, charcoal clouds. They were limned with red and orange fire, like staring up at a bed of coals.

No sun or moon could be seen through the infinite darkness of pregnant, hostile clouds.

Death pointed a skeletal claw off to his right and a pillar of white simply evaporated, collapsing like a demolished building. I blinked.

"Death is all around you, now. You sought this. You asked for this. But this is only the beginning of the decay, the heartache, the woe." He said it like a neighbor pointing out patches of petunias in the front yard while bragging about the garden out back. "This is all you can conceive at the moment, but as you descend, your horizons will be... broadened," he said with a mirthless, rasping chuckle.

"Tone down the crazy, Death. You know me. No need to impress."

Whip quick, his scythe was swinging at my face with the sound of a thousand dying screams rather than the whistling of air. Both Talon and Carl were suddenly before me, but the scythe turned to vapor, whisking right through them before solidifying on the other side of them –right before my face.

The blade appeared at my neck. I was caught so off guard by both its sheer speed and by its delivery – harmlessly passing through my friends – that I didn't even have time to flinch. White fire danced in the black sockets of Death's Mask. The scythe's razor edge barely touched my skin and I suddenly felt as if my whole body was submerged into the Arctic Ocean...

"Drop the blade, Rider, or we all die here. We've all come to dance, and it looks like you're the only one in a dress," Talon snarled, glancing at the Horseman's death-shroud robe.

Carl just hissed, holding two swords in a reverse grip as he crouched, readied to leap. His fanned hood rattled, and I knew he was ready to spit that odd venom of his.

But I could only stare at Death's skeletal claw holding the edge of his scythe a dozen feet away from me, and the blade itself resting against my throat. But between, where the staff should have been, was only vapor. His scythe shouldn't have been able to reach me.

So his scythe was able to reach impossible distances, and grant no harm to those he didn't intend to die. Which made sense, being Death, and all. Otherwise he might have received a lot of written complaints. My hand was creeping up to my necklace, inch by inch, the only hope left to me. The moment before my fingertip touched the metal coin – my Horseman's Mask – Death's scythe evaporated.

I collapsed to my knees, shivering violently, feeling on fire as the icy sensation left my skin.

Death grunted. "There are no friends in this place. I warned you. That I could not aid you here. That this was foolish. That..." he waved a hand, turning his back on us. As his robes swirled near the ground, more puffs of the white ash floated up into the air, and I tensed as I saw his feet. Skeleton, not feet. Just bone.

I stared at his robes, remembering the cobwebbed fabric, like a death shroud, but somehow thick enough to prevent seeing through it. As I stared now, I noticed a faint purple glow beneath the shroud, like light. None of it shone near his hands or feet.

I climbed to my feet, rubbing my arms briskly. I didn't retaliate. He was right. I should have known better than to press him. This wasn't Hemmingway. Not any longer. This was Death in his official capacity. And I was banging on his front door in the middle of the night.

"My apologies, Pale Rider," I said, eyes downcast.

His shoulders tensed, but he didn't turn. After a time, he waved a hand before him.

The sound of cracking ice in a silent pond at dawn rocked the world, and the ashes on the ground began floating up a foot off the ground. The vibration of something underneath us began banging as if we actually were standing on thin ice, and a sea dragon was trying to break through to get to us. As the thumping increased, the ash continued to bounce and lift into the air, clearing the space around us to reveal polished black stone.

The air hummed. The heat began to increase as if we were standing before an open oven door.

Suddenly, everything stopped and we stood in complete silence.

Death was perched in a squatting position on the inches long wooden handle protruding from the haft of his weapon, about halfway up the blade. The arced blade rested on the ground, impossibly keeping the weapon upright, but rocking back and forth like a rocking chair along the back of the blade, making Death sway like a spinster on the porch as he stared at us, that white fire in his eye sockets flickering brightly.

"Don't use the Mask. I cannot take it from thee, but beware the Horn of Servitude. You've heard it twice. Perhaps the third time's the charm," he said in a wheezing chuckle, unlike any voice I had ever heard him use. "If you call upon the Mask down there, and it *is* the final stroke... let's just say that I wouldn't recommend announcing a Rider – a Fifth Rider – of the Apocalypse in the depths of Hell, without his Brothers. Some of the... residents have long memories, and were present when the scriptures were written. It might attract unwanted attention."

I opened my mouth but gasped as he suddenly leapt thirty feet into the air, directly above us, wielding the scythe overhead like an axe. Black lightning struck the blade, tinged with the red and orange hellfire of the clouds...

And then he was falling like a comet. Like a Fallen Angel. Straight at us.

We dove to the side and Death's scythe slammed into the black stone where we had been standing. Orange and red fire spider-webbed the polished black stone with a sound like the earth had just cracked in half, and the ground shattered beneath us.

We fell, obviously.

I stared up at the Hellish world above us, remembering all the decay and destruction, and saw the robed Horseman floating as he stared down at us. He held a black feather in his skeletal claw, and I noticed a red orb at the tip. Then the black glass began repairing itself like crystals growing in fast forward until Death and the hole were gone, leaving only a smoky glass window.

As I thought about the feather – which had looked just like one of Grimm's feathers – I managed to wonder what could be worse than what we had already seen.

I didn't have to wait long to find out.

CHAPTER 35

We splashed into a pool of thick liquid, like mud. I tried swimming back up to the surface, not daring to open my eyes as I stroked and kicked, struggling against the density of the pool.

I finally broke the surface, and had to kick twice as hard to keep my head out of the muck. The stench of sulfur burned my nose as I eagerly swiped the goop out of my eyes before opening them. Talon and Carl were kicking desperately for the bank, which was only a dozen feet away. I followed after, wondering what the black pool was. I quickly decided I didn't want to know as I bumped against a few thicker, denser chunks. I bit back bile and pressed on.

"Pah," Talon spat, crawling across the surface. "Foul!"

I nodded as I finally reached them, pulling myself out. Carl was on all fours, blowing out his nostrils and wiping the black filth from his orifices – eyes, nose, ears, mouth. I reached into my satchel and found a spare shirt. I was mildly surprised it was dry, but then again...

I wiped my face and hands and then threw it at Talon. He wiped off and then tossed it at Carl.

Soon, we were all more or less clean, except for our clothes, which were drying stiffly in the baking heat, and checking over each other for injuries.

"What the... why was Death so different?" Talon finally asked.

"It doesn't matter. We press on. I guess..." I jerked my chin to the open cavern before us.

To say *cavern* leaves a lot to misinterpretation. It was more accurate to say we were in a new world, and instead of open sky and clouds, only the earth's crust sheltered us from the heavens. Bat-winged figures – too large to be bats – swooped back and forth in an erratic aerial display, snatching onto blue wisps that drifted lazily through the air in condensed figures the size of a man. I shivered as one screamed, snatched up by a bat-thing. Souls. Not blue wisps. Souls. Those winged things were catching souls and... eating them. Or torturing them.

Talon spat disgustedly, climbing to his feet. He placed his paws on his hips, studying the endless expanse of cavern, the thousand feet of air between us and the earth's crust. Not too far away stood an arch, and beyond the arch was a thin rock bridge without railings. Below the bridge was only orange light, illuminating the cavern around us.

"Like a moth to flame," I muttered, stomping past Talon. Carl was suddenly beside me, inky black teeth visible as he breathed through his mouth rather than nostrils. His ear holes opened and closed as if making sure no one was about to jump us.

I wasn't concerned about being jumped. It wasn't like anyone had to try very hard. There was nowhere to run. They could just walk up to us and overwhelm us. Even the bat-like things just watched us, blinking lazily with their red eyes. I couldn't get a close enough look to really categorize their details, but I was sure my eyes would see plenty before we were through here.

As we neared the arch, I noticed the hundreds of black shades drifting over the ground. I had thought they were fog. They moved without hurry. As if just taking a walk. Or a hover. Their bodies didn't shift as they drifted, so it looked like nothing more than an army of shadowy mall cops on Segways, muttering about the rascal teenager souls loitering near the entrance to Hell.

But they didn't seem to bother – or even acknowledge – us.

Which was creepy when several drifted right past us. One actually went *through* Carl. He froze, completely motionless, and the hair on the back of my neck stood up in fear. Had they just fucking *killed* fucking Carl? We just got here!

Then he turned his neck to me very slowly, licked his lips a few times and grumbled. "That tasted delicious… So much anguish while that one lived…" He stared after the soul as if debating jogging over for another quick nibble of his life memories, which gave Talon and I enough time to glance at each other in horrified disgust.

"Fucking Carl," Talon finally coughed, nose wrinkling at the sulfur permeating the air. Although foul, I had gotten kind of used to it already. Then again, I had anticipated it. I reached into my satchel and pulled out a small unmarked tin. I handed it over to Talon. He opened it curiously and sniffed. Then he greedily scooped some out to smear around his nose.

Carl turned back to us, a forlorn look in his eye as he gave up chasing down the specter. Talon held the tin of mentholatum – like what coroners used when working on cadavers – to him. "For the smell."

Carl leaned in to sniff it and instantly snorted, taking two hurried steps back, shaking his head. "I think it smells refreshing here."

Talon rolled his eyes and handed the tin back to me. Knowing that sulfur was likely going to be a bouquet of roses compared to what else our nostrils might encounter down here, I wiped some around my nose anyway and closed the tin. As I continued on to the arch I felt an itch at my shoulders. Remembering Death's advice about not putting on the Mask of Hope, I began to ponder if he had meant using my white magic as well, since it was tied to my powers as a Horseman in training. I could always rely on my wizard's magic, but sometimes the white flavor had a mind of its own and washed over my magic without conscious thought. I began regretting I hadn't chosen a weapon for myself. Not that I was that great with any of them, but a blade wouldn't have gone remiss right about now. I could always grab one of the extras I had stowed away for Talon or Carl, but they had picked them out themselves, and with these two crazy fucks, there was no telling what ancient powers were imbued in their backup weapons.

I shoved the tin can back in my bag, studying the arch. My hand brushed against something inside the satchel but I skidded to a halt, jerking my hand from the bag as I heard the sounds of Talon's spear crackling into existence and Carl drawing twin bone daggers as long as his forearms.

A human stood before us. He wasn't decayed, disheveled, or remotely zombie-like. He did look tired and pale, perhaps a smidge hungry, but he was human. And he was staring at us.

I shared a look with my companions before slowly approaching the man. He didn't look threatening or imposing and had no weapons. He just watched us. Expectantly. Was this a gift from Death? Our guide?

"Greetings," I said politely. "You, uh, don't seem as dead as your roommates."

He nodded. "I am dead inside."

I smirked weakly. "So is this guy," I said, pointing a thumb at Carl.

No one said anything so I let my hand drop.

The man nodded at Carl. "I'm well aware of Elders." He glanced at Talon, seeming to focus on the scars over his eyes as if he understood what they signified. "It is an honor, Faeline," he said, dipping his head. I frowned, shooting Talon an inquisitive look. Was it a mix between *Fae* and *feline* or a title? With only his eyes, he managed to tell me *I have no fucking idea.*

"Okay. Do we have to answer a riddle or something to use your bridge? Because I already know my answer." I was going to pull the old Monty Python on him. He definitely wasn't dressed like he had been around when that movie came out.

"A riddle? No. That would be a different entrance. Luckily for you. This is a... side door. If you would have me, I am your guide."

Different entrance? How many doors to Hell were there? And, wait... guide? I studied his clothing more intently. He wore a tan robe and sandals, nothing else. And I'd read a book or two recently. "You're *Virgil!*" I said, recalling the poet's name. "The poet who guided Dante through Hell!"

CHAPTER 36

*T*he man didn't even blink. He didn't react at all. Had Death been lying about this not being like the *Divine Comedy*? Because Virgil had guided Dante through Hell, giving him a... Hell of a tour, so to speak.

But I was playing it safe. Always wear protection. "How much do you cost?"

His lips peeled back into a faint smile. Almost as if it wasn't a smile. Nothing nefarious, but as if he had forgotten how to truly smile and was doing his very best.

"Before we get to that, you must state your purpose."

I realized that every single shade around us had frozen still. "I'm sure you already know that, Virgil," I replied warily.

"It must be stated. Witnessed."

I studied him, watching his eyes. Not a flicker of deceit hung there. Nor fear. Just... acceptance. Whatever happened to me here would not impact his schedule tomorrow. For better or worse. He was already having one eternally-long shitty day.

I glanced at the Arch behind him, wondering if we were even supposed to be here since he had mentioned other gates, other entrances. The corners of the arch held carvings of stone faces screaming in torment. As I looked closer, I realized they were moving. Not carvings... they were alive. Well, relatively speaking. I watched as one took a deep, silent breath and then continued to scream without sound, his eyes stretching wide. I averted my eyes to the arch itself that spanned overhead. This close, I noticed worn words carved into the stone.

Abandon hope, all ye who enter here. In English. I frowned. It had been written in Italian according to Dante's book, but perhaps it was seen from the eye of the beholder. Made sense.

Can't have only Italian signs in Hell. That would be discriminatory.

I read it again. The direct translation had been hotly debated. Not the words, but the order.

All hope abandon, ye who enter here. Or…

Abandon hope, all ye who enter here. Semantics. At least now I could consider myself an authority on the subject when I returned. I began to laugh. Talon shifted uncomfortably, leaning my way. "Stop!" he hissed. His tone added, *you fucking lunatic!*

I wiped at my eyes, careful to not smear them with the mentholatum. And I let my laughter fizzle out. Still amused, but more resigned.

I thought about my answer to Virgil's offer. Very carefully. Death had made it obvious that the reason I had been allowed to see my parents the first time was because I sought nothing of interest from them. Nothing valuable. My sacrifice – dying briefly – had been enough to grant me a brief meet. Death had even been allowed to offer my parents a figurative couch to crash on in the Armory for a time, but the price to that was paid by them. They apparently hadn't been allowed to bring up anything that they knew. None of the secrets that I hadn't even known existed at the time. Also, in repayment for that brief hall pass they were to spend the rest of their existence down below. At least that's what Death had told me – only recently – the dick.

They had chosen to live in Hell for eternity – just so that they could spend a little more time around me. Not even so they could do anything to help me. Just… get to see me the few times I had deigned to visit the Armory.

Which, in hindsight, made me feel like a moldy asshole. I should have spent more time with them. I should have simply hung out with them rather than—

I cut off that thought abruptly. That would do me no good down here. In fact, I wouldn't be surprised if self-pity could be fatal down here. Like a cancerous poison to the air, slowly seeping my will to live out of me. Killing me with guilt.

I took a deep breath. What was my purpose here? What was true, yet vague? What would have a price I might be willing to pay? I was pretty sure Virgil knew exactly why I was here, and the act of me stating my intent was somehow an act of futility, but that it might have consequences down the line. But there was really only one reason I would risk everything to come here, and whoever was in charge had to know it. Had to have expected it, or he never would have required my parents spend the rest of their eternity down here.

This meeting had been put in his books long ago, even though I never knew my parents had made the appointment.

I met the dead poet's eyes. "I come bearing a gift. In return for granting a request."

Virgil nodded after a very meaningful pause. My answer had… surprised him. Intrigued him, perhaps. "So be it."

"Are you going to take us through the Nine Circles and everything? Because I would rather take the elevator if possible."

"You're more than welcome to wander the Path of the Nine, but I wouldn't recommend it. You would do so without a guide, and…" his eyes grew distant for a good ten seconds, "it wouldn't end well for you." He said that with… conviction, as if he had just checked his future calendar and read about my death. It was enough to make me shiver coming from that dead poet's mouth. "Everyone who enters Hell must see things, but no two people get the same path. Not that we have many visitors, you see. But the path to Hell is paved with good intentions. Quite literally. And I fear the Nine Souls would destroy you," he said directly to me.

Carl cleared his throat. "Can we walk and talk at the same time?"

Talon punched him in the shoulder, dipping his head to Virgil in apology.

Virgil didn't even acknowledge the two, staring at me. "There is a price for a guide. Accept that price and we may proceed."

I was already shaking my head. "We'll talk price first, but nice try."

"No. Accept the price and we may proceed," he repeated in the exact same tone.

"Maybe you didn't hear me. I'm not stupid enough to agree to a price that hasn't been defined. Some prices are too high. This is where we haggle."

"We… contemplate things down here. Think on it. We will define the price later."

I threw my hands up. "No, Virgil. I'm not falling for it. After we begin, you could demand any price."

"And would you not pay any price?" he asked in a soft tone.

I felt Wylde's instincts backing me up. He was Fae, and knew better than to make a deal without a defined price up front. "No. Not any price." A new thought hit me. "Where is Charon? All he would require is a six pack of beer."

"He is… unavailable at this terminal."

I grumbled under my breath.

Virgil finally lowered his standards. "I'll tell you this. A life or a gift. But you will have the ultimate choice. If none are appealing at the time your decision is required, your life will be forfeit. Now, agree to the terms or I will depart. And leave you to them." He slowly pointed a finger.

I turned to find three Candy Skulls staring at me, heads cocked. I didn't see any of their crystal blades, but their depthless eyes made my heart stutter. "Motherfuckers…" I whispered under my breath, readying myself for a fight.

"You may still leave this place, but once you set foot beyond the arch, there is no backing out. And traveling Hell without a guide will guarantee that you all become permanent residents here."

I thought furiously. I wanted answers from my parents, but did I *need* them? Really need them? I already had a lot going on in my life, not even considering this Catalyst crap. White Fang was prowling St. Louis, and if I didn't do something, every faction was ready to turn on one another. Fat chance the Regular humans would miss something like that.

Then our secret would be out – magic was real – and there was no telling what could happen. Freaks could become Enemies of the State overnight. Fugitives. Criminals.

Pandora's words whispered in my ears and the hairs on the back of my neck stood straight up. *Pay the piper…* Had she been talking about this moment or something else back home? Something to do with whatever was going on with Alex? Or maybe it had been a warning about Matthias kidnapping the Knight. Or… it could have meant so many things.

But whatever my parents had discovered was obviously very important. Because everything had been set up like a house of cards. Me being a Catalyst. Their Armory. The Hand of God. The Hourglass. The War Hammer. The Round Table. The Mad Hatter. Everything led to another thing like some vast, intricate, infinite web.

And…

If what my parents had discovered *wasn't* important, why had the person in charge decided to lock them away in Hell rather than let me talk to them?

"The price will be paid, if I have to pay it myself," Carl hissed, stepping forward. "This place isn't so bad. Like a long vacation compared to my previous banishment," he boasted, and I was pretty sure he wasn't lying. So far, Carl had been remarkably unimpressed with Hell.

At the same time, Talon advanced. "My life before his. Forever." His tail twitched back and forth, fur puffed out to make it look like a club. And his ears were tucked back as if he expected – and hungered – for Virgil to make an issue of it.

The Candy Skulls watched, heads jerking back and forth in their spastic twitching mode of movement. I sighed. "Fine. I'll agree. But you can't have them. I'll contemplate…" I enunciated his word darkly, "giving up some of my powers before I let it come to their lives. I have enough to go around," I added with a confident smirk.

Virgil bowed his head, and for a moment, I thought he looked utterly relieved. Not in any personal satisfaction of what I would pay, but… something else I couldn't quite make out.

"Then we shall meet the Lord of the Dead, and see if he will accept your gift. If it pleases him, he may even grant you a request. If. But heed me. If granted, you may only ask for one thing. And the answer – even if it seems what you asked for – is rarely what you hoped for."

He turned, and drifted through the arch onto the long stone bridge. Only inches remained on either side of his sandaled feet. Inches from death. I took a breath and followed him, keeping an eye on the Candy Skulls behind us as Talon and Carl followed me.

They didn't move. But they continued to watch.

CHAPTER 37

$\mathcal{A}$fter what felt like a mile, we finally stepped off the bridge and I let out a relieved sigh. That much open space above and below us had been jarring. We walked down a path, slowly zigzagging back and forth as it crossed below where we had just been. I glanced up, wondering exactly how the level above us was supported if we were now walking directly beneath it. I shivered, averting my eyes at the impossibility of it.

I saw no one.

Heard nothing.

Not even a breeze.

As we descended, frost began to grow over the stones beneath our feet. I glanced down as the rest of the group walked in silence. The cobbled path was made of pale, round stones. A closer inspection let me see it was actually skulls. I grunted distastefully, careful I didn't trip into an eyehole or open mouth, because as we descended, the path gradually changed from the tops of the skulls to the faces of the skulls. Despite my careful steps, teeth occasionally broke beneath my feet, falling into the skull and making me stumble.

The architect had been thoughtful, though, because he had also incorporated arm and leg bones into the mosaic path, signifying directions when it forked. One thigh bone that was much too large to be human pointed to our left and had strange, almost geometric symbols etched into the surface, likely stating directions. *Napalm Hot Tub – Only 666 bajillion miles!*

The edge of the long bone featured a skeletal hand, also not human, in a parody of a pointing finger. I stepped back to try and get a wider view of the path and noticed that as we continued – left, if it matters – the path became more detailed, more artistic. No longer just skulls, but various bones from more creatures than I could count formed designs – arcs, squares, circles, stars, and more. I wondered if the Lord of the Dead – as Virgil had called him – had scooped up a few Renaissance artists in a two-for-one discount sale during the Black Death that plagued Europe.

Carl strode down the path without a care in the world, seeming to smile as he whistled to himself – I don't know how, so don't ask. Talon's eyes darted to each crevice of rock as if expecting an ambush. The ceiling was lower here, still more than fifty feet above our heads, but at least we could see it clearly.

"You'll want to see this," Virgil said, deadpan. "Everyone usually does, anyway."

He indicated a large circle in the path ahead. We approached warily and saw that an oval glass surface was set into the path – a dozen paces across – with familiar names etched into the beautiful bone border. The design was obviously inspired by the Greek culture, the same as they had used on their ornate pottery and other treasures. I stared down at the glass and gasped as my vision abruptly distorted. It was some kind of telescope. As I readjusted myself to see clearly, my jaw dropped wide.

Large, giant shapes meandered far, far away, but with the telescope they looked close. I only knew they were large due to readjusting my face in order to see through the glass clearly. As I had leaned closer, the shapes shifted from small to massive. And I saw more of those bat-like creatures flapping in front of one figure's eye – they were the same size. These figures were huge, but I hadn't needed proof. I had been able to read the names around the lip of the window.

Still, it was humbling. And frightening. And sad.

The figures stumbled wearily across a barren, rocky surface full of pools of magma and frost – as if the two naturally cohabitated the same climates. Craggy spires and mountains broke the surface here and there, and I saw more of these figures almost as tall as the mountains hammering away at the stone. Then, several more would scoop up the boulders – the size of houses or larger – and carry them over to the other side of their world. Setting them down.

Another large figure stacked these boulders together, hammering them together with his fist, before reaching for another. He was forming another mountain. Just like the one the other figure had destroyed.

I looked closer to one of the magma pools to see that a man stood *inside* it, muscles bulging as he dredged something up from the pool of knee-high lava. A giant bucket. He set it on the lip of the pool where another figure grabbed the handle – steam billowing up on contact with his hand – and carried it over to the one hammering the boulders into the new mountain.

The figure heaved the lava onto the stack of rocks, filling in the cracks. Mortar for the boulders that made up the new mountain.

Then they repeated the process. Never speaking. Never looking up. Just... working.

Some building, others destroying – using the destroyed mountains to build another.

"The Titans... Tartarus," Virgil murmured without a hint of his personal opinion on the matter. But as soon as he spoke, every single face in that hellish world turned to look up, right at me. Eyes full of starlight, their pupils and irises like celestial bodies, stared up at me with agony and despair. I turned away, shaking my head.

"How many mountains have they made?" Carl asked, scratching his cheek absently.

"We don't really count things down here. Bad for morale."

Talon and I shared a dry look before I motioned Virgil to continue on.

The Titans. Good grief. Tartarus was real. I had read the names around the window – Atlas, Typhon, Gaia... but it was still surreal to witness. I quickened my pace to walk beside Virgil, glancing over at him. He didn't breathe and his face didn't change – not a frown, sniff, or blink. Like staring at a cadaver with his eyes open.

"How does it all work?" I asked him. "Are these pocket dimensions or something? So many religions have gods and their own versions of Hell or the Afterlife. Those were Greek Titans, but what about the others? The Christians, Romans, the Norse..." I trailed off, waving my hand to indicate the dozens I hadn't named.

"Consider them... neighborhoods. In a city, there are districts where the inhabitants are... different, yes? Richer, poorer, more industrious, more...

predatory?" I nodded. "Like that. You can wander from one to the other if you wish, but don't expect a warm welcome, much like a rich nobleman wouldn't receive a pleasant reception if he wandered down to the slums at midnight." I nodded to let him know I understood, watching his face. Even with the explanation, there had been no motion other than his mouth moving like a robot.

"These... districts or realms all exist here, much as they all existed, once, in your world." He sensed my frown and continued. "Just because Christianity has become more popular, has the Norse faith disappeared entirely from the world? Is there only one God on earth now? One replaces another and all forget about the Gods of yesteryear?"

I grunted. "No. But many were from different time periods. Romans replaced Greeks, for example." He waved a hand as if to remind me of his previous statement. Had all belief in Greek Gods disappeared the moment the Roman Gods stepped into the picture? I sighed, still not satisfied with the answer, but understanding it. Then again, I didn't really want to understand Hell's infrastructure. I didn't plan on sticking around. I'd just wanted to talk. A conversation. Something familiar to, well, two living people.

We continued on in silence for what seemed hours, not much changing, other than the temperature and the fact that we were now miles below where we had started. Between one moment and the next, we reached the bottom of the stairs and I stared in disbelief.

At a forest of black, stunted, rotting trees. White sap oozed from the bark, and although obviously decaying, white leaves grew from the branches. They grew rapidly, because just as rapidly, other growth rotted away to fall to the earth in wet slopping sounds. As if the entire life cycle of everything had increased exponentially, both decay and life. Like zombie trees.

Virgil led us into the deep dark wood, pulling up a hood. I frowned, but as I took another step, I felt rain suddenly falling from above. I stared down at my hands to find red drops striking my skin in the steady downpour. I grimaced.

"Blood rain," Talon spat, yanking up his own hood. Cats hated to get their fur wet.

Carl on the other hand lifted out his hands and spun in slow circles, almost skipping as he closed his eyes and began to hum softly to himself. It took me a few seconds to recognize the tune and I blinked at him in disbelief. Still spinning, he didn't notice us staring. Even Virgil.

"Is Elder Voldemort singing *My Favorite Things* from *The Sound of Music?*" Talon asked incredulously.

I nodded and then froze, slowly turning to face him. "How would *you* know that song? Or Voldemort, for that matter?"

He stiffened visibly. "The... the Reds were watching movies with Yahn a few days ago. I happened to pass by. That is all."

I grinned at him, but he averted his eyes. His tail betrayed him, twitching in time with the beat of the song. I rolled my eyes before continuing after dancing, singing Carl and our silent guide. Sometime later, I was scanning our surroundings, trying to determine how much longer we would be down here, when my palm flashed with a sudden heat. I shouted, glancing down at it to find what had hurt me. The skin of my Crest was whole and unharmed. The pain was already receding as I jerked my gaze up at our surroundings, ready to destroy my attacker.

No one but us was present. I shot a glare at Virgil, but he was simply watching me with those cold, dead eyes. I had no way of knowing whether he knew what had just attacked me, or if he was just curious as to my outburst. Talon and Carl had blades out, circling me uneasily as they glared out at the forest of black trees. Nothing moved. Well, nothing other than the steady slap of rotting foliage falling from the trees and the eternal drumming of the blood rain.

I finally let out a breath. "Let's go."

Virgil turned and continued on. I didn't dare say anything to Talon or Carl. Not with Virgil here. I simply gave them a level look that told them to be alert. I fingered my palm absently, wondering what it had been if not an attack. Some part of me warning me to hurry, that I was too long in Hell? I shivered at that. I'd never met anyone who had come down here like me. Perhaps as the time passed, our bodies would slowly begin to die, infected by the natural order of the Underworld, and a sudden flash of pain was just a natural warning sign to the living.

But I didn't feel any different. I reached out for my magic and felt it there, as full as ever. I also felt that reservoir of Fae magic Barbie had given me. Not that she had really *given* me anything, but she had done more in restoring my balance with that two-minute lap dance than seven days of meditation could have done. I checked my other internal indicators, everything seeming to be normal, but that only made me more anxious. I needed to hurry, but that was nothing new.

But was Virgil aware of what the sensation had been? Dared I ask him? Would he even answer if he knew? I eyed the trees cautiously, wondering if anything lived here, or if the trees were alive. Which meant my shoulders were practically knots after a few more hours of walking.

Finally, Virgil rounded on us. "We rest."

I skidded to a halt, almost bumping into him in surprise. I'd been walking robotically, wondering when the hell we were going to get anywhere useful. "Um. I wasn't planning on taking a nap down here. We're kind of on a timetable."

"We sleep. Or we will never make it."

"No offense, but I have trust issues. How do I know you won't leave us to die? Or let us sleep for a thousand years?"

He cocked his head. "I have agreed to take you to the Lord of the Dead. I would not betray you. I *cannot* betray you. I promise that we will get to our destination as quickly as possible, without delay. You are considered a... high value guest. I was informed not to delay, but for you to survive what comes next, you should rest. We have walked far, and energy is burned up faster down here than you are accustomed to. You might not feel it, but you are more exhausted than you know. Without sleep, you will suddenly collapse from exhaustion without warning when you least desire it, having never realized you were at the brink of your endurance."

I grimaced. Was that what that flash of pain had been? I glanced down at my palm quickly, but still felt no lingering effects. Had my body been trying to warn me? Virgil had made a deal with us... I turned to Talon and Carl, arching an eyebrow.

Talon glared at Virgil for a moment. "I am quite proficient at naps. My body is trained to sleep no longer than I desire. If I wish an hour, only an hour shall pass."

"Hell of a thing to put stock in. Catnaps. You sure?" I waved a hand at our surroundings. "Even in this place?" He nodded confidently. "Okay. But only an hour. Hear that, Virgil?"

He nodded. "That will be sufficient." With that, he lay down under a nearby rock overhang that kept the blood rain at bay. He closed his eyes and lay still. Not breathing or moving in the slightest. Like a dead body.

198

"Carl, take first watch. Talon and I will nap this time, and you can nap at our next stop."

The Elder grinned back at me, nodding. "No worries." The crazy bastard looked eager to get a few moments of privacy in this land of death. Maybe to go pick berries or something.

I lay down, staring up at the rock overhang and the decaying trees dripping with red rain. I didn't think it was possible to get any sleep in this place. I was too amped up.

I closed my eyes.

CHAPTER 38

I dreamed.

I wandered the grounds of Chateau Falco in a slow, fast-forward, enough to notice everything without it being a blur. I saw Chateau Defiance, my old crumbled fort tucked away in the woods.

The dream shifted to show Othello working in my office, muttering under her breath.

Shift.

Yahn casting furtive looks down a hallway before a pair of scaled red hands yanked him into a room, giggling as the door slammed shut.

Shift.

The Huntress frowning as she shot her shining black bow, the string like a strand of spider silk coated with dew. *Draw. Release. Draw. Release.*

Shift.

Raego shouting into a phone.

Shift.

Tory shouting into a phone.

Shift.

Achilles laughing as he hoisted glasses with Leonidas at his bar.

Shift.

Pandora wandering the Armory with a wistful smile on her face as she hummed to herself. She stared at an empty stand that looked designed for a weapon, but now lay empty.

Shift.

Grimm chasing rainbow reflections on the ground, the treehouse in the distance. Pegasus lay sleeping nearby.

Shift.

Paradise and Lost lurking in a dark alley, stalking something unseen, eyes glinting in the moonlight.

With a gasp, my eyes shot open to see Talon staring down at me. I grabbed him by his scaled armor chest, panting. His eyes widened, and he pulled me to my feet. I scanned our surroundings anxiously, remembering the black trees. The blood rain. I was in Hell. Carl watched me, head cocked.

I spun to see Virgil patiently waiting, watching us. No one spoke.

"It has been an hour," Talon said. I turned to him, regaining control. Dreams. I had been dreaming. Or remembering the last few days I had spent on earth. Or random memories from my past. As I tried to organize the flashes of memory, I nodded to myself. Yes, that was it. I was just having flashbacks. Like... my life flashing before my eyes before I died.

I glanced down at my palm with a sickening feeling in my stomach. It *had* been a warning. That I was slowly dying. My life had just flashed before my eyes like everyone said happened the moment before death. I recalled Virgil's warning about growing weaker faster and not being aware of it. He was more right than he knew. We were dying.

"We need to hurry," I said in a gruff voice. Virgil simply turned, continuing on down the path. Sensing my companions' trepidation, I shook my head and gave them a look that demanded silence. I didn't want to tell them why my face was etched with concern. We needed to hurry.

After a time – which I was having a hard time defining – we were out of the woods. I barely had a moment to enjoy it before the world suddenly changed between one corner and the next. A dull roar echoed in the sudden white tunnel before us. The roar of a crowd. I glanced back behind me to check the woods and stumbled to a stop. A white wall of polished glass stood a foot behind me. Not the path we had just taken. There was no path. Just the wall.

I rounded on Virgil, fingers clenching. "What is the meaning of this? A trap?" I demanded.

He turned to look at me. He slowly lifted a necklace from beneath his robe. A black circle on a black chain. "My key between… districts. You don't expect us to leave the doors open, do you? No, that wouldn't do at all." He dropped the necklace back into the robes and continued walking. "We'll be out of this spot soon. Hopefully before anyone notices you…" he added the last in a drier tone than usual. I didn't see anyone in the tunnel, but the roars continued in the distance.

Not wanting to be left behind, I hurried after him. We soon rounded a bend, the roars growing louder, and then the area opened up entirely, no longer a tunnel, but an open path overlooking a vast cavern. A lip of stone to our left, about waist-height, lined our path on one side with a wall of white stone stretching to the high ceiling on our right. Beyond the lip, the ground dropped about ten feet into what looked like an ice-skating rink. Not that it was, but the blazing white stone – like salt flats at noon – made me instantly think of one.

Except… it was an arena. The roars pounded at my skull. The arena was full of fighting monsters. All types. Pools of blood from wounded warriors painted the floor in vibrant splotches, and more blood spatter marked many of the walls. I saw one dwarf-looking guy slice an elf in half – completely. Blood sprayed the wall and the dwarf howled triumphantly before running after a new foe – a thousand-pound boar with five eyes, antlers, and fiery hooves.

After a few seconds, the two halves of the elf slowly crawled back together, flashing with light as they fit back into place like a jigsaw puzzle. He wearily climbed to his feet, gripped his weapon, and sought out a new opponent. He was snarling murderously, ignoring the blood beneath his feet. Or maybe not aware that he had been two pieces only a moment ago.

I saw a hydra battling a handful of chimeras. A frost giant hammering a fire giant. Two robed bald figures staring at each other with snarls on their faces, their eyes glowing green. They didn't move as battle raged around them, and judging by the looks they received, none of the monsters wanted to get too close to them. I spotted Candy Skulls hovering at various empty points around the arena, oddly devoid of any monsters, as if they hadn't desired to get close to the Calaveras.

I realized something for the first time. Not all the Candy Skulls were humanoid. The ones I had seen so far had been, but apparently that wasn't the case down here. A great four-legged creature, resembling a wooly mammoth complete with tusks wore a Candy Skull bone mask that fit his obviously much-larger head.

A four-armed winged creature sported a Candy Skull mask that looked like a bat skull.

A great serpent, easily fifty feet long slithered around the arena absently, purple crackling tongue flicking out through a Candy Skull mask with purple flowers dominating the design.

I shivered, counting them, and gave up at a dozen.

The arena was easily as large as a football field, and almost every foot of it was full of monsters. One massive free-for-all.

One figure in particular caught my eyes and I felt myself freeze.

His golden scales glowed in the reflected light from the white floor. Blood coated his face as his massive, horned head swept past me. Then he froze, slowly turning to stare at me in utter disbelief. His eyes flashed with fire, and then great golden wings flared out behind him and he roared.

"You've got to be shitting me…" I muttered as I heard Virgil actually curse.

Talon gripped my arm. "Who is that?"

"Alaric Slate. Raego's dad. I, uh, sent him here, I guess."

Talon yowled, his white spear whipping into existence. Carl let out a hungry chuckle.

The rest of the fighters had stilled, somehow differentiating that roar from the multitude of others filling the arena. Silence slowly ensued as every monster turned to stare at us.

Alaric pointed a golden claw, and every monster surged forward in a wave.

And the Candy Skull Wardens did absolutely nothing to stop the prison riot.

CHAPTER 39

*A*s hundreds of monsters screamed, clawed, and scrabbled towards us, I readied myself for a fight even though it was pointless. I'd watched them die and come back repeatedly in their melee. "Virgil! What the actual fuck! Get us out of here!" I snapped, not daring to turn away from the oncoming horde.

"I didn't realize that one was in here today," he replied. "If the Calaveras don't stop them, I fear I am not allowed to assist."

I cursed, opening myself to my Fae magic, not knowing what else I could realistically do against so many. I clapped my hands and a section of white floor thirty paces wide and ten feet deep rattled weakly, but didn't shatter. I pushed harder, frowning as my magic struggled against... something unseen. Probably because this was Hell, not the regular old Fae elements it was used to manipulating. I pressed harder, seeing stars in my eyes, and the ground suddenly collapsed beneath them, sending fifty monsters plunging to their... well, out of the way, since death didn't really seem to be an inconvenience down here. Maybe they would fall forever.

Those behind the falling monsters didn't even hesitate, most leaping over the new hole in their arena with sheer glee in their eyes – the chance to *actually kill someone* after an eternity of fighting and killing foes that rose back up after a few moments.

Carl cleared his throat and I felt his hand slap against my chest, gently shoving me back.

Talon helped him, jumping in front of me and using his other hand to push me back further until I was standing beside Virgil, panting. I was fucking exhausted. Breaking that floor had been... so hard. Impossibly hard.

So what the hell was Carl doing?

I gripped Virgil by the robes, snarling into his face from inches away. "Get. Us. *Out!*"

Not a flicker of concern crossed his face. What could I do to him? He was already dead. Other than the slight inconvenience of dying and having to put himself back together after, he didn't have anything to worry about. Let the bully monsters slap him around a bit, eviscerate him, steal his lunch money, whatever. He would soon stand back up, brush off his robes, and continue on with his daily work.

But *we* weren't dead. We couldn't just walk away from this.

"You'll want to see an Elder at work. It's a rare sight..." Virgil said, glancing past me. I spun, frowning. I had seen Carl fight before. It was amazing, but not enough to stop the tide rolling towards him.

Carl gripped two swords in his hands, held high and out as if... No. What was he doing?

Then he began to sing. That *Sound of Music* song again. As he did, he flicked his swords back and forth like a conductor would direct an orchestra. His voice had never been designed for singing, not even close, but he gave it his full effort.

And as he flicked his swords back and forth, directing his nonexistent band of musical instruments...

Bodies exploded in clouds of frozen gore.

Then charred ash.

Then smoke.

Then motes of dust.

In fact, each tone of his voice seemed to hold a different finishing move. High pitches were shattered ice. Low pitches were dust – nothingness. Long, drawn out notes were explosive, gory detonations.

The army of monsters died screaming, one by one, several at a time, or entire sections where he pointed his ivory swords. Talon's eyes were wide and his jaws hung open, his spear the only thing seeming to keep him on his feet.

Carl glanced back at me over his shoulder, smiling delightedly. He even flung a hand my way and I jolted in horror as if he was attacking me. Then I realized he intended for me to sing with him. Not knowing what else to do, I joined in with a stunted, rasping voice. And felt something latch onto my mind like a rope, drawing something from me to wrap around those ivory swords like ribbons of white silk.

He drew those cords from me, twirled them around his swords, and then flung them out.

Alaric Slate, airborne and only a dozen feet away exploded in a shower of golden dust.

My eyes watered as I sang louder, stunned, but realizing that I was... smiling. This felt...

Good. It wasn't that he was taking anything from me, but rather like he was showing me how to efficiently use my power in this place. As if he was driving the car that was Nate.

Gateways of white fire appeared in the center of the arena, right where the rear faction of the monsters were now trying to run away from the musical onslaught of Elder Carl. They ran straight through the Gateway and only bones erupted from the other side, still smoking.

Talon joined in the chorus, and I saw red ribbons rip out of his chest, almost ethereal. They twined around Carl's other sword before he flung them out. Where he pointed his sword, the monsters collapsed into thinly sliced strips of steaming flesh – as if struck by a thousand swords simultaneously.

Only a minute had passed before it became obvious that all the monsters were fleeing from us.

Carl stopped singing, and then gave the arena a formal bow before sheathing his swords.

The Calaveras stared at us. The monsters were huddled against the back wall of the arena, as far from us as they could get. I stared at the dead bodies, what remained of them. They were going to get back up any second. None of this really mattered. I spun to Virgil. "I think we should leave now..." I whispered, hands shaking.

He nodded, and calmly turned to resume his walk away from the pits.

I kept an eye on the arena as I backed away. Some of the bodies began piecing themselves back together, but for others it would be a longer process.

Carl smiled at me. "You did well, Temple. With practice, you could do much more. Do you have something to eat in your purse?" I found myself reaching into the satchel blindly, not even correcting him. I pulled out a bag of jerky and handed it over. He tore it open, tossed the trash on the ground and walked past me, chomping on a long strip of jerky as he hummed to himself. He didn't look back at the arena. Talon shot me a very deep look.

"This is not the end, Temple!" a very distant, but familiar voice snarled. Alaric.

I just turned away, trying to remember how to use my legs as I followed Carl and Virgil. With the amount of magic Carl had... helped me use, I should have been unconscious. But I wasn't. Stunned, but not drained. As if him using it through me had prevented me from dipping into my well of power. Or was it just because we were in Hell and my body couldn't sense how close it was to exhaustion? To giving up. To dying. Because I was already dying.

"How do you feel, Wylde?" Talon asked in a hesitant purr.

"Hungry," I said, surprising myself.

He frowned at me. "I meant... emotionally."

I blinked at him. "Don't tell me hungry isn't an emotion, because I feel that shit in my soul."

CHAPTER 40

To prove the point, I reached into my satchel and pulled out two more bags of jerky. I opened one and handed it to Talon. He took it with a sigh, numbly popping a piece into his mouth as he stared at Carl who was actually skipping behind Virgil.

We left the white district without further fanfare. I glanced back to see a wall separating us and let out a sigh of relief. We walked down another set of descending bridges and sloped ramps that crossed back and forth impossibly, but these were made of diamond or clear crystal of some kind. Talon's tail twitched at every flicker of shifting light, but he managed to restrain himself.

We didn't speak. I was too lost in my thoughts, Talon was too frightened of Carl or possibly feeling inadequate as my Shadow – my protector. Carl was too busy sightseeing, frolicking, or singing.

Virgil was Virgil, the awkwardly silent taxi driver.

After what felt like a few more hours, we reached a yawning lake that stretched as far as the eye could see. A lake of blood. Boats drifted here and there full of clouded masses that resembled huddles of souls. I studied them, wondering if Charon was present, or if these were maybe trainees for his replacement when he was too hungover to come to work. Which was probably often.

No boat was at the shore before us, but Virgil waited patiently, not informing us of anything. I went back to studying the lake. Two waterfalls, each a thousand feet high could be seen in the distance – raging, white capped rivers of blood crashing down into the lake. Detritus fell down those waterfalls, too, looking suspiciously like drowning humanoid figures, but it was too far away to be certain.

A low gong echoed through the cavern, and Virgil walked out onto the roiling water. "Don't fall in," was all he said, not even glancing back at us. I blinked, turning to Talon and Carl. As they looked at me, I almost took a step back. Their faces were... slightly blurred. Like a charcoal sketch that had been smudged with a thumb. I could still make out their features, but only with effort. Their bodies were the same. Smudged.

They looked just as concerned upon seeing me, telling me all I needed to know.

I set my shoulders and strode after Virgil. "Let's hurry. There's nothing to be done about it."

I heard them murmur their agreement as I stepped into the water.

But my foot didn't break the surface. I glanced up to see Virgil calmly walking across the constantly roiling lake of blood, also not breaking the surface. He didn't stumble, even when the water dipped and rose beneath him. Almost like he was hovering over it, but he wasn't. He was walking on top of the blood in his sandals without faltering once.

I took another step and wobbled as the surface shifted up and then down beneath me. Like a fucking Ninja Warrior obstacle course. Not wanting to get too far behind, and knowing that Virgil wasn't the kind of guy to wait, I pressed on, hands out for balance as I struggled after our guide. Talon and Carl seemed to be faring much better behind me, but then again, reptiles were used to all sorts of awkward perambulation, and cats had an uncanny ability to always maneuver easily and land on their feet.

Fumbling, bumbling wizards, though? Not so much. I gritted my teeth and hurried as best I could. Just because my feet didn't break the surface didn't mean my body wouldn't if I fell. Remembering what Virgil had said, I crouched down and brushed my hand against the lake of blood. My hand dipped below the surface like any other body of liquid and came out bloody.

I shivered, quickly wiping my hands on my pants as I straightened. My companions grumbled at the revelation – that any misstep could send us into the lake, and that the results probably wouldn't be favorable. We had to keep our feet.

I had a few near falls, but Talon and Carl kept an eye on me, steadying me often.

At one point, a boat drifted before us, chopping the wake not a foot in front of me as I stared at the huddle of tortured souls in the boat. I didn't give them my full attention, because my eyes kept darting from the blood I stood on, to the boat cruising right through the same substance, the impossibility of it all making me stumble as the bloody lake shifted up and down, side to side.

We continued on once it passed, and spent the next hour crossing that lake. We reached the waterfall surprisingly fast, and I glanced back at where we had started. It seemed impossibly far away, too far for us to have walked so quickly. I suppressed a shudder and pressed on. Virgil walked under the waterfall, the blood striking an unseen dome that abruptly appeared over his head. He stopped, motioning for us to hurry.

I did, trying to urge my feet faster. That's when I slipped.

I felt Talon's claws slice through my shirt as he darted to catch me, but he missed. I struck the bloody lake and sank like a rock. I paddled and kicked as hard as possible, but it was as if I weighed a million pounds as I saw the surface stretch further and further away.

Mmmmm... a bubbled voice gurgled in my ears. I flinched, spinning back and forth to spot the threat, but saw only crimson darkness. *So sweet, a wizard's blood. Screams so delicious. Bones so crunchy, like shouts of ecstasy in our soul. Sweet spurts of lust and snarls of greed. This one has LIVED, but now he shall die. Forever.*

Forever, a new voice agreed.

Forever... A dozen voices this time, all around me.

A crashing sound from up above. I looked up, clawing my hands for the ever-distant surface, and saw a white shape slicing through the depths after me, black fangs extended and snapping like a pale crocodile. *Sobek,* I thought absently. The Egyptian crocodile God. I flinched, struggling to escape before it latched onto my hair, grabbing a fistful.

Then I was rising with impossible speed, unable to see anything through the swarm of bubbles around me.

Nooooo!

He was OURS! The other voices shrieked, screamed, and roared in those bubbling tones.

I suddenly gasped as I was tossed out of the crimson lake. Strong paws caught me, held me close to a cold chest, and then began jostling me up and down as if trying to shake out loose change. I heard a roaring sound and then I was dumped onto solid ground. Talon stared down at me, shaking me. I blinked at him. "I'm... I'm fine..." I rasped, coughing and wiping at my eyes.

He nodded and then spun. I saw Carl walking calmly towards us, spitting blood from his mouth. He looked more smudged, and not just with charcoal, but with a wine color mixed in.

Talon let out a breath upon seeing the Elder, and when I looked at him, I noticed he had purple smudges around his body and face. I scrambled to my feet and saw Virgil watching us. "We shall rest. We are almost there."

"If we're almost there," I growled, wiping more blood from my face, "then let's get moving."

Virgil shook his head. "The door opens in two hours, by your time. We don't want to wait outside the door. This place is safer. If any place is safe here."

I considered his words, with nothing about his face to tell me whether he was lying or not. I finally nodded. "Two hours."

He lay down on the rock floor and closed his eyes. I frowned at him. Why did he need to sleep? Wasn't he already dead?

A paw gripped my shoulder, gently forcing me down to the ground. I tried to fight it, but something about the touch made me obey. As I sunk down to the ground, even though I was arguing in my mind that I should stand watch this time, I felt lethargy deep in my soul. I finally sat down, letting out a deep breath. I wasn't sure if I was exhausted from trying to swim or walking across the damned lake.

Talon studied me. I could still make out the scars bisecting his eyes, but much of it was blurred. Like a smudged painting. "Sleep. We need you at full strength. I don't think – despite our strengths," he added, glancing back at Carl, "that we can leave this place without you. This man is hiding something, or at least not telling us the full truth. I fear his price."

"I'll pay the price and get us out of here. Don't worry, Talon."

He nodded distantly, and the smudged face wouldn't let me determine if he was confident in my answer. He placed a furred paw over my eyes, forcing them closed.

"Sleep, Wylde. Sleep..."

CHAPTER 41

*M*emories – like gossamer threads of love, illuminated by starlight, swamped me.

Chateau Falco stood below me, strong, defiant, a bulwark of hope against a world gone mad.

Roland and Alucard stepped through a Gateway of crimson liquid, like blood.

I stared at the treehouse, a leaf blowing past the white sapling.

Tory placed a hand on the Huntress' shoulder. They both cried.

Flash.

Flash.

Flash.

I woke with a gasp. It took me a moment to get my breathing under control, to remember where we were. I waved down Talon and Carl. I couldn't see their faces clearly, but their posture was aggressive. Defensive.

Those... dreams couldn't have been memories. Not all of them. I'd never hovered above Falco. Well, when I had been falling from Olympus after fighting Athena, perhaps. Or maybe when riding Grimm one day, but I didn't immediately recall anything like that.

Maybe... I was seeing through another's eyes. Thinking back, I analyzed the visions. I had felt... taller, as if seeing everything from a different elevation. I blinked. Alex? Was I seeing through his eyes? Had Pandora bonded us somehow? Or maybe the Ravens? Was I seeing through the eyes of Hugin and Munin? They were on my Crest, a part of me, whether I understood it or not. Then again, if Alex's last name was Arete, he was tied to my crest, too.

Not that it really mattered, but it made me feel... detached. Not knowing the answer left me troubled. Was it a warning? Or a sign? Was it in the past? Future? Present? Or was I simply having bad dreams because I was napping in Hell, high on vaping sulfur?

Whatever it was, I was here for a reason, and whining about dreams wasn't getting me any closer to leaving. Virgil waited for us to be ready, and then simply turned away.

We didn't see anything particularly horrifying on our walk. Mostly we just saw tunnels. For a long time. We came out of one – like a dozen others – and I felt as if I was walking in a trance. Nothing changed, maybe different rock walls, but just more of the same, on and on and on ad nauseum.

Virgil chose different directions at forks in our path – I no longer bothered to count how many, reminded of his comment about counting – as if he knew the way by heart.

Then, I realized he had stopped at an open space. I gasped, woken from my daze.

We stood at the mouth of the tunnel, staring down into a cavern of polished obsidian. The steps before us were as ornate as a palace, lined with large bowls of silent black flame that seemed to cast a silver light, leading down into an expansive courtyard. Frescoed ceilings were splashed with hieroglyphics, Greek battles, and Norse runes. Columns of freshly polished, crimson and black marble, easily ten feet in diameter stretched a hundred feet into the air as if supporting the painted ceilings. The floor was one solid sheet of mirrored glass. Or liquid metal, I wasn't sure which. It reflected the frescoes high above, creating a distortion, as if the place was much larger than it really was – and if any place needed to look larger than it was, it was not here.

In the courtyard, dozens and dozens of Calaveras lined a wide walkway that led to an empty black throne carved with roses. I jolted, suddenly wary of possibly meeting Lucifer himself.

The Candy Skulls watched as we descended, their heads rotated impossibly to watch us without their bodies shifting. They did twitch occasionally, cocking their skulls sideways as we walked between them towards the large, black throne. They didn't attack, but they looked ready to do so. Many of them were different forms of arachnid-like creatures the size of cows, but I saw a few that resembled the bodies of ogres, trolls, even some made of rock, not wearing robes. They all seemed to sniff the air as we passed, and a whistling noise escaped from behind their masks as if they were excitedly sucking in breath through their teeth. Or as if their windpipes were too decayed to simply let us hear them inhaling in a normal fashion.

Or maybe they were just fucking whistling in approval.

Behind the throne was a turbulent sea of fiery magma, black spires like oil derricks clawing up from the raging ocean. I couldn't see the ceiling, but black and green lightning hammered down across the horizon, slamming into the lava. Each strike birthed a new stone spire, but occasionally those forks of lightning would strike an already existing spire, obliterating it into a million pieces of rock that splashed back into the molten sea, then melted back to whence it came.

I turned back to the throne and froze. It was no longer empty.

A tall bare-chested man sat gripping a bronze staff with alternating stripes of blue glass, obsidian, and gold, the top of the staff a flail of sharp, glass beads that seemed to absorb the silver light from the bowls of black flame on either side of his throne. Light, athletic muscles were obvious under his oiled, bronze skin, similar to my build. Okay, maybe bigger, but not by much. White wraps of gauze covered his abdomen and he wore a shimmering golden kilt with sapphires sewn into the knee-length hem – unless the skirt was actually metal, like chainmail.

I couldn't see his face because he was wearing a tall black mask that almost anyone could have recognized, regardless of their faith – a black jackal.

The mask had two tall pointed ears and a long thin snout. Where his eyes should have been only a dark, almost indigo flame, like I was staring into the deepest part of the universe, a black hole devouring a star. He bowed his head slightly and thumped the butt of his flail into the floor. The Calaveras crashed to their knees, if they had them, doing that odd whistling sound.

"It's so good to see you again. Call me Lord. Or Anubis," he said, staring into my soul.

I replied with a slight dip of my jaw, wondering what the hell he was talking about. *Again?*

"Anubis..." I replied formally, surprised to find him in charge. I may not be an Egyptian scholar, but even I knew there had been a change in leadership – that Osiris had stepped in as Lord of the Underworld at some point.

"Of course it's a fucking dog. Hell is run by a fucking canine!" Talon breathed, barely audible, not sounding the least bit pleased.

Anubis barked at him and Talon flinched, fur puffing out like a blowfish all over his body as he fell to all fours, arching his back. He hissed instinctively, hopping sideways a few times.

I blinked at Talon in astonishment.

Anubis roared with laughter, his face unchanging. "Oh, this will be so much fun. I hardly get out anymore..."

CHAPTER 42

*A*nubis studied the three of us, still chuckling as Talon stood back to his feet, licking his fur dejectedly, pretending none of us had seen anything amiss. I let it go, because the fact that Anubis hadn't taken offense to it removed all shame. Well, some of it.

"When you made that sweet, magical decision, *I want to go to Hell*... I was quite *satisfied*, you might say. Odin – against his will, I might add – was forced to make good on a favor he owed me from *way* back. You remember now, yes?" he asked.

I tried to hide my surprise. "*You* were the guy in the hood..." The mysterious guy that Odin had brought before me, asking if he was *satisfied* after they watched me for a few moments.

He held out his hands dramatically. "Couldn't stay long, you understand. Can't leave this place unguarded. The residents get... uppity. But I sent my wardens to keep tabs on you in my stead." He pointed at the Calaveras. "I still had to wait for Death to arrange the meet. Formally. Pity the Calaveras never caught you. Your trip would have been so much easier, and less costly."

I blinked, opening my mouth and then shutting it. The Candy Skulls had been... trying to give me a ride? And I wouldn't have had to risk... I took a deep breath, not even wanting to hear the details or I would do something drastically stupid. I followed Othello's advice.

"Anubis..." I said instead, shaking my head. "I honestly didn't see this coming."

Anubis leaned forward. "Anubis gets all the chicks." I guessed he was technically right, being Lord of the Dead. He got all the chicks *and* dudes, in the end. Just... sloppy seconds. I very wisely didn't voice that thought.

"What about Osiris? I thought he took your place?" I said, hoping he couldn't read minds.

He waved a hand. "With Isis giving him that new golden... confidence-booster and then ditching him after she got what she wanted – her son, Horus – he found other ways to occupy his time. I discreetly took back the throne to leave him to his... hobbies. It's amazing what a woman will do for a bar of gold." He winked at me. "Or for a son. Like Horus." His eyes flared for a second. What the hell was that supposed to mean?

Talon and Carl shared a look, not understanding the conversation in the slightest. Their faces, if anything, were almost entirely smudged now. Like greasy, black stains.

Anubis scratched at his ear absently and I swore I saw his foot quickly tap the floor as he did. *No*, I thought to myself. *Did he just... like a dog when someone scratches his ear?*

"Well, what is your request? May as well get on with it. No use burning daylight."

Anubis was apparently very lonely down here in Hell. Like he had been saving these jokes for eons, and we were now his captive – double entendre intended – audience.

"Surely, you already know..."

"I don't get much conversation down here. Humor me, *Hope*." I stiffened as his eyes locked onto the necklace at my throat. "Unfortunately, you won't find much use for that down here," he said, suddenly pointing his flail at my necklace. "I must take precautions, you see, to keep my... citizens safe. Like any good King. Always looking out for their best interests," he said, waving a dismissive hand, as if mocking the words. But the way he said them hadn't sounded dismissive at all. "Even when they don't always realize it."

I hesitated. With my friends looking so... distorted, had my priorities changed? Was he subtly hinting that it was more important to take care of *them* than my personal ambition in speaking with my *parents*? Or he was trying to derail me from talking to them. Frighten me.

I realized Anubis was staring at Virgil, frowning, as if I had missed a conversation. Then those indigo black eyes latched onto the Candy Skulls and I saw them all wilt, practically lying prostrate on the floor.

Talon and Carl were both fingering their weapons nervously at the sudden tension.

"You were *attacked* on your way down here?" Anubis snarled in outrage. I frowned. How would he have not learned this until now? Was he playing a game with me? Trying to see if I would buy such a weak lie? He shot them another withering glare. "This should not have happened," he warned them in a low tone. As I watched, I began to think that he really might be annoyed, and I wasn't sure I wanted to witness the Calaveras punishment. If *life* was torture down here, what constituted *punishment*? "They must have been so interested to see you appear during the inmates' recess, that they forgot their job. I can't just kill them, though. Obliteration is the only exit from this place, and only a god can do that. And I won't grant them *that* mercy because good help is so hard to find down here." He finally turned back to me. "That being said, I now owe you repayment in addition to the original agreement you made."

I pondered the conversation, ignoring the topic of punishing the Candy Skulls. Anubis would hold to the original agreement *and* grant me repayment. Perhaps the repayment could be to not pay for the request. I doubted he would go for that. Probably why he openly stated that the original agreement still stood.

Maybe I could ask to heal my friends as this repayment. But one thing at a time. I had come here to talk to my parents, risked our lives for it. That came first. The fact that my parents had been stashed down here in the first place, so hard to reach, pretty much guaranteed they knew something important. And judging by several of Anubis' comments, I felt mildly confident that I could negotiate the safety of Talon and Carl as this *repayment*. I locked eyes with Anubis, doing my best to look confident and in control as I faced the Lord of the Dead.

"I want my parents."

"To take them back home?" he asked in a wry tone. I shook my head. Anubis watched me, curious. "Interesting. To see or speak to them?"

"Both."

His fingers tapped the arm of his throne thoughtfully, as if considering the dangers. "Hmm... Well, let me see your satchel," he finally said. "You obviously aren't carrying anything else useful, and you mentioned gifts.

Unless *they* are the gifts," he said, pointing at Talon and Carl. I shook my head quickly before they could agree. Something in his tone had sounded almost... eager at mention of my satchel. Could he sense the things inside? Not having much of a choice in the matter – because I could sense Carl and Talon didn't have long if the smeared look was any indication – I handed it over, keeping my face blank.

As I did so, I discreetly focused on my satchel. Anubis unceremoniously upended it like a bag of trash before his throne. Nothing valuable came out. At least... nothing that I didn't want him to see. Instead, a stream of weapons, blades, bandages, clothes, and food fell to the floor. I winced as I saw a thick glass vial fall, landing on a pile of silver chain Talon had wanted to bring – a cat-o'-nine-tails, ironically – a whip of sorts.

I let my face flush with guilt as he slowly looked up at me. Oh, he didn't look pleased. Nothing about his face had changed, but his aura suddenly seemed furious. "Quite a few... weapons. Does this imply you wished to attempt force? Against *me?*" he chuckled dryly, but his attention shifted back to the pile. He toed some of the items with a boot, grunting at the vial. "A sample from the River Styx... Interesting. Is this your *gift?* Water?" he spat.

I shrugged sheepishly. "I doubt you wanted any of that floating around up above," I said neutrally. "Unless you want more men like Achilles." Because the water of the River Styx was rumored to have made him all but invincible. Except on his heel.

Anubis scooped it up, hefted it in his palm a few times, and then set it beside him before resuming his casual search of the pile of items at his feet. Then he scowled. Maybe he had expected to find something specific inside. The Hammer? The Hourglass? The Hand of God? All were inside, safely tucked away. He lifted the satchel to his nose, sniffing. He snorted, and then stuck his whole freaking head inside, ears and all.

I blinked, sharing a stunned look with Carl and Talon. At least, I think their return look was stunned. The smear made it impossible to tell. Was there any danger to him sticking his head inside my pocket dimension? Could he see what I had hidden?

His muffled words made me flinch. "Something strange about this..."

Ice shot down my arms. "The satchel is very strong. Try slicing it," I offered in what I hoped sounded a casual tone.

He pulled his head out, shook it like a dog would, and then studied me.

His hand instantly changed to a black set of claws that matched the material of his mask – and he slashed at it.

Nothing happened to the bag. Anubis grunted in surprise. Then black shadows abruptly infused his arm and I felt the sudden power practically vibrating the air itself. He had turned on his godly steroids. The world dimmed at the arrival of the shadows around his arm, and screams echoed inside my cerebral cortex as he slashed again, a full body motion.

I hoped Darling and Dear had a good return policy. *A dog destroyed my satchel.*

CHAPTER 43

The smoke faded to reveal Anubis staring down at the satchel in disbelief. I tried to hide my own astonishment. Darling and Dear were hardcore, and apparently Anubis wasn't on their email list if he couldn't recognize it. At least I could tell Callie the leather-makers weren't Egyptian.

He hung the satchel on the arm of the throne and was suddenly crawling around in the pile of weapons. I heard the Candy Skulls murmuring uneasily, and even Virgil's eyes widened at the sight of his King on all fours digging through the items from my bag. He even scooped up a few to sniff, as if hoping to find it wasn't what it appeared to be. Some illusion, perhaps.

He jumped to his feet, breathing heavily. "Fine. You may keep it," he snapped.

The bag was suddenly on my shoulders again, sans the armory of weapons he had dumped onto the floor. I didn't feel a thing. One moment he had been holding the bag, and the next it was on my shoulders.

I dipped my head gratefully, waiting. He tapped his obsidian mask, looking angrier by the second – even though his mask didn't actually change. Something about his posture promised unrestrained fury, and he was struggling to keep that down. "None of the keys," he muttered under his breath. Virgil frowned at him for the length of a heartbeat before his face returned to bland nothingness.

Keys? What was he talking about?

Anubis slammed his palm down onto the arm of the throne, and a dozen bolts of lightning lanced into the lava ocean behind him, either erupting in more pillars or destroying those already in existence, depending on which lightning bolt I focused on. "Bring them out," he finally snapped at the Candy Skulls. He turned to me. "This is as much for you as it is for them, but speak quickly. You don't have long…" Then he laughed, a sad, disgusted sound. Maybe Anubis had a few screws loose after spending so long in the Underworld. His people skills – and personal control – were sorely lacking. The absurdity of pressing for time in Hell, where everyone suffered for eternity.

He didn't speak, and was obviously waiting for my parents to arrive. Or he had forgotten about us, because he was leaning back, staring up at the ceiling and breathing deeply, as if trying to calm himself.

Talon and Carl were only smudges of darkness, now, and I knew they wouldn't last long. "Why do we look like this?" I asked Anubis, pointing at myself and then my companions.

He lowered his head very slowly, chest heaving in silence. I forced myself not to take a step back. "They are dying," he finally said. "As powerful as they are, they cannot last long. Only a god can survive down here." His eyes twinkled.

"That would have been nice to know ahead of time," I growled, glaring daggers at Virgil.

Talon spoke up uncertainly. "We also glow gold?" he asked Anubis. I whipped my head to him. Talon was staring at his arms as if searching for proof.

"Gold?" I asked him. "No, you're smudged gray, like a charcoal sketch."

Talon and Carl both stiffened, then slowly turned to me. Anubis roared with laughter. He pointed down at the mirrored floor for me to look. I did, and almost jumped. Rings of concentric light spun about me – weak, but definitely noticeable. And my skin… glowed faintly. But my eyes… were sheets of molten gold. I looked from Talon and Carl back to myself. We looked nothing alike. When I had seen them staring at me, I had thought I wore the same smudged look. But I only saw the golden glow in the reflected floor, not when I looked at my arms directly.

"What is the meaning of this, Anubis?" I whispered.

He leaned forward, his pulsing aura directed solely at me, no longer amused. "You murdered a *God*. Athena... You're still stained by it, but not enough. Never *enough!*" He cackled, a harsh, pitiful sound. I stared down at my skin, searching for the once-familiar golden veins as I tugged my sleeves back. I hadn't seen them in quite some time. To be honest, I had thought they were long gone after I used the Hammer to destroy the tree and free my Beast, Kai.

After about ten seconds, I finally saw a flicker of golden light. So faint it was almost unnoticeable – I only saw it again because I stared for ten more seconds, and knew what I was looking for. As if it took a long time for that miniscule sliver of ichor to circulate through my body. I couldn't see the rings of light rotating around me unless I looked at the reflection. Same with the eyes, obviously. And in the reflection, my very skin seemed to glow with the golden light, but when I looked with just my eyes, no such glow was visible. Was this how everyone saw me down here?

"It is not enough..." Anubis whispered to himself. No one else seemed to have heard. His head abruptly shot up, staring past us. "Say hello to mommy and daddy for me. But remember, your friends don't have long..."

Anubis dismissed us with a flick of his hands.

And we were suddenly standing on the edge of a crumbling stone cliff overlooking the ocean of lava.

CHAPTER 44

$\mathcal{W}$aves of magma at least a dozen feet tall slammed into each other as the sea raged. I stared across the ocean of liquid rock, trying not to flinch at the occasional lances of green and black lightning that struck down from the impossibly high ceiling where clouds of black, tinged with red festered. I frowned, staring at a tiny cliff in the distance. It looked like it bore a black throne... Was that Anubis? Where we had just been? No wonder I hadn't seen the ceiling over the ocean. That cliff with the throne looked tiny and about to be swallowed up by the lava ocean.

I heard a grunt behind me and flinched. Two smudged faces stared across the ocean of fire at the black throne... at least I think they did. The lighter one spoke. "You should step back from the edge..." Carl said nervously.

I nodded, glancing down at the cracked, worn rock with sudden panic. I was only inches away from taking a dive.

The other figure – Talon – snorted in disbelief, pointing down at the ocean of fire.

I followed his gesture to see a lone boat zipping through the waves, looking like an elaborate canoe, but without a driver. A long black cord stretched from the back of the boat, tugging...

I blinked, my jaws falling open. A familiar robed figure gripped the cord with one hand, riding a long, thin sliver of stone like a wakeboard. His other hand held a beer. He poured it over his face, and I noticed the familiar, sewn up lips. He waved his beer at us and continued on, jumping over a particularly large wave, landing with a splash of magma.

"Charon..." a woman's voice murmured behind me. "The only smile I have seen down here."

I spun, heart wrenching into a knot. My mother stood before me, smiling sadly. She looked gaunt, dirty, and hollow, but at least she wasn't smudged. She wore tattered robes, like strips of dirty cloth that fluttered in the waves of heat. A sob bubbled up from her throat, her face anguished as she threw her arms out. I took two steps and scooped her up, crushing her to my chest.

She felt so *real*.

Not like a spirit at all. Which meant more to me than anything, that I was able to actually *touch* her rather than talking to her shade.

"Mom..." I whispered. The word broke her, and she almost collapsed in my arms, but I didn't let her. I clutched the back of her head, mumbling incoherently, forgetting all questions in my sudden swell of emotion. My mother. She was sobbing into my neck, rubbing my back in soft circles like she had done whenever I had nightmares as a child. She even murmured the same words she had told me then, now. "We don't tell fairy tales to teach you to fear monsters, but to teach you how to *beat* the monsters..."

I squeezed her harder, my vision a blur, my cheeks drenched with tears. "I know, mom. I know... I'm trying. I'm trying so *hard*..." I whispered, shaking.

A throat cleared and I stiffened, looking up. I wiped my eyes, staring at the other figure that I had completely forgotten. My dad. His face was pale, tear tracks trailing down from his eyes, smearing the soot on his bearded face. That was the only sign of his crying – just the tears – no sobbing, shaking, or shifting of jaw. Just tears.

"If that devil woman would let go for a moment... I would like to hold my son..." His false bravado did crack at that, but he weathered it well. Just one more tear rolling down his cheek.

My mom, Makayla, detached herself from me with a sad bubble of laughter. She shot him an arch look and then stepped aside. "Watch your tone, Calvin," she whispered, tears pouring down her face as she watched the two of us as if witnessing an impossible dream come true.

I held my hand out for a shake, but gasped as he lunged at me as if to tackle me into the lake. He picked me up like I was a boy again, spinning me in circles as he gripped the back of my neck with his thick, calloused hand, holding me like a lifeline. "Nate," he rasped, finally overcome with emotion as I felt him shudder as he held me tight, setting me back down.

I squeezed back just as tightly, missing his solidness. Like a boulder in a raging river. Even though he was overcome with emotion now, that inner confidence roaring inside him was still stronger than any man I had ever met. Not arrogance, like me, but a solid, unwavering center of self. "Wylde, dad. Wylde..." I whispered. He shuddered harder, his muscles bunching as if he'd just been struck by a whip, but it didn't shake his embrace, as if knowing and accepting those lashes with pride and relief... that I finally knew the truth. My birth-name.

"Talon?" I heard my mother whisper in a throaty cry. "It *is* you! Talon the Devourer!" she shrieked, giggling delightedly. My dad finally set me down, gripping my shoulders as he stepped back, studying me with glistening, proud eyes. A flicker of something else danced there, too. Hope? That his choices had resulted in this... in *me*?

Then he shook his head and laughed, a pure, sharp sound like a struck bell. As if nothing could break him. He wrapped an arm around my shoulders, turning me back to my mom who was squeezing Talon as if he would disappear if she let go. He stood awkwardly, but he did brush his chin into her neck, and his tail curled around her lovingly. Fucking cats.

Carl cleared his throat, extending a hand towards my father. "Hello," he said. "I am Carl." My father hesitated only a moment before accepting, and pulling him in for a hug, slapping him on the back in gratitude. "Thank you. For keeping Nate... Wylde safe. Thank you for being his friend, Elder Carl..." Carl nodded, matter of factly, before they detached.

Then he turned to my mother, studying her. Then he took two strides towards her, wrapped her up in both arms to pick her up, and then spun her in a slow circle. She gasped in surprise, but it soon turned to a joyful laugh. He sniffed her hair loudly before setting her down. My dad looked startled at the greeting, but he didn't interfere.

"My son," my father said. I wiped my nose before turning to him, remembering Anubis' warning about time. That my friends didn't have long. "We should talk."

I nodded, following as he led me a pace away from the edge of the cliff, a hundred feet above the raging ocean of lava. We sat down, Talon joining us to sit on my father's other side. They embraced warmly, speaking softly to each other, but my attention was distracted by Carl as he spoke to my mother. I glanced back, staring in startled disbelief.

"I must know the secret," he insisted. "A woman of your worldly experience must have vast understanding of the D..." If I had thought it impossible for a shade to blush, Carl just disproved it. Luckily, my father hadn't heard. Elder or not, there were some things that just shouldn't be asked of another man's wife. Or a guy's mom.

Fucking Carl...

To my surprised horror, my mother nodded with a wicked grin. "A little coaxing and passion can do wonders to find new life..." she began as they walked further away. Carl leaned in closer, nodding as he listened to her share the secrets of the D.

I was going to kill Alucard.

My father caught my attention with a question. "Is Falco well?" His face was guarded, as if unsure which lies to admit to first. I was angry, of course. All the secrets they had kept... but anger wouldn't help anyone. This was the last I would ever see of them. What was done was done. Now was the time to make their choices mean something.

To turn this fucking lemon into lemonade.

CHAPTER 45

$\mathcal{I}$ took a deep breath and caught him up to speed, knowing we were short on time. To help me best, he needed to know everything that had happened. So that he would know if it tied into any of his... lies of omission. The schemes they had set up. He would be the most help if he knew the full story, so in quick strokes, I told him everything.

My mother and Carl joined us not long after I began, so didn't miss much. Carl and Talon remained silent, seeming absorbed in Charon's lavaboarding skills as he zipped back and forth before us like a frat boy showing off to a sorority. It gave my eyes something else to focus on as I spoke, which was better than staring into my parents' faces, which were full of pain and guilt.

At all the pain I had been forced to endure because of them. They didn't look regretful of their decision, only resolved to hear every dark detail. What they had put their son through. Like spanking a disobedient child – hating every second of it, but knowing that the child needed to learn this harsh lesson in order to grow.

Even if delivering the punishment made the parents cry with guilt for the rest of the night in the privacy of their own bedroom.

When I finished, they shared a thoughtful look, as if silently discussing what they needed to say and how it fit into what I had told them. They didn't bother apologizing, or commenting on my new friends, asking about my love life, or anything like that. But I could tell they wanted to – desperately wanted to hear of at least one happy, frivolous moment in my life. But they knew that all my hardship was a result of their choices – and that it had led us to this cliff, me risking my soul to find them in the depths of Hell to finally get the answers I deserved.

The answers I needed.

"You're glowing…" my dad finally said. "It's beautiful."

I nodded. "Apparently, not enough," I sighed, feeling a brief flash of despair. Had this all been for nothing? What had Anubis been looking for? Keys? The Godly power flowing through my veins not being enough. Enough for what? Was he trying to use me? Take something from me? There was only one way to find out. I'd have to ask him.

My father interrupted my thoughts by suddenly grabbing me by the shirt under my jacket. He ripped it away in one swift motion and I gasped. Like yanking a table cloth from under a table set with china – not disturbing a single dish – my jacket remained in place. He tossed the shirt into the lava far below and then pointed at my chest. I looked down and saw the golden glow was much more prominent around… my heart. Still not strong, but definitely concentrated there.

"Follow your heart, my son," my father whispered sadly. "It is stronger than it seems…"

"Right. My heart," I mumbled with a frown. It sure didn't look like there was enough of the golden light to make a difference. And make a difference with what, anyway?

My mother placed a hand on my thigh. "Have you met a boy all alone? One unbroken by hardship?" She sounded resigned – as if hoping and fearing the answer at the same time.

I thought about her question. Who did I know that *hadn't* survived hardship? Tory had a whole school of kids who'd survived a terrible existence. I frowned as another face came to me. "Alex?" Pandora had sure been interested in him, and my parents had sure been interested in Pandora. I told them about Alex, what he'd been through in Fae. How I had kind of adopted him.

She sighed, drooping like a kite with cut strings. "This… Alex is vital to everything. Much like you, his situation is more than mere happenstance, whether he knows it or not."

My dad spoke up, absently scratching the ground with a loose rock.

"Family can save you. Protect your family, always. You never know when they will return the favor." I frowned at his doodle, my skin suddenly standing up on edge.

Sorry. They're listening... was scratched into the rock. My mother pointedly ignored it, gesturing at Charon as he did a barrel roll in the air. Only I had seen the message. My dad scuffed it out with a frustrated gesture, watching me out of the corner of his eyes.

We were being *watched*? I wasn't that surprised, really, but it pissed me off. That here I was, having risked it all to talk to my parents, and that now that they were finally willing to speak openly, they feared doing so. Meaning whatever they were not saying was very, very important, and must be kept secret. I paid very close attention.

"Like a later inheritance, for example," my dad continued in the same tone. "Passing on your wealth to your offspring like we did with you. Gives you a leg up in the world. And your inheritance is vital. Is Temple Industries doing well? It's important. I put my life into that," he said in a warning tone. In the dirt, he had scratched another message.

Fuck the company.

I blinked rapidly, trying to keep up. "I... lost it. With the Brothers Grimm..."

He growled, kicking out a leg in frustration, conveniently scuffing his message.

My mother sighed empathetically, squeezing my thigh. "Well, don't waste the rest of your inheritance. You should have plenty to rebuild as needed."

Her eyes flicked to my satchel, but the rest of her body didn't move. "I wish you hadn't come to this hellish cave. This ocean of stone. This mausoleum..." she said sadly, wiping her nose for effect. "I didn't want you to see us like this... In the House of the Dead..." her eyes again touched my satchel, but she disguised it well.

Those words... were specifically chosen. We had often played games like this. Hiding conversations within conversations. A family pastime.

Cave. Ocean of stone. She was talking about our cave in Fae, where I had been born. Where we had watched thunderstorms rolling in over the ocean of rock. Where Pan had given me the War Hammer.

And the *House of the Dead. Mausoleum.* She was referring to the Temple

Mausoleum... Where they had left the Hourglass and the Hand of God for me.

Inheritance, indeed.

I squeezed her thigh in a specific pattern, trying to calm my racing pulse. "I had to see you again." My squeezes spelled out *YES* in Morse Code. She sobbed at the gesture and message, placing her hand atop mine. If I had been wrong about the secret conversation she would have looked at me strangely, for squeezing her leg in such an oddly specific sequence. "As painful as this is, I will hold this memory close to my heart for the rest of my life," I said, letting my hand – seemingly coincidentally – brush my satchel. *They will always be safe beside me*, the gesture said. "I always hoped I would see you again," I added with a faint smile.

She nodded sadly. "Hope... such a small word. And, of course, the first letter has three parts, like you three heroes. Three lines that form something greater, a cornerstone. A foundation. Strong enough to come down to even this place..." She blinked as if at a new thought, then smiled. "Not unlike our family, back together against all odds," she smiled, nudging both mine and my dad's ribs playfully. She leaned forward, making a show of picking up a rock.

"Oh, not your doodling again. He's not a child, Makayla," my dad complained tiredly.

"Hush, Calvin," she chided sternly. "This is about how we met. I've always wanted to tell him myself." My father sighed in resignation, but his eyes were tight with concern. She turned back to me. "Humor an old mother for a moment, Wylde." She started, as if the name had been an accident. And perhaps it was. Or perhaps it wasn't. "Two arrogant wizards with the same goal, but not romantic together." She drew two parallel lines. "Then..." she added a horizontal line connecting the two, and forming an *H*. "You came along and brought us all together... Made us a family." Her eyes confirmed to me she wasn't just talking about us three. Or even Carl, Talon and me.

Was she referring to my inheritance? The three things they had given me?

The Hand of God.

The Hourglass.

The War Hammer.

"Three lines... Three... Such a powerful number," she mused, sounding lost in her thoughts. "Like a pyramid or tripod, perhaps…. It can't stand without that third leg, can it?" she murmured absently. The Hand of God was shaped like a pyramid… Or was she talking about Talon and Carl keeping me balanced? She drew the letter *A* into the rock, making it look like she was just fidgeting to avoid looking in my eyes.

She was trying very hard not to say something. *A* for… Alex? Arete?

"All vital. Without one, the tripod falls. A strong blow from a hammer can knock these sticks down, of course." She scored a line through her drawing, but her eyes flickered to where Anubis' throne sat in the distance, making her warning obvious. Anubis was a hammer that could destroy them. But… why didn't she hide this warning?

"But the right hammer can also forge things together with the right heat. Three legs… A young man can be equally important," she said, jerking her chin towards Talon and Carl. "But I guess it all depends on what the leg is made of. An empty pyramid wouldn't be valuable without treasure inside, of course. Bah, I'm just babbling now."

My dad spoke gently, placing an arm on her shoulder. "I think what she means is that you three are important. Friends are important. Family is important. Keep each other safe, and your heart will never be empty."

My mother nodded in embarrassment, but I was getting confused. Were we talking about us or the inherited gifts? Or both? At least I knew that if I was confused, anyone watching had to feel drunk. My mother smiled at us warmly. "My Three Musketeers. All for one and one for all." I glanced down at the dirt where my dad was scratching absently, but not looking at his hand.

For = are.

I kept my face blank. Switching words? I replayed my mother's statement, replacing the word *for* with *are*. All *are* one and one *are* all. I had no idea what it meant, but if I ever got out of here, I was going to have a migraine.

"We love you, my son. My Wylde…" she laughed messily, ruffling my hair. "I've wanted to call you that again for so long…"

"Never fear for us, Wylde. We love you, even if we never showed it properly. We gladly accept the consequences. Temples always pay the piper. No one else pays our debts."

I barely concealed my jolt at the phrase. *Pay the piper…*

As one, their gazes locked across the ocean of lava towards Anubis' throne, and they evaporated into puffs of smoke.

A moment later, we were suddenly standing before the throne again.

"So, your parents want you to pay the piper, do they?" Anubis said, sounding amused.

CHAPTER 46

I scowled back at him for good measure. "You listened in? How... considerate of you."

His fingers clenched the throne as he leaned forward. "This is my *home*, Wylde. I may do as I wish." He studied me skeptically, as if trying to decipher the rest of our conversation. I just glared back. I could barely understand what our conversation had been about, so I had little fear he could. Hell, maybe he could explain it to me.

We stared at each other in silence. Something was bothering me about him. I expected him to be grumpy, agitated, even a giant asshole. He *was* all that, sure, but something was... off. Like he was personally angry with me for something I had done. Or hadn't done. He'd mentioned keys, and that I didn't have enough of the golden light. And that his wardens would have taken me here without all this trouble. All this cost.

Maybe those glass blades had been offering hugs.

I suddenly realized I had no shirt and that my coat hung open. It was too late to hide it, so I just glanced down. My chest glowed with the golden light, visible to all. I looked back up at Anubis uncertainly.

He shook his head. I could have sworn I heard him murmur *still not enough!*

I was just glad that I hadn't just ruined everything by revealing what my father had shown me.

234

"Your request was granted, but now it is time to pay," Anubis snarled in a harsh tone. Even though his mask didn't show emotion, I was sure he smiled as he abruptly stabbed Virgil in the chest, ripping out his heart in one swift motion. My heart almost erupted from my chest, and Talon and Carl were suddenly gripping their weapons.

Anubis slowly lifted the still beating heart up before him, showing the three of us. Virgil folded to his knees, staring through vacant, pain-filled eyes. Was he still in there? He hadn't ever showed emotion before, but something about that blank look screamed agony.

"Eat. And welcome to your new home. One of you at least. I have need of a new guide."

I stared at the Lord of the Dead in horror. "What?"

"Dante has fulfilled his duty. It is time for the next guide to take his place. To learn the map."

"I don't care about Dante!" I argued. "I'm talking about Virgil!" I pointed at the dead poet.

"Those who accept the protection of a guide must replace him. In your case, you wisely brought two candidates with you. One of you must pay the price and become my new guide. Dante replaced Virgil, now one of you must replace Dante. The Circle of Life," he chuckled darkly.

I shook my head slowly, thinking. "One of us must stay and learn the map," I said.

Anubis grunted. "This is the map," he said, shaking the heart in his fist. "Take a bite and gain knowledge of the paths of Hell. All paths. All ways."

I shivered, even imagining eating the proffered fruit of knowledge and the disgusting twist on the apple from the Garden of Eden story. Then I had an idea. "Wait," I shouted, flinging out my hands as I sensed Talon and Carl readying themselves to take it before I could. They grunted, pressing against my palms as a sign that if my plan didn't work they were going to go through me to get to that heart.

"Virg— Dante said we could also pay with something other than a life. What is the price?"

Anubis almost shattered the heart in his fist and those indigo sockets of flame for eyes pulsed darker, if at all possible. He pointed at my glowing chest. "You don't have enough to pay!" he spat angrily.

And I suddenly understood why he had seemed so angry. He had wanted my god juice. But... I didn't have enough in me. Even seeing the concentration at my heart, it wasn't enough to slake his thirst. But for him to be angry meant that he hadn't wanted one of us to replace his guide.

He had wanted that power instead.

But already knowing I didn't have enough power, he had started off by killing Dante.

My parents had called me the Catalyst. Which meant the precursor. Maybe my time had ended. I had been the Catalyst. For whatever this was. I had kicked off... whatever was coming. I was the glue that held everyone together. The last piece... But by myself, I was just a lone *line*. I needed my friends – the other two lines – but they needed me, too. To form our triumvirate.

I couldn't let my friends pay this price. My parents had said that we all needed to watch out for each other. That three legs were strong. I didn't understand all of it, but I was confident about this. The three of us needed to survive. To keep each other safe. Which meant that whoever remained down here needed to escape. Somehow.

Carl, who had risked his life repeatedly down here to keep me alive and fight back my enemies. Even though he had repeatedly made it sound like Hell would be fun for him. But even as powerful as he was, he didn't stand a chance of escaping. And he didn't have the motivation. He would calmly accept his imprisonment, never trying to escape, because he hadn't understood the subtle messages my parents offered. He would proudly pay the price of his life to keep me safe, and that was that. He might even *like* it down here, judging from what I had seen.

Talon was physically strong, ruthless in battle, and loyal to a fault. He would pay this price for the young boy who had given him a name. He would pay the price of being my Shadow – my guardian – without blinking. He would be so satisfied with the fact that he had done me a solid, that he would never try to flee – to tarnish his last act of devotion to his friend.

It had to be me. I was the only asshole stupid enough to attempt a prison break. The only one possibly strong enough.

Temples always pay the piper. No one else pays our debts.

I still had my satchel. With the three items my mother had mentioned inside. Anubis hadn't taken my Horseman Mask away. He'd said he had nullified it, but maybe I could find a way around that. I was clever. Sneaky. And had always found a way to pick up some new magical trick that pulled my ass out of the fire. Whether I knew a way out or not, I was the only one who had even the slightest chance to get back out.

I knew that if I left one of them here, I would never be welcomed back to rescue them, and that even if I could, I would be right back in this same position – with someone needing to replace the guide – either Talon or Carl. Which defeated the purpose, because they would ultimately die. The only way out of this was to become the guide and find my own way out.

And that person had to be me.

Talon and Carl surged forward on either side of me, as if sensing my inner decision, but I suddenly cast a whip of red fire at the heart, snatching it up and yanking it back towards me. Anubis didn't even flinch in fear, although I heard the teakettle Candy Skulls hiss in outrage behind me, fearing I had attacked their boss.

I caught the ice-cold heart in my fist and took a bite before Talon and Carl could do anything to stop me. *Pay the piper...* I thought to myself.

Sugary sweetness rolled over my tongue as the flesh disintegrated like cotton candy in my mouth. It tasted like... an apple. I shivered at that thought, swallowing it. And liquid metal roared through my veins as the hammer of knowledge abruptly pounded my mind like it was an anvil. The paths to Hell were seared into my brain with each hammer stroke of my heartbeat.

Talon and Carl faced me, their faces slowly clearing of the smudges to reveal outraged horror.

"I thought it would be you," Anubis muttered. "Such a foolish mortal. To lose it all to talk to mommy and daddy again. Only to walk into your own prison cell right beside them." I flinched at that. His icy smile held no humor. "Figuratively speaking, of course. You won't be talking to them again. Ever." He shook his head, brushing off his hands. "Don't you realize how pointless that was? To risk your life to only pay with your life?" He sounded angry. Angry at the situation. Angry that I hadn't been able to pay him with power – the golden light of a dead God.

"I've never claimed to be that bright. But I always pay for my ignorance." I tried to ignore the constant pounding in my temples.

The fire in his eyes made me frown. As if briefly letting me know he would have given almost anything for Talon or Carl to have taken the heart first. Or just regretting my lack of god juice.

"Time to say goodbye to your friends," Anubis said coldly.

237

Talon shook his head at me, tears leaking down his furred cheeks. Both angrier than he had ever been and terrified for me. Perhaps even for himself. I was the only family he had.

Carl studied me with narrowed eyes, as if trying to read my mind, or find a way out of the situation. I smiled sadly at him.

"Brothers, keep my friends safe. Please. It was an honor to know you. To fight beside you."

I couldn't let them think of a rescue. I couldn't voice that I would do my best to be my own rescue. I couldn't give them false hope like that. It would eat them alive for the rest of their days. And I didn't want to alert Anubis of my plan, either. I was about to hand over my satchel – someone needed to take care of what my parents had warned about – when they simply disappeared. My hand hadn't even begun to move yet.

I gasped, rounding on Anubis angrily, ready to demand to know where he had sent them.

"Don't concern yourself with them. They are home in your world," he muttered. "I'll take you to your rooms." He climbed down the stairs in swift strides, grasped my shoulder before I could open my mouth, and we were suddenly in a world of darkness. We stood on a red stone dripping with blood, almost slippery with it.

But around us was nothingness.

I had the sensation of movement, but there was simply no way to tell.

I grunted, almost gripping my head as the pounding flared hotter for a moment. I closed my eyes and a massive, dauntingly complicated labyrinth was clearly floating in my mind. Paths, levels, stairs, holes, traps, caverns, crisscrossing all over this world.

The map to Hell. I hissed at the pain, but also the magnitude of it.

It was nothing like Botticelli's illuminated manuscript. That was a toddler's finger-painting.

The map was so large and complex that my hope of ever finding a way out died by suicide right there. I could never walk that far, and I hadn't been given a key like Virgil.

It would take years to truly understand the place, let alone map out an escape plan.

And every step I took would be through other prisons, other cells, not even counting trying to sneak past the Candy Skull wardens. It was hopeless.

Anubis grunted, still gripping my shoulder with his obsidian claw. Not hard enough to pierce skin, but not light enough to let me detach myself either. "The pain will fade soon." He let out a light laugh. "Well, the pain of the *map* will fade. Your position as guide is somewhat better than the other residents, but I only have one open cell that can contain you at the moment. Until you are called upon, you are much like any other prisoner. Confined to your cell." I looked up at him and realized how tall he was. His chest was directly in line with my eyes, that regal black jackal head staring straight ahead. Despite no opening in the mouth, his voice was clear, not muffled.

"I had such high hopes for you, Temple. Such high hopes."

I blinked at him. "I didn't really know what I was walking into. Maybe if I had been better prepared..." I muttered. "Like telling me those clowns were offering me a free ride."

He grunted. "You have never known what you are walking into, and are rarely prepared, yet you have always prevailed. I had hoped for the same today..." he trailed off. His tone was kind of like my father used to tell me *I'm not mad at you. I'm just disappointed.*

I opened my mouth to ask what he was talking about, but he interrupted me.

"I mentioned repayment for being molested on your way to my throne. If I were you, I would consider the advice many give on surviving the first day of a prison sentence."

I was suddenly standing in a small cavern – relative to the rest of Hell anyway. It was actually quite large, but closed off. It was a cell, not just a random cave. But at least it wasn't pitch black or anything. Ambient light illuminated most of the cell, only leaving pockets of shadow in the corners. I didn't question it. If invisible light wanted a certain section to remain dark, so be it.

I spun in a slow circle, shoulders itching from Anubis' parting comment. I snarled as something shifted in a shadowed corner. Apparently, Anubis' definition of taking me to my rooms was dumping me into a fight pit.

Because I wasn't alone.

Find the biggest, scariest bastard in the yard, and pummel him like a lunatic. That was the way to survive your first day of prison. Or at least your best chance. To make an example of the worst of the lot. Or at least someone with a lot of clout.

A hungry, familiar chuckle rumbled across the room and I readied myself for a rematch with one of my oldest friends.

CHAPTER 47

A hulking, winged monster stepped out of the shadows, puffs of steam clouding before him as his golden snout came into view.

Alaric Slate.

This was Anubis' definition of repayment? The old Dragon King stared at me with so much hatred, I should have just dropped dead.

"Temple..." he growled. "Oh, I've wanted to talk to you for quite some time."

"Funny. I had forgotten all about you, Al."

He snorted angrily at the nickname. I somehow managed to not feel guilty about it. "How is my son? That conniving black stain on my family tree?"

I tapped my lip, thinking. "Oh, Raego? He's doing wonderful. The dragons worship him, talking about how much better things are with Weird Al gone. Did you know he gave me a medal for taking you out? I would show you, but I must have left it on my trophy case back home. Oh, and I redecorated my throw pillows with some really flashy golden scales." I eyed him, frowning. "Kind of just like those," I said, pointing at him.

His eyes crackled with fire, but then he began to laugh. "Humor. I had forgotten about that. You just don't understand, do you? You can't die here. We get to fight each other for eternity... And... you without magic... Oh, this isn't Hell. This is HEAVEN!" he roared.

I blinked, frowning. What? No magic? I reached for my power and… felt nothing. Not even a whisper of it. I concealed my panic as I tried to tap into my Fae powers.

Nothing.

Alaric continued to laugh, each outburst like a punch to my soul.

What the hell kind of repayment was this? I swore to myself, right there, that I would kill Anubis if I ever got the chance. I would spend eternity making his life miserable. Somehow. Anything I could do to make him regret this. After all that talk, almost sounding like he regretted my plight. My failure. The bastard had conned me, and was likely laughing his ass off right now.

I needed to stall. I still had my satchel. Maybe something inside could help me. Not forever, but enough to give me time to think. Even the best blade wouldn't last for an eternity of heavy, daily use against a powerful golden dragon.

"Were you close with Gertrude?" I asked, stalling.

Alaric snorted, caught off guard. "That viperous bitch would betray anyone for power. It's why I banished her." I frowned, not being aware of that. "But then if I had remembered how much she hated your family, I might have sent her to St. Louis ahead of me to take you out. Or die trying," he muttered, not sounding as if he cared one way or another.

"Why would she hate *me*?" I asked, actually interested in the answer. I hadn't met her until after I killed Alaric, so how could she have hated me before *that*?

Alaric prowled in a slow circle around me, licking his lips. "Your parents. They stole from her. A blade of some kind. But it was the principle of the matter. She didn't like anyone making her look the fool."

Not that it did me any good now, but I cursed my fiendish, thieving parents.

"How about we don't fight?" I said, keeping my eyes on him as he continued to circle me. "Might be roommates for a while. Would suck for you to walk around like a cripple forever. Literally forever. We could draw a line down the middle of the cave or something," I said, quickly checking my surroundings. Only rock walls surrounded us, obviously, but something about the space directly behind him seemed different. A slightly different color to the wall.

Alaric noted my attention. "I wouldn't get too close to that door. If you get close enough you can somewhat hear the poor bastard on the other side. Then again, you won't have any time for exploring, what with the never-ending death you'll be experiencing."

"What does it feel like? To die and keep coming back? Is it like when you lizards lose a tail?"

He licked his long teeth in a relishing gesture. "You'll see soon enough. Not a pleasant experience, but you'll get used to it. Kind of." He let out a low laugh, crouching low in readiness to pounce. "This is the first joy I've experienced since you put me here. I'm going to savor it."

He launched himself at my face. I had already shoved my hand into my satchel, thinking desperately for anything that could help me. Something strong enough to keep this fucker away long enough for me to find a way out of this shithole. Because as impossible as it seemed, my only other option was to deal with this motherfucker for eternity.

I'd rather opt for the hopeless escape plan.

My hand latched around an unfamiliar haft of wood and I yanked it out.

A black spear appeared from those bottomless depths, throbbing faintly under my palms. I didn't have time to question it, but I knew for a fact I hadn't put it in there. The last I had seen it had been in the Armory. *Sneaky, sneaky Pandora.* I spun the spear as I lunged out of his swipe, the spear feather-light in my hands as it scored across his shoulder. He hissed in outrage, and the red gem on the stone throbbed as if eager for more blood.

Or as if drinking his injury.

We both frowned at that.

Then it winked out.

He laughed, and backhanded me into the wall behind me. I slammed into the stone, seeing stars. He didn't wait for me to recover, slicing across my stomach with his claws. I groaned in agony, falling to my knees. I stared down at my open stomach, the death blow.

I could see – quite too clearly for my taste – my insides.

And how torn and shredded they suddenly were. I gasped as I bled out, watching in shock as Alaric calmly walked back up to that wall and sat on his haunches, smiling at me. Waiting for me to die and come back. I struggled to hold onto my spear, using it was the only thing keeping me from falling over. I stared up at the black blade, too disgusted to continue looking at my wound.

It was the spear I had seen in the Armory. The intricate one with the red gem in the center of the wide, almost axe-like blade. It kind of looked similar to Talon's white spear. Except he didn't have a giant gem in his. Mine was cooler.

Not that it mattered now. My strength drained out of me as I slowly died. I fumbled with my satchel awkwardly, remembering that I had something I was going to grab before that golden taxi across the street hit me. And why was it parked facing me?

What was that rushing noise?

A traffic light above me flashed red and then fell, slamming into my stomach.

Of all the damned luck. St. Louis drivers were the worst!

CHAPTER 48

I hissed as the traffic light struck me, gasping as it scalded my stomach.

"No!" someone roared from not far away. Little late for a Good Samaritan to help me. A fucking taxi had just blind-sided me and then I was hit by the traffic light he had obviously ignored.

My head cleared in an instant. No. Not a taxi. Alaric Slate, a golden dragon. Raego's dad.

Not a traffic light... I looked up at the spear in my fist. The ruby held no light. I glanced down at my stomach, grimacing in pain, but transfixed as I watched the flesh knit back together. Not perfectly, but closing the wound. Healing it.

I glanced back at the spear with a frown.

It had... healed me? Whatever it had done, I could sense that it was entirely out of batteries now, unlike the faint thrum of power I had felt when first touching it.

I met Alaric's enraged eyes. "I'm not dead yet. Tis merely a flesh wound!"

He snarled back, flame dribbling from his lips. "Bet it doesn't work twice!" He lunged.

Still on my knees, I dropped the spear flat to the ground, dipping under his outstretched claws and bringing it up directly beneath his jaw. He grunted and gurgled as his weight wedged the spear into a small crevice in the rock floor. I slowly shambled to my feet. The blade had pierced clean through his lower jaw, his tongue, and his upper snout so that the ruby glittered between his dazed eyes.

Not wanting to waste a moment, I reached into my satchel, my hand clasping around a familiar hilt. The golden light around my chest winked out, and sucked into the War Hammer as I pulled it out. I willed every drop of godly power that still flowed in my veins from killing Athena, all that golden ichor, until I was sure not a whisper of it remained in my body or soul. Maybe it would be enough if I could combine the two.

Enough for Goldschlager here, anyway.

Obliteration is the only exit from this place, and only a god can do that… Anubis had said. The power of a God. True death wasn't possible here. Just never-ending torment. Despair.

The War Hammer fairly crackled with golden light, fingers of lightning dancing across its stone surface. Alaric's eyes danced in both pain and fear.

"Fuck obliterate. Taste Dominate!" And I hurled it at his face from two feet away with every ounce of power my muscles could muster as I screamed.

The hammer crushed his face entirely like a boulder thrown at a wet sheet. I watched, caught off guard as his entire physical being rippled, jerked backwards as the Hammer sailed through him. My spear toppled to the floor unbroken as Alaric Slate simply *melted*, sucked into the Hammer as it flew to the opposite side of the cell…

And slammed into the wall he had warned me about. The one with the crazy guy on the other side. The Hammer flashed even brighter as it struck the wall, sending golden bolts of lightning like a spider's web across the surface, cracking the stone. Then the hammer fell to the ground, lifeless.

And the wall crumbled to dust, glittering faintly as the cloud rolled into the prison.

I heard a rasping, throaty laughter from the dark depths beyond and shivered, reaching for my spear in desperation. What the hell had I just done? And what had happened to Alaric? And who the fuck was laughing? But no light came from that dark hole. He must have lost his light privileges at some point. Probably because of his creepy laugh.

A dark blur, like one of those sooty smudges drifted out of the cell, hovering over the hammer as if studying it. "Empty, now…" it rasped in a sound like a stone sarcophagus sliding open.

I stared in horror, wondering what the hell it was, and if my new roomie was nicer than the last one. Despite the obvious wards on my cell, this... thing dripped with raw power. Wild, erratic power, as if it couldn't quite be contained in the shade. That – without a body – it was now just a sentient storm cloud constantly stabbing lightning at anything that came too close.

It was more power than I had ever seen in one space, and I had the impression that it *had* been a human – once – because the shape was vaguely humanoid.

It seemed to turn its attention to me and I scooted back against the wall, gripping my spear before me defensively. "You're welcome, man," I said quickly, taking credit for his freedom.

The form shifted back and forth thoughtfully. Then that chilling voice echoed like dry leaves in the cell. "Thank you, boy. You just won't do..." it added, sounding disappointed. "You're almost empty as well. I'll just have to settle for the Nine Souls... Yes, they will suffice."

Then it simply drifted past me, right through the rock wall. I spun, pounding on the stone. "Hey! Tit for tat! Let me out of here! We're roomies!" I shouted.

But the form was gone.

The Nine Souls, it had said. Virgil had mentioned something like that, hadn't he? And how had it simply shifted through the walls? Hell was designed to contain shades, so how had that bastard broken out? The other wall had contained him just fine.

I glanced into that darkness and shivered. Whatever had been keeping him in there was stronger than the cell holding me now, and this cell had already muted my magic. Or taken it entirely. But... that smoke dude obviously had his power still. Why?

I studied the War Hammer thoughtfully, not daring to walk over and pick it up. Not yet. I didn't want to go anywhere near that hole. What if it sucked me inside, hungry for a new occupant?

I had filled the Hammer with the last of my Godly power – although not enough to interest Anubis – and obliterated Alaric, relieving me of the headache of constant death while I tried to find my way out of this place.

But that plan had backfired. I had freed something obviously quite dangerous. And now it was just a stone Hammer. Had I broken it? Whatever it really was? My parents had made it pretty obvious that it was important, but that shade hadn't seemed to care for it, and I had a feeling he would have picked it up for his own if it had been powerful.

So... my *birthright* – as it said on the stone hammer – was now just a lump of useless rock.

Or was it just sapped from spending time in Hell? Like...

I glanced up at the spear in my hands. Pandora had obviously snuck it inside my pack, and it had somehow healed me from death. Not that I was sure it had needed to waste its energy on that. I was in Hell. I couldn't really die here. But it had healed me, that stone flashing red. Holding it now, there was no thrum of power, almost as if I had imagined it. I tugged off the silk bags hanging from the base of the blade and gasped. Two feathers – identical to Grimm's – hung freely. Black, with dripping red orbs on the tips.

This was it. I just knew it. Pandora had saved me. I called out to Grimm, ready for the quickest prison break in Hell's recorded history, imagining the stories I would be able to tell.

A whole lot of nothing happened. I frowned at the spear, shaking it. The feathers swayed back and forth at the motion, doing nothing remotely magical. I glared at the weapon, muttering Grimm's name a few more times. Still, nothing. The blade itself even looked like the feather, now that I thought about it. Fat lot of good that did me.

Just a spear.

And across the cell, just a hammer.

I waited for some kind of alarm to go off and Candy Skulls or Anubis to come storming in, demanding to know what I had done. But no one did. Maybe they didn't even know anything had happened. I had made a lot of noise, but this was Hell. Kind of a noisy place, what with all the inconsiderate victims screaming and whining as they were mutilated for eternity.

Maybe the noise had gone unnoticed. *Must be Tuesday again. Damn Larry and his weekly flaying. All that screaming is enough to keep a guy up at night. I'm going to complain to the wardens. This time I promise. I've had enough. He's gone too far.*

I realized I was having an entirely fictional sitcom in my head and stopped with a sigh.

After an hour of waiting in silence, watching the Hammer, the opening into the adjacent cell, and my spear, I finally gave up. I spent a considerable amount of time with my eyes closed, letting the pain of the map to Hell sear through me, relishing the sensation. It was better than fear, and I couldn't do anything until I got used to it, became numb to it.

I needed to know the place, map my way out. It truly was a labyrinth.

I remembered the arch from the beginning of our trip so long ago.

Abandon hope, all ye who enter here. Then I began to laugh. Wow. If that hadn't been a warning... My friends had been forced to abandon me, the Horseman of Hope.

Talk about irony.

I saw the districts Virg— *Dante* had mentioned. The different realms. I saw the Field of Reeds. Elysium. The Christian Hell. Nirvana. Tartarus. Even what looked suspiciously like Heaven with a towering set of Pearly Gates. I saw Purgatory.

Although it initially didn't make sense to me – seeing all the conflicting religions' versions of the afterlife all in the same... city – it slowly began to make vague sense to me. Like the five boroughs of New York. Rough areas. Pleasant ones. Each soul categorized and filed away into their respective retirement home.

I didn't receive any insight on exactly how that filing system worked – for example, a Christian going to either Hell or Heaven – but I saw the distinct, convoluted path to physically get to either destination. Which meant I wouldn't be able to publish my book *What really happens when you die – a memoir.* I realized I was humming Carl's song from the Sound of Music and cut off abruptly.

"Too soon to get stir crazy," I said aloud to the empty room.

But I would have given anything to hear him ask about the D again. Anything.

"This place sucks. Maybe I shouldn't have killed Alaric..." my words echoed back to me, somewhat distorted from that open cell shrouded in darkness. I stared at it curiously, wanting to know what was inside. Then I shuddered. Maybe later. Curiosity killed the... I sighed.

Talon. I hoped he would have a long life without me.

I hadn't gotten any real sleep in a long time, and I felt drowsy. I checked to make sure that I wasn't actually bleeding to death again, verified I was as healthy as possible, and closed my eyes for some shut eye. Thankfully, none of my neighbors made any noise.

CHAPTER 49

I was retracing my steps through Hell. Whether more of those odd flashbacks or a result of studying the new map in my mind, I wasn't sure. It almost felt like I was seeing it from one of those drones that adrenaline-junkies use to follow them on their mountain bike rides or surfing videos. Watching my steps through Hell from a slightly higher perspective.

Tartarus.

The white arena.

The black forest.

The ocean of blood.

Staring into Anubis' face as I felt a faint humming in the air, but heard no sound. Since I couldn't read his motionless lips, I just got to see him for a solid minute, staring back at me intently. I saw his fingers tighten on the throne a few times, but that was it.

I woke with a groan, my eyes crusted from the dirty air. "Need to replace the air filters," I muttered, climbing to my feet. I ached from sleeping on the stone floor. Even using my coat as a pillow – although I didn't remember taking it off – hadn't helped much. My fingers also ached from gripping the stupid spear, which I had apparently slept with like a security blanket.

I walked the room in an effort to alleviate my tight muscles.

Also, to make sure I was still alone and that no one else had moved in.

I realized I was staring at the opening to the darker cell. "Or moved out," I said out loud.

No one answered. "Hello?" I asked, peering inside, but not taking a step closer. No one responded. I scanned as much as possible from the safety of my own cell before taking a deep breath. In an intimidating shuffle, I scooped up the War Hammer and bravely ran away from the opening, breathing nervously as I glanced over my shoulder. No one attacked me.

I studied the War Hammer in my hand, sitting down where I had gone to sleep. I hefted it curiously, trying to sense it with my mind. But I gave up with a grunt, because I had no magic available to me. It was just a rock on a stick to me. A pretty one, but that was it.

The word carved into the side mocked me.

Birthright.

With an angry sigh, I set it down so the hilt stuck straight into the air.

I soon pulled out the Hourglass from my satchel, the one my parents had stolen from the Fae Queens so long ago. It controlled, or at least prevented time slippage between the two realms – earth and Fae. So that one didn't have to worry about spending an hour in Fae and returning to find a month had gone by. I set it before me and stared at it, replaying everything my parents had said. All the cryptic shit that didn't matter anymore since I was trapped down here, in Hell, with these oh-so-important things that somehow needed to help protect the world upstairs.

To protect my friends.

And the items were locked up here with me, Anubis' new enslaved Uber driver, working only for tips, thank you very much.

I set it down beside the Hammer. No magical solution appeared.

Just to be thorough, and because my calendar was pretty open, I pulled out the Hand of God. A glass pyramid with the crumbled sand from the original stone Hand of God I had stolen from Athena. I lay on my stomach, lifting it up occasionally to study it from every angle. I tapped at the glass with a fingernail, making sure different sides didn't have a different sound or something. I even shook it lightly and made a wish like a magic eight ball. I stared at the sand inside, scowling as I imagined a response.

Ask again tomorrow...

I almost hurled the glass pyramid across the cell at the imagined response. Instead, I calmly set it down beside the other two items my parents had left for me.

I waited, studying them one after another. I even rearranged them in all possible orders. I stacked them. I spoke nicely to them. I cursed them.

They stared back at me with pompous sneers.

I found a sharp rock and began drawing on the wall. Thinking of my parents, I drew an *H*. Then a letter *A*. I stepped back, studying them. I glanced back at the three items on the floor and then back to the letters on the wall.

I continued writing the letters, hoping that repetition would yield the desired answer, like with sports, dribbling a basketball for hours every day paid off in the long run. I wrote the letters in different sizes, fonts, and angles, peering at them studiously. I found myself very angry after half an hour or so of this when the piece of rock suddenly broke in my hand, halting my very important analysis.

I stepped back to inspect my work, and realized I was staring at a wall that said…

Ha hahahahahahahahahahaha. Ha. Ha. Ha. Hah!

The wall was laughing at me. I sat down with my back to the laughter so I wouldn't see it and lose what little sanity I had left. The three inherited items before me laughed anyway.

I closed my eyes, thinking on my conversation with my parents. Because I needed it, I spent the most time remembering those first few moments. Hugging my mom. My dad. Carl asking my mom about her vast experience with the D. I felt myself finally smiling, so moved onto the rest of the conversation. Their words had been so freaking cryptic. They knew we were being watched and, finally, had wanted to tell me everything. To come clean.

But because of whoever was watching us, they couldn't.

After going over it what felt like a hundred times, I came up with no new answers. At least, no answers that would help me now. These items were important, and I needed to do something with them. To stop something from happening on earth – or in Fae, possibly. But now they were trapped down here with me. Untapped potential.

I spent some time studying the spear, but other than being exquisitely pretty and well made, it was just metal and wood. I could sense nothing special about it. Probably due to the wards on my cell, since I had failed to touch my magic – about a dozen times now so far. It looked like one big feather from Grimm, and the two feathers hanging from the blade were also identical to my alicorn. I again considered Talon's spear. It was very identical in style to this one.

I reached for my necklace and unclasped it, staring down at the coin. I closed my eyes and tried to feel something. Anything. The metal disc was cold in my fingers, not even a flicker of response. I didn't need magic to use it, at least I was pretty sure, so it should have worked.

I tried imagining it into looking like one of those Candy Skulls. Maybe I could use it as a disguise. Changing it from Mask to a random item that could be concealed had never taken magic before. It simply changed if I needed it to. Like the other Horseman Masks. A way to conceal what it was. Also, so they didn't have to walk around with those frightening Masks on all the time.

The coin sat in my fingers, unchanging.

"Looks like Anubis was right," I muttered. He'd said he had blocked my Horseman's Mask, but then again, Death had warned me not to even attempt using it, so it was probably for the best. I might accidentally end up letting some other poor bastard out of his cell.

I reached inside my satchel, pulling out a large, black feather. Grimm's feather. It was a perfect match to the feathers on the spear. I closed my eyes, took a deep breath, and deciding it couldn't hurt, I called out to my friend again.

"Grimm."

Nothing happened.

"Grimm, Grimm, GRIMM!" I shouted.

I waited ten seconds before cursing, tossing the feather on the ground as I bumped the back of my head against the rock wall. I felt nothing. Heard nothing. Sensed nothing. Grimm's arrival was always... climactic. Black lightning, murderous scream, sparking hooves, enemies dying...

Looked like the architect of this place knew his stuff. Either these things didn't work in Hell, or they didn't work in this *cell*. Seeing as how I had been able to use magic as I traveled with Dante, Talon, and Carl, it must be the cell. If I could only find a way out...

A whole lot of nothing happened for a few hours.

At one point, I glanced down at the spear to see that Grimm's feather had landed beside the other two. I frowned, studying them, but gave up. It didn't really matter if I couldn't find my way out of this fucking cell, did it?

More hours went by.

I spent a good two hours stacking rocks in aesthetically pleasing piles around the cell in an effort to establish some Zen in my afterlife.

Then I spoke to the rocks, asking how long they had been down here. What kinds of things they had seen. What their favorite place to visit was. How old they were...

Realizing what I was doing, I spent ten minutes kicking them all down as I cursed up a storm.

Good grief, I wasn't good at this whole solitude thing.

I realized I was staring at that open cell again and looked away angrily.

"Not a good idea. Only bad things can happen from going in there..." I told myself as I climbed to my feet. "What if it closes up behind me?" Maybe I would be able to spot something from the outside, from a safe distance away, of course. I flung out my hand to cast a fireball of light inside. Nothing happened. "Right, no magic, you dumb boob," I cursed myself.

With a sudden thought, I went back to my satchel, reaching inside in hopes that Anubis hadn't shaken it out in his search for... whatever he had been looking for. The keys.

With a triumphant shout, I brandished three glow sticks, courtesy of raiding Yahn's sock drawer – rave accessories. I snapped the tubes, the cavern suddenly glowing with neon light, and tossed them into the open cell, spaced apart for maximum light.

My eyes widened in disbelief. The hole was... tiny. Maybe ten paces across and six feet deep. "Heh. Six feet deep. Hell..." I sighed, refocusing back on the walls. The green light cast strange markings on it so I took a few steps closer, not enough to let anything grab me, but close enough to squint.

I froze, blinking several times. The same few words were written thousands of times on the entire wall. The reason I hadn't at first recognized them was because – as the occupant had used up the last clear space – he had begun to scratch the words in a second layer over his previous etchings. My skin pebbled, both in confusion, curiosity, and amazement. To do this... thousands of times... he had either loved or hated these things. Since we were in Hell, I was leaning towards hate.

Camelot.

Arthur.

Merlin.

I stared at the wall for a very long time, wondering if I had just made things upstairs one hell of a lot worse – even from my locked prison cell.

I closed my eyes and said a prayer. "Help me, Brothers…"

I spent a long time waiting, but no one came to do so.

CHAPTER 50

*I*n my dreams, I sat on the cliffs over the edge of the lava ocean. Charon zipped back and forth, doing tricks or drinking beer behind his pilotless boat.

I was crying, but I didn't turn my head to see my mother and father behind me. I just stared out over the ocean of fire. Well, that was a shitty part to remember. It would have been nice to see—

My mother's face suddenly hovered before me, crying and sobbing uncontrollably as she nodded her head at me. Then my father's face, complete with tear tracks, and his face appeared desperate.

Then, nothingness.

I slowly woke again, this time holding myself with both arms wrapped tightly around my chest. I was curled in a ball and I could see my breath. Was it a change of season or was this some new form of torture? I pondered my dream. Memories. Whatever. Some form of torture?

I had at first hoped that it was Grimm or Hugin or Munin flying down through Hell to save me. But I had been here too long for that to be likely. I'd even considered it being Alex, since Pandora had been so adamant about me needing his help one day. And he was taller than me. Since the dreams always felt like they were aerial, it made sense.

But none of them could make it into Hell. Not without Death's help. And that would take time. It had taken him months to arrange for my trip here.

Had it *been* months, topside? I waved away that thought. Unlikely. Even if Death did help them in, none of them could survive the long way down here. I knew that now, being the new guide and all. There was literally zero chance any of my friends, even a swarm of them, could make it past all the Circles of Hell.

To put it bluntly, I wasn't even sure if the Four Horsemen and I, at full strength, could have fought our way down here. Because I realized where I was now. I was in one of the deepest pits that existed in the Underworld. Not as punishment – my pit was actually quite pleasant, even compared to some of the Nirvanas down here. Well, that was pushing it, but it wasn't a lake of fire or anything.

I was near Anubis' pyramid. Really, it was just a palace shaped like a pyramid, but it was the simplest way to put it. Basically, I was in his personal prisons. Not for a crime, but so that he could keep an eye on me.

Not that he had visited, the bastard, or he would have realized I was close to boredom-induced insanity by now. I wondered if he cared.

The only other option for my friends to come down here was to acquire a guide – me.

I would have been called to… well, *guide* them.

I realized I was laughing at the ridiculousness of it. Called out of my cell to guide one of my friends down to Hell to save me – their guide – from my cell. Which would culminate in Anubis ripping out my heart and handing it over to them to eat and take my place.

Worst rescue mission ever.

Which meant the dreams were probably just memories. Or something to do with the map. Or it was a form of torture unique to Hell. Or I was hallucinating from not eating or drinking anything in quite some time. Regardless, it wasn't helpful.

I sat up with a sigh, looking to my left out of habit, again checking to make sure I was alone. Not that it really mattered. I could have been murdered twenty times in my sleep, only to wake up again alive and well a few minutes later.

In case you're wondering, I was still alone.

Then I turned the other direction, yawning. My yawn turned into an awkward shout as I saw a cloud of tightly condensed mist not two inches away from my nose. I scrambled back instinctively, trying not to breathe any of it in, just in case it was a being of some kind. Accidental possession, or something. The cloud zipped back a few feet, quivering as if just as agitated as me. I didn't sense any malevolence to it, not like that dark cloud from the other cell, but it was still enough to scare the shit out of me.

"Wh-who the hell are you?" I finally gasped, realizing that it wasn't intending to apologize. "Don't you know to never creep up on a ninja when he's sleeping?" I panted, trying to regain my breathing. As I looked closer, I realized it wasn't entirely opaque. Faint green light shone through almost a silvery sheen, but maybe that was just a result of the glow-sticks not far away.

"Dad?" it said in a soft, frightened tone.

My heart stopped.

CHAPTER 51

I opened my mouth and then closed it. The cloud quivered harder, drifting slightly back and forth as if afraid. I stared harder, noticing the green flecks inside weren't caused by the glow-sticks. They were brighter. And the silver was actual silver, like mercury. They were familiar.

I gasped in disbelief, my eyes welling up as I slowly shook my head. My jaws ached in that way when you're watching a sad movie and you're struggling not to cry in front of your girlfriend. Or so I've heard – softer men describe it that way, at least...

I didn't quite know how to answer, but I managed to smile. A painful smile.

Like seeing a lost child reunited with his frantic mother after being missing for an hour.

"Your mother must be very worried..." I whispered gently, slowly lowering my hands before me. "This place is very dangerous. You should go. Your father would want you to go..." I whispered to...

The Baby Beast.

Falco's son.

Kai's son.

My... family.

It shifted back and forth uncertainly. Then it dipped down to the ground, lifting it up somehow. I unfolded my fingers to reveal the brand in my palm. The Temple Crest. A lone drop of silver and gold liquid splashed down onto the brand, and my body rocked with sympathy at the celestial teardrop. My crest suddenly grew warm and I felt something deep in my bones. Something alien and...

Protective as all hell.

"This is my mother..." the cloud whispered in a quivering voice, on the verge of more tears.

Ohmygod.

This was too much. My heart was ripping in half. Something about a child in danger just shredded me. But a Baby Beast? *My* Baby Beast? I suddenly recalled my palm flashing with heat and pain while walking through Hell. Had that been... Falco giving birth? My brand had flared with heat at this cloud's teardrop. Falco *had* felt it. But the sensation had been weak. Full of rage and anxiety and relief, but far, far away. Whether it was the distance that held her back, or whether she was too tired from giving birth, I didn't know. Too far away to protect her baby.

Tears poured down my face as I nodded, sucking in ragged breaths. "Yes, my boy. That is your mother, and she is very... special to me. She keeps me safe. Has always kept me safe..."

"I love her," the Baby Beast whispered longingly. "I miss her, but she was so scared for you."

My spine froze rigid, but the Baby Beast continued.

"I searched everywhere for you," it said. "I didn't know who you were, but my mommy misses you. She's so sad. I followed the signs," he said, another green and silver teardrop striking my palm for emphasis. "I followed them all. Then I followed your friends. Anyone who spent time inside my mother. I thought you must be my father. I wanted to protect you. To keep you safe for mom. To meet you... Aren't you proud of me?" he asked nervously, as if terrified to hear the answer.

I broke down, dropping my face into my palms and wept. I didn't know where to begin. To thank him, to scold him for being so reckless, to hold him tightly...

To tell him how incredible his father was. How he had sacrificed his life to keep me safe?

How his mother had kept my family safe for generations. Centuries.

How his father had done the impossible... That this beautiful Baby Beast

– who wanted nothing more in his so far short life than to go find and protect his unknown dad – was the first Beast born into freedom, perhaps in millennia. Or ever.

"You have no idea how proud I am..." I rasped. "Or how proud your father would be to see you now. Or your mother... You are extraordinary, my boy."

Suddenly, the silver and green cloud pressed against me, wrapping misty arms around me in a hug that only a child can give.

Those hugs that wrap around you like a Bandaid, conforming to every fold, crevice and bulge in your body without fear, judgment, or concern.

Pure.

Unconditional.

Love.

And it was the only thing that held me together as I gasped to suck in a breath over my tears. I wrapped my arms around him, squeezing as tightly as possible, the same as I had hugged my mom.

No.

Harder.

I hugged this Baby Beast as hard as my inner child had always wanted to hug my father. And mother. Surprisingly, the misty Baby Beast had enough substance for me to actually feel the body within. Either that, or the cloud conformed himself into the shape of a small, helpless child.

I finally detached, keeping my hands on the outside of his cloud, much like my father had kept hold of my shoulders after our hug.

"Would you like me to tell you about your father? His name was Kai," I whispered, smiling.

The Baby Beast seemed to bob up and down wonderingly, lowering down to the ground of my cell as if it was a throne in our secret hideout.

In the depths of Hell, one of the lowest points that existed in all of creation, a broken man told a boy about his hero of a father.

And the celestial boy listened in rapt attention.

A boy and a broken man found love in that land of despair, where Hope had no name, long since abandoned in the city of woe...

CHAPTER 52

I had fallen asleep at some point, overwhelmed by the unexpectedly pleasant storm of emotions that had bombarded me in the depths of Hell. As if they had scoured my soul clean. I woke to discover that the Baby Beast – B, for short, I decided as a temporary name – had huddled up against me, as if seeking protection. And I had subconsciously held him as I slept. He didn't shift, so I assumed he was sleeping. I didn't want to give him a true name, because then his name would be forever tarnished by the man he had met in Hell that one time, since I still had no way of getting out.

Thinking of that, B needed to get going. He couldn't just hang out down here with me. What did he eat? What did he need to stay alive? What if someone found him and attacked him? Imprisoned him? I began to panic, and this, apparently, woke B up.

He darted away in a blink, and metal spines like a thousand needle-thin razors suddenly erupted from the soft, huggable cloud. He zipped back and forth aggressively, but not against me. Against... whatever it was that had made me afraid. He was essentially barking at the burglar that had woken me up in the night, ready to rip him limb from limb.

"It's okay," I said with a smile, hiding my surprise at his sudden ability to kill. "I was just thinking of your safety. That you should probably go home soon. To your mother." I patted the wall behind me. "I'm not going anywhere. I don't even know where the door is," I admitted.

"I don't think my mother would like that answer," B said slowly, the silver spines slowly retracting back into the cloud.

I grunted at the understatement. "Well, you obviously know the way down here. You can find your way back out. How did you even find me?" I closed my mouth, realizing that it sounded eerily close to *do you know how far from home you are, how worried your mother will be?!*

And that would only serve to scare him. And make me sound like a grouchy old man.

B didn't even hesitate. "I followed your soul. I could hear you crying out. You are... a part of me, I think. But I don't know how to find my way back. Your parents said you could help me. Help your family. I'm very tired..." he said, drawing the words out as if he really was at the point of exhaustion. I stared at him. My parents...

I suddenly knew what my dreams had been. It had been B searching for me. Listening in on conversations with my friends, stalking everyone. I wondered if they had been able to see him. Many had acted like they could not. But my parents had.

I watched in horror as he ever so slowly began to descend lower to the ground. When kids got like this, they were minutes away from a coma. Like a sugar crash. Oh, no.

"B, listen to me. You have to go home. Right now. I can't keep you safe. I have no *power*."

"You have powerful toys, they are just tired, too. And you know the way out. I heard the black one say so. Maybe it's this room..." he said sleepily.

I blinked at him, feeling a surge of excitement. "When did you get tired, B?"

He shifted lazily, sinking lower to the ground. "After I came in here to talk to you."

"Shit..." I cursed. The cell was exhausting him. He didn't have a body, and I was pretty sure he wasn't a soul, since he'd had no problems traipsing about Hell. He was a Beast, something I barely pretended to understand. Maybe he *was* celestial, a being from another place, or a realm I simply *identified* as celestial. Whatever it was didn't matter right now. He'd gotten in here without a problem. I needed him to help me get out. Not only because

I wanted to get out, but because he couldn't find the way out on his own. He needed someone with a map.

The new guide to Hell. Me.

And I had unleashed something deadly into my world – because I was sure my brief roommate was an asshole of the highest caliber.

And he sure seemed interested in some of the same hobbies as Matthias and me.

Arthur. Camelot. Guinevere.

B had said my toys had power, but they were just tired. Did that mean... outside the cell they would work fine? "B, I need you to do something. We'll take a nap in just a minute. Can you... get rid of this wall? Quietly?" I asked, not knowing how to phrase it so that he might understand, not sure how many words he knew. It sure seemed like he knew a hell of a lot, but I couldn't waste time. We had to act fast. He was my only way out. And I was his only way out. We had to work together.

"As you wish, Catalyst," he murmured as if in a trance. I jumped, but seeing how slowly he drifted over to the wall, I didn't pester him about the word he'd so casually used. He bobbed in a weaving pattern, like a child dragging his feet on the way to bed. I quickly gathered up my stuff, took one last look at the glow-sticks in the dark cell behind me, grunted, and turned back to B.

The wall shimmered, and a thousand pounds of diamond grit collapsed to the floor, some of it rolling over my feet. I hefted my spear and dove through, not caring what was on the other side as B suddenly sagged completely to the ground like fog in a valley. I grabbed a hold of his... fluffiness where I thought his hair would be and tugged him after me.

Startled whistles shrieked at me from my right, and I cut loose with my spear as three Candy Skulls lurched after me with their glass sword-hands. With each second, another arm appeared with another blade until each of them sported six or more arms – a shitload of glass.

Magic surged up inside of me, and I smiled at their prettily-painted faces.

"Early checkout, Candy Asses."

And I threw myself into them, drawing deep on the Fae powers that Barbie had rejuvenated me with. Remembering how difficult it had been when trying to take out the monsters in the white arena, I gave it more effort than probably necessary.

A dozen silver spines – like I had seen B use – erupted from my hands, impaling the first two Candy Skulls. I didn't stop, even as they shrieked, higher pitched, like teakettles about to explode. I swung my spear laterally, decapitating them. Their robes crumpled and their Candy Skull Masks bounced on the ground loudly as the ruby on my spear flashed twice, drinking in their... souls? The third Candy Skull warden took one look at me, the spear, and turned to run. I scooped up one of their Masks – not a full skull like I had seen others donning – and pointed my spear at the fleeing warden. A bar of blinding red lightning hammered into his spine.

He simply ceased to exist, and my spear gobbled him up, too, the gem flashing brightly one time, devouring whatever it was that kept the Calavera vertical. I frowned at it before spinning to check on B. Now that we were out of the cell, he should be fine. Less sleepy.

But he wasn't. He was a deflated lump of cotton, not moving. Dying or dead.

"NOOOOOOOO!" I roared at the top of my lungs, loud enough to... well, wake the dead.

And not knowing what else to do, I pointed my spear at B, unleashing a torrent of arcing red light into the Beast. The walls exploded all around us, shrapnel pelting my body and face.

And I fell from these Hellish Heavens.

CHAPTER 53

J managed to open my mouth to scream but I touched the ground too soon for it to become more than a surprised grunt. As if I had fallen only a few feet. Still, I jumped instinctively as if to grab onto the lip above me before whatever I was standing on *also* collapsed.

And it took entirely too long for me to return to the floor, like there was no gravity. Open air surrounded me, and it was windy as all hell. My feet finally touched the ground again.

"That should have hurt a lot more," I murmured, crouching against the ridiculously loud wind.

Wait, I knew this sensation… It reminded me of a time when – as a five-year-old – I had been riding down fifty floors in an elevator with my dad and a bunch of his executives. I had looked at him, grinning and said, *that makes my balls tickle.* The group had erupted in laughter.

I felt my balls tickling right now, folks.

"Oh, shi—" I realized too late what was happening.

I crumpled to the ground like I weighed a million pounds as the floor I was standing on suddenly hammered into something just as hard.

And molten rock flared up around me in a complete circle. I gasped, eyes wide.

I'd landed on a piece of rock from the hall that had *also* been falling. Then we struck the ocean of lava together.

I groaned, lying on a black circle of stone now in the center of the lava ocean. I glanced up to see a rock bridge, shattered in the center, the two ends like broken teeth reaching towards the new hole I had made. I blinked, still aching from the impact of falling...

Christ, that was a long way up.

My prison cell had been above the ocean of lava? Checking the Map in my mind, I nodded. Yeah. That was right. I just hadn't ever attempted to search the Map any deeper than my cell, not considering to check what was below me, assuming it was just more rock, not the fucking lava ocean. I grunted as I climbed to my feet, studying the edges of my island, watching as lava slowly oozed over the perimeter, swallowing it.

I was still standing on the bridge I had destroyed. And it was now sinking.

Frantically trying to decide how the hell I was going to get out of this, I didn't see the sodden cloud until it was too late. It slammed into me like a pile of wet laundry, knocking me perilously close to the molten lava. My skin dried in a heartbeat, only moments away from serious proximity burns or something.

Suddenly, I was yanked back into the center of our temporary rock island.

I stared in relief to find B quivering in midair, sharp crackles of red zapping within his soul.

"I was sleeping, and something woke me up. It feels... stained..." he said uncertainly.

I just nodded. No time for explanations. "We need to get off this rock," I told him.

Without a word, he wrapped himself around me and began to rise, but before we had gone a few feet, he struggled, and we began to drift back down to the ever-shrinking circle of rock. "I can't fly any higher with you. You're too heavy. Or I'm too tired," he said, terror creeping into his voice.

"Fly..." I repeated dumbly. I reached into my satchel and pulled out a feather. "GRIMM!"

I grabbed onto B, holding him like a football under my arm as black cords of lightning the size of miniature tornados slammed into the lava all around us, exploding in geysers of liquid rock. My Alicorn swept us up into the air not a moment too soon. I could smell burning leather and rubber from my boots. B shivered under my arm, wrapping himself around me in fear.

"Fucking idiot!" Grimm snapped angrily. "You trying to get yourself killed? And why cloak yourself? I heard you calling, but couldn't find you!" His fangs actually clicked shut at the end.

"Virgin ears," I snapped back at him, indicating B.

He snorted most indelicately, pumping his shadow wings until we reached one of the broken edges of the bridge I had destroyed. "Land here for a second, Grimm."

"Why – *the fuck* – do you want to land, you crazy bastard?" he snapped, but he did obey, skidding his silver hooves across the black rock.

I climbed off his back, holding B at arm's length for a moment. "You okay, kid?"

He quivered, which I took for a nod.

"Okay. I need you to do me a favor. Hop into my satchel. I need to keep you safe." Without a word, he shifted into the satchel as I held it open. "Keep your... top close to the top," I said lamely, not familiar with Beast biology. "Just, stay near the open part."

He did, and I made sure he wasn't about to fall into oblivion or anything. I would have asked him to hop into one of the other things inside, but they were all incredibly dangerous, and there was no telling what might happen.

I looked up at Grimm who was eyeing the spear in my fist. He looked... very alert. But we didn't have time to worry about that yet. We needed to get out of here. I carefully slid the spear into my satchel, preferring to have my hands free in case I fell off Grimm or needed to grab onto B or something. And if anything approached me, I wanted to feel them die up close.

I stared down at the Candy Skull Mask, and a very slow smile split my cheeks. I turned it back and forth, studying it. I even reached inside it with my Fae magic, verifying that it was just a mask. A powerful material, but not anything that would do me harm. I held it out to Grimm. "Sniff this. Does it feel dangerous?"

He did and snorted. "The previous occupant was... decaying rapidly, but it's just a mask."

I nodded, and popped it on over my face. Then I climbed onto Grimm's back, telling him where to go with a lightning quick assessment, the Map seeming to understand my desire. He launched into the air, flapping those great shadow wings like we were fleeing an erupting volcano. Perhaps we were.

I shouted commands into his ears on instinct, the Map seeming to speak to me, as he flew. It was much faster astride Grimm, flying over various labyrinth's and mazes, pockets of cells that would have guaranteed a deadly fight, and the vast open ocean of blood that would have taken me forever to walk across.

That didn't mean it was uneventful. Not in the slightest. The initial shock of seeing the Candy Skull mask over my head saved us from quite a few conflicts. But in those large open spaces where we had nowhere to hide, they soon realized we weren't what we pretended to be.

A handful of Candy Skulls peeled off from the ceiling, those arachnid ones.

I grunted. Stupid idiots. I opened my mouth to tell Grimm to simply dodge them, letting them fall past us, when giant wings made of spider webs erupted from their backs, one great big pump of those sticky wings sending them gliding straight towards us at impossible speeds.

I lashed out with whips of red flame, and then thinking of Talon's cat of nine tails weapon, I made sure each tip broke off into nine tips instead of the one. I even made the tips shaped like crucifixes, just to be an asshole. The added focus hit me heavily, but it also created a ridiculous number of streams of fire for the Candy Skulls to avoid.

Each whip that struck a wing lit it up like flash paper, and the Candy Skull hissed as it fell. Grimm made short work of the last Warden, not bothering to let it fall after I sliced off its wings, but deciding to stab it through the face with his horn. He shook it off violently, the mask ringing around his horn where he had pierced it. Like ring toss.

After that we tried harder to stay concealed. Not that we feared taking on any more of the Candy Skulls, but we knew it was only a matter of time before alarms went off, or one of them decided on calling in backup rather than taking us on directly.

So Grimm kept his fiery eyes alert for dangers, staying close to walls and corners rather than flying through the center of the various caverns. We still attracted attention from the hordes of souls, all shouting, cursing, and screaming at us for leaving them behind.

I reached into the satchel, placing my hand on B's... head, I think. "You okay?" I asked, keeping my eyes out for danger.

"Yes. I'm feeling better."

"Good. Just a little longer. We're almost there," I said. "I've been seeing through your eyes... And you called me the Catalyst..."

"Yes," he replied.

"What *is* a Catalyst?" I asked, scanning our surroundings quickly.

B hesitated, the flickers of green and silver popping back and forth inside him faster for a few seconds. The red had faded, but was still there. "It's like a whisper to me. A memory of a dream. A promise to my kind, I think. But I don't fully understand. Maybe I can ask mother..." he said, sounding sorry he couldn't offer a better answer.

I smiled down at him. "That would be great. I don't understand it myself. You caught me off guard when you said it is all."

I leaned forward to pass on a few directions to Grimm after a quick assessment of our location with the Map. We were moving fucking fast. I'd almost missed telling him to turn down the tunnel that would save us an hour of flight time.

I felt his muscles bunch up beneath me as he shifted course. He should be good for a few minutes. Unless we were attacked. We were almost upon the Arch where I had first entered Hell so long ago. I knew the only way out was to break the smoky ceiling window high above, but I wasn't sure if I had anything strong enough to do it. I would just use overwhelming force. 'Merica style.

"B, I need to know what else is happening up there. What else you've seen. We may have trouble when we return..." I said, suddenly thinking of the wolves, and Raego, and White Fang. God, they felt like they were a million years in the past after everything else I'd seen. But I needed to know what we were walking into. If it had anything to do with the... thing I had released from Hell. He obviously hated King Arthur and his pals. And my dear old ancestor had just taken one of those Knights into Fae – the only lead on Avalon we had yet to find.

B suddenly wrapped himself around my palm, and my mind exploded with visions.

Wolves tearing through the streets at night, hundreds of them.

Dragons arguing hotly with each other, on the verge of violence.

Yahn and the Reds arguing with Tory.

Alucard and Roland talking in a dirty, dilapidated building that looked like an old church.

I gasped as B let go. I gripped Grimm's feathered mane with both fists, reeling with dizziness to find I was flying hundreds of feet in the air, not standing in St. Louis. I panted, shaking my head. I glanced down at B. "Thank you, B. When... when was this?" I managed.

"Before I came to find you. I don't know time very well yet. They spoke of war coming soon when I left. Perhaps he has already left again?"

I flinched. "War, a person?" I asked nervously.

Grimm answered for me. "No. Not the Rider. The bubbling cauldron between factions that White Fang has riled up." He snorted suddenly. "Looks like they're expecting us."

I glanced up to see masses of shades and Candy Skulls on the other side of the Arch where we had first entered Hell so long ago. I placed a comforting hand on B's head and then closed the satchel. I gritted my teeth as Grimm flapped his wings harder.

"Looks like they're throwing a going away party," I muttered.

CHAPTER 54

*W*e sailed upon the army of shades ready for an all-out, hair-pulling, eye-gouging fight.

But... they didn't even seem aware of us. They were fighting... each other. No, wait. One person. I think it was a person. I squinted as Grimm flapped his wings, changing course to aim for the exit, noticing we might avoid a fight after all.

If Grimm was anxious to run from a fight, the odds were not in our favor.

My blood chilled as I recognized the one creature standing against Hell's army. "Grimm, we need to get out of here. Now. Before we become collateral damage in their fight."

But I needn't have bothered.

My old roommate stood near the bubbling pit of oil I had first landed in after falling into Hell. He faced the horde of shades and Candy Skulls and simply flung his hands up. Every single creature toppled over, slamming into the monster behind, row upon row, collapsing like deathly dominos.

My roommate brushed off his hands, looking much more physical now but still smoking, and then shot up into the air like his cloud form I had seen, straight up towards the exit.

Rather than wait for everyone to get up, I urged Grimm after him. I knew I had no chance of defeating him. Not now. Not after all I'd been through. Maybe not ever. I needed help.

We very quietly followed the insanely strong cloud out of Hell, as quiet as three mice.

Except, as we entered the vertical tunnel, the black glass ceiling was solid. Had it already resealed? As I was frowning, I failed to notice the bat-like Candy Skull suddenly launching off the wall just above us, aiming straight for Grimm.

I flung out a sudden whip, but didn't do more than annoy him before he struck Grimm in the face. I prepared to lash out over Grimm's neck, but was surprised to see the bat hanging limp, his torso firmly gripped between Grimm's jaws and his neck neatly impaled on Grimm's horn, leaving a few inches poking out the other side.

He spat out the body, grunting as he flapped his wings harder. "Hold on very tightly."

Then the tip of his horn struck the glass ceiling above and over the thunderous crashing sound, I heard a familiar roaring behind us.

"Don't let Mordred escape, you fool!" Anubis. But... hadn't my roommate already escaped?

That's when I saw a dark shadow zip past us, having been hiding on the rock wall below the glass ceiling. As he flew by, he murmured in that chilling, rasping voice. I almost managed to make out the features of his face in the black smoke.

"That's twice you've broken me out of a cage, wizard. Perhaps we'll meet again soon..."

Then he was gone, fading to nothing like fog before a sunrise.

Grimm landed in the powdery ash, snorting and shaking his head free of the dead Candy Skull. It crumbled to nothingness, leaving behind only the mask. Since this one seemed less damaged than mine, Grimm picked it up with his teeth, tossing it back to me.

I took off my own mask, compared the two, and then tossed my old one aside.

I opened the flap of the satchel, making sure B was still there. "We're out. Not home yet, but we're out of Hell." I wrapped my arms around Grimm's neck. "Thank you, old friend. You saved our lives."

Surprisingly, he didn't comment, simply leaned into me, neighing happily.

I smiled, pulling away, gauging this wasteland. Then I patted him on the neck.

"I think I can take it from here, Grimm." Not entirely sure what I was doing, I just did what the Map advised, and waved my hand in front of us. With a flash of darkness, a black Gateway erupted into existence, smoke shifting around the circular hole.

Grimm stamped a hoof, emitting sparks, as a view of Chateau Falco appeared before us. Several very startled faces turned to look at us, and their faces paled. But they had been sitting in lawn chairs eating popcorn as monsters fought in the distance. My lucky chair was outside with a beach umbrella propped up beside it. It was empty, or I might have started off by killing someone.

I stepped through, face like thunder, smoke billowing at mine and Grimm's legs. "B, go to your mother. She'll be wanting to see you. I'll be along after I clean this mess up." Grimm laughed, shaking black blood from his horn, the fog billowing around us.

I hadn't even noticed that the Candy Skulls bled. I stared down at my hands to find them covered in the black liquid. I wiped it off on my pants before glaring at those before me.

I let the Gateway close behind me.

CHAPTER 55

I didn't have time for pleasantries. I was a ball of barely restrained fury at finding such chaos on my property. I briefly swept the VIP area around me. Achilles sat with Leonidas, drinking beers and eating popcorn.

Tory sat alone, near the edge of the small group.

Callie was on her feet watching me steadily. She wore tight white jeans, a dark plain tee and a red hoodie. And she was wringing her hands uncertainly before her stomach. She looked like she'd been crying recently, judging by her red-rimmed eyes. Not in the past few minutes, but as if she'd had a rough night or long day. Not knowing what else to do, I tossed the Candy Skull on the grass between us. "Problem solved," I said in a gruff voice. There. Nice and considerate.

Maybe that would make her not sad anymore. She didn't even look at it.

Feeling uneasy under her gaze and angry at the fighting, I turned my attention to the wars on either side of this VIP area. The death and destruction was illuminated by the setting sun. Falco – still weak from giving birth – hadn't been able to put a stop to this madness herself. And my friends had just… watched.

Drinking beer. Eating popcorn.

Sensing our area was safe from immediate danger, I glanced about fifty yards to my left, past the small white treehouse sitting like a tranquil haven in the grass.

Tides of wolves fought in tight units – Ghosts and Paws striking like surgical scalpels. But they fought other wolves, so it wasn't as efficiently ruthless as usual. Still, many died before them. Survivors of skirmishes fled to rejoin a new hasty gathering of their fellow wolves before turning back to the fight – safety in numbers. There had to be almost eight hundred wolves still fighting, not even counting the torn bodies of naked people strewn across the fields and bushes…

Ruining *my* lawn.

Like empty red cups after a kegger party. That's how I saw them.

Whomever I let survive was going to clean this mess up. Or Dean was going to be impossible.

I spotted two shaggy black wolves with crimson eyes – Paradise and Lost – each leading their own Paws of five werewolves that shared their body type. The Kansas City breed looked very different than the stocky St. Louis timber wolves. They were taller, longer, narrower at the waist, but more barrel-chested. Their necks stretched higher and their snouts were more elongated. They had wavy, silky hair that formed thick manes around their throats and down their broad chests. Basically, the two breeds were equally lethal, but different in aesthetics and functionality.

The KC Crew were nimbler and faster, but didn't look as powerful in a direct charge.

They could jump further, but they couldn't shake their prey as violently.

Weight-wise, I didn't think they were any bigger than Gunnar's wolves, but the Kansas City breed almost made my hair stand up on edge. They just looked… more demonic.

Like Hellhounds. Especially Paradise and Lost with their crimson eyes, but that had something to do with their bond to Roland, the vampire ex-Shepherd.

But why were there so many Kansas City wolves here?

I spotted Drake and Cowan – at least wolves that matched the description Gunnar had given me before leaving for his honeymoon – each leading their own Paws, and I realized that the four clusters – Paradise, Lost, Drake, and Cowan – actually formed one Ghost, working together as if they'd done it their whole lives. I let out a breath of relief, glad to find that Paradise and Lost hadn't been fighting Gunnar's wolves while he was on his honeymoon.

After a few minutes, the wolves slowly separated into two distinct packs, glaring at each other over…

My fucking lawn.

At least this let me clearly see the battle lines, better able to discern enemy from ally. The enemy was larger, but not twice as large or anything, and it looked like Gunnar had lost a quarter of his pack so far. But that loss had been mitigated by about a hundred Kansas City wolves.

A giant black wolf with a white spot on his chest – for ease of reference with so many wolves running around, I dubbed him Spot – stood in front of the enemy pack. The Midwest King, I guessed. He was bigger, much bigger than the others. Then again, Spot was the only one in Alpha form, standing on two legs. At a quick glance, he seemed shorter than Gunnar, but wider in the shoulders and chest, believe it or not. And the mangy mutt was… staring right at me.

Luckily for him, he broke eye contact after a few seconds and then snarled at his pack. "Ten minutes!" he roared. His wolves took a few more steps back before gathering to nurse their wounds. He didn't look at me again. The St. Louis and Kansas City wolves also rested.

Well, wasn't this just *professional* of everyone. Why hadn't I ever faced an enemy like this?

But more importantly, why was this happening on…

My lawn?

No longer distracted by the sounds of the fighting wolves, entirely different roars to my right made me turn to study the other battle, also about fifty yards away. Dragons tore up the earth and shrubbery where they fought. I saw a few in the woods, knocking down small trees but I didn't notice any fires. Others were in the sky, slamming into each other with machete-sized claws and teeth, or blasting each other with a rainbow of different streams of magic. Blue jets of ice, red gouts of flame, even a green blast of acid that smoked on contact. Dragon skin was tough, though, so most of these blasts injured their opponents, but weren't enough to bring them down on their own. Hence the fangs, horns, and claws.

But in combination, it was doing serious damage to…

My fucking *lawn*!

I didn't see Raego in the chaos of battle and my scowl deepened.

"I leave everyone unsupervised and I come back to *this*? Who's responsible? Give me an update." No one around me spoke, simply staring at me in stunned silence. I didn't have time for this. I was done with all the infighting between factions. All the drama. The hurt feelings. The egos. I had some serious shit on my plate with my brief roommate from Hell – Mordred – breaking loose, Matthias kidnapping my Knight, and Anubis... well, he probably wouldn't be pleased by my quitting the job without giving the standard two-weeks' notice. His Guide to Hell had done walked out because the benefits sucked.

I realized no one had yet answered. "NOW!" I roared, slamming my black spear into the ground beside me. The red ruby crackled with arcs of crimson electricity, and everyone flinched in fear. I hadn't even realized I'd taken it out of my satchel. I also realized that no one seemed to have noticed B's departure. I sure hadn't. I glanced down to see that at least the black fog had dissipated, making me look less, well, like I had just stepped out of Hell to clean up a mess.

Leonidas seemed to be pretending I couldn't see him, hunkered low in his chair. Achilles watched me from over his shoulder, looking very cautious. He slowly lifted a bottle of beer. "You're home..." he said in the same tone a teenager would use when his parents unexpectedly returned home early from their vacation during the middle of his out-of-control house party.

My brow drew lower, the crimson sparks popping louder. Leonidas sank further in his chair.

"We, um, brought your chair out in... memory. In honor. Carl and Talon made it sound like you wouldn't be back..." My face didn't change. He jerked his head tensely. "Um, we didn't do this. And... Gunnar should be here any minute! I had some guys waiting to pick him up at the airstrip." Seeing my face still hadn't changed, he blurted out, "Someone get this man a beer!"

No one moved.

A *week*, I thought, processing the worthwhile tidbits from Achilles' nervous blabbing. A week since the wedding. Not months or weeks – just a few days – in Hell. It had felt a lot longer. I let out a breath of relief. Not that things were great, but at least it hadn't been a year or something.

I sensed Callie slowly approaching me as if I was a wild, unbroken horse. I realized I was still standing beside Grimm, who looked very... intense, reflecting my mood. I placed a palm on his mane, patting his feathers soothingly. His muscles relaxed under my touch and he neighed.

Dragons continued fighting in the background, but they didn't seem concerned with our VIP lawn party, so I let them continue as I stared at Callie, suddenly recalling – in entirely too vivid detail – the... gift Pandora had shown me outside her hot tub. My cheeks blushed.

"How are you, Nate?" she asked, but didn't wait for an answer. "Talon and Carl were... quite distraught when they arrived yesterday morning," she said carefully, studying my leather coat, my lack of shirt, the black blood covering my bare chest.

"Passing fair," I said roughly. "Since when was it my turn to host the Olympics?" I asked, pointing at the two wars on my lawn. "I thought I was everyone's best enemy, not a public park."

She abruptly stepped closer, eyes flashing with rage but... also relief? "Since when is going to the *Fae* the same as going to *Hell?*" she hissed, loud enough for only me to hear. Grimm snickered and she snapped her finger. "Quiet, you!" she shouted at my Alicorn in a voice loud enough for Dean to hear from inside the mansion. Grimm's mouth snapped shut with a click, and he disappeared. I frowned in surprise before turning back to Callie. She had her arms folded, and I could tell that she was about ready to lose her faint grip on control. She was angry. And happy. Angrily happy. It became perfectly clear, and I wondered how I hadn't seen it. She had thought she would never see me again. Someone had told her where I really went. Carl or Talon.

I let out a breath. Then another. "Later. Please, Callie. Later."

She continued to glare at me for a few tense moments, and then finally nodded. "Later."

We both paused, faint smiles flickering over our cheeks as we remembered that word from our last conversation inside Chateau Falco.

"Where are Carl and Talon?" I asked in a gentler tone, changing the topic for... well, *later*.

She hesitated, as if clearing her own head and debating whether or not I needed to know the answer right now with everything else going on around us. "Inside, watching over Alex."

I had taken a step closer and was gripping her shoulder with one hand, my spear flaring brighter in the other. "Is Alex okay?" I whispered.

She blanched at me, frightened at the sudden movement, the red light, and whatever she saw on my face. She nodded jerkily. "He's... fine. Distant, but fine," she whispered.

I let out a breath and released her shoulder. "Oh. Okay. You just… the way you said it…" I added. Then I just stopped talking. If she didn't know about Pandora's… lesson with Alex, I wasn't going to bring it up. If I thought about that conversation too much – what Pandora had shown me – I might just end up letting everyone duke it out while I scooped up Callie, carried her inside my mansion and slammed the door shut, telling Falco to put up the *do not disturb* sign.

Indefinitely.

"Why is everyone just watching?" I jerked my chin at Achilles who was trying to hide the fact that he was now exchanging gold coins with Leonidas. *Betting?* I thought incredulously.

This was all so… gruesomely callous. My friends watching as blood was spilled all over…

My lawn!

Callie grimaced. "We were told by all parties to not get involved. *All* parties," she enunciated. I grunted to show her what I thought of that. "I don't know what their deal is," she jerked her chin at the dragons before turning to the wolves, "But Drake and Cowan showed up first, to fight this Midwest King. The Midwest King showed up to fight *Gunnar*, for some reason believing he was back in town. The two packs were very confused for a few moments. Then Paradise and Lost arrived as if the world was about to end, but seeing the two packs gathered, *they* looked even *more* confused. Especially when *this* guy," she pointed her finger, "showed up out of nowhere with a pack from Kansas City that have been in hiding for almost a *year.*"

I followed her finger to see a rangy, shaggy, gray wolf standing near – but still a respectful distance apart from – Paradise, Lost, Drake, and Cowan. He was a big bastard. I blinked. Instead of saying anything, I forced a nod, letting her know I was following along. She continued.

"Everyone seemed ready to turn on another until this newest arrival casually trotted up to Paradise and Lost, all alone and in front of everyone, and *bowed*. I couldn't tell who was more surprised. Paradise and Lost, the Midwest King, or Drake and Cowan. As easy as that, everyone teamed up against the Midwest King – who was *still* waiting for his grand duel against *Gunnar.*" She shrugged. "Things escalated." *Then it started to rain*, her dry tone said.

I shook my head in disbelief, but I was pretty sure I knew at least a small part of *what* was going on – even though I didn't understand a lick of the *why*. Callie frowned at me, silently noting the calculating look on my face.

I lifted my hand. "That's White Fang. The trickster. The puppet master," I said, pointing at the big shaggy gray wolf. The one who had led the Kansas City wolves here. I was pretty sure he had somehow led *everyone* here. Probably telling them all exactly what they wanted to hear in order to get them all in the same place at the same time.

She was shaking her head. "No, I heard his name is Jessie. I'm sure of it."

Everything stopped, my mind going blank for a moment or two.

My smile evaporated. I slowly turned to face her, unable to speak for a few moments.

"I'll be right back. I think I'm going to go kill him," I finally said without any emotion in my voice. Then I hesitated, thinking about it harder. "Or kiss him," I amended. I wasn't quite sure *what* I felt like doing at the sudden revelation.

Deciding I would figure out that little detail on the way, I stepped forward, ready to—

The gates to Chateau Falco suddenly opened and everyone turned to look. Two massive wolves, both in their Fae forms, which was so much scarier than a simple Alpha, stepped forward. One was white, and one was black. I folded my arms as a smile slowly crept over my face. "Let them clean up their own mess," I decided. Gunnar and Ashley swept the armies of wolves before them with a silent, considering look.

I heard Achilles pleading with Leonidas to take his bet, but I didn't bother to look. I simply tucked my spear into my satchel, approached my leather throne, scooped up a tub of popcorn, and sat down. I ate a few bites, watching the spectacle before us, considering taking Achilles' bet. I felt Callie's hand touch mine as she reached inside my tub of popcorn.

She didn't immediately move it, so I slowly followed that arm up.

To find her sitting on the arm of my leather chair, inches away, smiling at me with a guilty shrug. The setting sun illuminated her hair with vibrant pinks and oranges, like neon highlights, making her look deliciously savage.

I decided I could get used to that.

CHAPTER 56

I realized that the dragons had ceased fighting at notice of Gunnar and Ashley's arrival. I spotted Dirty Gerty's giant blue and gold dragon glaring venomously at the wolves, making me frown thoughtfully.

"Is this normal?" I said out loud. "Taking breaks?" Gunnar and Ashley still hadn't moved.

Achilles chimed in, seeing that I seemed to have calmed down a little. "Not that I've ever seen, but there seems to be a lot of confusion. Been a hell of a scrap anyway, though. You should have seen Paradise and Lost and those crimson eyes of theirs. Like death walking. Made some of Gunnar's wolves look like new pups."

I nodded, studying the dragons absently. I wondered how my own little scheme was playing out. The deal I had made with those demons. I didn't relish making good on that payment, but Temples always paid the piper. I chuckled to myself, sensing Callie's hip brush my shoulder.

I refocused. Maybe my little games were helping with the confusion. A little. Enough.

Tory was rubbing her arms absently, looking anxious as she stared at the dragons. No doubt looking for the Reds. Something about the way she sat told me she didn't want me to come over.

Her daughters were dragons, and she feared for them. I didn't see Yahn – but that was understandable since he could turn invisible – or the Reds in the fighting. Luckily, there were only about two dozen dragons in the fight, not hundreds like the wolves.

I turned back to Gunnar in time to see him striding up to White Fang. Jessie.

It really wasn't fair since Gunnar was in his bipedal Alpha form and Jessie was in his four-legged wolf form. Then again, the son of a bitch didn't deserve fair – not for what he had done. Gunnar gripped him by the back of the neck and hoisted him up as if to bite off his head.

Gunnar was a problem solver. Old school.

I realized I was gleefully gobbling my popcorn now, distant ideas and decisions tumbling around my head – things I had only first truly considered in my prison cell – as I waited for my friend to do the damned thing. Everyone around me had gasped, wondering why Gunnar was about to kill an obvious ally of his pack. I waited.

Gunnar snorted and abruptly tossed him aside, cocking his head and snarling. He looked... confused. I grinned, sensing Callie watching my reactions just as closely as the confrontation. I let her. It felt nice to catch onto something before she did.

Ashley turned from Gunnar to the submissive large gray wolf, sniffing the air. She sneezed. Gunnar barked at him, and Jessie – White Fang – finally climbed to his feet, shaking his fur. Then the three of them turned to the Midwest King, who was glaring at Gunnar with pure hatred...

And anticipation.

Gunnar rolled his shoulders twice, and then lazily strolled up to the challenging Alpha. He stopped a pace away from him and just fucking stared with his one eye. The Midwest King snarled. Gunnar didn't react or respond. The Midwest King raised his claw suddenly, slashing down towards Gunnar's face, but stopped when Gunnar...

Still didn't move. I blinked. Spot had tried to make Gunnar *flinch*? Was that a *thing*?

Gunnar let out a yawn and I burst out laughing, the only sound on the property. It boomed like thunder, rolling across the lawn bathed in the light of the setting sun. *My* lawn.

Callie was gripping my arm, eyes locked on the fight. I might have flexed. You always flex when a pretty woman grabs your arm. *Man rule number thirty-eight.*

The Midwest King's outrage finally bubbled over, maybe a result of my laughter, and he brought his claw all the way down in one blazingly fast swipe.

But Gunnar was faster. His body was motionless as he shot his claw forward like a spear – those diamond claws glittering in the fading sunlight – and stabbed directly through the Midwest King's forearm and then retracted just as quickly – almost too fast to believe it really happened. That was it. He didn't do anything else. In fact, both of Gunnar's furry arms now hung lazily at his sides, one covered in blood, the other still pristinely white.

The Midwest King darted back two paces, gripping his forearm as he howled in both pain and anger. Gunnar watched him.

Ashley turned away from the fight, studying White Fang – or Jessie – as if he was infinitely more interesting than her husband's little argument with the new neighbor. Mama wolf had her puppies to take care of.

As if her decision had flipped a switch, every single werewolf on Gunnar's side… turned their backs on the larger opposing army. They hunkered down in the grass and lowered their heads as if to take a nap.

"Wow. Talk about disrespect," Callie breathed.

"There was never a fight," I said, grinning proudly between mouthfuls of popcorn.

The Midwest King saw this wave of disrespect and it was just too much to take. He lunged at Gunnar, snapping his jaws at my best friend's face. Gunnar took one single perfect step to the diagonal and swung his other paw up, slicing off the Midwest King's head. Blood fountained in the air as the head spun in lazy circles. Gunnar was already walking away when the head landed a few paces ahead and to the right of him. He glanced at it as if a thought had just struck him.

He looked at his pack, all facing away from him. "I forgot to ask his name. Did anyone catch it?" he asked them, pointing at the head. "That one," he clarified since they weren't looking. A few had glanced back, tongues lolling as they panted lazily. "Anyone?"

My voice shattered the silence. "SPOT!"

Gunnar looked at me, waved a crimson claw in gratitude, and then nodded at the severed head, the matter settled.

Gunnar's wolves were napping, and the Midwest King's pack looked as if they had been turned to stone. Then they all hunkered down submissively to their new king.

Still, Gunnar didn't look back for a long minute. He finally turned.

"Anyone who has even *one* positive thing to say about how... *Spot* ran things has one hour to leave town. Everyone else, talk to these two." Drake and Cowan – even though not named, stood and trotted over. "You're all in charge of cleaning up my best friend's lawn. Or his butler will kill you and use your hides for fur rugs. I've got a few things to take care of. Dismissed."

Paradise and Lost shared a long look with Ashley before she gave them a brief nod. Then they were following after Drake and Cowan to help.

Gunnar and Ashley were already walking towards us. I saw no sign of Jessie. White Fang.

Dirty Gerty shouted in the silence. "Forget the wolves! Where is your *King*? Raego led us to this, but he is nowhere to be found. As you die to defend his supposed honor, he hides, unaware – or unconcerned – of your allegiance! Is this what you want in your King? He doesn't care about you. The Council does!"

A line of dragons hunkered low, eyes narrowing as they snorted flame, standing against Dirty Gerty and the four Council members, looking determined, but not entirely confident.

An ear-splitting roar boomed through the grounds. I glanced up to see Raego – in giant black dragon form – perched on my roof. He spread his wings wide, shooting a geyser of black flame into the sky, fanning the fire with his wings to make it larger. Then he lowered his snout, dark smoke puffing from his nostrils, and leapt off my mansion. I noticed a dozen dislodged tiles sliding down the roof and glared at him as he glided over to land beside my chair. He locked eyes with me and dipped his head. "Family, right?" he said with a disgusted snort, staring at his grandmother.

Dirty Gerty screamed something not very nice about us, but the dragons ignored her, intent to hear what Raego had to say about... whatever it was that had brought them all here. Obviously, where he had been would also be a hot topic, if I were a betting man. But they kept their battle lines just in case. Raego turned to look at her, and something about that look made every dragon grow very still. "I'll be with you in a moment, *grandmother dear...*" he snarled, snorting a small puff of black fog that turned a patch of my lawn to obsidian grass.

My lawn!

Her pupils dilated at his words, and she gathered her four Council members around her in a huddle, speaking in low, gruff tones with them.

"What's really going on here, Raego," I asked, confident the dragons weren't about to bring the fight over here. "Or should I say *Jessie?*"

His lips pulled back in a slight smile, but both of us ignored the gasps of surprise from my friends. "I thought you would find out sooner, but then you took a vacation," he said. I grunted, shooting him a wry look. "My grandmother came to retrieve a stolen item from your vault."

I frowned at the way he emphasized the last word. "I don't have a Vault here..."

"Oh? No vault? How... unfortunate for her. She must have received bad information..." He glanced pointedly at the wolves. "I wonder who else received bad information... Something to bring them all together..." He turned back to me, his black eyes sparkling for a moment. Then he winked. "I guess it's a good thing we had Tory looking into that theft. As an impartial third party. Good thing the Council agreed to hire her or things might look... suspicious." He sounded very pleased, but Tory wasn't smiling. She was staring at the dragons. And she looked *pissed*.

What the hell? Why had *I* been dragged into this shit show? I suddenly wished I'd had time to talk to the demons I had hired. It didn't seem like they had done their job very well.

"I'm not killing your grandmother, Raego." I said at a sudden thought, leaning closer so only he could hear me. And Callie, of course, since she was practically laying on top of me in her eagerness to eavesdrop. I didn't tell her to move. That would have been rude.

"You've already killed one of my relatives. What's one more? If I do it, the entire nation could turn on me." I didn't need to tell him I had just obliterated his father in Hell. Not that I thought he would really care, but it wasn't really a good time right now. Maybe later.

"So, you would rather have them turn on *me?*" He shrugged as if saying *I'm open to ideas*. "Just... take care of this, Raego. I'm feeling grumpy."

"Aye aye, Captain," he purred mockingly. Then he let out a roar, calling off Dirty Gerty's huddle and motioning her over to come explain herself.

I rolled my eyes, settling into my chair as I let out an annoyed breath. *Aye aye, Captain* had been something my employees used to say to me at my bookstore, Plato's Cave.

This wasn't over yet, but things had just gotten a lot more interesting.

Because I had remembered the name *Jessie* when Callie said it. He'd been a worthless employee of mine at Plato's Cave many years ago. Right around the time dragons began invading my city. I later found out that Raego had been hiding from his father in plain sight, disguised as my terrible employee, Jessie.

Because that was something I had forgotten about a black dragon.

They could shapeshift into… well, anything. Anyone.

And I was pretty sure… *Jessie* had been doing it for quite some time now.

He was White Fang. I was almost sure of it.

But that brought up an interesting question.

Would the fake White Fang please stand up?

CHAPTER 57

*R*aego slowly sauntered up before his grandmother. The four ancient dragons on the Council stepped up beside her, facing the Obsidian Son. Simply put, they were stunning. Majestic. And powerful.

"Everyone is aware that I could simply turn you all into new lawn ornaments, right?" Raego asked with another puff of smoke that turned yet *more* of my lawn into obsidian blades of grass. "Or that I could mind-fuck the lot of you to get what I want?" He didn't sound the least bit concerned. As if the effort might be easier than the act of stating it out loud.

The Council shared cold, but considerate looks with each other, Raego, and then...

"Resorting to threats! If we don't—" Gertrude began.

Raego silenced her with another blast of smoke at her feet, trashing even *more* of my lawn.

"But I'd rather talk things out. I think discussion will be... enlightening."

The dragons considered this, sharing looks.

Gunnar and Ashley had finally reached us. "Your throne is pointing the wrong way," he said.

I looked up at him, realized he was right, so made a pompous gesture for him to move it. He blinked at me for a moment. And then with a snarl, he and Ashley fucking picked up the chair, knocking Callie into my lap – bonus! – and rotated it to face the dragons.

They set it down harder than necessary, and something about their snarling faces looked amused. I slid over for Callie to make herself comfortable, and then wrapped an arm around the back of the chair. Not around Callie, but the back of the *chair*. Gunnar gave me another one of those amused looks and I scowled before turning back to the dragons.

Baron was the slate gray dragon with orange eyes – which was strange. Normally the eyes matched the skin. His scaled hide looked to be made of stone – like the kind used at Stonehenge. His head more resembled a triceratops than a dragon, complete with almost yard-long horns above the eyes, on the nose, and a wicked sharp beak at the tip of his snout. His wings even seemed to sport moss like the damp stones back in England.

Chu was the pale blue dragon. He was long and thin, easily twice as long as the others, but much shorter with stubbier legs and wings like fins down his sides. He had a long, thin snout. And yes, he did have turquoise catfish whiskers hanging from his chin, matching his goatee.

Enya was a vibrant emerald dragon, her scales seeming to glisten like the gemstone. She was the one I had seen spitting poison at another of the dragons. Her scales were much smaller and uniform, making her flesh look sleek like a python, but she was much taller than the others, with a long, gracefully thin neck. She smirked at me in my chair. I think. I felt Callie glance at me and wisely pretended not to notice either woman.

Malik was a yellow dragon with white stripes, which looked pretty cool. There was exactly nothing special about him. Just a big yellow dragon – as boring as he had been as a human in the meeting where I had first met him.

I saw Ivory standing behind him, a pale dragon covered in spikes and spines as if he was actually made of bone, like a skeleton of a dragon. He didn't have wings. Two smaller sapphire colored dragons stood within view of Chu, side by side like identical twins. They had black spikes down their backs, but were otherwise unremarkable. I was sure they were the asshole guards I had immediately disliked. None of them bore signs of the battle. No wounds.

Which meant they had either hung back during the fighting or they were dangerous.

Then there was Dirty Gerty, a large blue and gold dragon, standing a few paces ahead of her Council members. Horns and spines trailed down her back leading up to the horned crest around her head. I knew she could spit an almost napalm-like fire, and she looked ancient.

None of them looked eager for a fight, but neither did they think they should back down from their cause – whatever that was. Their cold, predatory eyes respected Raego's powers, and his position, but they were not pleased with him. I could tell they would oblige Raego with a fight if he didn't answer them the way they wanted. Maybe even if he did. And with their superior numbers, Raego might have a decent fight on his hands, even being the Obsidian Son. Because these dragons were old. Their scales were thick, and their claws looked more like aged ivory than shiny claw. Like they could tear through anything.

Still, they watched Raego warily. They knew his power. That he could control other dragons with his mind. Possibly even ancient dragons like them. Or he could simply turn them to stone.

But they probably had tricks as well.

Gertrude cleared her throat, and then pointed a claw… at *me*! "I have eyewitness accounts that you helped Raego steal from me. I brought guards to help me retrieve my property, and to prove their King's deceit. Some of his dragons thought to stop me from doing so until Raego could explain himself. My dragons thought to press the matter," she snarled. The dragons behind her stirred aggressively. Both those for and against her accusation, all of them pissed. "Hand it over. I know it's here."

I blinked, placing my finger on my chest as if checking to make sure they were talking about me. "Pardon?"

Tory piped up, finally. "It's all out of the bag, Nate. She knows." Dirty Gerty snorted thankfully, pinning her gaze on Tory. "Raego has not been taking care of his dragons. He's been otherwise occupied," Tory said, loud enough for all to hear.

"*Occupied* meaning consorting with Nate Temple!" Dirty Gerty clarified.

I frowned, shaking my head. "I've been through Hell."

She scoffed, but everyone seemed to freeze in sudden terror, staring over my shoulder. I felt a skeletal claw settle on my shoulders, mainly because Callie let out a startled gasp. I looked up, fearing Anubis had come to rehire me. Forcefully.

But with a sigh of relief, I saw it was just the Grim Reaper! Death stood behind me. "Bell," I hissed at him for good measure.

He gave my shoulder a reassuring squeeze as he spoke. "I think the kids would say *Lit Hell*. As in, he *literally* went through *Hell*. Not even an hour ago, in fact," he indicated the black blood covering me and he handed me the Candy Skull I had tossed at Callie's feet.

I glanced down at it like Hamlet holding a skull, and tossed it in the grass at *my* feet. "Totes lit," I agreed in an overly serious tone, recalling the odd teenager slang I had heard the Reds teaching Alex.

Speaking of, I spotted Talon, Carl and Alex walking up to the group. I scowled as I recognized my fedora – the one with the red feather! – on Alex's head. He'd been raiding my closet again, the sneak. "Has a little sex and thinks he can put a feather in his cap, does he?" I murmured under my breath. Callie whipped her head in my direction, eyes wide. *Later*, I mouthed, patting her thigh.

Talon and Carl stared at me as if at a mirage, struck still. I raised a hand, smiling guiltily. They let out a collective breath and dipped their heads. Achilles and Leonidas were watching curiously, still eating popcorn. We were getting quite the audience.

Tory stepped up, clearing her throat. "The Council hired me to find a thief. It didn't take me long to find the stolen goods. A necklace. In Raego's private safe."

Gertrude had a surprised look on her face. Then her eyes flicked back at the dragons as if searching for someone. I squinted at her suspiciously, but no one else seemed to have noticed that first look.

Raego sighed, pulling out a jeweled necklace that looked to be worth a lot of money, judging by the number of gems covering it, but I didn't get a close enough look since he tossed it at his grandmother's feet. She looked... hesitant as she scooped it up. In a blink, that look evaporated, replaced with open anger, but I could have sworn I saw a faint breath of relief. She slowly lifted her head, staring at Raego, eyes calculating. "A fake," she muttered, snapping it in half. It broke much too easily to be authentic, like cheap wire or plastic.

Tory nodded. "Weird, right?" Silence fell over us, and I knew everyone was thinking *why would he put a cheap plastic replica in his Vault?* What the hell was going on here?

Gertrude snorted. "Because the real one is *here*. In Temple's Vault. I have witnesses." Again, her eyes swept the dragons behind her, but she didn't seem to find who she was searching for. But the Council members were nodding their agreement, which didn't make me feel any better. I had a sinking feeling that I knew who her witnesses were, but I let it play out, wishing I had more popcorn and hoping Tory would get back to the part where I wasn't the center of attention, because I sure didn't know anything about her stolen necklace.

Tory began to pace. "I obviously realized something much bigger was going on, so asked Raego for access to the state of the art surveillance he had recently installed." She glanced at Dirty Gerty. "Around the time you showed up, ironically." As if suddenly remembering something, she reached into a pocket, withdrawing a slip of paper. She held it out to Dirty Gerty, but the dragon didn't move. Tory let it fall to the ground with a shrug, turning her back on the older dragon. "That's a signature card for your recently opened deposit box at the Vaults."

I leaned in to whisper to Callie, and found she was closer than I had thought. "The magic bank," I murmured before pulling back, trying to shake off her strawberry scent and focus.

Dirty Gerty didn't even have the audacity to look surprised. "I have a safe deposit box. What's inside is private. Nothing to do with this. After the theft, I put all my valuables there, not trusting Raego's minions. Search it," she said, folding her arms.

Tory nodded. "No need. I know where the necklace is," she said, waving a hand as if it hadn't been her point. I frowned. If she knew where this necklace was, what were we all doing here? "Did I mention those security feeds yet?" Tory asked, letting out a slow whistle. "Top of the line. Tamper proof. Oh, and it showed you placing this fake necklace in Raego's private vault."

Dead silence. The dragons shared long, considering looks. Well, everyone but Dirty Gerty. She just looked about to explode. I could tell she was desperately trying to find a way out of this clusterfuck, because Tory had caught her red-handed. But red-handed in what? A fake frame-job? To take Raego down a peg? Why rope *me* into it?

She finally growled, shooting Tory a fiery, dangerous look, one promising retribution. "Fine!" she snapped. "But that doesn't change the fact that the necklace is *here*! In *his* vault!" she snarled, pointing a finger at me. "I just needed to nudge the Council into hearing me out until I could show them real proof of Raego's theft. I needed a way to show the dragons how unfit for leadership he is. He's never present. I'm interested to find out what he thinks is more important than his own people. Perhaps it's his friendship with *Temple* – a *dragon killer.*" Her words, unfortunately, seemed to strike a chord with the dragons, even *with* her admission of guilt.

Their judgy eyes looked at me as if I had just birthed a sphincter sneeze in a small elevator.

A new voice spoke up, as if trying to talk to his wife at a concert, accidentally speaking a bit too loudly right when the music stopped, taking the attention away from me.

"I would have chosen friendship over family, too, if I had been in his shoes," Gunnar said. Then, sensing all eyes on him, he straightened, feigning embarrassment.

Gertrude bared her teeth.

He grinned back. "Bring it, you old scaly bitch."

"*Ancient* scaly bitch," I admonished. "I think the word *old* is one of those new offensive terms, and I'm fresh out of safe spaces for her to retreat and recover in." I didn't know what, exactly, was going on, but I couldn't resist an opportunity to razzle the old girl.

Gunnar dipped his head at her apologetically. "*Ancient* scaly bitch," he amended. "I'd hate to offend the *ancient* scaly bitch before I smash her face in."

She snarled in outrage, turning to her Council for support.

Chu, the silent angry son of a bitch, flew off the handle. *Always needed to watch the silent ones*, I thought to myself. He lunged like a sky-blue cobra, slithering past Gertrude as his side fins flared out. "You do *not* speak to an elder dragon like—"

And he was suddenly screaming in pain. One moment he was lunging for Gunnar, and the next he was screaming from a horrendous gash down his side, the bright red blood vibrant against his blue scales. I saw bone within. Twin red comets erupted out of thin air to slam into his side, sending him hurtling a hundred yards with shattered ribs. A glass man shimmered into view out of thin air, standing between Gunnar and the rest of the Council. His glass claw was bloody. The Reds paced back and forth at his feet, hissing protectively in dragon form.

In the resulting silence, my voice was very clear.

I glanced at Chu's body. "Ah, Chu…" I said, shaking my head sadly.

"Bless you," Alex offered politely.

Gunnar chuckled, but Achilles lost it, belting out a wheezing laughter.

Dirty Gerty looked about to have a seizure, her claws digging into... my lawn! "How DARE you! I offered you everyth—" she cut off abruptly.

Yahn burst out laughing as the Reds deemed it safe enough to return to human form, naked as the day they were born.

Sonia smiled acidly. "You mean when you commanded us to go to your safe deposit box, retrieve the real necklace, and then *hide* it here? Or when you commanded us to tell the Council we *found* it here?"

Arya chimed in. "Or when you threatened to marry us to Fook and Yu if we *didn't* obey?"

The Council looked stunned, snorting and backing up a step, glaring at Gertrude in disbelief.

"Wait!" I called out. "Did she just say Fook and Yu?" I asked incredulously. Achilles was now sobbing with laughter. I pointed at the blue sapphire dragons. "No, I think this is really important, guys. Their names are Fook and Yu? I really need to know the answer to this. I'm not concerned about the necklace. This is *way* more important."

Fook and Yu glared at me, eyes livid, but they were crouched lower, as if this were somehow their fault. It obviously wasn't. If Gertrude had wanted to bribe Chu, offering up the Reds as potential brides wasn't unheard of. And it would definitely earn his allegiance. To have his boys married into the house where the King lived. Or the Council... if Gertrude had managed to take Raego down.

No one answered my question, but Callie gave me a silent fist bump.

Yahn had a dark look aimed at Gerty. The Reds sauntered up to him, tucking under either shoulder and nuzzling against him as if he wasn't made of glass. They seemed to be reminding Fook and Yu that their dreams would never crystallize, in case the boys had been unsure.

"We... well, I guess you could say we fucked you," Yahn said. I was really wishing I had that tub of popcorn now, trying to bite back my grin. Yahn kissed the top of both girls' heads lovingly. "And *this*," he enunciated, mocking Dirty Gerty's words, "is *everything*."

Sonia smiled sweetly at Dirty Gerty. "We might have lied about there being a vault here. But the necklace looks much better on me anyway."

And Yahn lifted his hand to reveal a ridiculously expensive, gemmed golden necklace from the Middle Ages. He placed it around Sonia's neck, letting it hang between her breasts. This reminded Alex – quite suddenly, judging by his gasp – that she was naked.

If a dragon's face could blush, Gertrude would have looked like the purple dinosaur.

Arya clucked her tongue. "We might have lied about Raego being away, too. Forgive us?"

Gertrude's ears could have been steaming and I wouldn't have been surprised.

Baron did not look pleased. He looked downright furious. He was grinding his teeth as he glared at Gertrude. "I will personally take care of this matter." Gertrude crouched aggressively, but seemed to realize she didn't stand a chance. Baron shot an inquisitive eye towards Raego, and there was a slight dip of his head. Very slight. "But I *do* want to know where our king has been lurking all this time." The three other Council members suddenly voiced their agreement, latching onto the potential life raft.

Raego held out a hand to Tory, who nodded. "Raego's been disguising himself as a werewolf, speaking with the people of the city, encouraging union. Better relations. People began calling him White Fang. He's been doing this for months, apparently." The dragons just stared in confusion, so Tory continued. "But then someone *else* started meeting up with those same factions in town, sowing rumors and fear. Anarchy. That person somehow made them think they were White Fang. That the friendly White Fang they knew and trusted was looking out for them, warning them of the dangers in associating across species. Or dealing with Temple."

"Lies!" Dirty Gerty roared. "Where is your proof? Will you deny—"

Yahn interrupted her. "I have been following Raego. Saw it with my own eyes. He even brought the Kansas City pack to help in Gunnar's absence. I just confirmed this with Paradise and Lost, who had also been trailing him." He shot Raego an apologetic shrug, but Raego didn't seem to mind. "Then I saw a person meeting with those same groups. Not a wolf at all. When I spoke to those groups afterwards, they swore on their lives they had just had the most alarming meeting with White Fang where they were warned of all sorts of things coming to St. Louis, and that Temple was behind it all." Yahn slowly lifted his glass finger to point at Dirty Gerty. "She used her mind control to trick them into thinking she was White Fang."

Dirty Gerty looked like she wanted to roast Yahn alive. He blew her a kiss. Baron, seeming to surprise *himself* at Yahn's gesture, laughed out loud. Then, surprising all of us, he walked over to crouch before Raego. "My king... it seems I've been fed lies. My apologies. I accept your judgment, but know it was never my intent to dethrone you for personal will. And I have no offspring to bribe or extort," he added drily. "I believed you were neglecting the dragons." He glanced at Gertrude, his eyes pulsing brighter. "It seems I fell for a long con. If they were complicit in her scheme, I wouldn't be against proving my allegiance by combat..." he growled, staring right at Chu, who was just now getting to his feet a good distance away, and then the two elder dragons.

The two ancient dragons snarled back, hunkering lower, daring him.

CHAPTER 58

$\mathcal{T}$ory studied Baron as if the three dragons weren't about to destroy my VIP party. She then turned to Raego – who had been watching her – and nodded one time, giving Baron her stamp of approval. She didn't give this stamp of approval to the other ancient dragons. Raego didn't look pleased that only one of them might be trustworthy.

Enya didn't look happy. Resolved to follow through with her stance, but not happy that she'd been played. I wondered how complicit she was, or if she had just been a pawn, too.

But Chu... he had returned, walking up to his sons, his head hanging low in shame. They had snorted and walked away from him without looking back. Chu slowly lifted his head and glared at Gertrude with utter hatred. Then he calmly – peacefully – took his place in the spotlight. I wasn't sure if that made him a good guy, or if he was just accepting the price for his mistakes.

Malik... looked surprised. As if he had missed half the conversation. But I wasn't sure I bought it, especially noticing Ivory looking so anxious behind him. I'd keep an eye on those two.

Tory then began walking back and forth before Dirty Gerty, who looked desperate for any way out of this mess, of the scheme that had collapsed around her. Any way to point a finger. Use her little old lady charm. But we all saw through it, now, too.

"Here's where you really fucked up. You *knew* that I, being a Beast Master, was immune to your little mind tricks, so you thought to use the *Reds* against me, hinting that Raego intended to marry them off without my permission."

She took a calming breath, and finally gave Dirty Gerty a merciless smile. "But did you know I spoke with Raego that first night? Right after our initial meeting? He told me all sorts of horrible things about you. What you would do, how you would try to get to me. Then he swore that he would never play those games with me, and that I was free to pursue the investigation as I saw fit. And that he would never use the *Reds*, or anyone *else*, against me. He even offered to let me take control of his mind and catch him in a lie. I walked away from that meeting very... troubled. Surely, I was being used somehow. I just didn't know by whom. But then you proceeded to do everything Raego warned me about. And when you hinted that Raego intended to send off my kids, I knew the truth of the matter." She spat on the ground.

"But to drag Nate into it? How stupid can you be? He and Raego haven't spent much time around each other in quite a while. Every dragon knew this. Except you and your little club of out-of-towners. You might have gotten away with it if you hadn't tried adding him to your plate."

Then she began to laugh harshly. "You stupid thundercunt. I'm a Beast Master. I *own* shifters. And you are going to pay very dearly for that over-sight." And her eyes began to glow a smoky green. Callie leaned forward, not even breathing.

Dirty Gerty was panting, eyes darting back and forth for a way out.

Baron spoke up, shaking his head in awe. "I, for one, am *honored* to have such a devious King. How long have you been setting this up?" he asked curiously. "Letting her smear your name while you set up this house of cards against her..." Raego willing to damage his own reputation seemed to impress him the most. That he had done it for his dragons.

Raego shrugged. "Ever since she came to town. I broke ties with Nate and began building relationships across neighborhoods. I didn't know what she would do, but I figured it would involve Nate, and since he was friends with a lot of people in town, I decided that was the first line of defense.

Baron nodded in disbelief. He finally turned to Dirty Gerty. "You fool."

"Temple has to pay for his disrespect," she shouted in a last-ditch effort.

"He killed Alaric! Stole his throne to give to his friend! They're working together! I only did what I had to do for *all* the dragons!"

I frowned. "From the sound of it, I would think you and Alaric were very close."

"As close as family can *be!*" she snarled.

I nodded. "Funny, because I recently had a chat with Alaric." Death made a noise, urging me to silence, but I waved a hand. "I was his roommate for a while. In Hell," I clarified, pointing down. "Had to kill him. Again. Permanently, this time." I dusted off my hands. "But you should have heard how much he loved dear old Gertrude..." I laughed wickedly. "Okay, not so much. I think he said something that rhymed with *power-hungry old bitch.*"

"Ancient," Alex piped in, correcting me.

I pointed at him, silently thanking him with a nod. Everyone else was staring at me in shock, reminded of the fact that I had really been in Hell less than an hour ago. And that I had apparently killed Alaric. Again.

I jerked my chin at Yahn and the Reds.

The demons I had hired. Made a deal with.

Here's where Tory might not be so happy with me. "They've been working for me ever since our meeting. I didn't know what was going on, but I needed to know what you dragons were doing behind closed doors, because Tory is my friend, and I have a soft spot against harming kids. Extortion is abuse, in my book. I promised them my protection. From you *or* Raego." I shot Raego a shrug, letting him know it hadn't been personal. He nodded back. "And I told them I would stand to support their relationship," I added, glancing up at Tory from under my brows, hoping she wasn't about to pummel me. You never knew with moms. Or women. Tory blinked, and a very warm smile split her cheeks. I let out a sigh of relief, turning back to Gertrude.

"You have no soul, lady. And after my recent vacation, I believe I'm the authority on the matter of having a soul or not."

"Your filthy parents stole from me!" she seethed.

With that, the last piece of the puzzle clicked into place as I remembered what Alaric had told me about my parents robbing her. She hadn't done all this because I embarrassed her at the Dueling Grounds. "You set this crazy scheme up... all of it. Not just to take down Raego, but to take back what my parents allegedly stole from you years ago?" I asked in disbelief. That's why she had wanted the Reds to plant the necklace here. To take me down *and* retrieve what my parents had stolen. A double win. "You set every nation on fire with fear to... get some *treasure* back?"

The fire in her eyes told me the answer.

Raego chortled. "I'm hurt, grandmother. We're blood. How could you betray blood?" he said, voice dripping with false pain.

With a scream, Dirty Gerty lunged for the Reds, the weakest and closest enemy to her.

CHAPTER 59

ory took her mind whip-quick, her Fae side leaking out. Dirty Gerty stared dumbly at the Reds from only a few feet away. Yahn calmly walked up, formed a glass fist the size of a bowling ball, and punched her between the eyes.

Then Tory, the tiny Beast Master, smiled. Gertrude's eyes went wild, flicking back and forth as she choked and gagged, unable to flee as the air was shut off from her throat. Tory didn't end it. She just watched as Gertrude slowly died. She held it for another minute before letting the body drop to the ground.

Then she looked at Chu and Malik and they began to choke to death, too. Their eyes were wide, but they didn't try to run. Couldn't try to run. Because Tory held their minds and throats with her power. Enya looked both grateful and horrified. Grateful that she wasn't choking beside them, and horrified that whatever she imagined coming for her afterwards might be even worse.

Raego cleared his throat politely. Tory glanced back, but the two dragons kept struggling for air. Her look wasn't subservient, but acknowledging his position. "Yes, Obsidian Son?" she asked. "I was hired as an impartial judge. I don't work for you, but for the dragons as a whole. These two betrayed your people." Enya blinked her eyes in relief, glad that Tory hadn't said *three dragons*. "I'm just doing my job. Although I won't deny enjoying it."

He nodded neutrally. "Do as you will, but this actually leads into an idea I've been having. I wouldn't mind if your position became more permanent – the police of this city. You'd have my vote, and I don't think anyone else would challenge it. But we'll talk of that after you... deliver your justice."

She nodded, the dragons still choking. "We *are* on Temple's property..." she said slowly, as if just thinking of it.

Raego turned to me. "She has a point, my brother. Do you want to decide their fate? At this juncture, I think you're the only salvation left to them..." he said with an easy shrug. "I think everyone else would rather just kill them. But we'll take care of it if you have no opinion on the matter."

Tory growled territorially, and Raego smiled. "Well, *Tory* will take care of it."

Everyone waited. I heard someone munching on popcorn, the only sound over the choking dragons before me. I considered everything I had heard. The betrayal, the backstabbing, the infighting. And I thought fondly of Hell. The torture, the anguish, the misery. And I thought of what I had let escape. Mordred.

A shudder crawled up my spine at that. He was powerful. Too powerful. He'd taken down an army of shades with one wave of his hand. And now he had taken the Nine Souls... whatever they were.

And he was encroaching on my interests whether he knew it or not. Camelot.

And I remembered Barbie. Her... enthusiastic healing, but more so her advice. Thunder rumbled in the almost setting sun, but it wasn't from me. Just regular old weather. But I let them think what they would.

I walked up to the two choking dragons, glancing at Tory, who nodded for me to proceed. "You want salvation?" I whispered in a cold tone.

They nodded hurriedly. They gasped as air suddenly filled their lungs. Tory kept her eyes on them, watching as they struggled to regain their composure. They slowly turned to look at me, and there was none of the previous disinterest, disdain, or hatred. Just... terror.

The last of the setting sun struck their obedient eyes. We were only minutes from darkness, and I realized I had made my final decision.

"Take this city," I said in a voice as cold as wind over a frozen pond. Like a Fae King. "Announce it far and wide that I claim St. Louis as *mine*. Don't kill, but let them know you are serious. And that they should expect a summons from their new king soon."

The resulting silence was palpable as I turned and walked back to my leather chair. Callie leaned against the side of it now, watching me thoughtfully.

Gunnar and Ashley were the first to kneel before me. In my mooseknuckle throne.

Then Achilles and Leonidas.

Then Raego and Baron. Then the rest of the dragons.

Death didn't kneel, but he did look amused. Callie continued to watch me.

Alex walked up and handed me the fedora he had stolen from my closet. "I don't have a crown handy, but thought this would work in a pinch."

Callie took it from my hands and stood, inspecting. She set it on my head, and straightened it minutely. "There. It does look rather dashing," she finally smiled and gave me a curtsy.

I rolled my eyes at her.

Four of the oldest dragons in the world snorted steam from their ancient nostrils, and then began snarling, lining up their followers with short, harsh commands. And as darkness finally fell, dragons took to the skies of St. Louis to let my subjects hear the name of their new king.

It was catchier than *Master* Temple.

CHAPTER 60

$\mathcal{I}$ didn't realize the wolves had surrounded us. They all began to howl, staring up at the horde of dragons racing towards St. Louis. At least it was night. Maybe the Regulars wouldn't notice.

"This... changes things," Gunnar said. It didn't sound judgmental. Just... a fact.

"Thanks to Dirty Gerty, everyone already thinks I'm a power-hungry tyrant," I said. "It's about time for some changes. If I have to do this to keep everyone safe from what comes, I will. When it's over, I'm walking away."

"Maybe you shouldn't walk away. King of St. Louis... Sounds catchy."

Ashley spoke up, assessing the howling wolves. "We'll see to the pack, although it looks like that's a bigger problem than I thought." I turned to look at the giant mass of wolves. Hundreds upon hundreds. Twice as many as before their honeymoon.

"We'll need a new home..." Gunnar said suggestively.

I sighed. "Send me the bill. I'm going to have to look into raising taxes or something. You can use the five million tents from the garage if you guys need to crash here for a while." Because this wasn't the first time I'd had armies living on my lawn. We'd kept all the camping gear, enough for ten freaking circuses. They nodded and left, gathering the wolves.

"What are you going to do, Nate? You seemed pretty focused on something when you returned," Callie said in a soft voice. I realized we were alone. Everyone had left with Gunnar. Well, I saw Talon not far away, watching over us from a respectful distance. Or maybe just wanting to give me a moment of privacy with Callie. I could see his tail twitching, though, and knew he desperately wanted to talk to me. I didn't see Carl anywhere.

I nodded to Callie. "I'm going to do what every new king does..."

Callie frowned. "Which is?"

"Invade."

"You just... took St. Louis. What are you going to invade?" she asked incredulously. A pause, then, "Don't even *think* about Kansas City..." she warned, but she was smiling.

I met her eyes, but was unable to smile. "The Fae. Mordred is free, and I think he's going after Camelot. Merlin. Arthur. But I have something he needs..."

She leaned closer. "The Round Table..."

I smiled at her, then, nodding. I glanced around. "Where's Roland? And Alucard?"

She waved a hand. "Still in their meeting. I spoke to Roland earlier. They're fine."

I nodded, thinking of what else I had to take care of now that I was back home. Pan. I needed to talk to Pan. See how Baba Yaga and Van Helsing were doing. And B. And Falco. And Pandora. And Alex. My mind began to race, anxiety slowly creeping over my shoulders.

Callie tugged me to my feet, not letting go as she led me back to the house. I didn't fight her, just watched as she tugged me along as if to walk over Talon. "It looks like it's *later*..." she said in a soft tone.

I opened my mouth to answer, unable to hide the sudden grin on my face, when I heard shouting. I spun, hands out defensively only to see Carl on his knees before the tiny sapling near the treehouse. He was cursing and chanting to himself. Very, very loudly.

"What is he doing?" Callie asked, still holding my hand.

Talon piped up, suddenly beside us. "That's what I was waiting to tell you. He's been sitting there this whole time, muttering to himself. Your mother put some fool notion in his head—"

"Grow, D! *GROW!*" Carl suddenly crowed, slicing a claw down his forearm and holding the dripping wound over the lone sapling. The thunder grumbled above, much darker and ominous than it had been earlier. Power washed over Carl, buffeting over us like a wind, forcing us back a step. And that tiny sapling erupted like Jack's beanstalk, racing for the skies as lightning struck the earth three times. Less than a minute later, my vision slowly returned from the flashes, and the ringing in my ears faded somewhat.

And I clearly heard Carl cackling to himself. A giant white tree stood where the sapling had been, scooping up the tree house as it grew so that it now sat fifty feet above the ground, barely halfway up the tree. I thought I saw the door to the treehouse open and then slowly click closed.

White scales covered the bark of the tree, and black leaves filled the branches as if it had stood for a hundred years. It had a very pale glow. I shook my head in disbelief.

"Behold Carl's glorious mighty D!" the Elder bellowed, throwing out his arms and spinning in a slow circle.

"Fucking Carl," I breathed in disbelief.

"I thought it was a *joke*. Your mother truly *is* a master of the D…" Talon whispered.

Callie muffled a cough, but I didn't turn to look at her.

My house rumbled faintly behind me and I knew things had just gotten a whole lot weirder.

∾

*N*ate Temple will return in Summer 2018... *Turn the page to read the first chapter of* UNCHAINED *- Book 1 in the Amazon Bestselling Feathers and Fire Series - and find out more about the mysterious Kansas City wizard, Callie Penrose... Or pick up your copy* HERE!

UNCHAINED (FEATHERS AND FIRE #1)

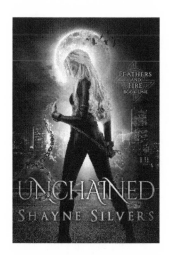

*T*he rain pelted my hair, plastering loose strands of it to my forehead as I panted, eyes darting from tree to tree, terrified of each shifting branch, splash of water, and whistle of wind slipping through the nightscape around us. But... I was somewhat *excited*, too.

Somewhat.

"Easy, girl. All will be well," the big man creeping just ahead of me, murmured.

"You said we were going to get ice cream!" I hissed at him, failing to compose myself, but careful to keep my voice low and my eyes alert. "I'm not ready for this!" I had been trained to fight, with my hands, with weapons, and with my magic. But I had never taken an active role in a hunt before. I'd always been the getaway driver for my mentor.

The man grunted, grey eyes scanning the trees as he slipped through the tall grass. "And did we not get ice cream before coming here? Because I think I see some in your hair."

"You know what I mean, Roland. You tricked me." I checked the tips of my loose hair, saw nothing, and scowled at his back.

"The Lord does not give us a greater burden than we can shoulder."

I muttered dark things under my breath, wiping the water from my eyes. Again. My new shirt was going to be ruined. Silk never fared well in the rain. My choice of shoes wasn't much better. Boots, yes, but distressed, *fashionable* boots. Not work boots designed for the rain and mud. Definitely not monster hunting boots for our evening excursion through one of Kansas City's wooded parks. I realized I was forcibly distracting myself, keeping my mind busy with mundane thoughts to avoid my very real anxiety. Because whenever I grew nervous, an imagined nightmare always—

A church looming before me. Rain pouring down. Night sky and a glowing moon overhead. I was all alone. Crying on the cold, stone steps, and infant in a cardboard box—

I forced the nightmare away, breathing heavily. "You know I hate it when you talk like that," I whispered to him, trying to regain my composure. I wasn't angry with him, but was growing increasingly uncomfortable with our situation after my brief flashback of fear.

"Doesn't mean it shouldn't be said," he said kindly. "I think we're close. Be alert. Remember your training. Banish your fears. I am here. And the Lord is here. He always is."

So, he had noticed my sudden anxiety. "Maybe I should just go back to the car. I know I've trained, but I really don't think—"

A shape of fur, fangs, and claws launched from the shadows towards me, cutting off my words as it snarled, thirsty for my blood.

And my nightmare slipped back into my thoughts like a veiled assassin, a wraith hoping to hold me still for the monster to eat. I froze, unable to move. Twin sticks of power abruptly erupted into being in my clenched fists, but my fear swamped me with that stupid nightmare, the sticks held at my side, useless to save me.

Right before the beast's claws reached me, it grunted as something batted it from the air, sending it flying sideways. It struck a tree with another grunt and an angry whine of pain.

I fell to my knees right into a puddle, arms shaking, breathing fast.

My sticks crackled in the rain like live cattle prods, except their entire length was the electrical section — at least to anyone other than me. I could hold them without pain.

Magic was a part of me, coursing through my veins whether I wanted it or not, and Roland had spent many years teaching me how to master it. But I had never been able to fully master the nightmare inside me, and in moments of fear, it always won, overriding my training.

The fact that I had resorted to weapons — like the ones he had trained me with — rather than a burst of flame, was startling. It was good in the fact that my body's reflexes knew enough to call up a defense even without my direct command, but bad in the fact that it was the worst form of defense for the situation presented. I could have very easily done as Roland did, and hurt it from a distance. But I hadn't. Because of my stupid block.

Roland placed a calloused palm on my shoulder, and I flinched. "Easy, see? I am here." But he did frown at my choice of weapons, the reprimand silent but loud in my mind. I let out a shaky breath, forcing my fear back down. It was all in my head, but still, it wasn't easy. Fear could be like that.

I focused on Roland's implied lesson. Close combat weapons — even magically-powered ones — were for last resorts. I averted my eyes in very real shame. I knew these things. He didn't even need to tell me them. But when that damned nightmare caught hold of me, all my training went out the window. It haunted me like a shadow, waiting for moments just like this, as if trying to kill me. A form of psychological suicide? But it was why I constantly refused to join Roland on his hunts. He knew about it. And although he was trying to help me overcome that fear, he never pressed too hard.

Rain continued to sizzle as it struck my batons. I didn't let them go, using them as a totem to build my confidence back up. I slowly lifted my eyes to nod at him as I climbed back to my feet.

That's when I saw the second set of eyes in the shadows, right before they flew out of the darkness towards Roland's back. I threw one of my batons and missed, but that pretty much let Roland know that an unfriendly was behind him. Either that or I had just failed to murder my mentor at point-blank range. He whirled to confront the monster, expecting another aerial assault as he unleashed a ball of fire that splashed over the tree at chest height, washing the trunk in blue flames. But this monster was tricky. It hadn't planned on tackling Roland, but had merely jumped out of the darkness to get closer, no doubt learning from its fallen comrade, who still lay unmoving against the tree behind me.

His coat shone like midnight clouds with hints of lightning flashing in the depths of thick, wiry fur. The coat of dew dotting his fur reflected the moonlight, giving him a faint sheen as if covered in fresh oil. He was tall, easily hip height at the shoulder, and barrel chested, his rump much leaner than the rest of his body. He — I assumed male from the long, thick mane around his neck — had a very long snout, much longer and wider than any werewolf I had ever seen. Amazingly, and beyond my control, I realized he was beautiful.

But most of the natural world's lethal hunters were beautiful.

He landed in a wet puddle a pace in front of Roland, juked to the right, and then to the left, racing past the big man, biting into his hamstrings on his way by.

A wash of anger rolled over me at seeing my mentor injured, dousing my fear, and I swung my baton down as hard as I could. It struck the beast in the rump as it tried to dart back to cover — a typical wolf tactic. My blow singed his hair and shattered bone. The creature collapsed into a puddle of mud with a yelp, instinctively snapping his jaws over his shoulder to bite whatever had hit him.

I let him. But mostly out of dumb luck as I heard Roland hiss in pain, falling to the ground.

The monster's jaws clamped around my baton, and there was an immediate explosion of teeth and blood that sent him flying several feet away into the tall brush, yipping, screaming, and staggering. Before he slipped out of sight, I noticed that his lower jaw was simply *gone*, from the contact of his saliva on my electrified magical batons. Then he managed to limp into the woods with more pitiful yowls, but I had no mind to chase him. Roland — that titan of a man, my mentor — was hurt. I could smell copper in the air, and knew we had to get out of here. Fast. Because we had anticipated only one of the monsters. But there had been two of them, and they hadn't been the run-of-the-mill werewolves we had been warned about. If there were two, perhaps there were more. And they were evidently the prehistoric cousin of any werewolf I had ever seen or read about.

Roland hissed again as he stared down at his leg, growling with both pain and anger. My eyes darted back to the first monster, wary of another attack. It *almost* looked like a werewolf, but bigger. Much bigger. He didn't move, but I saw he was breathing. He had a notch in his right ear and a jagged scar on his long snout. Part of me wanted to go over to him and torture him. Slowly. Use his pain to finally drown my nightmare, my fear. The fear that had caused Roland's injury. My lack of inner-strength had not only put me in danger, but had hurt my mentor, my friend.

I shivered, forcing the thought away. That was *cold*. Not me. Sure, I was no stranger to fighting, but that had always been in a ring. Practicing. Sparring. Never life or death.

But I suddenly realized something very dark about myself in the chill, rainy night. Although I was terrified, I felt a deep ocean of anger manifest inside me, wanting only to dispense justice as I saw fit. To use that rage to battle my own demons. As if feeding one would starve the other, reminding me of the Cherokee Indian Legend Roland had once told me.

An old Cherokee man was teaching his grandson about life. "A fight is going on inside me," he told the boy. "It is a terrible fight between two wolves. One is evil — *he is anger, envy, sorrow, regret, greed, arrogance, self-pity, guilt, resentment, inferiority, lies, false pride, superiority, and ego." After a few moments to make sure he had the boy's undivided attention, he continued.*

"The other wolf is good — he is joy, peace, love, hope, serenity, humility, kindness, benevolence, empathy, generosity, truth, compassion, and faith. The same fight is going on inside of you, boy, and inside of every other person, too."

The grandson thought about this for a few minutes before replying. "Which wolf will win?"

The old Cherokee man simply said, "The one you feed, boy. The one you feed..."

And I felt like feeding one of my wolves today, by killing this one...

~

 et your copy today! Book 4 releases April 2018...

MAKE A DIFFERENCE

Reviews are the most powerful tools in my arsenal when it comes to getting attention for my books. Much as I'd like to, I don't have the financial muscle of a New York publisher.

But I do have something much more powerful and effective than that, and it's something that those publishers would kill to get their hands on.

A committed and loyal bunch of readers.

Honest reviews of my books help bring them to the attention of other readers.

If you've enjoyed this book, I would be very grateful if you could spend just five minutes leaving a review (it can be as short as you like) on my book's Amazon page.

Thank you very much in advance.

ACKNOWLEDGMENTS

First, I would like to thank my beta-readers, TEAM TEMPLE, those individuals who spent hours of their time to read, and re-re-read Nate's story. Your dark, twisted, cunning sense of humor makes me feel right at home... I also couldn't have done this on time without Carol T's incredible editing services.

I would also like to thank you, the reader. I hope you enjoyed reading *NINE SOULS* as much as I enjoyed writing it. Nate Temple returns in Summer 2018, and Callie's book 4 in my new bestselling *Feathers and Fire* urban fantasy series releases in April 2018...

And last, but definitely not least, I thank my wife, Lexy. Without your support, none of this would have been possible.

ABOUT SHAYNE SILVERS

Shayne is a man of mystery and power, whose power is exceeded only by his mystery…

He currently writes the Amazon Bestselling **Nate Temple** Series, which features a foul-mouthed wizard from St. Louis. He rides a bloodthirsty unicorn, drinks with Achilles, and is pals with the Four Horsemen.

He also writes the Amazon Bestselling **Feathers and Fire** Series about a rookie spell-slinger named Callie Penrose who works for the Vatican in Kansas City. Her problem? Hell seems to know more about her past than she does.

Shayne holds two high-ranking black belts, and can be found writing in a coffee shop, cackling madly into his computer screen while pounding shots of espresso. He's hard at work on book 10 of the Nate Temple Series - coming Summer 2018 - as well as Callie's book 4 in the Feathers and Fire series for April 2018. **Follow him online for all sorts of groovy goodies, giveaways, and new release updates:**

Get Down with Shayne Online
www.shaynesilvers.com
info@shaynesilvers.com

BOOKS BY SHAYNE

CHRONOLOGICAL ORDER OF BOTH SERIES IN THIS MULTI-VERSE ARE LISTED ON THE NEXT PAGE...

NATE TEMPLE SUPERNATURAL THRILLER SERIES

FAIRY TALE - FREE prequel novella #0 for my subscribers

OBSIDIAN SON

BLOOD DEBTS

GRIMM

SILVER TONGUE

BEAST MASTER

TINY GODS

DADDY DUTY (Novella #6.5)

WILD SIDE

WAR HAMMER

NINE SOULS

BOOK #10 - *COMING SUMMER 2018...*

FEATHERS AND FIRE SERIES

UNCHAINED

RAGE

WHISPERS

BOOK #4 - *COMING APRIL 2018...*

CHRONOLOGICAL ORDER BOTH SERIES

Made in the USA
Coppell, TX
27 March 2020